PENGUIN BOOKS

A TASTE FOR MURDER

Anjana Rai Chaudhuri was born in Kolkata, India, and obtained a PhD in Chemistry from the United States. She lived in America for six years, married her Singaporean husband there, finally settling in Singapore. Anjana worked for many years as a research scientist in premier universities (including the University of Oxford, UK) and is the author of a science book chapter, fourteen research papers and review articles published in prestigious chemistry journals. Anjana's love of English Literature led to a BA in English Language and Literature from the Singapore University of Social Sciences in 2012. She is a double gold medal winner, for her master's in chemistry and BA in Literature, respectively. Motivated by her husband's diagnosis of chronic leukaemia, Anjana became a founder/moderator of cancer patient support groups, volunteering at the Singapore General Hospital, which led to the hospital awarding her an inspirational caregiver award. Her work with cancer patients led to two publications, one in the prestigious *British Medical Journal*. Anjana is the author of two works of fiction. Her first novel, a historical romance, *The Scent of Frangipani*, was published in 2019 by Monsoon Books, UK. In 2021, Penguin Random House SEA published her second novel, *A Time for Murder*, a contemporary murder mystery. She is a National Arts Council/Singlit Station grant recipient and a featured speaker at the Singapore Writers Festival. Anjana is an avid reader, and in her spare time, watches theatre, movies and TV with her husband of thirty-two years.

A Taste for Murder

A Das Sisters Mystery

Anjana Rai Chaudhuri

PENGUIN BOOKS

An imprint of Penguin Random House

PENGUIN BOOKS

USA | Canada | UK | Ireland | Australia
New Zealand | India | South Africa | China | Southeast Asia

Penguin Books is part of the Penguin Random House group of companies
whose addresses can be found at global.penguinrandomhouse.com

Published by Penguin Random House SEA Pte Ltd
9, Changi South Street 3, Level 08-01,
Singapore 486361

First published in Penguin Books by Penguin Random House SEA 2022
Copyright © Anjana Rai Chaudhuri 2022

ISBN 9789815017045

Typeset in Garamond by MAP Systems, Bangalore, India

www.penguin.sg

Contents

Monday, 29 August 2011

1

His hands on the car's steering wheel seemed to have a life of their own. Young Pritam Singh giggled as the Padang zoomed by, a dark patch at this time of night, lit dimly by streetlamps. Vivid memories of cricket matches played there crowded his mind. His eyes were barely focused on the road.

'Those were the days, my friend, we thought they'd never end,' he sang drunkenly, swerving sharply to avoid a road divider. Laughing uproariously, he zigzagged along the road, turning into a street leading to the next pub on his list.

The road sped away, illuminated by the car headlights. *Like a yellow tunnel snaking into the past, taking him to his parents.* They had never seen the Taj Mahal, and it was his mother's greatest wish to see the Mughal Emperor Shah Jahan's tomb of love built for his favourite wife, Mumtaz. His parents had embarked on a busy itinerary in India, travelling in style by luxury train that took them from Delhi to the pink splendour of Jaipur, the last stop being Agra and the Taj Mahal. While travelling in the night from Jaipur to Udaipur, tragedy struck. The train derailed and his parents sleeping in a coach at the front did not stand a chance. They died without knowing what killed them.

Pritam's nostrils flared as an ember sparked, in the alcohol-ridden fog of his mind, from the dying fires of the past. His uncle told him the news of his parents' deaths, his yellow face gleaming like old parchment, his eyes alive even then with the seeds of the diabolical plan that had started taking root in his mind. Pritam did not know where his uncle found a lawyer who produced the fraudulent document purportedly written by his grandfather stating that the ancestral house in Siglap reverted to the son who survived, leaving no provision for his dead son's family. Pritam, at the age of fourteen, bereaved and devastated, literally found himself on the street. He laughed maliciously. He had heard his uncle was in the last stage of cancer; he would raise a glass in celebration when the fangs of the disease squeezed the life out of that evil man who would now not have the time to enjoy his wealth. *But his children would.*

Intent on his murderous thoughts, Pritam did not see the other car coming until it was too late. His feet reached for the brakes at the same time as his hands desperately turned the steering wheel. But his feet were numb; he could feel neither the accelerator nor the brakes, his legs seemed suspended in air. He screamed as he swerved away from the other car, his car headlights illuminating the frightened face of a child peering out of the rear window.

Pritam continued screaming soundlessly. *Why couldn't he feel his toes?* He thrashed around. He was sinking into a cesspool of darkness, and he fought it vigorously. There was a light shining, and he had to move towards it. Like a swimmer surfacing from under deep dark water, he swam towards light and life. His eyelids flickered and he opened his eyes. The bedroom chandelier beamed down on him, and a Chinese woman's frightened face swam into his field of vision. Someone he did not recognize.

'Dolly! Where is Dolly?' he shouted.

Sunlight was streaming in through the windows of his bedroom when he next opened his eyes. The curtains had been drawn back and a mild breeze floated in. Pritam shook his head before hunting for his glasses on the bedside table. What a nightmare he had had, recollecting the accident and then the terror when his legs went numb. He cautiously moved his toes and then his legs. He gave a sigh of relief. His legs were fine. It had all been a dream.

Professor Pritam Singh sat up on the bed and saw, with surprise, his wife, Cheryl, sitting in the winged chair in a corner of the bedroom, looking at him with frightened eyes.

'Sherrie, what's wrong?'

'You woke up last night, shouting for Dolly.' Tears pooled in Cheryl's eyes, trickling down her cheeks. She was in her early thirties with a pleasant face, a snub nose, and curly hair that fell over her shoulders in waves.

Pritam frowned at the mention of his ex-wife's name. While he and Inspector Dolly Das of the Singapore CID had tried to remain civil after their divorce, tensions remained, especially when co-parenting their son, Ashok. They disagreed on what Ash, during his National Service stint, should and should not do as he faced a host of problems at camp. This resulted in verbal wars followed by icy silences on the part of the ex-spouses.

Pritam now gave a dry laugh. 'You're kidding, right? Why would I call out for Dolly?'

Cheryl rose awkwardly from the chair. She was in her seventh month of pregnancy, and husband and wife kept their fingers crossed that this time there would be no miscarriage.

Cheryl's first pregnancy when Pritam was still married to Dolly had been the reason for the couple's quick divorce after twenty-five years of marriage. Pritam admitted his infidelity before a judge and the couple was granted a divorce within six months of applying, thanks to adroit management by Dolly's lawyer, Frankie Kennedy, who was now married to her sister, Lily. Two months after their marriage, Cheryl lost the baby. The doctor shook his head, proclaiming Cheryl was prone to miscarriages. When she became pregnant again six months later, Pritam forced Cheryl to give up her postdoctoral research job and become a housewife, hoping adequate rest at home would prevent another miscarriage.

'You could not recognize me at all,' Cheryl whined, coming over to the bed. 'You said your legs had gone numb.'

'Eh, that explains it.' Pritam, fifty-nine, tall, muscular with a craggy profile, gave a relieved sigh. 'I was having a nightmare. I was driving a car and I had to push the brakes down and found my legs had gone numb. I avoided crashing into another car by a hair's breadth. It was a bad dream, sweetheart. Go and take rest, darling. We mustn't disturb Baby too much.' As his wife bent over him, he dutifully pecked her cheek.

Cheryl began moving towards the door. 'I don't know.' Cheryl's voice was doubtful. 'You've been different lately, irritable and short-tempered.' She nodded at the clock on the wall. 'Better get going if you want to reach the university on time.'

After an invigorating shower and a good breakfast, Pritam felt rejuvenated. He kissed his wife goodbye and hummed a tune as he got into his white Honda in the condo carpark. It was when he was driving that anxiety hit him. What if his legs went numb again? He should have taken a cab to the university.

He gently pressed on the brakes and found his legs were working fine. After driving for some time, Pritam slowed down. Where was he going? He looked at an unfamiliar neighbourhood, and waves of panic washed over him. Which road led to the university?

He parked the car in an alley and began to practise deep breathing. What was wrong with him? He wiped his face and neck with a large white handkerchief and clumsily fiddled with the car air-con buttons. Finally, when cool air blew gently over him, his heart slowed into a normal rhythm, and he looked around. At once the lane was familiar. He had taken a wrong turn five minutes back on the main road. Reluctantly, he turned the GPS tracker on and started the car.

When he finally parked at Temasek University's basement staff carpark, Pritam was very shaken. For he understood that had he not turned on his GPS, he would not have reached his place of work.

'I'm going crazy,' Pritam muttered to himself as he took the lift to the ground floor.

As he strode down the path towards his office in the Science building, the contents of his dream overwhelmed him. At least in his dream he had not crashed into the other car. Dreams were what you wanted the past to be, not what it was.

2

Dr William Eddington gazed out of the window of the small office he shared with another postdoctoral fellow of the chemistry department of Temasek University. The clouds had cast a blanket over the noonday sun. The leaves in the trees were motionless as Singapore waited for the storm to break. At least the shower would be brisk, wholesome and short, not like the incessant trickle that leaked out of the grey skies of Oxford, Bill thought. In Singapore, the sun would peep out soon and, before long, bake the land like a humid oven.

His attention wandered from the research paper he was writing on the computer. It was difficult to focus on his work when the alluring image of Ursula danced along the passages of his mind. Nothing had changed for him from his Oxford days. She was Professor Ursula Botham now, married for eleven years to Professor Graham Botham and the mother of ten-year-old Tom. She headed the Natural Products section of the Department of Organic Chemistry while, Graham oversaw the newly built 'Surface Science' laboratories. In his early thirties, Bill still hoped to find the right woman with whom to share his life, but his shyness held him back. Instead, he hung on to his infatuation for Ursula, a married woman he had loved years ago. In his fantasies, Ursula returned his love and divorced Graham. Fantasies were enough, or were they?

Bill looked at the closed blue door facing him and bit his lip. All those years ago, he had let Ursula go. Shy and diffident, afraid of relationships after his parents' divorce, Bill had few girlfriends while pursuing his PhD degree at Oxford. He had fallen hard for his fellow graduate student in Magdalen College, Ursula, but did not have the temerity to ask her for a date. Ursula, popular with other students, had flitted from one romantic relationship to another, blissfully unaware that Bill, whom she liked very much as a friend, had romantic feelings. And suddenly their graduate student days ended, and they went their separate ways—Bill to the USA to do postdoctoral research with a Nobel Prize winner, Ursula to Germany on a prestigious scholarship to pursue postdoctoral studies.

Mutual friends had informed Bill of Ursula's pregnancy in Germany and of her hurried marriage to Graham Botham. Bill, who had visited Ursula's opulent home, Banbury Hall, on the outskirts of Oxford, could only imagine Ursula's mother Bianca Asquith's horror at the news of her daughter's shot-gun wedding to a man unconnected to any English families of title. While it was true Ursula's father, Michael Asquith, was a distant cousin (twice removed) of a titled lord, to hear Bianca Asquith talk, one would think they were blood brothers. Michael had made his money in construction and, unlike his wife, was not snobbish. Bill disliked Bianca and admired Michael. He had read with sadness of Michael's death last year from a massive cardiac arrest.

Bill sighed. It was time for him to apply for lecturer positions in England instead of whiling away his time as a research fellow. He had managed to secure two fellowships in USA, one in New Zealand, one in Europe, and now in Asia. It had been more than ten years from the day he had proudly worn his cap and gown and accepted his doctorate degree. He liked travelling, tasting different cuisines, and his fellowships had enabled him to live in different parts of the world. Now it was time to set his roots down in his homeland. Not having a wife and family had lengthened his bohemian life, but universities did not like their lecturers to be too old when they applied for the job, and it was time to go home.

The blue door opened and a short, grey-haired man in his early sixties, with a pock-marked face, entered the office. He smiled widely at Bill, showing off two gold-capped front teeth, and sat down at the second table in the room. The office was small, the starkness of the whitewashed walls broken by a lone, tattered hanging of the Periodic Table.

'How is the paper coming along?' Dr Dong-wook Pak asked jovially, switching on his computer and settling into his chair.

'Slowly, DW,' Bill said, morosely, to the South Korean scientist. 'I don't seem to be able to concentrate on my calculations. I had a chat with the new postdoc, Kiong, and yeah, he seems to know quite a lot about theoretical calculations. I was not aware of that as his PhD degree was on thin films of molybdenum compounds on graphite. Pure experimental work.'

Dong-wook leant forward, conspiratorially. 'How come he is only a junior research fellow?'

Bill smiled. 'Because of you, DW. Kiong is a joint fellow, works for both Pritam Singh and Graham Botham. Graham pays his salary, and it is that of a junior research fellow because you are paid a senior fellow's salary. Poor Kiong lucked out. He applied for a senior fellow position as he had prior postdoctoral experience at Harvard, but Graham said you had that position, and he did not have any vacant positions other than a junior fellow. I wonder why he accepted the lower pay and position.'

DW's face fell. 'Oh dear, I took his job. I hope he is not angry at me.' He laughed pleasantly before adding, 'A junior fellow's salary is quite high at this university, so I am not surprised he accepted the offer.'

Bill nodded. 'The Singh and Botham group members are friendly, in general. As for the bickering going on between the two graduate students, Cheng Yong and Latha, I, for one, think it's all a show. They're in love with each other!'

Dong-wook nodded. 'I think so, too. Salma Ahmed and Terence Tan, the undergraduates, are nice too. Salma works hard, and I think she will score a first in her Honours Exam.' He frowned and swivelled his chair to face Bill. 'I like it here though I had thought twice before applying to Graham Botham as my supervisor. His reputation is not good. There was a scandal in Australia; a student of his died, took her own life because of him.'

Bill sat up straight, his face turned fully to DW. 'You mean the student fell in love with Graham? How do you know all this?'

'The student was Korean, and her father is my friend. Yes, he had an affair with her and ditched her. Kim, that was her name, hung herself from her dorm room ceiling fan. There were no charges or investigation as Kim had written a suicide note saying she was dying by her own hand because her lover refused to marry her. She did not name Graham; her friends told her Papa that the lover was probably Graham. I cannot understand why he is being considered for the headship of this department. The head of chemistry must have good moral character.'

Bill frowned. 'The department does not know Graham well. He and Ursula joined here only two years ago. Anyway, I think his peers will elect Pritam Singh as the head based on his longevity in this department. But yes, if the department gets to know of Graham's past, he can kiss the headship goodbye. Anyway, Graham pays your salary, DW, better not spread tales about him.'

DW shrugged. 'Well, his personal life is not my business though I agree that the department should have vetted him better before hiring him.' He swivelled his chair back to face his desk. He stretched out a hand to his satchel, burrowed in it, and took out a small slim flask of whisky. After taking a tipple, he cleared his throat with pleasure.

Bill looked disdainfully at the bottle in DW's hand. 'You're lucky the department voted against installing CCTV cameras in offices, old chap. Shall we go and see what the students are up to? How was your doctor's appointment?'

Pak glanced at his friend and smiled. 'Yeah, thanks for asking, Bill. The doc said to continue my heart medication, but he will wean me off soon. My daughters are arriving for a visit next week. They will get leave from their jobs and come visit me. And of course, tour Singapore. They have never been here, though my late wife and I toured here ten years ago.' A shadow crossed his face.

'Lunch!' Bill announced, not wanting a maudlin conversation on the illness that had put an end to Dong-wook Pak's wife's life before her time. He pondered on counselling his friend on his drinking later. If it came to Professor Botham's notice, that would be the end of DW's working life at Temasek. 'Come, let's go to the common room.'

DW reluctantly put his liquor bottle away. The two men switched off their computers and exited their office companionably. When they came out in the open corridor, they saw that the storm had broken outside, and rain was coming down in torrents.

* * *

Bill and DW walked the few yards to a blue door, opened it, and entered air-conditioned comfort. Common rooms and research laboratories lined both sides of the corridor. The common room shared by the Singh and Botham research groups was near the end of the long corridor. The room faced the Singh research laboratory with its fume cupboards and dry boxes. Glancing into the lab, Bill saw the honours project student, Salma, hard at work at her fume cupboard.

Bill poked his head into the laboratory. 'Salma, I have already done the theoretical calculations on your bis-benzene cobalt compound. I can't wait to see whether they tally with the actual photoelectron spectral results.'

Salma, a scarf covering her head, smiled warmly at Bill and said, 'Cheng Yong helped me prepare the compound this weekend. I will be running the spectra with him tomorrow, Dr Eddington.'

Bill nodded. 'Great! Coming for lunch? Lily's Corner?'

Salma shook her head, still smiling. 'I need to set my compound to sublime, and it will take me a bit of time, Dr Eddington, you all carry on.'

Bill nodded and moved away. DW opened the common room door and the two postdoctoral fellows entered, interrupting a heated debate between Cheng Yong and Latha, Singh's two graduate students.

Cheng Yong was saying, 'The food in Mainland China is bland to the taste? Rubbish! Where did you go?' He was a tall, thin man with rimless spectacles, hailing from Beijing and planning to settle in Singapore with a job in one of the big multinationals. He was a second-year graduate student and would earn his PhD degree in another year.

With a retort on the tip of her tongue, Latha stopped, seeing Bill and Dong-wook enter the room. She was a tall, dark girl with exquisite features and long, silky hair that she tied into a severe bun at the back of her head. Like Cheng Yong, she was a second-year graduate student with big dreams of doing her postdoctoral studies in America before applying to Temasek for a professorship. Her father arranging her marriage to his business partner's son stood in the way of her dreams.

'Oh, don't let us stop you two from your constant arguments,' Bill said cheerfully, his spectacles glinting in the light of the harsh fluorescent lamps beaming down from the ceiling. 'What is it now?'

Latha gave an elaborate sigh while looking mischievously at Cheng Yong. She was seated at the long table in the middle of the room. 'We are discussing Chinese food. There are different types, right. I went on vacation to Beijing with my family and we ate out at restaurants. The food had no taste at all! I mean, here, we have Chinese food and it's so tasty! Take the food from Min Jiang restaurant for instance, the one at Goodwood Park Hotel. I could die for their chicken with dried red chillies!'

'That's a Sichuan restaurant,' Cheng Yong retorted, hotly, from the other end of the table. 'Sichuan food is spicy. Beijing food has its own subtle taste and aroma.'

'Well, the subtlety was lost on me, CY,' Latha giggled, pleased at having riled her friend.

The new postdoc, Kiong Tan, a man of medium height with black-framed glasses spoke from a corner table. 'Personally, I like Yunnan cuisine. Before I came here, I spent a month vacationing in Chengdu. The food there is delicious.'

'Again, that is spicy food,' CY protested. 'In Singapore, you like your curries and chilli-hot food. No wonder you found Beijing food bland. I find your food too spicy. The chilli masks the taste of the meat and vegetables. Such a waste!'

'You seem to enjoy the curries at Lily's Corner, CY,' Bill said, smiling, running a hand through his blonde, thinning hair. He tended to scratch the bald circle on his crown, and he did so now while looking at CY.

CY grinned, his good temper restored. 'Punjabi food is my favourite. The Indian spices blend well, and Mrs D doesn't make the dishes hot, so one can taste the meat and vegetables. Prof. Singh is Punjabi; he is Mrs D's ex-brother-in-law.'

'By Mrs D, you mean the Indian canteen stall owner?' DW looked puzzled. 'Who told you she is Prof. Singh's sister-in-law?'

'I did,' Latha said. 'I know Mrs D as Auntie Lily; she and my mother are friends. Auntie Lily's sister, Dolly, was married to Prof. Singh; they have a son together. They divorced two years ago and now he is married to a Chinese lady, Cheryl.'

'Cheryl Sim was a postdoctoral fellow working for Prof. Singh,' Terry Tan, a quiet boy, sitting next to Cheng Yong, who talked little of his personal life, spoke up. 'Talking of Prof., do you know what's wrong with him? He is so irritable. He scolded me last Friday when I gave him an update on my experiments for my honours project. He ranted on about how Salma was so much ahead of me. It hurts to be compared constantly with Salma. I know she is good and slated to get a first in honours. Each has their own rhythm, right?'

'Don't worry about it, Terry, I am sure Prof. did not mean it, he has been odd,' Bill said. 'I went to his office in the morning to show him the draft of a proposal, and he seemed confused. He looked at me as though he did not know who I was and did not remember asking me to write a proposal. Is he sick?'

'He was fine last week when we had the group meeting,' offered Latha.

CY spoke to Kiong. 'Has Prof. Botham found an office for you yet? It must be difficult for you to concentrate on your reading with us chattering on.'

The postdoctoral fellow stood up and glanced at Dong-wook Pak, who looked away guiltily. 'Not yet,' he said shortly.

Bill glanced at his watch. 'It's past noon and all that talk about North Indian food has made me hungry! Lily's Corner, everyone?'

The students and postdoctoral scientists hurried out of the door, looking forward to their Indian thalis at Lily's Corner.

The rain had eased, but the day remained bleak and gloomy.

3

Lily Das stood behind the boiling pots in the Indian food stall situated at one end of the Science Canteen of Temasek University. She was wearing a multi-coloured 'Hello Kitty' apron over black trousers and tee shirt, lending her a festive look. Appropriate for welcoming the students back after their summer holidays, Lily thought, as she vigorously stirred a pot of lentils.

Without her trademark thick glasses, Lily looked less Tootsie-ish in her appearance. She had traded in her glasses for contact lenses when she had fallen in love with a professor, and even after the affair ended, she continued with them as her new boyfriend, Eurasian lawyer Frankie Kennedy, liked gazing into her beautiful brown eyes. After marrying Frankie, she coloured her hair bronze. To look Eurasian, her sister, Dolly, told her, waspishly. Lily's large brown eyes softened an otherwise stern face with an overlong nose. But her smile was sweet.

The canteen had ten food stalls arranged in a semicircle around the crowded sitting area with its benches and tables. Lily's stall was the most popular in the canteen. A long line of students stood in front with Lily's assistant, Vernon, a Chinese cock-eyed youth, busy ladling portions of delectable Indian food on to plates and serving customers. From time to time, he looked up and grinned at his wife, Angie, a Chinese girl with blonde hair and a nose-ring, who was manning the cash counter. The hum of excited student conversation rose and fell around them as the sun began to peep out from behind clouds, like a hesitant beacon.

While she smiled at the customers, a film of worry clouded Lily's eyes. Newly married, she was having a hard time adjusting to life with her husband, Frankie Kennedy. This was her second marriage; her first one had been arranged and deliriously happy, ending with the tragic death of Joy, her first husband, from terminal cancer.

Lily had dated Frankie for six months after a previous affair had ended. Lily often wondered if she had married Frankie on the rebound. Her previous beau had asked her to settle with him abroad, but Lily refused. She was attached to her eighty-year-old mother, Uma; her sister, Dolly; and her nephew, Ash. Also, Joy's memories floated around Singapore like frequent mirages, making Lily settle for marriage to Frankie Kennedy, who had skilfully managed her sister's divorce from Professor Pritam Singh.

She had not known Frankie suffered from obsessive compulsive disorder when she married him, although she had raised her brow sometimes at his insistence on cleanliness, frenzy over items lined up in a certain way and other acute symptoms that she had failed to notice in their courting days. As she lowered the gas flame of the burner under the pot of lentils to allow it to simmer gently, Lily thought her married life with Frankie was almost intolerable.

He would make her take off her shoes before she entered their condo unit, which was fine, but she had to have a bath before she could sit on the sofa in the living hall or the satin smooth bed in the master bedroom. She did not always like taking a shower immediately on entering her home and would rather flop down on the sofa and turn the TV on; but no, Frankie went berserk if she did so, and to avoid that, Lily did what he wanted. If she came home before him and assured him, later, she had showered before she sat on the sofa, he would disbelieve her and have a row. So Lily made sure she entered her home after he returned from work, electing to spend the evening at her mother's house in Silver Springs Condo on Holland Avenue, her former home. Frankie cleaned the bathroom at 10 p.m. every day so that it would look sparkling when they woke in the morning. Obviously, after a hard day's work at his law firm and the cleaning, Frankie felt tired, resulting in Lily's nocturnal love life grinding to a halt.

After six months of married life, giving the excuse that her mother was ill and needed her, Lily left the luxurious condo in Pasir Ris that Frankie had bought as a wedding gift and escaped to Uma Das's condo unit, where her mother lived with her domestic helper, Girlie. It had been easy to slide back into her old life, and while Uma had raised fierce eyebrows, the sadness etched on Lily's face stopped the old woman from wording a vitriolic response to her daughter leaving her husband. Lily knew her marriage was failing.

Work kept her busy. While her dreams of graduating from operating a small coffee shop to opening a restaurant in a shopping mall had not materialized because of lack of funds, Lily had managed to secure a stall at Temasek University's Science Canteen, cooking and selling North Indian food, and three months into the enterprise, Lily was making such good money from her business that it sometimes made her forget she was estranged from her husband.

At first, Frankie had called night and day, but when that had failed to entice Lily back into her marital home, he had preyed on Dolly to talk to her younger sister and counsel her into returning home. Dolly, a shrewd police officer, had refused to intervene and finally Frankie had relinquished hopes of a reconciliation, reluctantly waiting for Lily to serve him divorce papers. So far, Lily had been too busy to think of divorce.

'Can I have the non-veg thali, please? Chicken, and not mutton, thanks, Vernon.'

Lily looked up, smiling, and nodded at Latha, her ex-brother-in-law Pritam Singh's graduate student. While Dolly only spoke to her ex-husband about their son, Lily was on pleasant terms with her former brother-in-law. With Pritam married to Cheryl and Dolly married to Joey Pestana, Lily considered the estrangement as belonging to the past, and shrewd businesswoman that she was, knew she had to be on good terms with the professors and students of the science department for her Indian stall to be successful.

'All of you are eating at my stall today?' Lily asked Latha, pleasantly, peering over Latha's shoulder at CY and Bill chatting animatedly with each other in the queue. She patted her close-cropped curly bronze hair and smiled through thin lips covered with gloss.

'Yes, Auntie Lily,' Latha said. 'Us students and postdocs. Prof. is having his lunch at the Teacher's Club today; they have some function there. Oh, and Salma will be down, later; she is seeing to an experiment in the lab.'

'So, when are you getting married?' Lily asked, chattily.

Latha's face lost colour. She gave a wan smile and said, 'Date has not been fixed yet. My father is consulting with the astrologer for an auspicious date.'

Lily smiled at Latha's discomfiture. 'I had an arranged marriage, Latha. And my husband, Joy, was the love of my life. At our book club meeting yesterday, I was talking to your mother. Why, you and Nagarajan have known each other since childhood!'

Latha's face set into a hard mask. 'Yes, Auntie, but I am not in love with him. He is my childhood playmate, and I have never thought of him in a romantic way.'

'Love comes later,' Lily said, pragmatically.

'Your non-veg thali is ready; it's butter chicken today. Please pay at the counter, we have a long line.' Vernon looked so fierce with one eye rolling randomly that Latha directed a shy smile in Lily's direction, grabbed her plate, and went over to Angie at the cash counter.

'Such a long queue today, Mrs D. No need to chit-chat and hold up the line,' Vernon scolded. Although she was married two times, Lily had retained her maiden surname, as had her sister, Dolly.

Lily's long nose quivered. 'Really, V! You forget I am your boss.' By 2.30 p.m., the stall had emptied, and Angie was busy washing the dishes at the back. Lily, seated on a high stool, glanced at Vernon cleaning the counters and asked sternly, 'You left the stall for a while before the lunch crowd started coming in. Where were you?'

Vernon avoided Lily's eyes and mumbled, 'I was taking a call from Mr Kennedy.' He glanced at his boss and said virtuously, 'He calls me every day. To know about you. Whether you are minding your diet and limiting your sugar. He worries about your blood sugar levels.' Vernon stopped wiping the counter and leaned over, conspiratorially. 'It's been some weeks you are staying with Auntie. Such a shame if you divorce Frankie, Mrs D. He really loves you; his voice is so sad over the phone.'

Angie stopped washing the dishes to listen to the conversation. She flung back her blonde hair and said, 'Mr Frankie nice man, Mrs D.'

'Stop being silly and romantic.' Lily laughed and blushed at the same time. She said, 'You don't know what it's like to live with Frankie; it's like being in a sanitized hospital.'

'So, he has OCD, Mrs D,' Vernon said, reasonably, continuing cleaning the counter. 'It is a mental condition; one of my uncles is like

that. Mind doctors can fix it. My uncle and aunt have house rules. Work
it out, Mrs D.'

After Angie and Vernon had finished their work, they took two
butter chicken thalis to a nearby table in the canteen to eat their lunch.
Lily took her mutton rogan josh thali to another table and ate hers.

At 4 p.m., Lily sat at her stall register and counted the days' takings
and put the money away in her handbag. Angie, who had been sitting with
Vernon outside as he smoked a cigarette, sidled into the stall.

'I will make some tea, Mrs D,' she said, turning on the gas burner and
putting the kettle on.

They joined Vernon at a table outside to take tea together. Some
students had lined up at the *sarabat* stall to buy their afternoon beverages.
Lily reflected on whether she should sell finger foods like samosas and
curry puffs for this time of the day. There would be enough customers for
the stall to make a better profit.

Biting into a biscuit and then sipping his tea, Vernon said, 'The
students, Latha and Cheng Yong, are in love. Plain to see. What for Latha
want to go for an arranged marriage?'

Angie was gazing dreamily at the banana plants bordering the canteen,
the leaves fluttering in a mild breeze. 'I don't understand arranged
marriage.' She focused her gaze on her employer. 'Mrs D, you never meet
your first husband at all before marriage? Ooo, if I don't know what V
is like and meet him only after wedding, I sure run away.' She laughed at
Vernon's mock-angry face.

'I saw Joy's photo before the wedding!' Lily said, indignantly. 'He was
the sweetest guy ever.' Tears pooled in her eyes.

Vernon said hurriedly, 'Sure, Mrs D. So sorry for your loss. Modern
marriages are different. Dating, meeting parents, then marry.' He brooded
into the dregs of his tea. 'Latha's father is very fierce. CY told me that.
I don't think he want Chinese son-in-law.'

'Definitely not,' Lily agreed, finishing her tea. 'Krishna is traditional
and Latha's future father-in-law is his business partner.'

Angie drank her tea and frowned. 'Marriage should be for love, not
business.'

'I agree.' Lily looked at her employees. 'So, Latha and CY love
each other?'

'Early stages,' Angie said and finished her tea.

Vernon glanced at his watch. '4.30 p.m., already! Angie, come, let's hose down the stall.'

Lily sat at the table, remembering the wedding night of her first marriage and how solicitous Joy had been. Her reverie was interrupted by Latha and Salma running towards her from the path connecting the canteen to the Science building.

Lily jumped up. 'Latha, what's wrong?'

'DW has food poisoning!' Latha looked frightened. 'Dr Eddington found him half an hour ago slumped across his table. He had vomited his lunch. He had the vegetarian thali. Oh, Auntie Lily, your stall has an "A" certificate.'

Salma nodded. 'We eat here with no worries.'

Lily stuttered, 'He didn't get poisoning from my food! We follow strict hygiene, and my food cannot be contaminated. He must have eaten something later.'

Vernon and Angie came running out and stared at the two girls, shocked. Vernon finally found his voice. 'Has someone taken him to a doctor?'

Latha shook her head. 'DW didn't want to go to the clinic. He said he wanted to go home. Bill and CY took him to his quarters and settled him on his bed with plenty of water bottles. He told them if he got sicker, he would go to the clinic.'

Salma said, 'Please clean the stall and make sure you follow good hygiene standards when cooking, Mrs D. We like you, that's why we came to see you. So you are prepared when we don't take lunch at your stall tomorrow.'

The two girls nodded sadly and began walking back to the Science building.

Lily slowly sat down on her chair and buried her face in her hands. 'This is the end of the road for my catering business. Rumours are the best reason for a stall to shut down.' She rounded on Vernon. 'Who else took the vegetarian thali? How many? Do you remember, V? If it's food poisoning, more people will be affected.'

Vernon scratched his head, his bad eye rolling. 'Most took the non-veg thali, but the Pharmacy Indian girls took the veg thali. I think there were five of them.' He looked worried. 'I hope you don't shut down, Mrs D. We have so many bills to pay. I better go and work at my father's stall tonight at Newton for extra money.'

Lily glared at Vernon. 'You are so disloyal, V! How can you think our food is contaminated? We are a clean stall. Go then, work at your Pa's stall. See if I care.'

After Vernon had sadly left, Angie came to sit with Lily, her eyes filled with commiseration. She said decisively, 'If more customers who came to our stall complain of food poisoning, it is our fault. If it is only Dr Pak, he must have eaten something after lunch that caused a stomach upset. We have hosed down the stall. Shall we go home, Mrs D? I shut the stall?'

Lily nodded, gathered her handbag, and waited till the stall was shut and she had the keys.

'Give me a lift in your car, Mrs D? Vernon's granny is sick again. She keeps crying for Grandpa; it's been a year since he died.'

Lily nodded and the two women walked to the open-air carpark where Lily's yellow Honda Jazz was parked. The sun was out and the leaves of the trees lining the path to the carpark rustled in a strong breeze. The university campus was filled with so many buildings that trees and open spaces were scarce.

Angie said shyly, 'Oh, Mrs D, I think I'm pregnant. I go to see doctor tomorrow. Can you come with me?'

Lily exclaimed in delight and hugged Angie. 'Of course, I will come with you. Oh, Angie!'

'Don't tell Vernon anything until confirmed.' Angie looked darkly at Lily. 'Baby will cost money.'

They had reached the carpark and Lily flicked her remote, and the lights of her car turned on. While walking to the driver's door, Lily said, 'Don't look to me, Angie, for a raise in salary. I may lose my business tomorrow.'

They got into the car and Lily reversed out of her parking space. Soon she was driving down the expressway towards Holland Avenue and her mother's home, Silver Springs Condominium.

Tuesday, 30 August 2011

4

Lily's worst fears were realized when customers avoided her stall the next day. Word had spread that Lily's Corner served contaminated food causing someone in the chemistry department to suffer from poisoning. Naheed, the Malay food stall owner, waddled over to Lily's stall after the lunch crowd at the canteen had thinned.

'Lily, you so clean! What happened?' The buxom lady dressed in a pale blue *baju kurung* and matching *tudung* looked slyly at Lily sitting behind her counter, gazing morosely at the food she had cooked so enthusiastically and which no one had bought.

Lily bristled. 'It's not my food that is the problem,' she replied, spiritedly. 'I cooked the food hygienically, and my stall is sparkling clean. Look for yourself!'

Naheed peeped in and nodded. 'I know, but who will believe with the rumour going around? Give us all a bad name!'

'You did very well at lunchtime. You had more customers coming to your stall because they avoided mine.'

Naheed's double chins wobbled as she laughed, jovially. 'Business good, what to do, Lily?'

A small voice piped up. Rani Menon, a dark girl, a first-year Pharmacy undergraduate, had approached the stall. 'Mrs D, can I have lunch at your stall? You still selling? Just to let you know, five of us took your vegetarian thali yesterday, and we are fine. No food poisoning.'

'See?' Colour flooded Lily's cheeks as she looked triumphantly at Naheed, who hurried away. Lily got busy behind the pots of food. 'Yes, Rani, today no eggplants, okay? Paneer mattar, dal, and okra for the vegetarian thali.'

'Sounds yummy,' Rani said, smiling, and paid Angie for the thali. Lily, herself, doled out the food on to a stainless-steel plate as Vernon had gone to work for his father.

'Your friends not with you today?' Lily asked, pleasantly.

Rani looked uncomfortable. She spied her four friends at the Malay stall and silently pointed them out to Lily.

'Hm. I will give you some free mango chutney for your loyalty,' Lily said, trying to smile. After Rani had gone, she allowed tears to pool into her eyes. She looked at Angie and shook her head. 'I must clear my name. This is ridiculous. I am being shut down by rumours!'

Angie sighed. 'No more customers today, Mrs D. It's 2 p.m. already. I pack the food in containers and take to Silver Springs. We can all have a good dinner.' She glanced at Lily. 'Still coming with me to doctor, Mrs D? To find out if baby will join our family?'

Lily smiled through her tears, wiping them away with a small handkerchief. 'Of course, Angie. We can take our lunch first. Then I will help you pack up the food, and as soon as you clean up and hose the stall, we can go to the doctor.'

The sun hid behind clouds, and it was suddenly dark.

* * *

Dong-wook Pak lay on his bed, breathing torturously. The ceiling fluorescent light beamed down on him. He was unable to get up from bed, and he had not eaten for more than twenty-four hours. His fingers reached for his mobile phone to call for an ambulance, but he was trembling so much that the phone dropped on the floor. He struggled to rise, but fell back, his strength gone. His fogged mind registered the insistent ringing of his mobile phone before he suffered a seizure, his limbs thrashing wildly.

DW forced his eyes open, his body seemed to be shutting down. He gasped for air. Blearily, he made out a figure standing near the bed, gazing down at him. His limbs refusing to move, DW's eyes were full of entreaty as he looked at the dim figure. His heart pounding, he croaked, 'Need doctor! Get ambulance! Please!'

The mobile phone on the floor trilled again, and DW watched incredulously as the visitor casually kicked the phone to the far corner. When the visitor finally left DW's quarters, the Korean scientist was in a coma, his head lolling on his pillow. The phone in the corner trilled again and again as his daughters from Seoul desperately tried to reach DW.

* * *

Bill Eddington was in his office working at the computer. He glanced at his watch. It was 5 p.m. Half an hour more and he would call it a day. There was a knock on his door.

'Come in!' Bill said.

Salma's face peered around the door. Her eyes swivelled to DW's empty chair. 'DW taking the day off? How is he, Dr Eddington?'

'Resting, I would imagine. Come and sit, Salma.' Bill liked the intelligent, hard-working Malay girl. Salma sat down in the visitor's chair opposite him. 'I looked in on DW last night about nine. He keeps a spare key under a flowerpot in front of his apartment and I used that to enter. DW was asleep on his bed, so I did not disturb him. He must have taken sick leave today to get over the food poisoning.'

Salma looked at DW's empty chair. 'Something is bothering me, Dr Eddington.' She cleared her throat. 'Does DW drink alcohol at work?'

Bill's eyes guiltily swivelled towards the satchel DW had left behind yesterday on the table, and he mumbled, 'Why do you ask, Salma?'

'After lunch, at around 1.45 p.m. yesterday, I came to the office to ask DW a question on the NMR data of my compound. He is good at explaining NMR spectra, so I wanted to get his opinion. He appeared drunk, Dr Eddington. He was laughing at his computer and when I asked the question, he slurred and talked nonsense. I quickly came away. When he vomited all over the table, I wondered if he had too much alcohol. You can vomit when drunk, right? And poor Mrs D's food was blamed for him being sick.'

Bill looked grim. 'He did bring a whisky flask into work, and I was going to warn him about this. He will lose his job if the department finds out he is drinking at work. He has never been drunk before as he just takes a tipple. Maybe yesterday he had more to drink. We can check, his satchel is still here.'

Bill rose, went to DW's desk, burrowed in his satchel, and brought out the flask of whiskey. He opened the bottle and looked in. 'No, he hasn't drunk whisky from *this* flask. See, it is nearly full like it was before we went down to lunch yesterday. He just had a bit then.'

DW's phone on his desk came to life, ringing insistently. Salma's eyes rounded and Bill looked at the instrument. 'Maybe, it's DW,' Bill said, 'but he usually calls my mobile.' Bill picked up the phone.

Even from where she was sitting, Salma could hear the anxious tone of a female voice on the other end of the line. The voice was so shrill that Bill was forced to hold the phone receiver some inches away from his ear. As he listened, Bill's face grew concerned and lost colour.

'Yes, yes, I will go and check. I will let you know, Ms Pak, don't worry,' Bill finally said and put the receiver back in its cradle. He looked at Salma, his eyes worried. 'That was one of DW's daughters. They claim DW is not answering his phone and fear something has happened to him. He does have a bad heart. His two daughters talked to him last night for five minutes on the phone and he rang off saying he was sleepy. They have been trying to call all day today and the phone is going to voice message. I must go to his apartment and see what's wrong.'

Salma nodded. 'I will come with you.'

* * *

Bill and Salma left the Science building and took the shuttle bus to the staff quarters. Bill and DW lived in Block A. Bill checked Salma in with the guard at the door, and they took the elevator up to the fourth floor. DW lived in a corner apartment at the end of a long corridor. Bill lifted the flowerpot in front of the door, took the spare key, unlocked the door, and entered the apartment with Salma close on his heels.

The apartment was in darkness except for light spilling out of a bedroom at the end of the corridor. Bill flicked on the light switches in the hall and called, 'DW! Are you okay? It's Bill and Salma!'

There was no reply and Bill hurried along the corridor to the lighted room, Salma following him. They stepped into the room and stopped short. There was a stench of urine coming from the bed, and Bill saw a mobile phone lying on the floor in the far corner. The bottles of water on the bedside table had been knocked down to the floor.

Uttering an exclamation, Bill rushed to the bed. DW was lying motionless in his own urine, his eyes half open, his mouth slack. Salma, peering over Bill's shoulder, screamed. Bill grabbed DW's wrist and felt for his pulse.

'I can't find a pulse!' Bill shouted. 'But his skin is still warm. Salma, call for an ambulance!'

Salma whipped out a mobile from her handbag and quickly dialled for an ambulance. After speaking on the phone, she looked at Bill, her large eyes filled with tears. 'Oh, Dr Eddington, I think DW is dead!'

Bill, his face white and shocked, began to shake his friend's shoulders. 'DW! Wake up!'

He did not resist when Salma drew him away. Stunned, Bill and Salma went to the living room, sat down, and waited for the wail of the ambulance siren.

5

Lily and Angie waited at the doctor's clinic for Angie's pregnancy test results to come through. Angie's face shone with trepidation in the harsh fluorescent lights of the waiting room. Lily sat, her thoughts turning to her miscarriages. Now that she was forty-five and past child-bearing age, the anguish of lost motherhood cut deeper. The waiting room was crowded with sick people, some coughing loudly.

The room was very cold. Angie shivered, wishing she had brought a jacket with her. She muttered softly to herself, 'I do want children. I love kids. I could die for my sister's ones. But with no stable jobs for either of us, I can't help feeling worried, Mrs D.'

Lily patted Angie's cold hands. 'Well, if needed, Vernon can hold down two jobs, one with me and the other with his Pa at his Newton stall. Don't worry so much, Angie. A child is God's blessing.'

Angie shrugged, looking unconvinced. The doctor's assistant came out of the consulting room and called Angie's name. Both women rose and went into the doctor's office.

Susan Heng, the GP, smiled at Angie. She had her clinic on the ground floor of Block C Silver Springs and was well liked by her patients. She looked after Lily's mother, Uma, very well, and Lily gave the doctor a friendly smile as she took the visitor's chair. Angie plonked herself down in the patient's chair, her eyes wide with consternation.

Dr Heng beamed. 'I am happy to give the good news that you are going to be a mother, Angie. Congratulations! Your pregnancy test is positive. How many months did you miss your menstrual cycle?'

'Two months.' Despite her misgivings, Angie smiled in wonder. 'Are you sure, Doctor? I'm really pregnant?'

'Yes, you are. I have examined you as well. I recommend you see a gynaecologist for the duration of your pregnancy. Dr Emma Lim at the General Hospital is good, and my receptionist can make an appointment for you.' Susan Heng busied herself looking up phone numbers on her computer.

'Wait, do I need to? I worry about the fees.' Angie's face set into stubborn lines.

Lily intervened. 'Let Angie talk with her husband about this first, Doctor. Maybe later she can come to the clinic for the appointment. No hurry, right?'

Lily was walking across the courtyard with Angie to Block D and her mother's apartment when her mobile phone rang. Lily looked at the phone caller ID display and frowned. 'What does the drinks stall owner, Uncle Wang, want?' She switched on her mobile.

While she listened to Uncle Wang, Lily's face became so white that Angie cried out. 'Mrs D, what's wrong? What's happened?'

Lily spoke tersely into the phone before disconnecting the line. She turned to Angie. 'The NEA officers are at my stall. They want to close it down because they think my food poisoned Dr Pak. The poor Korean gentleman just died.' Lily burst into tears. After sobbing for a while, she rallied determinedly. 'My food is not contaminated, whatever they say. I must go to the stall now. NEA wants the key.'

'I come with you, Mrs D.'

The two women rushed to the carpark.

* * *

The science canteen was deserted except for two men sitting at a table, drinking tea. Uncle Wang, a white-haired man in his sixties, who ran the *sarabat* stall, came to the table and spoke to the two men as soon as he saw Lily walk into the canteen with Angie. The two men rose from their chairs and walked towards Lily.

One of the men said, 'You are the owner of Lily's Corner?' He peered at the signboard above the stall.

Lily stepped in front of her stall. 'I am Lily Das, and I run this stall.'

'You need to shut down the stall until further notice,' the man said, sternly. 'We are from the National Environment Agency.' He fished a badge out of his pocket and flashed it. 'A man suffered severe food poisoning in the chemistry department yesterday, and his colleagues said he ate his lunch here. Unfortunately, he was found dead in his quarters about an hour ago. Our officers will come to inspect your stall but till then you need to remain closed. Please hand over the key.'

Lily gulped. 'The poor gentleman.' Then her eyes flashed. 'How come the other people who ate at my stall yesterday are not sick?'

Angie chimed in, 'Many students and fellows had our lunch thalis. If our food is the problem, how come no one else is sick?'

The NEA officer shrugged. 'The Korean gentleman had the vegetarian thali. From what we understood, eggplant is only served on that thali. Your eggplant dish was probably the problem.'

Lily drew herself up to her full four feet eleven inches. 'My stall has an "A" certificate,' she said in a trembling voice. 'Dr Pak wasn't sick from the food cooked here. We follow strict hygiene, and our standards are high. There must be some mistake.'

The second NEA officer looked intimidating. 'Give us the key to your stall or we will call the police. NEA will investigate the hygiene standard in your stall. Please hurry up!'

Lily brushed the tears away from her eyes and fished in her handbag for the key to her stall. She quietly handed it over to the man.

'We will be in touch with you,' the NEA officer told Lily, grimly, before leaving.

'Bullies!' Angie muttered.

Lily sat down on an empty chair and wept. 'This is the end of the stall and my career in the restaurant business,' she sobbed. 'I take such good care with hygiene and then to be blamed like this.'

Angie's nose ring glinted. 'Dr Pak must have taken something else after yesterday's lunch. Mrs D, the Indian Pharmacy students all took the vegetarian thali, there were five of them. NEA will open us up again, no worries.'

Uncle Wang came over to Lily with two cups of tea. 'Sorry, Lily, they ask me to point you out when you come in. Take some tea, on the house.' He sat down on an empty chair, his eyes glinting with curiosity. After Lily muttered her thanks, he told her in halting English DW died of a heart attack in his flat and was found by Bill and Salma. Glancing uneasily at Lily, he told her everyone believed food poisoning from her stall brought on his heart attack. Uncle Wang avoided Lily's flashing eyes and looked at the trees in front of the canteen.

Despite her predicament, Lily felt curious. She sipped her tea and said, 'Why did Bill and Salma go to Dr Pak's house?'

'The Korean gentleman's daughters call the English gentleman. They worried their Pa not answering his phone. He have a bad heart.'

Lily finished her tea and said, 'Thanks again for the tea. Well, Uncle Wang, the doctor will find out the Korean gentleman did not die of food poisoning. I am sure of that.'

While Angie was finishing her tea and after Uncle Wang had left, Lily mourned, 'We will never live down the shame of being a dirty stall. No one will buy our food again. I will talk to my sister. She is dropping by to see our mother tonight. A police officer can surely make enquiries about how the poor gentleman died. Come, Angie, I'll give you a ride home.'

When Angie stood up, Lily suddenly hugged her. 'Don't let the news about our stall lessen your joy of being pregnant, Angie. Believe me, not everyone is given the chance.' Lily smiled mischievously. 'I want to see V's face when he hears the news.'

The two women giggled and made their way to the carpark.

* * *

Lily was remonstrating with her sister in the large sitting-room of their mother's condo at Silver Springs. She sat on a long, low ottoman glowering at her elder sister, Dolly, seated opposite her on a roomy single sofa. Dolly had dropped in to see her mother on her way back home from work. She raised a cup of tea to her lips as she looked at her younger sister. It was raining outside, and the window was closed.

Dolly and Lily were unalike in appearance. Where Lily was short and some would say plain, Dolly was tall, statuesque with a slim waist. Lily was dark to Dolly's fair skin but was not envious of her sister's beauty and was the first to tell friends that Dolly had once been a runner-up in a beauty contest. Lily, though, was secretly jealous of Dolly's intelligence, with memories of their late father lauding Dolly's academic achievements while throwing reproachful glances at his younger daughter still haunting her. Praises heaped on her for helping to solve her sister's murder case at Silver Springs condo about a year ago had done wonders for Lily's self-confidence. Her feelings of inferiority surfaced only now and then.

Right now, Lily was an angry ball of fire and Dolly's large brown eyes, delicately accentuated by eyeliner, looked at the divan where a frail bent figure in a nightie sat in all her pathetic grandeur. Anxiously hovering around, like a well-meaning fly, was a short round woman in her thirties, in shorts and tee, the domestic helper, Girlie. Girlie, who had left Uma's employment to return to the Philippines a year ago to her husband, had returned to Singapore to work a month ago after her husband mortgaged their house to pay off his gambling debts.

Uma Das, at eighty, was plagued with osteoporosis, her bones slowly disintegrating into fine dust. Her eye lenses had started turning foggy, but Uma refused to have her cataracts removed. Instead, she wore powerful glasses that she bought at periodic intervals from her optician. Her hooked nose (that her younger daughter had inherited) hung predator-like over thin sucked-in lips. The living hall was lit by shady lamps placed on low tables. The chandelier hanging from the ceiling remained unlit as bright light hurt Uma's cataract-ridden eyes.

'My stall is not to blame for this food poisoning, and I am not going to have my reputation spoilt in this way.' Lily's voice trembled, her face a dark purple. 'I demand you open an investigation into this poisoning case at Temasek University, Dolly!'

Dolly, dressed in a sensible trouser suit, stirred uneasily. She said softly, 'And I am telling you the NEA oversees investigations into food poisoning. There is nothing I can do.'

'Do you know how much income I will lose?' Lily squeaked.

'That cannot be helped,' Dolly said tersely.

Uma's eyes were round with wonder behind her glasses. 'Oh dear, Lil, your food actually killed somebody. What did you serve? What else could it be but food poisoning?' Uma quavered. Her eyes bored into her younger daughter. 'The gentleman only ate your food before he was sick.'

Lily glared at her mother. 'How do you know that? And explain to me why we have not had reports of anyone else suffering from food poisoning! Why would the food poisoning target only Dr Pak?'

Dolly stirred. 'Dr Pak is a heart patient, you said. Maybe his heart was already in a bad state and the food poisoning made it fail.'

'I want to know something,' Uma said. 'The non-vegetarian thalis had dal and vegetables, too, right? What was different with the pure vegetarian thali?'

Lily said, 'The extra eggplant curry. Mummy, the non-vegetarian thalis had the dal and cauliflower masala in common with the vegetarian thali. I offer dal and two vegetables for the vegetarian thali. Usually I serve paneer butter masala, but I had run out of paneer, and I served a potato and eggplant curry instead. So, those who had the vegetarian thali ate the extra eggplant dish. That is the reason NEA shut me down. They said my eggplant dish caused the food poisoning. But the Indian pharmacy girls who ate that seem fine, so my stall is not to blame.'

Uma frowned. 'Eggplant doesn't usually spoil. It's meat and fish dishes that can get bad.' She looked askance at her daughter. 'Your stall was cleaned as usual before the cooking started?'

Lily looked outraged. 'V opened the stall and hosed it down and Angie cleaned the counters. Even though it had been cleaned the previous evening, I always insist on double cleaning.' She tossed her head. 'Let the NEA people come and do their inspection. My stall is clean. And when the doctor at the hospital confirms DW died from other causes, NEA will have egg on their faces. Shutting down an "A" grade stall just like that!'

'Even if the Korean scientist's heart failed from natural causes, that doesn't put you in the clear, Lil.' Dolly finished her tea and looked at her watch. 'His heart problems could have worsened after the food poisoning. Unless doctors can prove the gentleman did not have food poisoning at all, you will still be blamed for his death. It's nearly 8 p.m. Joey is making an Italian dinner at home. I need to go.'

Uma gave an enormous yawn and smiled toothlessly at Girlie. 'What's for dinner? Did Lily bring back some food from her stall? Butter chicken tonight, Girlie?'

Dolly looked horrified. 'Surely, you are not thinking of having food cooked by Lily until her stall is in the clear.' Getting up to go, Dolly cleared her throat and looked furtively at her sister. 'I had lunch with Frankie today. Joey joined us as well.'

Lily looked surprised. 'Whatever for?'

'Joey saw Frankie drinking at Wine Connection one night when he was having dinner there with a client. Frankie got so drunk he passed out and Joey had to see him home. So, my husband went to visit Frankie to ask if everything was all right. Frankie started crying. He said he feels like ending his life because he cannot help having OCD and that is breaking up his marriage. Joey was afraid he would do something stupid, so we met for lunch today. I tried to counsel Frankie,' Dolly said, looking at their mother for support.

'Stop interfering in my affairs, Dolly,' Lily said in an icy voice. She rose from the ottoman and said, 'It's been a long day and I have a headache. I am off to bed.' She looked at Girlie. 'Leave my casserole in the oven, Girlie. I will have it as a late-night snack. Yes, Mummy, vegetable casserole for dinner with toasted garlic bread.' Her eyes flashed at Dolly. 'Nothing fancy and NOTHING from my stall. There was a lot of leftover food from my stall today since no one bought it. Angie has taken all the food for their house and will also share with her neighbours. I thought loyalty started at home.' She stormed out of the room.

'Mummy, you should talk to her.' Dolly walked over to her mother. 'She can't give up on her marriage just like this. She will listen to you. Frankie has agreed to talk to a counsellor. That's the first step in this sort of thing.'

'A marriage counsellor?' Uma stared at her older daughter.

'No, Mummy. A mental health counsellor. OCD is a form of mental illness,' Dolly said, patiently. She pecked her mother's cheek. 'Goodnight, Mummy.'

Girlie shut the door after Dolly and went to the kitchen to warm up the casserole for Uma.

Lily, lying on her bed, could hear the door opening and closing, snatches of conversation and then the squeak of Uma's wheelchair as Girlie wheeled her to the dining room for dinner. The moon shone in through the window, lighting up the bedroom in an eerie glow. Lily's lips trembled. She had lost her husband, and now she might be losing her job and career. The stall was her baby, and she could not help sobbing bitterly.

After spending some time on self-pity, Lily reached down inside herself and found the courage to face tomorrow. She would find out whether anyone other than DW had fallen sick. And if not, she would not rest until she had solved the case of the mysterious poisoning.

Wednesday, 31 August 2011

6

The sky was clear blue and the sun shone brightly. Lily had spent a sleepless night worrying about her catering business and found she had no appetite for breakfast. Uma was feeling poorly with fatigue and a slight cough. Lily resolved to take her to the medical clinic in the afternoon if she got worse. She was grateful to have Girlie, who cooked oatmeal just the way Uma liked it and patiently fed her in her bedroom from a tray. Lily's mind was on her stall. She took a brisk shower and decided to visit the canteen to find out more about the Korean scientist's death.

At 10 a.m., Lily walked along the covered path connecting the condo blocks to the carpark. There was a film of tears in her eyes. Her mother's ailments were increasing in number. A diabetic with hypertension, Uma had recently been diagnosed with early-stage Parkinson's Disease. *Singapore is not the cheapest city in the world when it comes to healthcare,* Lily thought to herself. Living with her mother, she did not like asking her sister, Dolly, for money to pay for her mother's visits to a neurologist at a private hospital. No, she had to make a living and help her mother with expenses. She quite forgot she was still the legally wedded wife of a lawyer with a lucrative practice who would readily pay for his mother-in-law's medical expenses.

'Hi, Lily! Taken your breakfast?'

Lily grinned as she saw her friend, Ashikin Ali, walking towards her, smiling widely. Ashikin was dressed in a purple baju kurung with a matching tudung and her big brown eyes were warm and friendly. Ashikin lived in Block C, and Lily had made friends with her during a baking class they had attended together. Ashikin shared Lily's interest in cooking, and Lily enjoyed hearing about the trials she had with getting her four children to live peacefully with each other without squabbles breaking out every minute. Whenever she was free, Ashikin worked in her sister's stall at the Takashimaya Shopping Centre's basement food court.

'Yes, and you? Nasi lemak, right. Oh, your nasi lemak is delicious, Ashikin. The coconut rice so moist and the chicken fried exactly right.'

Ashikin giggled, before her face became serious. 'Ali was reading the newspaper this morning and said your stall was shut down by NEA. Someone died after taking your food. I can't believe it! You are so clean and tidy. I was going to ask to work at your stall.' Her face became sad. 'My sister's stall has closed. She did not make enough profit any more. She is taking a break from work now and I am out of a job.'

Lily looked dismayed. Everyone in Singapore now knew her stall sold contaminated food. How would she live this smear down? 'I did not know the newspapers printed the news of every stall that is shut by the NEA for investigation.'

'I think it's because someone died,' Ashikin said in a small voice.

'We will see about that,' Lily said, grimly. 'The gentleman who died had the same food as a dozen others so how come he was the only one affected? No, there is more to this.'

'You are so clever, Lily.' Ashikin smiled. 'I still remember how you solved your sister's case in our complex. You will find out how this gentleman died. I am sure it's not because of your food, either. Hey, if you reopen, can I come work for you?'

Lily sighed and slowly shook her head. 'I already pay Vernon and Angie good wages. If I take on another person, I won't make much profit.'

'We share the lease and the profits, 30–70, maybe? No need to pay me salary. I was thinking we have a Malay-Indian stall,' Ashikin said, conspiratorially. 'I cook the Malay dishes and you make the Indian ones.'

Lily's eyes sparkled. 'Not a bad idea, friend, but there is already a Malay food stall in the canteen. They don't sell breakfast, though. Hmm, your nasi lemak will draw many more customers to my stall for sure. Some staff and students come in early and have breakfast at the canteen, so we can sell your nasi lemak and I will make roti prata with curry. You can make rojak for teatime and I make my samosas. This is a good idea, Ashikin, and I will think about it.'

Ashikin smiled in appreciation. 'Thanks, Lily. Got to fetch Zainab from pre-school. Talk to you, later, Lily, okay?'

Lily walked thoughtfully to the carpark and got into her Honda Jazz. As she drove, she thought hard. Dr Pak had to have taken some other food after he had eaten his lunch. She hoped one of the Singh research group students or fellows could tell her more of Pak's movements after he had taken lunch at her stall.

* * *

Lily walked from the carpark to the canteen. She entered, smiling at customers and other vendors, the smile fading as people turned away from her. Only Bill Eddington, sitting at a table, sipping tea, greeted her, warmly.

'Hello, Mrs D, why don't you join me for a cup of tea?' He said and when Lily nodded, he went to the drinks stall and got her tea.

Lily looked at the masala chai, aghast, and then glared at the drinks stall vendor, who was grinning at her. 'What cheek! Uncle Wang never sold masala chai before my stall closed, it was a specialty sold only at my stall!' Lily exploded. 'Look at him now. Making the most of my absence to take over my business. Let me see how his tea tastes,' she fumed, before taking a sip. A grin spread over her face. 'Bitter! Yes, you must know how to blend the Indian spices so the tea tastes pleasant and invigorating. Pooh!' She gave a thumbs down sign to Uncle Wang in the distance, wiping the grin off his face.

'I knew the masala tea would not taste like yours, so I ordered *teh tarik*,' Bill said. Sadness etched his face. 'DW liked your tea very much, Mrs D.'

'Oh, the poor gentleman.' Lily looked morose. 'You found him, Dr Eddington?'

Bill nodded, and while sipping his tea, narrated the events that occurred after Pak had been taken home on Monday. His face reflected the horror he experienced on finding his friend's lifeless body. 'The hospital pronounced him dead on arrival. I accompanied the body in the ambulance.' Bill finished his tea, his hands on the tumbler trembling.

Lily had been listening attentively. Now stubbornness set on her face. 'But my food did not poison him. The Pharmacy students ate the vegetable thali along with him and did not get food poisoning.'

Bill decided to articulate the worry he had been experiencing. Lowering his voice, he said, 'Mrs D, what I am telling you is confidential. Latha said your sister is a police inspector. Please repeat what I tell you to her. DW liked to drink and would take a sip or two from a whisky flask he brought to our office. He was never drunk before, at least not during the day, but the way Salma described him before I found him slumped on his desk indicated he had been intoxicated. Salma was the last to speak to him on Monday before he lost consciousness, and she says he was slurring and acting drunkenly. He had taken a bit of whisky before lunch, but not enough to be drunk.'

'He was an alcoholic then,' Lily stated.

'Yes, but here's what's puzzling, Mrs D. I never smelt any alcohol on him when I found him Monday afternoon. He was not reeking of alcohol. Yet, he had been slurring and was in a state of euphoria. Salma told me all this last evening before we went to DW's house. I looked in DW's satchel on the desk, expecting his liquor flask to be empty. But, Mrs D, it was two-thirds full, like it was before we went down to lunch on Monday. If he had not taken alcohol from his flask, then how was he drunk?' Bill frowned. 'I believe there is some mystery about DW's death. His daughters are on their way to Singapore; they will arrive sometime this evening and stay at his apartment. I will tell them all this too. It would be good to know if there were high alcohol levels in DW's body. That would explain whether he was drunk from alcohol consumption or only had symptoms of intoxication.'

Lily's eyes had rounded, and she was breathing fast. 'An autopsy could determine that, right? I wonder if his body is still in the hospital morgue, and who signed his death certificate? But why would he appear drunk if he were not drinking? Oh, Dr Eddington, I will ask my sister about this and let you know.'

'Not a word to anyone else, mind,' Bill warned. 'I don't want his daughters to hear rumours.' Bill thanked Lily and rose from his seat.

Lily nodded, reassuringly. 'I will only tell my sister. See if she can talk to DW's doctors. As you know, I have a vested interest in knowing how the poor gentleman died as everyone is saying it is from my food.'

As Bill walked away from the canteen, he felt relieved. Bill had good instinct: it was screaming at him that all was not what it seemed about Dong-wook Pak's death. As he switched his computer on in his office and set to work on his funding proposal, glancing from time to time at Dong-wook's empty chair, he felt DW's presence around him. It was almost as if DW was urgently trying to communicate with him from the nether world. Bill shook his head at himself for being fanciful.

7

The sun was blazing in the afternoon. Dolly parked her car at the VIP section, walked the few feet to the glass doors of a glittering lobby and entered the air-conditioned comfort of Temasek Teaching Hospital. She had taken Bill Eddington's concerns seriously and assured her sister she would talk to the doctor who had written Dr Pak's death certificate. To better facilitate discussions on the possible causes of DW's demise, she had sent the forensic pathologist, Benny Ong, to the hospital beforehand as Dr Alex Gan, the doctor who had treated DW when he was alive and signed his death certificate, was a friend of Benny's.

Dolly took the lift to the eighth floor and was directed by Dr Gan's receptionist to a meeting room at the end of the corridor. She knocked and entered. The room was small, but with bay windows and a view of shimmering greenery. Benny Ong rose from a chair behind a round conference table as did a silver-haired, bespectacled man in his fifties. Benny motioned Dolly to a chair, and everyone seated themselves. The forensic pathologist was a short, rotund man with a bald pate, and his kind, jovial manner made him popular with the police officers. Now his face was sombre as he looked at Dolly.

'Good afternoon, Inspector Das,' Dr Gan said. 'Benny has filled me in on Dr Eddington's concerns. I was the one who wrote Dr Pak's death certificate. He was my patient. I am a cardiologist, and from the time he joined the university, Dr Dong-wook Pak was under my care. He had hypertension and a bad heart. In fact, I told him he may need to be fitted with a pacemaker soon. He had a documented history of heart disease, and when I examined him after he was brought to the hospital, I found he had a heart attack, probably brought on by a seizure from the food poisoning. I did cardiological tests and am certain he expired from a massive heart attack.'

'He may have died of a heart attack,' Dolly said, looking candidly at the cardiologist, 'but on Monday before he was taken ill and after he had taken the food that may have caused poisoning, he appeared intoxicated. I have not known heart disease or food poisoning present with intoxication symptoms.'

'Maybe he had several drinks. I did warn him to limit his alcohol intake. I am aware he liked drinking whisky.' Dr Gan frowned.

Benny Ong intervened. 'His whisky flask was two-thirds full. I think the police want to know about his alcohol levels.'

Dr Gan was shaking his head. 'We did not do a toxicology or blood and urine alcohol panel. Pak's heart stopped beating and that was it. Even if we find alcohol in his body, he still died from a heart attack.'

'But what if you don't find alcohol in his body?' Dolly's eyes were shining. 'Maybe he was poisoned.'

Benny Ong nodded. 'Yes, some poisons can give symptoms of intoxication, retching and seizures.'

Dolly saw that Dr Gan was unconvinced. She was thoughtful as she looked out of the window at the sunlight glinting from the leaves of the trees. She turned back to Gan and said, 'Pak was slurring and laughing. He was behaving like a drunkard. So, odds are that you will find alcohol in his body, and we will all be satisfied that he had too much to drink. What is the harm in doing an alcohol levels test? He may have gone somewhere with a friend and had drinks, though the time factor is there. He seemed to have been in his office after lunch. People saw him there.'

'Is the family asking for such a test?' Dr Gan said, stiffly, his eyes narrowed in disapproval. 'We have to budget resources and I have to give justification for extra tests.'

'His daughters are on the way here from Korea,' Dolly said, 'and I will ask one of my officers to liaise via text or email with them and meet them at the airport and take them to their father's apartment. We cannot force you to do alcohol tests, Dr Gan, not if you are entirely convinced that Pak died from pre-existing heart problems. Was he at great risk of a heart attack?'

'No, no, absolutely not. He was keeping well. The food poisoning taxed his heart.'

'But, Dr Gan, we are not at all certain that Dr Pak suffered from food poisoning. You see, no one else who ate the same food was poisoned,' Dolly spoke sharply and concisely.

Benny said, 'Come now, Alex. From all symptoms described, it does seem that Pak's death is a bit of a mystery. The cause of death may be a heart attack, but we need to know for certain what brought it on. Do you have urine and blood samples from the deceased?'

Dr Gan sighed. 'Yes, we did take samples. Okay, I liked Pak, we shared travel tales together. I can do some alcohol tests and put it on his medical bill. But he died Tuesday early evening and he may have consumed alcohol on Monday. So, alcohol may not show up in the blood. I will need to check for alcohol in the urine, Benny, if we have enough of a sample. But it would be good if one of his daughters gave me a call and authorized it. Then I can do the EtG test on the urine sample. I will let you know the results, Inspector Das.'

Dolly nodded, satisfied. She thanked Benny with a nod, knowing that his friendship with Alex Gan had tilted the balance in favour of doing an alcohol test. She left the room and made her way outside, a niggling feeling in her heart that there was more to Dong-wook Pak's death than a mere heart attack.

* * *

Dolly buzzed for her sergeant, Charlie, as soon as she reached CID HQ on New Bridge Road and was seated in her office. Charlie immediately came over and Dolly motioned him to the chair on the other side of the desk and began narrating the circumstances surrounding the mysterious death of Dr Dong-wook Pak.

Senior Staff Sergeant Charles Goh had worked with Dolly for a long time. He was overweight, with a goatee beard, and wore rimless spectacles. He was a family man and his Indian wife, Meena, who was a good cook, was firm friends with Lily Das. Dolly sometimes wondered what she would do without Charlie. He was astute, hardworking and jovial, traits that endeared him to his colleagues.

Charlie listened to Dolly with interest. 'So, the Korean gentleman had lunch at Madam Lily's and within the hour was slurring and acting drunk. And his whisky bottle was untouched. I wonder if the gentleman had some dessert or a beverage after his lunch when he was back at his office. Food poisonings, Madam, are usually on a large scale. It is odd the Pharmacy girls who had eaten the same food did not report any food-poisoning symptoms. That's got me thinking the gentleman had something else to drink or eat later. And he had vomited and fainted around 4 p.m.? Hmm, I have had food poisoning a couple of times and the reaction is quite immediate. Diarrhoea and vomiting are within an hour of ingestion.'

'Maybe he vomited in the toilet, we wouldn't know,' Dolly said. 'The main thing to focus on is that he had the symptoms of intoxication but had not taken whisky in the afternoon as far as we know. Sometimes, Charlie, poison can give these symptoms. It seems to be a suspicious death. Benny has talked to Dr Gan, the Korean gentleman's cardiologist, and he has agreed to test the dead gentleman's alcohol levels, from the urine, I think, once he has the go-ahead from Pak's daughters.' She opened her notebook and flipped through some pages. 'When Dr Gan informed the daughters of their father's death yesterday, they decided to fly here immediately. They contacted Dr Eddington to say their plane reaches Changi Airport at 7 p.m. Someone from our team can meet the daughters at the airport, take them to Dr Pak's quarters and tell them they need to call Dr Gan if they want to know what really happened to their father. Gan wants the family to authorize the alcohol test. You are wrapping up the North Changi Street industrial homicide case this evening, right?'

'Yes, Madam, Mok and I will be arresting the killer this evening, but I know whom to send to the airport to meet Dr Pak's daughters. Leave this to me, Madam. We will get the daughters to call Dr Gan and request the alcohol tests.'

Dolly nodded and said, 'Keep me updated about the arrest in the North Changi murder case, Charlie.'

When her sergeant had left, Dolly checked for email messages before switching the computer off. Then she gathered her handbag and went down the lift to her car. Her husband, Joey, was working late before flying off the next morning for an assignment in Bali, and Dolly decided to visit her mother and sister at Silver Springs Condo.

8

Dolly was in the living room of her mother's Silver Springs Condo unit sipping after-dinner coffee when her mobile phone rang. She frowned on seeing her ex-husband's name on the caller ID display. *What did Pritam Singh want with her?*

It was not Pritam but his wife, Cheryl, who was on the line.

Cheryl's voice was hesitant. 'Really sorry to disturb you at this hour, Dolly. Pritam is out and forgot to take his phone with him. I don't know what to do.'

'What's up?' Dolly's voice was crisp. While she had resented the young Chinese girl for wrecking her marriage and estranging her son from his father, Cheryl's subsequent miscarriage and the trauma she had suffered had mellowed Dolly. Knowing Cheryl was seven months pregnant, Dolly decided to help her 'former rival' in whatever way she could. She could not care less, anyway, now about Cheryl and Pritam, being happily married to her Eurasian husband, Joey Pestana.

'Pritam is having psychological problems.' Cheryl's voice was teary. 'He goes into a deep depression some weekends and has nightmares daily. Sometimes he calls out for you and can't remember me.' Dolly heard Cheryl burst into tears at the other end of the line.

Dolly frowned. Pritam calling out for her? She tried to make her voice casual. 'Stress at work, maybe?'

'Oh, it's more than that,' Cheryl said in a more composed voice. 'He sometimes shouts at me for no reason, and he has trouble remembering events. Once, he even forgot he has a son!'

Dolly bristled. 'Cannot be! Ash and Preet are so close. Why, they call each other every weekend! Ash may call him late as he is busy in the camps, but they do talk.'

'That's just it. Preet did not take Ash's call last Saturday and told me at dinner that someone called Ashok is hounding him on the telephone!' Cheryl's voice became high-pitched. 'Do you know if anyone in Pritam's family suffers from mental problems?'

Dolly's brows drew together in a frown. She did not know how to answer Cheryl as she knew next to nothing about Pritam's family. She cleared her throat. 'Pritam was living in a bachelor pad when I met him. There was a burglary at his house, and I investigated the case. His family cut off ties with him long before I came on the scene.' She coughed discreetly. 'Pritam had a wild youth. His parents died when he was young, and his uncle was after the family property and palmed him off to a distant relative to raise. Pritam was into drink and drugs when young. He only mentioned this to me once or twice. He does not like talking about his past. During our marriage, we never visited his family, not even the distant aunt who raised him. So, I don't have an answer to your question.'

'This is so upsetting,' Cheryl bleated, 'and I'm seven months gone. I'm sure it's all building towards another miscarriage.'

'You'll be all right,' Dolly said, kindly. 'I'll drop in on Pritam, don't worry, maybe when I visit my sister's stall once it's open. You take care.'

Dolly sat back in her chair and thought hard. She had always found Pritam's reticence about his family intriguing. Who knows, she mused, there may be a mad woman in the attic from his past. There was a cough and Dolly looked up. Her mother and sister were looking expectantly at her. Sighing, Dolly told them Cheryl's news.

'Forgetting Ash? That man has Alzheimer's for sure,' was Uma's unsympathetic view.

Lily was more tolerant. 'Poor Preet. He looks unhappy nowadays. He comes into the stall to eat his lunch looking preoccupied. He told me he is one of the candidates standing for the elected headship of the department. Maybe he is tense about that.'

Dolly finished her coffee and said, 'I will text Ash. He talks to Pritam often and will know more about his dad.'

Lily said, 'Thanks for talking to Dr Gan about the alcohol tests, Dolly. I really need to clear my name.'

Dolly nodded. 'Charlie texted that Pak's daughters have authorized Dr Gan to do the tests. Results will be in tomorrow. Pak's death is sudden and odd.' Dolly could not help being interested in Pak's death. She was naturally analytical and curious.

Lily thought back to all the crime thrillers she had read and asked with shining eyes, 'Is there a poison that mimics drunkenness when ingested?'

'We are not doctors, how should we know,' Dolly observed, waspishly. She glanced at her sister. 'Lily, do go home to Frankie.'

Lily's face went dark, and she left the room. Girlie, who had been sitting at Uma's feet, said sadly, 'Mr Frankie loves Ma'am so much, but all she sees are his bad habits.'

Dolly glanced at her watch. 'Joey should be home now. He is leaving for an assignment tomorrow morning, and I will be alone.'

'Stay here, of course,' Uma said in a sleepy voice.

Dolly smiled. 'Thank you, Mummy. You look half asleep. Take her to bed, Girlie. I will let myself out.'

Dolly walked down the dimly lit path of the condo complex towards the main gate. The night was dark and silent. A trained police officer, Dolly knew someone was stealthily following her. She walked on and then suddenly whipped around and ran towards her stalker and caught him before he could understand what was going on.

Dolly dragged her stalker towards the lamppost and in the dim glow, she examined his face. 'Frankie!' She exclaimed on recognizing her brother-in-law. 'Why are you stalking me?'

Frankie Kennedy reeked of alcohol and looked morosely at his sister-in-law. 'I want you to make Lily return to me,' he slurred.

Dolly shepherded Frankie along the path until they came to the gate where Bahadur, the security guard, was sitting in his kiosk, gazing out at the road. He stood to attention on seeing Dolly and looked with surprise at Frankie.

'Mr Kennedy,' Bahadur smiled. 'Long time no see. Your new house nice?'

Dolly realized Bahadur recognized Frankie as a former resident of Silver Springs Condo; in fact, it had been here that Frankie had first met Lily. 'Bahadur,' Dolly said, sternly. 'Please call a cab.'

While waiting for the taxi, Dolly sat her brother-in-law on a bench, seated herself next to him and began talking softly.

'Frankie,' Dolly said, kindly. 'Lily loves you. I am sure of that. But she cannot cope with your OCD. Joey told me you are consulting with a therapist this week. The doctor will help you to live with a spouse without problems.'

'You make me sound like a madman,' Frankie accused, loudly, and glared at Bahadur, who was inching forward to eavesdrop on their conversation. 'What do you want?' Bahadur melted away into the darkness. Frankie continued, his brown eyes moist, his hair dishevelled, 'I have always been manic about cleanliness ever since I was a child. My parents did not leave me because of it. I stayed in the same house as them.'

Dolly sighed. Her large eyes surveyed her brother-in-law with pity. 'Parents have no choice,' she said, knowing for a fact that whatever her son, Ash, did, she would always be by his side. 'A spouse is different. Any normal newly married couple takes time to adjust to each other, so it was a bit of a shock for poor Lily to confront your OCD. But I am sure the therapist will give you pointers on how to manage your mania. It is not right of me to interfere, Frankie,' Dolly added sternly. 'You are a lawyer and a good one. You know Lily must return to you of her own free will. Here is the cab. Come on, get in.'

After the taxi had driven off and before Dolly made her way to the carpark to get into her car to drive home, she glanced kindly at Bahadur. 'How is your little son?'

The Nepalese security guard beamed, his small eyes lighting up. 'Naughty, Madam. I go see them December, Manager Babu give me two weeks holiday, Madam. I show you video of my boy?'

Ten minutes later, after making appreciative noises about Bahadur's video of his son, Dolly was in her car driving home to the eastern part of Singapore. She could not help wondering what the alcohol test would reveal the next day. Dolly was fond of her sister and knew Lily was stringent about hygiene. She did not believe there had been any food poisoning from her sister's stall.

Her thoughts switched to her husband, and she smiled fondly. Joey Pestana had been her JC classmate, and she had met him again when she hired him as a private investigator during her divorce from Pritam. After her divorce, Dolly dated the fun-loving Eurasian for three months and quickly married him. She was happily married and only wished that Joey's work as a PI did not take him away from Singapore as often as it did. He was sure to have cooked a delicious dinner and Dolly looked forward to spending time with her husband before he flew off the next day.

Thursday, 1 September 2011

9

It was past noon on a sunny warm day and Dolly, in sisterly camaraderie, decided to have lunch with Lily at the science canteen of the university. She did not want Lily to feel isolated and wanted to be on hand if Dr Alex Gan needed to see her when the results of Pak's alcohol tests came in. The Temasek Teaching Hospital was within walking distance of the canteen. It was the peak lunch hour and students ate and talked in loud voices. Birds pecked on the ground inside the canteen, at scraps of food that had dropped from the tables.

Dolly's mobile beeped urgently when the sisters were eating fish-ball noodles soup from a stall. She looked at the text and gave an exclamation. Lily glanced at her sister, enquiringly, her eyes had been on her shut stall and her mind wandering back to the days when she was doing good business there.

'That was Dr Gan. The tests for alcohol did not show overly elevated levels, but the urine sample gave a surprising result. The doctor found small amounts of calcium oxalate crystals in the urine, a by-product of ethylene glycol poisoning. That explains why DW appeared drunk when he wasn't, as ethylene glycol poisoning gives symptoms of intoxication without alcohol consumption. DW was murdered, Lil! Poisoned!' Dolly's voice rose excitedly above the babble of conversation. A few students turned to look at the two sisters.

Lily's eyes were round and gleamed with excitement. 'Wow, DW was poisoned with anti-freeze.' She told her sister of the time she had seen steam rising from the bonnet of her car in very hot weather and the car-shop mechanic told her the engine needed a coolant called anti-freeze. He brought out a bottle of the anti-freeze and cooled the engine down and from that time, she always had a bottle of anti-freeze in the car trunk in case the engine heated up. Lily said she had looked at the ingredients of anti-freeze and the primary one was ethylene glycol. 'Who could have poisoned DW and why?' Lily's mind whirred back to crime thrillers she had read. She absently spooned a fish ball out of her soup and popped it into her mouth. Then her eyes widened. *This meant she was off the hook. DW had not suffered from food poisoning.*

Dolly was busy calling Dr Alex Gan on the phone. After she had finished talking, she ate her cooling noodle soup while saying, 'When the pathologist told him there was a chemical substance called calcium oxalate in DW's urine sample, Dr Gan ordered the ethylene glycol test. Oxalic acid seems to be a by-product in the body when ethylene glycol metabolizes there, and the acid later forms a salt that was found in the urine. If there was no ethylene glycol in the body, calcium oxalate crystals would not be detected in the urine. Ethylene glycol is readily available in a chemistry laboratory, Lil.'

'Also, in car and DIY shops,' Lily countered, while finishing the last of her noodle soup.

Dolly got busy on her phone texting. She said, 'I am asking Charlie to inform Dr Pak's daughters of developments. They arrived here last night and are staying in Dr Pak's apartment. My team is liaising with them by telephone and text.'

'Your soup is getting cold,' Lily pointed out. 'Are you authorized by Supt Dragon Lady to run the investigation?' Lily asked innocently. 'Seems to me you are doing a lot of unofficial investigation.'

'Well, first you wanted me to investigate what really happened to DW and now you are backtracking,' Dolly said, grumpily. 'There's no pleasing you, Lily!' Dolly's mobile beeped again, and she got up from her chair and moved away from the table to take a call, leaving her noodles half eaten. When she returned to the table, she said, 'That was Supt Dragon Lady,' she said, referring to her boss, Superintendent Siti Abdullah. 'Dr Pak's daughters have been informed of the poisoning and are requesting us to investigate his homicide and catch his murderer. We have a case to solve, Lily, so I will be off. Supt Dragon Lady has put me in charge of catching DW's poisoner and wants to see me ASAP. Benny Ong, the forensic pathologist, will now take over the autopsy since it's a murder case. Joey left for an assignment in Bali, so Mummy asked me to stay at Silver Springs for a few days. See you at home, later tonight.'

'See you, Doll!' Lily watched her sister disappear into the sunshine and quietly started on her lime juice.

Supt Dragon Lady was the mischievous nickname Dolly and her sergeant, Charlie, had given Superintendent Siti Abdullah of the Special Investigation Section, Major Crime Division of the Singapore CID. Siti was a strict disciplinarian, very set in her ways. While Dolly and Siti had got off to a rocky start in their relationship when Siti became Dolly's boss two years ago, Dolly's success in solving the Silver Springs murder case had thawed the relationship and instilled a grudging admiration in Siti for her subordinate.

Lily's pulse rate quickened with excitement. She knew Dr Pak and his colleagues well as they had eaten at her stall every day, and she had liked the jovial gentleman from Korea. Her mouth set grimly. She resolved to help her sister catch his murderer. Lily rose from her chair and walked away, a determined figure making for the carpark.

* * *

Dolly stood at her Level 14 office window of CID HQ on New Bridge Road and looked out. The cars on the road looked like toys. She felt the familiar rush of adrenalin pulse through her as it always did before she started work on a murder case. So far, she had solved every murder case that had come her way and locked up the killer. She was puzzled about Dr Pak's murder, though. The killer was daring enough to operate in broad daylight. The poison had to have been administered sometime after lunch, and students and fellows were about at the time. How had the poison been given? She had to interview the students and fellows to find out. And to take the ethylene glycol from the solvent cupboard needed boldness, though that could have been done at night if the killer were a staff or a student; they all had keys to the doors after the janitor had locked up for the night. And why use a poison as the weapon of death? Because it was handy in a chemistry laboratory?

There was a knock on her door and Charlie entered.

Charlie seated himself after Dolly had sat in her swivel chair. He opened a file and glanced at some reports. Then he looked up and smiled. 'So, yet another case to solve, Madam. I have looked at your notes and yet again Madam Lily pointed you in the right direction. If not for her heads up, we would not have asked the doctors to look for poison in Pak's body.'

Dolly smiled. 'Lily can't help being nosy. But yes, her sunny nature makes her accessible to people and Bill Eddington told her his worry that Pak appeared drunk without smelling of liquor.'

Charlie nodded. 'But poison, Madam? This is our first case investigating a poisoning. Do you think the killer used poison because it is easily accessible in a chemistry laboratory?'

'It looks that way, Charlie. But we have a very bold killer to murder in broad daylight. We have our work cut out for tomorrow. You and I will interview the students and fellows of the Singh and Botham groups in the morning. At the same time, have Mok and the team question everyone on that floor, especially ask whether they saw anyone behaving suspiciously near Pak's office on Monday afternoon. The forensics team is not going to be of much help two days after the murder when the crime scene has been compromised.'

'The time of the poisoning has been established.' Charlie looked at Dolly's notes. 'Pak finished lunch around 1 p.m., and no one reported he was unwell then. When the Malay undergraduate went in at 1.45 p.m., Pak was showing signs of intoxication. So, he started ingesting the poison during that interval of time.'

Dolly looked at her watch. 'Let's see if we can narrow that timing down by talking to the students and fellows. We must ask them if they saw DW taking food or a beverage any time in the afternoon after lunch. I must speak now with Supt Dragon Lady. We can discuss some more about the case after I return. I will give you a buzz.'

Charlie nodded and left the office. Dolly made her way to the lift and was soon on the way to see Superintendent Siti Abdullah. While she and her boss had ironed out their differences and shared mutual respect, Dolly was still apprehensive about meeting her supervisor knowing that fundamentally they shared dissimilar work ethics, with Siti not placing any emphasis on psychological profiling of murder suspects.

Siti glanced up from some papers on her desk when Dolly entered, and Dolly was dismayed to see her boss's eyes angry and her face set and unfriendly.

'Sit down, Inspector Das,' Siti said in an icy tone. 'May I ask why you spoke to the journalists about the poisoning at Temasek University before clearing it with me?'

Dolly's face went slack with astonishment. 'Ma'am,' she stuttered. 'I never spoke to journalists about Dr Pak's murder. I only came to know he was poisoned at lunchtime when Dr Gan texted me the news.'

Siti's black eyes flashed ominously. 'I have it on authority that a police officer from our division spoke to the press about half an hour ago. The newspapers are going to run the story that a researcher in a chemistry laboratory in Singapore has been poisoned with a chemical from the lab. Imagine how readers will feel! I won't be surprised if chemistry major students start dropping out of the university. I have told you that I deal with the journos.'

Dolly's face was ashen. 'Ma'am, I did not talk to the press, please believe me. And I am sure Charlie did not either.'

'Someone from your team did,' Supt Abdullah said, angrily. 'This is sensitive news. We all know chemistry laboratories keep industrial poisons as they are needed for the practical experiments and research. But if the way the press puts it is that these poisons are easily accessible and that students or teachers are on a killing spree, we are in trouble. First identify the leak in your team, Inspector Das, and update me on that as well as your investigation, starting now.'

'Yes, Ma'am,' Dolly said with a worried face and hurried out of the room.

10

Dolly walked back to her office, breathing hard. It would be a disaster if the press reported the poisoning at the university in lurid details. Who could have talked to the journalists? Seated in her chair, Dolly buzzed for Charlie. When he was seated opposite her, she told him what had transpired between her and their boss.

'Charlie, you have been texting Dr Pak's daughters and liaising with the hospital about the poisoning. Who else from our team knows so much that they can spill to the press? Mok?'

'No!' Charlie said, his face red. 'Adrian Mok would never do such a thing. You know him, Madam; his work ethics are exemplary. He runs clear of the press, he says they are into sensationalism. No, it's not Mok.' Charlie sat still, his wooden face hiding the chaos in his mind. Finally, he said, 'The only officer I can think of who might have talked to the press to gain attention is the recruit, Corporal Fauzia Khan, the lady who transferred into our department from Brendan Gan's division.'

Dolly's face froze. Assistant Superintendent Brendan Gan was feared in the division because he tended to take over other officers' investigations and spoil their careers. Dolly had a close brush with him in the Silver Springs murder case where he had come aboard, and she had thought she would be told to retire while he took over.

'Why are you working with Fauzia on this case? She is new, Charlie.'
Dolly was angry, she had to take the blame for any officer in her team
not following police ethics. 'She should have been assigned to one of the
burglary cases. How did she have access to your notes, Charlie?'

Charlie began to perspire and drummed his hands on the table in
agitation. The hands of the clock on the wall moved to 4 p.m. 'Fauzia
is highly intelligent, Madam. As you know, Mok is diligent, but slow.
Corporal Khan is also savvy on the internet and got me the email
addresses and phone numbers of Dr Pak's daughters. She was a great
help in getting in touch with them. We needed the daughters to quickly
approve our request for the alcohol tests and then later their request to
start a homicide investigation. It was Corporal Khan I sent yesterday to the
airport to receive Dr Pak's daughters and take them to his flat. Corporal
Khan was assisting me in all this as Mok and I were winding up the North
Changi murder case, Madam. Corporal Khan and Corporal Mok are the
only team members who know the details of Pak's death. The poisoning
was revealed just this afternoon; we have not had a meeting on the case
yet, Madam, for other team members to know. Are you sure, Madam, that
she is the leak?'

'That can be easily verified, Charlie. Aarti Shah is our contact at the
newspaper office. Call her and find out who talked to the press. Report
back ASAP.'

After Charlie had left to get busy on his office phone, Dolly sat back
in her chair and mopped her brow. Her mind meandered to the recruit,
Corporal Fauzia Khan, a smart thirty-five-year-old single mother of two
with a harsh face and a pleasant disposition. She had joined their team
two months ago and had shown aptitude and intelligence. Dolly could
understand Charlie asking her to help him when speed was of the essence,
Corporal Mok being slow on the uptake. But why would Fauzia speak to
the press without clearing it with Charlie?

There was a knock on the door and Charlie entered with Fauzia. The
corporal was wearing a smart business suit and trousers, her hair tied into
a chignon and her face apprehensive. With an undulating nose and narrow
eyes, Fauzia looked pleasant when she smiled.

'Ma'am, so sorry. I did not know we were barred from talking to the
press. I only gave a short interview about Dr Pak's poisoning.' Fauzia's
eyes flicked over Dolly's face, uneasily.

'How long have you been at CID?' Dolly's voice was sharp as she noted the cunning in her subordinate's eyes.

'A year, Ma'am. I was working for ASP Gan, but Auntie transferred me to your department, Ma'am.'

Dolly's eyes widened in shock. She coughed discreetly and asked, 'Your aunt is Supt Abdullah?'

Fauzia nodded, a nasty smirk on her face. 'Auntie said it would be better exposure for me to work with you. You get all the murder cases in the division, Ma'am. You are an ace at solving crimes. You are awesome, Ma'am.'

Dolly composed herself and smiled sweetly. 'Thank you, Corporal. Well, the damage has been done. I will have a short chat on the phone with the press and ask them not to reveal all details of the poisoning. I doubt they will listen to a word I say. Sergeant Goh will spend an hour every day for the next week going over work ethics for corporals, and you will realize that talking to the press is not included in your job scope. Supt Abdullah has asked me to find out the leak in our team, and I am sending an email to her now. I am sure she will have a few words of advice for you. The superintendent is angry you talked to the press. Please explain to her your motivations and your willingness to being taught the ethics necessary for you to excel at your job. That is all.' Dolly gave a dismissive nod and turned to her computer.

Fauzia had begun to look uncomfortable and said, 'So sorry again, Ma'am.'

When she had left the office, Dolly composed a terse mail to her boss about the leak in her team and sent it off. She looked at Charlie quizzically, 'Did you know Fauzia is Supt Dragon Lady's niece?'

Charlie sat opposite Dolly, looking stunned. 'No, Madam. ASP Gan wrote an excellent referral and the Supt signed off on it. Nepotism, Madam!' He uttered ominously. 'Fauzia thinks she can do what she likes because she is the Supt's niece.'

Dolly shook her head. 'No, Supt Dragon Lady will give her hell, I am sure of that. Fauzia may think she can get away with grabbing the limelight, but I don't think the Supt is going to buy it. Charlie, please stick to Mok from now on as your subordinate and assign Fauzia to that burglary case in Joo Chiat. Okay? She is quite cocky and wants to grab attention. What about the forensic investigation of the university murder case?'

'At Dr Pak's flat? Yes, Madam, the forensics team has gone there, and my team has also searched the flat. Since we knew Dr Pak's death to be a homicide only a few hours ago, the apartment is compromised. His daughters arrived last night, and their traces are all over the place.'

'Nothing we can do about that. Bring in his mobile phone and laptop, and see if anything interesting pops up from there. His flat was not the crime scene. He was poisoned in his office at the university. And the poison is there in the lab,' Dolly said.

'Today is Thursday and Pak was poisoned on Monday. I don't think any incriminating evidence has been left behind at the university, Madam. I did not ask Mok to seal the solvent cupboard, just to let the forensic officers bag the ethylene glycol bottle. The fingerprint team can have a go, but I am sure the killer took precautions and whatever we find, it could be traces of innocent people handling the chemical later.'

Dolly sighed. 'Yes, I know. It's difficult to solve a case with no forensic backup. I talked to Pritam briefly on the phone, and he has locked up the solvent cupboard in his laboratory and the students who need solvents must sign in and sign out solvents so there will be a record. Dr Eddington is overseeing the solvent cupboard log and keeping the key to the cupboard.'

Charlie nodded. 'I wonder what Supt Dragon Lady is saying to Baby Dragon?' He smiled as Dolly burst into laughter.

Siti Abdullah was not amused. She sat in her office and glared at her niece seated opposite her, examining her nails. She asked harshly, 'What the hell did you think you were doing, Fauzia? How dare you talk to the press without permission! And don't tell me you did not know that you are not supposed to. It's Police Ethics 101 for lower ranked officers to take permission from their supervisors before releasing sensitive information to the public. What were you looking for? Attention? And when the home minister holds me accountable for scaring the public, what am I to say? That I have a foolish niece in the police force who should know better?'

Fauzia looked up with narrowed eyes. Her face was red. 'A journalist approached me, and I told the truth. As for my duties in this division, Auntie, you transferred me here to keep an eye on Inspector Das—find loopholes in her detection methods, any unethical methods she uses, etc. and report to you so you can retire her for good.'

Siti Abdullah sat back in her chair and looked at her niece, speculatively. 'And did that job scope include talking to the press? By doing what you did, you are endangering my career, girl. This affects me!'

'Sorry, Auntie,' Fauzia said, laconically. 'Can I go now?'

'I am sure Inspector Das is going to implement disciplinary measures for you. Follow those and think twice before placing my career in jeopardy. Tell me, girl, why did Dolly Das ask for alcohol levels to be measured in the first place after Pak's death?'

'Her sister, Lily, told her,' Fauzia mumbled, examining her nails again. The polish had come off from one of them and she gazed at it, angrily.

'Look up when I am speaking to you, Fauzia!'

Fauzia looked up and shrugged. 'Lily Das runs a food stall at the university canteen and one of the other scientists told her that Pak was not smelling of alcohol but was behaving like a drunk after lunch. She told that to her sister, and Dolly Das then talked to the doctor who had signed Pak's death certificate.'

'Dolly Das should not have pressured the doctor at the hospital to measure the alcohol levels. Police ethics state that unless we are requested to investigate a suspicious death, we do not do it. We do not go around proving deaths are homicides. Doctors must tell us their suspicions; only then can we investigate. This is the other way around. Dolly Das took matters into her own hands. That's a loophole, and I will note it down.'

'Those two sisters are smart.' There was an admiring note in Fauzia's voice. She turned on her aunt. 'They did good work, Auntie, and that's how a murder was discovered! Everyone thought Pak died of a heart attack, and if the sisters had not investigated, no one would have known that the guy was murdered. I don't know why you dislike Dolly Das! Because she is beautiful, and you are not? She certainly did not climb up the career ladder because of her beauty; it was because of her brains. Auntie, I don't want to snoop on Dolly Das.'

'Now, now,' Siti Abdullah cajoled. 'The DCP wants new blood in the team, and I must retire the old ones, but my actions need justification. Why would you think it's personal, Fauzia?'

Awareness and intelligence gleamed from her niece's eyes. 'Oh, it's personal, Auntie. After all, you are getting on, yourself, and if Dolly Das shines too much, why, she will be promoted and you will be retired.

It does not take a rocket scientist to figure out your motives.' Fauzia rose from her chair, her eyes cocky. 'I need to go now, Auntie.'

Supt Abdullah nodded, a small smile lurking on her lips. 'You may go, Fauzia. Just remember that your father owes thousands of dollars to moneylenders because of his gambling habit. Your salary matters to your family. You are living with your parents after your divorce and burdening them with two tiny tots as well. You better contribute financially to the family. I would hate to break the news to my brother-in-law that you have been sacked from a job where you could, if you tried, do very well.'

Siti smiled to herself as the door banged shut behind Fauzia, but not before Siti had seen the colour recede from her niece's face. Supt Abdullah took out a file from the bottom of her drawer, a file on Inspector Dolly Das, and added some notes. There was the sound of distant thunder and Siti glanced at her watch. It was 5 p.m. Soon she could be on her way to keep a dinner appointment.

Friday, 2 September 2011

11

Latha Krishnaswamy looked out of the window of her home on Dairy Farm Road. Her bedroom was on the first storey of her father's bungalow. Dawn was breaking on the far horizon, a streak of light peeping between land and sky. Birds twittered in the tree in the garden, and the strong pungent scent of durian came with the mild breeze. Latha watched the driver wash her father's car in the portico, a black Mercedes-Benz that glimmered in the half-light. A sliver of fear clutched her heart as her father's rotund figure in shorts and tee jogged into the drive. He had finished his morning run. She constantly feared he would choose a date for her engagement to Nagarajan, and she wasn't ready.

Latha turned away from the window. The walls of her room were decorated with Tamil movie posters. Latha sighed. Her research kept her busy, and she had not gone out with her friends to the cinema for a long time. Latha entered her bathroom and turned on the shower.

Soon, dressed in a maroon Punjabi suit, her hair glistening curly and wet, her face powdered, her backpack slung over her shoulder, she came out of her bedroom, locked the door, and climbed down the curving stairwell into the dining room.

Her mother, a thin wiry fair woman in a housecoat, seated at the dining table, smiled at her briefly before resuming her breakfast of cereal and fruit. Separated from the dining room by an ornate gateway, the living room was generously furnished with sofas, colourful cushions, and display cases. Latha could see the muted TV there playing a Tamil serial. Her father, seated at the head of the dining table, looked up from the newspaper, the idlis on his plate steaming and untouched.

He had sparse hair, a thick neck and a belligerent expression. 'Where do you think you are going, young lady?' His voice was a pleasant baritone.

In the act of sitting down to her plate of hot idlis, Latha paused. Her throat was dry as she said, 'I am going to the U, Appa.'

Her father laid down the paper neatly on the table, glanced at his wife who had developed a deep interest in her plate of fruits, and said, still pleasantly, 'No, you are not.' He pointed to the newspaper. 'Your university is no longer a safe place. A Korean research fellow in your group was poisoned and killed. The police will be starting their investigations. There is a murderer roaming around there.' Krishnaswamy began to eat an idli using a bowl of sambar as a dip.

Latha's face fell in shock, her eyes grew round. She slowly seated herself and looked at her father. 'Dr Pak was killed? No, that cannot be true. He suffered from food poisoning and died of a heart attack. Auntie Lily's food was contaminated.'

'Really?' Latha's mother, Savithri, looked up from her plate. 'Why, Lily's stall is the cleanest I've ever visited.'

Latha's father, Krishnaswamy, interrupted his wife. 'Savithri, it does not say in the newspaper that the gentleman died from food poisoning. The reporter says that his death was *thought* to be from food poisoning, but the body was sent for an autopsy and tests showed he was murdered, poisoned with an industry chemical.'

'Which chemical?' Latha whispered.

Her father finished eating his idli, peered at the newspaper and said, 'Ethylene glycol. Isn't that anti-freeze we use in cars?'

'Some of us work with ethylene glycol. We have a bottle of it in our laboratory.' Latha's voice was still a whisper. 'We use it as an organic reagent.'

Krishnaswamy nodded, his face stern. 'Yes, and somebody in your laboratory has used that chemical to murder the scientist. You could be next. Tell your supervisor, Professor Singh, that you will not be continuing with your degree. The fees for this semester have been paid and cannot be recovered, but that cannot be helped. The engagement ceremony is next week, the pundit has approved the date. You will be getting married.'

Latha leapt up from her chair, her face white. 'Appa, I *must* get my PhD degree! One more year of work and I am done. The police will be investigating the crime, and I am sure they will catch the killer.'

Her father's voice rose, and Latha shrank back into her chair. 'Sit down, young lady! There is a murderer running around in your department, you foolish girl. Yours is a chemistry department, Latha, and industrial poisons are stored all over that place. If a lunatic is on the loose, who knows who will be next?' He lowered his voice to a cajoling tone. 'You are soon to be married and we must do all we can to safeguard this alliance. It's not that Muru readily agreed to this arranged marriage. He told me Nagarajan could find a more suitable bride, but it seems he really likes you.' Krishnaswamy's voice became high-pitched and strident. 'We are going ahead with this alliance, and you will do as you are told.' He looked with disinterest at the remaining piece of idli on his plate, pushed it aside and took a drink from a steel tumbler. The freshly brewed coffee soothed his nerves, and he began to look calmer.

Latha held back her tears and said in a trembling voice, 'My degree means the world to me, Appa! I will do as you ask, marry Nagarajan, but not at the cost of my education. Appa, I know your restaurant business is in the red and the merger with Uncle Muru's catering business after my marriage will save you from bankruptcy, but my life is important, too.'

Krishnaswamy finished his coffee and rose. He looked at his wife, held her in a piercing gaze, and said, 'Lock her up. See to it that she does not leave the house. Go on, Savithri!'

Latha's mother rose from her half-eaten breakfast, scraping back her chair so that it made a scratching noise on the marble floor. She came to stand by Latha's chair. 'Come, darling. Let us go upstairs and Usha Attai will bring the idlis there.' Savithri looked at a thin woman in a white saree standing by the door of the kitchen and nodded, encouragingly.

Latha wailed in distress and her lament was full of pathos, touching the heart of Usha Attai, a distant relative who had raised Latha and worked in the house for room and board.

'Appa, please! Don't take my life away from me! Chemistry is my life. I want to be a professor. My career will go down the drain.'

Krishnaswamy bellowed as he strode into the living room, 'All that has changed now. Your laboratory is a danger zone. Go upstairs to your room at once.'

In her bedroom, her eyes red from weeping, her plate of idlis untouched, her mother and Usha Attai looking on in distress, Latha announced, 'If I cannot continue my studies, I will kill myself. You tell Appa that!' She sat down on her bed and buried her head in her hands.

A flock of birds rose in the sky, spooling towards the distant horizon, mapping out their destination, away from their nests.

* * *

The wall clock read 9 a.m. in the Singh common room. Bill, Kiong, and the students were seated around the long table in the middle, their faces sad and anxious, discussing the death of their colleague, Dong-wook Pak.

Salma was in tears. 'You should have seen his face. His eyes were half-open, and he looked peaceful. Bill and I thought his heart gave out. And now we hear he was poisoned by ethylene glycol. Who could have killed him?' She wailed. 'He was a nice gentleman.'

Cheng Yong raised his eyebrows at Terry. 'You're working with ethylene glycol, right?'

Terry, thin and belligerent, said coldly, 'So? That means I poisoned him, is it? Why would I do such a thing? I liked DW, and he helped a lot with my project. I would not have had the breakthrough in my research if he had not helped me. Thanks to him, my honours project is almost ready to be written out and presented to my advisory committee. I owe him a lot.' He looked around at the others. 'The bottle of ethylene glycol sits in the laboratory across the corridor, anyone could have used the solvent. The solvent cupboard is never locked.'

Salma shivered and looked frightened. 'It is now. I am afraid to work here any more.'

Kiong Tan intervened. 'An outsider could have poisoned DW. Ethylene glycol is anti-freeze and can be bought at car shops.'

Cheng Yong, who was repeatedly looking at the texts on his mobile phone, said, 'Where is Latha? Does anybody know? I need to know where she kept one of the compounds I need to test. She is usually in by 8.30 a.m.'

Salma said, 'Her family is conservative. They probably want her to stay at home until DW's murder is solved. The news of the killing is all over the newspapers. My family may say the same thing when I return home tonight.' She burst into tears. 'I cannot stop thinking what a nice guy DW was.' She sobbed, 'One day, I was working late, and the photoelectron spectrum machine was malfunctioning. I was panicking, what if the machine broke? Prof. would be furious. Dr Pak was working late, and I went to him for help. He immediately came and fiddled with the machine and in half an hour, it was fine. He cheerfully helped me and made jokes all the while. I will miss him.' She took a tissue from the box on the table, wiped her eyes, and blew her nose.

CY's face was sad. 'I will miss him, too. He used to tell me stories of South Korea and his wife. She liked travelling and because DW did not make much money, he could not show her all the tourist spots in the world she wanted to see before she died of cancer. His poor daughters. They were coming for a holiday here, and he was going to show them the sights, and now he is no more. Imagine what this news will do to them. I hear they have arrived in Singapore and are staying at DW's university quarters. I think we should visit them and pay our condolences as a group. What do you think?'

Bill nodded. He was still in shock. He had shared his office with DW for more than a year and his friend's murder shook him badly. He was glad, though, he had communicated his suspicion of DW not being drunk to Lily Das. That information had propelled her inspector sister to talk to the doctors and get to the bottom of how DW had died. 'Yes, it's a good idea. I've already met them. I paid a visit last night as I live downstairs from them. They are nice girls, deeply affected by their father's death. They were crying.'

Cheng Yong's phone beeped, and he looked at the text, uttering an exclamation as he did so. Then he quickly got up and went to the door. 'I have to run an errand,' he explained. The door closed.

'Why do I think CY got a message from Latha?' Kiong's lips twisted in amusement.

Kiong's words put a smile on the faces of his colleagues. Salma said, 'You may be right, Kiong. On the surface, CY and Latha are forever arguing with each other, but underneath? I think love is blossoming.' She giggled.

Terry said, 'The police are coming down to question all of us about DW's murder. Guess who heads the investigation. Our Indian canteen stall owner, Lily Das's sister, Inspector Dolly Das.'

'I hope the NEA allows Mrs D to open her stall soon,' Salma observed. 'I miss her delicious food. Poor Mrs D was wrongly blamed for DW's death and spent some anxious days.'

Kiong nodded. 'It is sure to open now that everyone knows DW was not poisoned by the canteen food. Well, I need to head over to the laboratories. See you all later!' The door closed behind him.

Bill and the students resumed their reminiscences of DW as the clock's hand moved to 10 a.m.

12

The students were still discussing DW's murder in the Singh common room when there was a knock on the door and Abdul, the Malay janitor, entered. He had his broom and dustpan with him. He gave Salma a sad smile and offered her his condolences in their mother tongue. While Abdul could follow English conversations and could speak the language enough to be understood, he was most at home when conversing in Malay.

Terry's brow was furrowed in thought. 'I went to ask DW to explain a reference right after lunch at around 1.15 p.m. I noticed a large cup of coffee on his desk.'

Salma nodded. 'I noticed a coffee cup on his desk as well when I went in at 1.45 p.m. DW had kept it aside, so I think he had finished drinking his coffee.' She looked around and her eyes were scared. 'Do you think the poison was in the coffee?'

Terry turned to Salma. 'You can ask Uncle Abdul if he knows anything. He was mopping the floor outside DW's office when I went in to talk to DW. He may have seen someone enter the office with a cup of coffee.'

Salma said in Malay to Abdul, 'Uncle, you were mopping the floor outside the Korean gentleman's office last Monday? Did you notice anyone near the office? I went to see him at 1.45 p.m., and he had just finished drinking a cup of coffee then. We're wondering if the poison was in that cup of coffee. Did you see anyone take a cup of coffee to him?'

Abdul gave a strangled cry and cried out, 'The poison that killed the Korean gentleman was in the coffee? Oh, I am going to jail, soon, I know it! Who will take care of my wife? Her knees are so bad, and she can't go to the market on her own.' Tears started in his eyes.

While the others in the room looked surprised, Salma went to the janitor and patted him on the arm. She asked softly, 'Uncle, why would anyone take you to jail? What have you done?'

'I gave the Korean gentleman his cup of coffee,' Abdul wailed. 'It is better to die than spend my life in Changi Prison.'

Salma looked around at her colleagues, her eyes wide. Bill asked, 'What's going on, Salma? What's Uncle saying?'

Salma said, 'Uncle took the cup of coffee to DW, he says. Let me talk to him more about this.'

Salma and Abdul engaged in a heated conversation, after which, Salma turned to her colleagues. 'Uncle says he went to take his lunch at noon on Monday. When he returned an hour later, there was a large Styrofoam cup of coffee on his desk with a note to deliver it to DW. Since we sometimes send beverages to the staff and faculty through Uncle, he thought nothing of it and took the cup of coffee to DW.' Her eyes were round and scared. 'The killer put a poisoned cup of coffee on Uncle's table knowing he would do his duty and deliver it to the recipient.'

Bill looked puzzled. He glanced at the coffee dispenser at the corner of the room. 'It's true the dispenser is not working. But we had just come up from downstairs after taking lunch at the canteen. If he wanted coffee, DW would have bought it at the drinks stall and taken it up with him.' He glanced at the janitor standing petrified by the door, his broom and dustpan forgotten.

Terry said thoughtfully, 'It's usual for professors to send money through their students to Uncle and order their beverages through him, on account of the faculty having their offices in a different building and far from the canteen. I, myself, have left notes on Uncle's table for a cup of tea or coffee to be delivered to Prof. Singh. But DW's office is right down the corridor. Why would he order coffee through a student? He just came up from the canteen.'

'He never ordered it. His murderer left the poisoned cup of coffee to be delivered,' Salma said. She looked at Abdul and asked, 'Did you see the person who left the coffee?'

Abdul replied, 'No, Salma. I saw no one. I am not a criminal. But I will go to jail anyway.' His face became melancholic.

Bill asked, 'What did DW say when Abdul took him the coffee? Can you ask Uncle that, Salma?'

When Salma put the question to Abdul, he said, 'The gentleman looked surprised. But he sipped the coffee and said it was sweet. He loved sugary food, the poor gentleman.' He began moving towards the door. 'I go now to sweep the other offices. I come back here later. I don't know how long I have before the police take me to jail.'

'Wait!' Bill said. 'Salma, can you ask Uncle if DW ordered coffee or tea this way before?'

When Salma repeated the question, Abdul shook his head vehemently. He replied in halting English to Bill, 'No, but others do it. Professor Singh do all the time. His students leave kopi on my desk for him. So, I take Korean gentleman the coffee. How to know it has poison?' Shaking his head, he opened the door.

After the door had closed, Bill said, 'The ethylene glycol was in the coffee. That is why the coffee tasted sweet. The solvent has a sweet taste. We must tell the police all this. Professor Singh said the officers will interview us this afternoon.'

Terry said, 'Maybe DW thought you had sent the cup of coffee to him, Bill! There are police officers in the corridor outside asking people if they had seen anything suspicious on Monday afternoon. Many on this floor buy their beverages from the stall in the canteen and walk with them down the corridor after lunch. How are the police going to find out who was carrying the poisoned coffee to Abdul's office?'

Bill said, 'Someone must have placed the cup of coffee in Uncle's office sometime after 12 p.m. We will leave it to the police to carry on the questioning. Let's get back to work. Now remember, you can use the solvents in the cupboard for your experiments. I must check it out for you, and I will open the locked cupboard. Have your beakers ready and as soon as you have poured out the solvent, I will lock the cupboard again.'

'More work for you,' Salma said, sympathetically. 'See you all, later.'

Sadly, Bill went back to his office. He had been fond of his colleague and office room-mate, and was sorry DW had been robbed of his retirement years. He had been looking forward to building a Japanese garden. Sitting in front of his computer, looking at the blank screen,

Bill was in no mood now for a luncheon date with Ursula Botham. She had
called him up some days ago asking to have lunch and he had been elated.
Events unfolding in the last few days had changed his mood. When the
clock struck 12 p.m., he made his way dejectedly to the Science canteen.

* * *

The sight of Ursula sitting at a corner table, though, cheered Bill up.
He ordered two prawn noodle soups from a stall and walked back with
the food tray. Lily Das was sitting at a nearby table having a cup of coffee
and Bill smiled at her.

'I am sure you will reopen soon, Mrs D,' Bill shouted.

Lily said, 'Yes, on Monday, Dr Eddington. I am really sorry about the
death of the Korean gentleman.'

Bill nodded and made his way to where Ursula was sitting. She was
looking particularly lovely in a flowery dress made from a thin fabric that
accentuated her small, rounded breasts. Bill hurriedly averted his gaze
from them and found Ursula smiling at him, her blue eyes friendly, her
blonde hair blowing in the breeze that had whipped up outside.

They discussed DW's murder and were halfway through their meal
when Ursula leaned back in her chair. She was no longer smiling but had
a dark brooding look.

'What's wrong?' Bill asked with concern, noting her glance of anger.

'I have decided to divorce Graham,' Ursula said in a low voice.

Bill laid down his spoon and fork to look at Ursula closely. 'You've been
married for a long time and … there's Tom,' he began tentatively.

Using chopsticks, Ursula spooned noodles expertly into her mouth,
chewed for a while, and then said, 'I have thought about divorce so many
times during our marriage, but the thought of Tom always deterred me.
But there's only so much a woman can take!'

'What's Graham done?'

Ursula's nostrils flared. 'You may not be aware of his character, that he
is a serial cheater. Keep it quiet, though. I have. He is up for the headship
of the department. Rumours can hurt his career. Did you know he had
to leave his last academic post in Australia in disgrace? He was having a
fling with a student, and she reported him to the authorities. His head of
department was a friend who still wrote a good recommendation letter to

Temasek. I have suffered so much for Tom's sake! Thanks to Daddy, I will always be well-off; he made a fortune out of building houses. Banbury Hall is mine, and I can take care of Tom.'

Bill remembered what DW had told him about the Korean girl who had killed herself in Australia because Graham had spurned her. He said, 'There was some scandal with a Korean girl in Australia, right?'

Naked fear flashed through Ursula's eyes. 'That girl had a Korean lover. Graham was wrongly blamed there. How do you know, anyway?' Ursula demanded.

Bill shrugged. 'DW was a friend of the girl's family. He told me.'

'Don't spread rumours about Graham, Bill. Keep it quiet. The headship,' Ursula hissed.

Bill looked indignant. 'It's none of my business, no worries. Surely, then, this is not the time to divorce Graham. What will that do to the headship?'

Ursula pursed her lips. 'I am saying I will ask him for a divorce, obviously after the head has been elected. I am still trying to stop his philandering. He has started seeing my cousin, Lorna, and that's the limit!'

'You mean Lorna the Leech?' Bill's mild blue eyes were incredulous as the image of a lanky redhead trailing their footsteps at Banbury Hall floated into his mind. Younger than Ursula by five years and an awkward sixteen, Lorna had fastened herself to her cousin's group of friends, spurring them on to nickname her 'leech'. They had been as rude as possible but there had been no budging Lorna, and the group of friends up for a holiday at the manor had to resort to plans and strategies to shake her off, wasting considerable time they could have spent on cinemas and theatres.

Bill woke from his reverie as Ursula's voice cut into his thoughts.

'Yes, that's who. Except now, she is no longer awkward but a fiery redhead with a model's figure, eyeing my husband.' Ursula was wiping her eyes with a small lace handkerchief, impervious to Lily gawking at her from behind her table.

Bill bitterly cast his mind back to the past. He remembered Lorna the Leech was one of many reasons he had not been able to tell Ursula his true feelings. That girl had never left them alone. 'I remember Lorna,' he said, his voice on edge.

'Well, she is a visiting lecturer at the geography department here, and Graham is carrying on with her.' Ursula's voice shook with anger. 'I am going to invite you to dinner this weekend, Bill, and I will invite Lorna as well. I want you to renew your acquaintance with her and dissuade her from breaking up my marriage. She may listen to you. I remember she had a crush on you.'

The memory of an adolescent's hot breath on his face as she thrust out her lips to be kissed sprang up in Bill's mind, and he winced, his mouth twisting into a moue of distaste. Bill frowned, intensely disliking the idea of playing mediator in an estranged couple's marriage breakup by hooking up with the other woman. Bill had been a bachelor long enough to feel uneasy and frightened when dealing with emotional situations and hysterical women. He did not feel it his place or business to save Ursula's marriage.

He cleared his throat and said apologetically, 'I'd rather not, if it's all right. I have no interest in Lorna so it would be unfair to egg her on amorously, if you know what I mean. Why should she even listen to what I have to say? She is a grown up now. No, I must politely decline to help you, Ursula, although you have my sympathy. I do hope that Graham sees sense and stops his dallying. Why don't you remind him that he is under scrutiny for the headship? He may stop then. I know he wants to be Head of Chemistry very much.'

Ursula's eyes blazed blue fire at him and abruptly, she rose, her soup half-eaten, and stormed away from the table. Bill desultorily finished his meal and walked back to his office.

Lily looked at Bill's retreating figure. Ursula and Graham Botham had lunch occasionally at her stall, and they had not been friendly of late—Ursula scolding her husband in a loud voice and Graham looking taciturn and sullen. Lily had shamelessly eavesdropped on the conversation between Bill and Ursula and now knew Graham was having an affair. What a cad, Lily thought, and as her phone beeped, she glanced at her sister's text. Dolly was having lunch at HQ before arriving to interview the students and fellows and told her not to wait lunch for her. Lily, looking grumpy, walked over to the Malay food stall and chatted with the owner while ordering rice and mutton rendang.

Remembering Ashikin's interest in collaborating with her to cook Malay dishes at her stall, Lily asked the Malay stall owner, 'So, Naheed, are you selling breakfast at your stall?'

Naheed, dressed in a green baju kurung and tudung, her face flushed from the steam rising from the curry cauldrons, shook her head. 'No, no. Who's going to wake up so early? Customers can take Chinese breakfast at Uncle Goh's stall. Rice porridge and noodles. I make enough from lunch, Lily. When's your stall opening? The poor Korean scientist was killed, they say.'

Lily nodded and said tentatively, 'You mind if I sell nasi lemak for breakfast?'

Naheed's deep brown eyes set in a round face, widened. 'You can make nasi lemak? Lily, you are so talented.' She grinned.

'Oh, it's my friend, Ashikin, wanting a job at my stall. Her sister's stall in Orchard shut down, she was working there. She is a wonderful cook.'

Naheed's eyes narrowed. Then she smiled dismissively. 'Oh, it's okay, Lily. No competition for me since I don't cook breakfast.' Her voice was not as friendly when she said, 'Is she going to cook Malay lunch too?'

'Well, some customers want nasi lemak for lunch,' Lily said, evasively and then gave a bright smile. 'She will be no competition for you, Naheed, you can easily work in the restaurant of a five-star hotel,' she lied, knowing Ashikin's rendang could rival that served at the restaurant of Rendezvous Hotel.

Naheed looked mollified and smiled. 'We will be friends, don't worry. I may need help in my stall, maybe she can work for me if free?'

Lily smiled insincerely, waved to Naheed and walked away to a table to eat her rendang and rice. She had no intention of lending Ashikin to Naheed. Lily sat down to her meal.

After eating, she leisurely made her way to her car to drive home. She felt happy that soon she would be back at work. NEA had inspected her stall and re-issued an 'A' certificate. In the light of DW's poisoning with a chemical, the NEA officers had been apologetic, and Lily was appeased.

She wondered whether Dolly would find out by the end of the day how Dr Pak had been poisoned. Dolly was staying at Silver Springs, and they could discuss the case at night. Lily shivered a little. She had nearly lost her stall because of the poisoning case. She felt uneasy at the thought that it was so easy to kill someone with an industrial poison.

13

Abdul's office and storeroom were in a cul-de-sac at the end of the corridor from the Singh common room and laboratories. There were shelves of detergents and cleaning aids stacked against walls, and Abdul sat at a table by the small window. Neatly compartmentalized in one corner was an open cupboard containing brooms, dustpans and mops. Clothes hung to dry on a mobile clothes hanger. The storeroom had its own large sink with a stainless-steel tap, where Abdul washed the dirty rags.

Abdul wore loose trousers and shirt, and a cap over his head. He was about fifty years of age with a pointed chin covered by a straggly beard. He stood up, looking enquiringly at the police officers as they entered his office.

Charlie flashed his warrant card and introduced Dolly and himself. Charlie, proficient in Malay, offered to conduct the interview with Abdul. It was best to carry out interviews of important witnesses in the language they were comfortable with.

Abdul's face became pale and sweat sprung up on his forehead. He looked around, spied two low stools and motioned Dolly to his chair and pointed Charlie to a stool. Abdul's eyes gleamed with fear.

'There is no need to be frightened of us. We talked to the students, and they told us about the cup of coffee you delivered to the late Korean gentleman. We just need to ask you some questions,' Dolly said in a soft voice and was gratified to note that Abdul's stiff shoulders relaxed, and the ghost of a smile tugged at his lips. Dolly knew from the students Abdul understood English but did not speak the language well, and had accepted Charlie's offer to conduct the interview.

Charlie asked in Malay, 'There was a cup of coffee left on your table with instructions to be delivered to Dr Pak. Do you still have the piece of paper?'

Abdul's hand began shaking. He said, 'The cleaner is always blamed. I did not put poison anywhere, Sir. The only poison I have in this office is rat poison, and it is locked in a cupboard.' He pointed to a low cupboard beside the door.

Charlie's voice was impatient. 'We are not suggesting you did anything bad. We would like to know more about the coffee cup left on your table for the gentleman who died. Poison was found in his body, and it is likely it was in the coffee. We know you deliver beverages to the staff, and at this point, we are not suspecting you of wrongdoing.'

Abdul looked with dislike at Charlie. 'I did not know the note was important and threw it away. The professors have their offices in the next building, far from the canteen. They do not want to walk all the way to the *sarabat* stall to get their coffees. So, they send students with notes and money to me. I buy their coffees and teas and take the beverages to their offices. This is the custom here, Sir. Sometimes, students buy drinks for professors and leave them on my table to deliver. This is the first time a fellow wanted coffee this way. When Professor Singh and Professor Botham bought the beverage dispenser in the common room, it was easy for me. I went next door and got the drinks. There was no need to go to the *sarabat* stall. But the dispenser is always breaking down. And some professors do not like drinks from there. They say it is not freshly made.' He stemmed his garrulity at a frown from Charlie.

'Dr Pak never had a drink delivered this way before?' he asked.

Abdul shook his head. 'Something is not right. If a student wanted to send a drink, all he had to do was walk down the corridor to Dr Pak's office. Why ask me to deliver? Fellows have their offices in this building and near the sarabat stall. They usually get their drinks themselves. Yes, this is the first time such a thing happened.' He hastened to add, 'But at the time, I did not think it was strange and took the gentleman his drink. It is part of my duties.'

'What was his reaction?' Charlie asked, interested.

'The gentleman was surprised. He thought someone sent him the drink. He took a sip and liked it. He said it was so sweet.' Abdul gazed out of the window at two *mynah* birds bickering over a scrap of food on the ledge opposite.

'What did the note say?' Charlie asked.

'It said, "Coffee for Dr Pak, Room 302". That was the gentleman's office room number, Sir. That is all the note said.'

'What time did you take the coffee to Dr Pak?' Charlie asked, looking at his watch impatiently.

Abdul said, 'Around 1 p.m. I left for lunch at noon and returned to my office an hour later. I saw the cup of coffee and note. I took the gentleman his coffee. Then I started mopping the corridor outside.'

Charlie leant forward. 'Did you see anyone enter the office?'

'The one they call Terry. He entered around one plus and was there for around ten minutes. About half an hour later, Salma entered the room, but she came out soon. I was mopping further down the corridor.' Warmth laced Abdul's voice. 'Poor Salma. She is so clever, but she must fall in love with that rascal, Junaid. I know their family,' he said in explanation. 'I eat at the coffee shop with her father and other friends; we are neighbours. Junaid is ten years older than Salma and jobless. Nowadays, young people are so reckless in love. They don't think of the future!'

'Did you see anyone else?' Charlie asked.

'No, nobody else that day. But two weeks ago, a visitor came to see the Korean gentleman. She was a Korean lady, and they had a fight inside his office. I was mopping the corridor and I heard shouting from inside. She ran out of the room in fifteen minutes. I went in to make sure the gentleman was okay. Dr Pak's face was red. He told me the lady was his wife's sister, and she was no good. Stole money from his wife, he said.'

Charlie's eyes shone, and Dolly looked excited. She had understood most of the Malay conversation. 'Thank you, Abdul,' Dolly said. She added in halting Malay, 'You have been helpful. Everyone thought Dr Pak was suffering from food poisoning after eating at my sister's stall. Now we know otherwise.'

Abdul's face became animated. He replied, 'Your sister's food is very good. I take food at her stall twice a week. You tell your sister I am very happy her stall will open again soon.'

Dolly smiled and nodded pleasantly before rising from the chair. Leaving Abdul mumbling about being a chief suspect in any wrongdoing on account of being a cleaner, the two police officers entered the corridor.

'Charlie, we need to visit Dr Pak's daughters and ask them about their aunt. We need to find out about her. She looks like our chief suspect. She quarrelled with her brother-in-law two weeks ago. The girls should be able to give us their aunt's name and hopefully her address in Singapore. But the sister-in-law would have to know that leaving beverages on the janitor's desk for delivery to staff was a common occurrence. How would she have known that? We need to know if the sister-in-law was in the habit of visiting DW. It's obvious the murderer poisoned the coffee and had Abdul deliver it to escape suspicion; so the murderer must be aware of the department's customs.'

Charlie said, frowning, 'Maybe the coffee delivered by Abdul did not have poison. Someone else may have come in later and poisoned DW somehow.'

Dolly shook her head. 'Look at the evidence. Terry and Salma saw the coffee cup Abdul had just delivered to DW. And when Salma came in, the poison was already working, with DW showing intoxication symptoms. No, the poison was in that cup of coffee. Also, look at how it was delivered. To throw off suspicion from the killer.'

Charlie nodded. 'You are right, Madam. Yes, we cannot rule out the students, teachers and fellows here as suspects. They know the customs. Madam, we can leave in the car now for Pak's quarters. It's only five minutes' drive from here.'

Dolly nodded, stopping to text Lily that she might be late home from work. She had a long afternoon ahead of her.

14

The staff quarters were red-brick dwellings built around a small green park that doubled as a children's playground and a place for adults to sit and chat on benches amid trees and shrubs. Charlie parked at the open-air carpark and flashed his warrant card at the guard sitting inside the lobby of Block A, a five-storey building. The lift lobby was brightly decorated in blue and white, and the officers took the lift to the fourth floor. Dolly smoothed her hair, looking at her reflection in the lift mirror.

Charlie knocked on the plain wooden door of Pak's apartment, and it opened to reveal a petite bespectacled Korean girl with long hair and eyes red from weeping. There were two flowerpots standing on either side of the door. Charlie flashed his warrant card and introduced Dolly and himself. The girl nodded and ushered the police in.

The curtains were drawn in the living hall and one dim overhead bulb illuminated another Korean girl sitting on the sofa gazing into space. She quickly rose on seeing the two officers.

The first girl said, 'I am Soo-ah, and this is my sister, Seo-yeon. Inspector Das and Sergeant Goh,' she informed her sister.

The two girls ushered Dolly and Charlie into a roomy sofa and sat on chairs facing them. The living hall was sparsely furnished. It was obvious DW had not intended to spend too many years there.

Soo-ah turned to Dolly, her big eyes wide. 'Inspector, who could have murdered our father? Have you got any leads?'

Seo-yeon said, 'When can we see him? Is it okay if we take him to Seoul for burial? We want him resting next to our mother in the cemetery there.'

Dolly nodded. 'As soon as our forensic pathologist releases the body, we will inform you and help make arrangements to fly your father back to Seoul.' She cleared her throat. 'You have an aunt living in Singapore?'

Seo-yeon looked surprised and shook her head, but her sister said, 'You must mean Aunt Eun-jin.'

Seo-yeon looked with disbelief at her sister. 'She's *here?*'

Both girls spoke good English, and Dolly wondered whether they had been educated in America as they spoke with an accent. 'We want to talk to your mother's sister,' Dolly said. 'We understand she visited Dr Pak two weeks ago in his office and there was a quarrel.'

Seo-yeon's brows had knitted in a ferocious frown and her voice was angry as she said, 'We don't speak to our aunt. Not after what she did to our father in Seoul.'

'What did she do?' Charlie leant forward intently; his pen poised over his notebook.

The sisters had an unspoken signal between them as to who was to speak next. It was Soo-ah who said, 'Our mother had only one sibling, our Aunt Eun-jin. Our mother came from a wealthy family, and they had a country estate. Our father was poor, and when Ma married Pa, our maternal grandmother cut off connections. Later she asked for our mother to visit when she was sick, but Ma did not go. Aunt Eun-jin looked after our grandmother and poisoned her mind against our mother so that our grandmother left the country house to her. Our mother received nothing.'

Seo-yeon continued, 'But that was not all. Our mother was close to our aunt, and we think our aunt did care for our mother. She did not like our father. When our mother died of cancer, our aunt told the police our father killed our mother by euthanasia. She said he helped our mother to die by giving her an overdose of morphine for the cancer pain. The police arrested him, and he spent six months in jail before he was cleared. Aunt Eun-jin was generous to us, loved us. But we cut off ties with her when she sent our father to jail.'

Dolly could see why DW would want to murder Eun-jin, but did the sister-in-law have a motive to murder DW? 'Your aunt visited your father two weeks ago and witnesses overheard them quarrelling over money.'

Soo-ah nodded. 'Pa was going to sue Aunt for false accusations and was also going to challenge our grandmother's will. He felt some of her money should have come to us.'

Eyes shining, Charlie asked, 'And your aunt works in Singapore?'

Soo-ah nodded. 'She called me five months ago saying she was coming to Singapore to work. My sister does not talk to her, but I do.'

'I don't know why you do,' her sister turned flashing eyes on Soo-ah. 'She made Pa spend months in jail with a malicious accusation just because she was jealous of how much Ma loved Pa.'

The room was claustrophobic, and the fan overhead did nothing to alleviate the humidity. Dolly took out a handkerchief from her handbag and mopped her brow. 'How did your father get out of jail?'

Seo-yeon said, 'We are forgetting our manners. May we offer you some tea?' When Dolly smiled her thanks, she went to the adjoining kitchen, and they could hear the kettle boiling.

Soo-ah settled herself into her chair and said, 'I will tell you what happened. Our Ma had Stage IV breast cancer. Pa hired a nurse to take care of Ma in her last days. She was supposed to give the usual dose of morphine at 5 a.m. But at 2 a.m., Ma cried out in pain and begged the nurse for morphine. The nurse was distracted as her daughter was going to go into labour in her village any time, and she was glued to the phone. She gave the morphine dose to Ma but forgot to record it on the roster. Then she received news her daughter needed her and asked Pa to get another nurse and allow her to travel to her village by the early morning train. The nurse left for her village. At 5 a.m., Ma cried out for her morphine dose and unaware, that the nurse had given an extra dose at 2 a.m., Pa gave Ma her usual shot of morphine. At 7 a.m., Ma was agitated and sleepy by turns and her lips were turning blue. Pa called the doctor, but by that time, Ma was gone. The doctor suspected morphine overdose and Aunt Eun-jin, who had arrived, urged the doctor to do tests to find out if Ma had overdosed. When the doctor found out that Ma had died from an overdose of morphine, Aunt told the police that Pa had performed euthanasia. Pa was jailed.'

'But why didn't the nurse come forward to say she had given a morphine shot at 2 a.m. and forgot to log it on the roster?' Dolly asked in surprise.

Soo-ah said, 'The police had trouble locating her. When Pa's case came up for trial and all the newspapers reported it, somehow the nurse got to know, and she came to the police and told them that she had given Ma a morphine dose at 2 a.m. but forgot to log it in as she was worried about her daughter and distracted. Then the court ruled Ma's death as due to accidental overdose of morphine and not euthanasia, and Pa walked free.'

Dolly and Charlie remained quiet for some time reflecting on the information gained. There had been bad blood between Eun-jin and DW regarding the court case, and it was important to locate the woman. Seo-yeon arrived with a tray holding cups of tea. Her sister helped her serve tea to Dolly and Charlie. The sisters settled themselves with their own cups after they had served their guests.

'You don't know where your aunt works in Singapore?' Charlie asked, sipping his tea.

Soo-ah shook her head. 'I don't know where she lives or works. Her line of work is translations so she may be working for a Korean company here. Translating documents from Korean into English and vice versa.'

Charlie held his pen poised over his notebook. 'Your aunt's name?'

Seo-yeon said, 'Eun-jin Choi. If she contacts us, we will let you know.'

Dolly nodded. She held the cup of tea to her lips and took a sip. It might not be hard to track down Eun-jin Choi; she could get Mok to check all the South Korean firms and their employee names in Singapore. She cleared her throat. 'You last talked to Dr Pak Monday evening on the phone?'

Tears pooled in Soo-ah's eyes. She placed her tea on the low table and then nodded. 'We called him at 8 p.m., and he answered. We called him earlier as well, but the phone went on ringing. He told us that he may have food poisoning. He had vomited and had diarrhoea. He sounded weak and tired. We told him to visit a doctor, and he said he would if he felt worse. He wanted to sleep, so we rung off. On Tuesday, we called him once in the morning but he did not answer. We assumed he felt better and had gone to work. We called him in the afternoon and when he did not answer us even then, we got worried. If he were at work, he would answer his mobile when we called. We called him repeatedly and then finally called his office landline. Dr Eddington answered and said he would immediately go and see what was wrong with our father. The rest you know.' She took up her mug of tea from the table and began to drink in earnest.

Seo-yeon sniffed hard. 'It was so hard to imagine someone had poisoned our father. He was a good man and never harmed anybody.'

'Do you think your aunt had anything to do with your father's death?' Charlie asked, finishing the last of his tea. After hearing of their dark history, he was sure his sister-in-law had poisoned DW.

Soo-ah's face lost colour and her eyes glistened. 'We don't know.' She sniffed. 'It is hard to believe Aunt killed Pa. We did try to dissuade Pa from initiating the lawsuit; after all, Eun-jin was our aunt, and she was sorry for what she had done. Pa said he would think about it. But it is true he was angry with her for us not inheriting Grandma's house.'

Seo-yeon said, 'I don't know why. We are not at all interested in that crumbling country mansion.' She gulped down her tea.

Charlie asked pleasantly, 'What are your occupations?'

Soo-ah said, 'Our parents gave us a good education. We went to a posh school that sent us for an exchange programme to America for two years. When we returned, we joined the premier university in Seoul. We work now as engineers in a semiconductor company.'

Dolly finished her tea and asked, smiling, 'Are you two twins?'

Seo-yeon laughed. 'Yes, though we don't look alike.'

The police officers assured the two girls that they would do all they could to bring justice for Dr Dong-wook Pak. Leaving the teary-eyed girls, Dolly and Charlie left DW's apartment.

'We need to find Eun-jin Choi,' Dolly said.

Charlie was busy texting Corporal Mok. 'I am on it, Madam.'

'Drop me off at the Science building, Charlie, and I will later take a cab back to the office. I want to speak to Pritam. I told his wife I would look in on him.'

Charlie nodded, and the officers got into the squad car.

15

Dolly rode the lift of the science faculty building to the sixth floor and knocked on a blue door bearing her ex-husband's nameplate. She had called ahead saying she wanted to speak to him. A gruff voice asked her to come in. Pushing open the door, she entered. Dolly had not seen Pritam Singh in over a year and was surprised at how much he had aged. He was standing near his chair and seeing her, he said, 'Let's go somewhere else. I feel claustrophobic in my office and want to spend as little time here as possible. We'll use the conference room at the end of the corridor.'

The room was large, with an oval table and chairs around it. One wall sported a large screen where PowerPoint presentations could be made. Dolly noticed her ex's dishevelled appearance. He was wearing somewhat frayed trousers and a shirt that had seen better days. After a brief interlude during his courting days with his second wife, Cheryl, when he had refrained from wearing his turban, he was back to wearing his maroon turban that Dolly had bought for him when they were married. Dolly felt a small twinge of nostalgia on noting the turban.

After motioning her to a seat, Pritam said, 'How are you? What a terrible thing to happen to Botham's research fellow! Dong-wook collaborated with me as well, though I did not pay his salary. Want some coffee?' When she shook her head, he poured himself black coffee from a carafe and seated himself opposite her.

'Ash will be home from camp for two weeks; he is arriving next Friday,' Dolly said, brightly. 'I am sure he has told you already.'

Pritam looked nonplussed. 'I have not spoken to Ashok lately. My home computer broke down. So, can't Skype.' His eyes sparkled. 'It will be good to see him. I'll tell Cheryl to have him over for dinner. I didn't think he would take to National Service, but he is proud of his stint as an NS man.' Pritam laughed and took a sip of his coffee.

Dolly nodded and cleared her throat. 'Pritam, a murder has been committed. Tell me about Dr Pak. Did he work for you?'

Pritam nodded. 'Professor Graham Botham and I shared him; he worked for both of us. Graham paid his fellowship salary out of his research funds, but Pak did one project for me that was important. He used to be a professor in a small university in Seoul, then he lost his wife to cancer and decided to tour the world on research fellowships. He joined us about a year ago.'

'He seemed to have been poisoned on Monday afternoon. I believe he drank coffee with ethylene glycol in it.'

Pritam Singh shuddered. 'How diabolical! I was at a function at the university club on Monday and had lunch there. There was a small conference and I listened to some talks. I was there the whole afternoon and early evening. Pak and I were on formal terms. He never talked to me about issues other than our project. Someone must have a grudge against him and me, too.'

'What do you mean you as well?' Dolly asked sharply.

Pritam rummaged in his pocket and brought out a sheet of paper. He passed it to Dolly. On the paper, in red ink, was written: "YOU will be the next to die, Pritam Singh!"

'When did you receive this, Pritam?'

'Sometime this morning. I was taking a class at 8 a.m. and when I returned to the office, this note was shoved under my office door. Is there a murderer on the loose in the department, Dolly? Or is someone trying to scare me?' He took a long calming sip of his coffee before pushing the Styrofoam cup away.

Dolly frowned. 'Does anyone have a grudge against you?' She noticed that her ex-husband's beard and moustache were both grey and the wrinkles on his face more pronounced than when she had last seen him. She said, 'Try to think back over your academic life, Pritam. Any rival professor or disgruntled student you can remember?'

Pritam Singh looked out of the window, lost in thought. He said, 'There was an ex-student who might have had a grudge against me. His name was Manjunath Reddy, and two years ago, he joined my research group as a doctoral student. He hailed from Andhra Pradesh in India and boarded at the student dorm. His paper qualifications were good, and he seemed interested in his studies. But in chemical research, you need to have a curious mind and he lacked that. He did very well in examinations where there was rote learning but to qualify for a doctoral degree, you need to have a research-oriented mind. He failed his oral preliminary examinations. He could not answer most of the probing questions his steering committee fielded. He was angry after that, and when I told him it was not possible to fund his scholarship any longer, he became nasty and issued threats.'

'What kind of threats?' Dolly asked, eyebrows raised.

'Manju said he came from a powerful political family in India and if I did not give him another chance, the Indian mafia would get me. Obviously, I lodged a complaint with the Police Post; you may be able to retrieve my complaint. The police talked to him, and the university told him to leave. I don't like being issued threats, and this boy imagined himself the goonda you see in Hindi movies.'

Pritam stopped talking and sank into a reverie, then awoke suddenly. 'I would not put it past him to reapply to the university as a doctoral student in another discipline. His family is wealthy and well connected. It would be worthwhile finding out if he is enrolled again at Temasek.' He pointed to the piece of paper and said, 'This kind of note and threat would be just what he would send.'

Dolly decided to get Charlie on to Admissions and find out if Manjunath was studying again at Temasek.

Pritam Singh mopped his brows. He seemed to be feeling warm although the air-conditioner was whirring away. He looked at his ex-wife and said, 'I really do wish you happiness with your husband, Dolly. I am sorry for the unpleasantness I caused in your life. We are good now, right?'

Dolly smiled thinly but nodded in agreement. Pritam's folly was still vivid in her mind. She could not forget the anguish his extra-marital affair had caused her and Ash. She gave herself a shake. He was, after all, her son's father. She said cheerfully, 'I hear you can't stay away from Lily's food.'

Pritam laughed the jovial laugh of better days. 'Yes, she is a great cook. I am glad to have connected back with her.' He looked sad. 'I made many mistakes in my life, Dolly, and one of the biggest was not lending money to Lily when Joy was so gravely ill with cancer. Your mother is right to be angry with me about this even now. Joy and I got on well. He was an engineer with a curious mind, and we chatted about science so many times in coffee shops. I was sad to hear of his diagnosis but at the time my tenure had just been approved and I began thinking, what would happen if I had cancer? I need to save money, I thought, with a son to raise. But you and I should have helped Lily during that time.'

It was a long emotional speech from Pritam, and Dolly was touched. She was glad he was now friends with Lily and that her sister had forgiven him. Poor Pritam, Dolly smiled to herself, he could not help being a worrier and miser.

'I worry about Ashok,' Pritam said, right on cue. 'The newspapers are always reporting some mishap or the other at the camps.'

'Pritam, Ash is nineteen years old. National Service and the Army are toughening him. He will be all right.' Dolly was laughing. 'He may have a girlfriend. Did he tell you?'

A smile lit up Pritam Singh's saturnine face. 'No! Who is she?'

'Her name is Amita Singh, and she studies at Ash's junior college. A year younger than him. She will soon take her "A" levels. He says they met at a party and not at JC, but who knows. He raves about her. I think he will be out on dates with her in the two weeks he is at home.'

'Singh … Punjabi,' Pritam said, approvingly. His eyes were gentle as he looked at his ex-wife. 'You did a great job raising him, Dolly. Thank you.'

'And you're a great father,' Dolly said, warmly. She remembered Cheryl's words and asked, 'Are you keeping well, Pritam?'

Immediately, Pritam Singh's face closed. 'What do you mean? Of course, I am well.'

'You look a bit tired, that is all,' Dolly said, soothingly.

Pritam sighed. 'Yes, to be honest, I have been feeling weird. I have nightmares, and I have numbness and tingling in my limbs. I also have memory lapses. It must be age catching up with me.'

'Get checked up by a neurologist,' Dolly advised kindly. 'You can consult for free at the Temasek Teaching Hospital.'

'I can't drive on the road without the GPS tracker on,' Pritam whispered, miserably.

Dolly's eyes rounded in alarm. 'Pritam, please see a doctor. Check yourself into the hospital and have the doctors run some tests.' She lowered her voice. 'Joey and I are rooting for you, Cheryl and Baby Singh. Cheryl worries about your health, and she needs to be calm so that the baby can be safely delivered.' Dolly rose from her chair and made her way to the door.

Pritam nodded docilely. 'Okay. See you for dinner then. Chinese, tonight?'

On the act of leaving, Dolly paused. *Had she heard right?* 'Pritam, what did you say?'

Pritam looked at her in bewilderment. He shook his head and looked around him, alarmed. 'Why am I here?'he asked, piteously.

'Come with me, Pritam,' Dolly said and shepherded her ex-husband out of the meeting room and marched him along the corridor, down in the lift and on the road towards Temasek Teaching Hospital.

Monday, 5 September 2011

16

Dolly was late for work. Pritam had been admitted to the Temasek Teaching Hospital Friday evening, but the doctors could not discover what was wrong with him. Sunday evening had been spent at the hospital talking to more doctors while Pritam threatened to discharge himself and go home. Cheryl had been no help at all, bursting into tears at the slightest provocation and refusing to deal with the family crisis, bemoaning the fact that she would surely lose her baby. Cheryl was certain Pritam was mentally ill and would receive better care at Woodbridge Hospital. This resulted in a vicious spat between Cheryl and Dolly, leaving Dolly upset and worn out. Back home, Dolly discussed Pritam's health and the case with her mother and sister late into the night. It had been a bad weekend for Dolly.

As soon as she entered her office, a constable immediately told her the Supt wanted to see her. So, at 10 a.m., Dolly found herself in Superintendent Abdullah's office. The Supt was looking through some reports on her desk, and Dolly was glad to see that she did not seem angry. She motioned Dolly to a chair.

Her words, though, dispelled Dolly's first impressions. 'So, Inspector Das, I am looking through Charlie's notes on the university murder case, and I do not see any doctor requesting a police investigation into Dong-wook Pak's death. Pak was taken to the hospital on Tuesday evening and declared dead on arrival. His cardiologist, Dr Alex Gan, examined him and wrote on his death certificate that he died from a heart attack. Pak had a history of heart problems. The doctor deduced the death to be from natural causes. Yet, I see from Charlie's notes he was busy contacting Pak's daughters on Wednesday, and after they arrived here, asking them to request Dr Gan to do alcohol tests. Did Dr Gan talk to you, Inspector Das? Was he, perhaps, suspicious of the death not being natural and contacted you?'

Dolly squirmed in her seat. Slowly and precisely, she told her boss of Bill Eddington's suspicions that DW had not died a natural death based on not having smelt alcohol on his breath on Monday and his flask of alcohol remaining untouched after lunch.

'And Dr Eddington approached Dr Gan to look into his colleague's death?' the Supt prompted.

Dolly shook her head and proceeded to inform her boss that it was she who had talked to Dr Gan with the forensic pathologist, Benny Ong, and requested him to test Pak's alcohol levels.

Siti Abdullah's eyebrows disappeared into her hair and her eyes began flashing. 'Let me get this straight, Inspector Das. On your own initiative, you approached Dr Gan. You are not one of Pak's relatives or colleagues, and his family had accepted the doctor's verdict of Pak dying from natural causes. Why did you intervene?' Siti's eyes narrowed into slits. 'I think I know the reason. Your sister, Lily Das, had her stall closed because her food was thought to have poisoned Pak. So you wanted to clear your sister's name and began meddling in the cause of Pak's death.'

There was a photo of the Supt receiving an award from the commissioner proudly displayed on her desk. Studying it, Dolly said in a soft voice, 'I was searching for the truth, Ma'am, as was Bill Eddington.' She looked up and gazed fearlessly into her boss's eyes. 'Dr Pak's daughters were not here, someone had to raise questions with Dr Gan on the cause of Pak's death. It appeared mysterious. He was found to have been murdered because of our questioning. Otherwise, his death would have been ruled natural.'

Siti shuffled some papers on her desk and said sharply, 'The police will investigate a suspicious death on the request of a physician or family member of the deceased. Not otherwise. You used your friendship with the forensic pathologist to get the doctor who had written out Pak's death certificate to initiate an investigation into Pak's death. You are not to take matters into your own hand. Is that understood?'

'If I had not cast doubts on the cause of death, we would not have found out Pak had been murdered,' Dolly said stiffly.

'That is beside the point. You can go now. I don't want this to happen again. You are to clear all actions you take with me before you meddle again,' Siti said rudely and dismissively.

'So the public cannot approach the police to look into a suspicious death?' Dolly asked, scraping back her chair and standing up.

Siti said, 'Of course they can. They must follow protocol, right? Why are police posts there? Dr Eddington could have approached a police post and lodged his complaint against Dr Gan for negligence. Then the police could have started an investigation into Pak's death. You know this well, Inspector Das. It was inappropriate of you to question the treating doctor based on allegations by Pak's colleague and to pressure him to do further tests on the cause of death.'

Dolly's nostrils had flared, and she asked, 'Am I still in charge of the investigation into Dr Pak's death? We have a lead. Pak was on bad terms with his sister-in-law and quarrelled with her two weeks before his death. My team has located the sister-in-law in Singapore, and Charlie and I were going to interview her at 11 a.m.'

Siti waved her hand. 'Since you have meddled into this case, go ahead with the investigation, but know I am keeping a strict eye on whether you are following police protocol.'

'Ma'am,' Dolly said and marched out of the room.

In the corridor, Dolly found herself trembling and breathing hard. Instead of commending her for sniffing out a murder and setting the force on the track of a killer, her boss was berating her for not following protocol. Siti would rather Pak be buried as the victim of a natural death and his daughters receive no justice for their father's murder? Siti's precious protocols mattered more than justice? Dolly fumed as she got into the elevator.

In her office, she vented her feelings to Charlie, who was patiently waiting to accompany her to interview Eun-jin Choi.

Charlie was ruminative as the officers walked down the corridor to the lift lobby. He said, 'Fauzia keeps asking questions about Pak's death even though I have taken her off the case. I wonder if she has been sent to spy on us for the Supt.'

Dolly's eyes widened. 'It is strange Fauzia transferred to our division.' She gave a short laugh. 'Maybe the boss wants to sack me.'

Charlie said, 'There are rumours the division is going to be trimmed, Madam, and jobs will be made redundant by year's end. Retrenchment from the police force in Singapore is rare, so I am hoping the rumours are just that.'

The officers entered the lift and Charlie pressed the button for the Level 1 lobby. Dolly said, 'I heard Supt Dragon Lady has a new boss. Deputy Assistant Commissioner John Nathan. He is sharp and fair. I briefly worked under him when I was a sergeant, Charlie. I met with him last week, informally, to welcome him to our division. I don't see him sacking me unless there is a good reason.' Dolly tossed her head. The two officers exited the lift and walked across the lobby to the door leading to the carpark.

'Yes, I heard about his appointment as well. I just feel uneasy with Fauzia around.' Charlie looked at his watch. 'We have an appointment to keep. If we solve cases, Madam, no one can touch our jobs. Let's hope we can sew this case up fast after interviewing Eun-jin Choi.'

Dolly nodded as Charlie opened the front passenger door of their squad car. 'Congratulations to our team for the speed with which they found Choi's workplace. Let's go, Charlie.'

* * *

Charlie drove Dolly to Shenton Way and a skyscraper office building where Dong-wook Pak's sister-in-law, Eun-jin Choi, worked as a translator and business analyst in a multinational South Korean conglomerate. Dolly looked glum; she was getting tired of her boss watching her every move, probably to find an excuse to terminate her job. Unlike Charlie, she doubted Eun-jin Choi was the killer; she would not have known about the arrangement that students and professors had to leave drinks on Abdul's table to be delivered.

Charlie sighed as he made a right turn in heavy traffic. 'Here we are then, Madam. I will drop you off and hunt for parking; it's a nightmare to find parking in the business district.'

'Use your warrant card,' Dolly said, shortly, as she alighted in front of a glass-fronted skyscraper.

The interior was stark, the atmosphere hushed. Dolly took the lift to Level 23 and walked along carpeted corridors with glass-fronted offices on either side, stopping at the end office.

She flashed her warrant card and asked the receptionist at the glittering chrome counter to call Eun-jin Choi. The startled Korean receptionist scuttled into the inner sanctums of the office. She returned and asked Dolly to follow her inside. They went into a small conference room where a slim, tall woman with bobbed hair, dressed in a smart business suit, was waiting. She looked to be in her early fifties.

The receptionist waved Dolly to a chair and left the room, closing the door behind her.

The Korean woman spoke. 'I am Eun-jin Choi. May I know what this is about?' She spoke good English with a slight accent.

'Are you aware of the death of your brother-in-law, Dr Dong-wook Pak?' Dolly motioned to the Korean woman to be seated. She noted the loss of colour from the woman's face.

'Dong-wook?' Eun-jin cried, her voice shaking. '*Dead?* How?' The woman stood standing, her face white and shocked.

'He was murdered. Poisoned on Monday, 29 August. His death was reported in the newspapers. Did you not read?'

'Murdered?' Eun-jin screeched. 'Poisoned?'

Dolly looked patiently at the dead man's sister-in-law. If she was the murderer, she was doing a good job of feigning shock and surprise. 'When did you start working at this firm? When did you arrive in Singapore?'

Eun-jin gazed at the floor, and when she looked up, her eyes were still startled. 'I came to Singapore four months ago. I was retrenched from the firm I worked in for ten years in Seoul, and I was lucky to get a translator's job here. I now also work as the firm's chief business analyst.' She slowly sat down in a chair opposite Dolly.

Dolly said, 'Dr Pak arrived here a year ago. Did you meet your brother-in-law often?'

Eun-jin's face stiffened. 'No, we never met in Singapore, nor did I have any contact with him.'

'But you were aware he worked at Temasek University?'

Eun-jin inclined her head. 'Soo-ah, my niece, mentioned it once when I called her before I left Seoul.'

'You are on speaking terms with your nieces? Do you know they are here now?'

Eun-jin blinked behind her spectacles and mutely shook her head. She appeared to be in deep thought.

'I need to know of your movements on 29 August.'

Eun-jin raised her head. Her eyes were dilated with horror. 'Is that when Dong-wook died?' she whispered. Then she said in a stronger voice, 'Surely, you don't think I killed him?'

'Well, you were lying when you said you never met him in his office at the university. We have witnesses saying you and he quarrelled when you met him there two weeks ago. That is suspicious.'

The woman could not look whiter, Dolly thought.

In a whisper, Eun-jin said, 'I want to be on good terms with my nieces, but I could not because of my brother-in-law. He forbade them to interact with me. Soo-ah is merely polite when I call her, and Seo-yeon puts down the phone when I ring. I went to Dong-wook to request him to allow me access to my nieces. My sister, Binna, was my only sibling.' Eun-jin's voice trembled.

'And what did he say?'

'We quarrelled,' Eun-jin said, shortly. 'But that was the only time I met him in Singapore, and it was over two weeks ago.'

'We need to investigate all angles,' Dolly said and added, 'You are a person of interest in this case given that you and your brother-in-law had been on acrimonious terms in Seoul. You accused him of murdering your sister, but he was acquitted. You may still think he murdered your sister and were taking revenge.'

There was silence in the room. Two tears trickled down from Eun-jin's eyes. She drew a handkerchief out of her handbag and vigorously blew her nose. Composing herself, she said, 'I see you have talked to my nieces. I was wrong to accuse Dong-wook of euthanasia. My action cost me my cordial relations with my nieces. I love my nieces and now they only talk with me as a formality, or not at all. We used to confide in each other, visit museums, eat at restaurants. All that has stopped because I was stupid enough to think that my brother-in-law would assist in my sister's suicide. The nurse proved me wrong. I went to their house to ask for forgiveness but Dong-wook had left for Tokyo, and my nieces shut the door in my face. No, Inspector, I was hoping to reconcile with my brother-in-law, not murder him.'

'Your nieces said Dr Pak was going to take you to court for falsely accusing him of killing his wife and challenge your mother's will.' Dolly looked sharply at the Korean woman.

The colour receded from Eun-jin's face. 'I think my nieces persuaded Dong-wook not to take me to court. But that day at the university, he said he was going to challenge Mama's will. That was what the quarrel was about.' Eun-jin gave a sharp sigh. 'Mama wanted to see my sister when she was ill, but Dong-wook did not allow Binna to visit. Mama was angry and left the country house to me.' Eun-jin looked piercingly at Dolly. 'I told Dong-wook then and I am telling you now. I have made a will leaving that house to my nieces. So he was quarrelling for no reason. My nieces inherit that house, anyway.'

'We need an account of your movements on 29 August,' Dolly said.

Eun-jin sighed. She whipped out a tablet and switched it on. After viewing it for some time, she said, 'Last Monday, isn't it? My firm is Korean, and sometimes I need to visit Seoul on business. I left Singapore on Sunday, 28 August in the evening for Seoul. I returned on Friday, 2 September. Maybe that is the reason I never read about Dong-wook's murder in the newspapers. I was not in Singapore.'

'I will have my sergeant check it out. He will talk to your receptionist here about the flight details.' Dolly nodded. 'Tell me more about the quarrel with your brother-in-law.'

Eun-jin exploded, her eyes pinpricks of anger. 'What was I to do if my mother leaves me her country house? Dong-wook saw to it that Binna seldom visited our mother in the country. He was possessive of her. My mother was resentful, and when she was taken ill, I left my job to nurse our mother. I asked Binna to visit her one last time, but she said Dong-wook would disapprove. Is it abnormal then for our mother to leave her country house and estate to me? Dong-wook wanted the spoils without putting in effort into relationships.'

Eun-jin could not tell Dolly anything more, and the inspector left the conference room. She spied Charlie talking to the receptionist, and together, they rode the lift down.

'Choi was not in Singapore on the day of Pak's poisoning, she says. Charlie, check with the receptionist at her office about flight details and double-check with Immigration at the airport. We need to be sure she was not in Singapore on the day her brother-in-law was poisoned.' Dolly nodded when Charlie shook his head in disappointment. He had been so sure Eun-jin had poisoned DW.

Outside, clouds were rolling across the sky and a sharp pre-shower breeze began to whip up. Charlie asked Dolly to wait inside the lobby while he brought the car around from where it was parked.

Dolly sat in one of the lobby chairs and watched with interest Eun-jin Choi hurrying out of the lift and rushing out of the door of the lobby. Through the glass, Dolly watched her stand on the road trying to flag down a cab.

17

Lily's mother, Uma, insisted Lily bring along the pundit, coconuts, and the necessary puja paraphernalia before she reopened her stall in the canteen. Only then would the stall remain blessed with good fortune, Uma told her daughter, and not be prone to rumours bad for business. Lily took this opportunity to take Ashikin on board, and her Malay friend, dressed in a bright green baju kurung and tudung, packed all the ingredients she needed for nasi lemak in plastic bags stored in the boot of Lily's Honda Jazz.

At 8 a.m., dressed in a heavy blue silk saree and with jasmine flowers in her hair, Lily supervised the pundit perform the puja in front of her stall, break the coconut, all the while chanting words in a lilting tone, watched smilingly by Ashikin and a bemused Vernon and Angie. Finally, convinced the blessings on the shop would prevent further catastrophe and instead bring prosperity, Lily paid the priest and he left. Lily motioned Vernon and Angie to bring in all the ingredients for the breakfast specials, a bright, happy smile on her face, looking forward to frying pratas for the breakfast crowd. She had already prepared the potato curry at home and Vernon brought in the large pot from the car, a big grin on his face. He was happy to be back with Lily as he did not get along well with his father and had not enjoyed working for him.

'You going to cook in that saree, Lily?' Ashikin said, tying a big apron around herself. 'We hear stories of sarees catching fire from the gas burner.' She peered into the pot of nasi lemak boiling on the burner, an enticing aroma filling the stall.

'No, no. I am going to get changed into jeans and tee; they are in the satchel over there.' Lily laughed, pointing to a high stool. 'The heat from the stoves is too much, what with you cooking as well.'

After Lily changed into work clothes, she expertly began to make the dough for the prata, watched closely by Angie, now Lily's helper. Vernon, with great enthusiasm, followed Ashikin's guidance in frying eggs and chicken for the nasi lemak. The aroma from the stall soon drew a long queue of students and teachers who breakfasted at work. Naheed, who had come in early to prepare her food at her Malay stall, glanced darkly at Ashikin, smiling insincerely when Ashikin gave her a grin, shouting out a Malay greeting. Lily was back in business!

After she finished frying the pratas and leaving Angie to serve new customers, Lily wandered outside her stall to take a breather. At a table sat Professor Ursula Botham and her husband, Graham. Ursula was not a great beauty, Lily thought, but her fragility lent her charm along with her long blonde hair and pale blue eyes. Lily always wondered what Ursula had seen in Graham, with his thick head of untidy hair, straggly beard, and black-framed glasses adding years to his age. Lily pricked up her ears on hearing them mention Pritam.

Graham's deep voice carried easily in the air. He was having breakfast from the Western stall and enthusiastically speared half a sausage with his fork. 'Pritam Singh has to resign from this university for me to be appointed to the Head of Chemistry position. We are both in the running, but Pritam has been at Temasek for years and all our peers will vote for him. The incumbent head has already nominated him. My million-dollar research doesn't count,' he gave a dry laugh. 'But if Pritam is out of the way, it's a cert I will be Head of Chemistry here.'

Ursula ate her pork congee enthusiastically. 'Is that so important, Graham? I am happy with my associate professor position; why aren't you?'

Graham turned his head away and Ursula continued, 'We have moved a lot, Graham. Your jobs were never stable, and we had to go from one place to another in the UK and Australia. Tom's schooling was affected. I intend to remain in Singapore for the foreseeable future whether you want to or not.'

When he turned to his wife, Graham's face was red. 'You don't have any ambition, Ursula, that's always been your problem.'

Ursula tossed her head. Then she looked at her husband, her intense eyes probing into him to such an extent that Lily felt uneasy. 'Remember what happened in Australia, Graham. Leave Lorna alone.'

Unknowingly, Lily had edged close to the Botham table and found Graham Botham's light-brown eyes on her. 'Yes, what is it?' he barked. Ursula clamped her mouth shut and concentrated on finishing her porridge.

'Oh, no, no, not to worry,' Lily said in dulcet tones. 'I was just coming to inform you that I now serve breakfast at my stall. Both roti prata and nasi lemak.'

Graham's eyes bored into Lily. 'Aren't you Pritam Singh's sister-in-law? Do you know if he is planning to retire? He is pushing sixty.'

'Really, Graham, what a question to ask!' Ursula smiled kindly at Lily and pushed back her blonde hair from her face. 'Don't mind my husband, he tends to say strange things. I am done here. Yes, Mrs D, I will be in the queue for the roti prata tomorrow. Is your curry spicy?' She smiled and got up from the chair. She left her husband eating his breakfast and walked away towards the Science building. Lily strolled back to her stall where the crowd had thinned.

'All the nasi lemak is finished!' Ashikin announced triumphantly. 'Must make some more tomorrow. I misjudged the number of customers.'

'What? None for me?' Lily cried in dismay. She had been looking forward to having Ashikin's delicious breakfast.

'I kept some for you, Lily,' Ashikin assured her friend before turning to Angie. 'Two roti prata for me please, Angie. Come, Lily, let's have our breakfasts together at the table in the corner.'

Lily nodded, collecting her plate from Vernon. She turned to Angie, anxiously. 'How did the roti prata do?'

'All finished, Mrs D, except for two plates for us,' Angie said, grinning widely. She jerked her head at Vernon who was gazing at his wife, a silly grin on his face.

'Oh ho, he knows. How does it feel to know you'll soon be a father, V?' Lily grinned.

Vernon said, shyly, 'Good.'

'Now make sure Angie does not smoke any more. It is dangerous for the baby. Have your breakfast and then clean the counters thoroughly before we start preparing for the lunchtime crowd.' Lily smilingly moved away to join Ashikin at her table.

After Ashikin finished her breakfast, she went to make friends with the Malay stall owner, Naheed. Lily sat at the table sipping her tea. She smiled as Bill Eddington walked into the canteen and waved to her. He got a coffee from the drinks stall and shyly asked if he could join her. He grinned when Lily nodded.

Sipping his coffee, Bill said, 'Last evening, we all went over to DW's apartment to pay condolences to his daughters. Seeing them broke my heart. DW had been looking forward to their visit and showing them Singapore. How cruel life is.' He took a sip of his coffee.

Lily liked Bill's compassionate nature and nodded, sympathetically. 'The poor girls. Now they have lost both their parents.' She looked at Bill, piercingly, knowing Dolly was interviewing Eun-jin Choi. 'They have an aunt, though.'

'Bad blood there,' Bill observed, putting down his kopi glass on the table. 'She came to visit DW two weeks ago and they had a row. DW told me she had stolen his daughters' inheritances from them.'

Lily nodded. 'She is a prime suspect for his murder then. No one else held a grudge. DW was a nice gentleman and got on with everyone.' She finished the last of her tea.

Bill's eyes gleamed. 'I should probably not be saying this. On the day he was poisoned and before lunch, DW and I were chatting in the office. And he said a strange thing. There was a scandal with a Korean girl in Graham Botham's last place of work, and she ended up killing herself.' He told her the story DW had narrated.

Lily's eyes shone with conjecture. 'If DW had informed the university authorities about the scandal, Graham would have lost his candidature for the headship, right?'

Bill finished the last of his coffee and sat back. He looked sombre. 'Yes. The head is supposed to be a role model to the other professors so yes, his character must be beyond reproach. I don't think DW talked to Graham about the scandal, though. And Ursula denied the liaison. She told me the girl's Korean boyfriend was responsible for her suicide. But I think Ursula was lying to save Graham's skin.'

When Bill had left, Lily sat back in her chair, her eyes far away. What if DW had talked to Graham about the scandal with the Korean girl? That would give Graham a motive for murdering the Korean scientist to prevent him from spreading the tale of his past philandering. Graham wanted the headship so much. Would he kill for it? He would know of the habit professors had of leaving notes to the janitor for delivering beverages. Had Graham Botham put the poisoned cup of coffee on Abdul's table to be delivered to DW? Last night, Lily and Dolly had discussed the case at great length, and now she needed to tell Dolly there was a second suspect. Lily got busy texting information to her sister on the phone.

Lily glanced at her stall and saw Ashikin instructing Vernon to chop vegetables for the Malay lunch specials. Lily rose and sauntered into the stall to get busy preparing the Indian lunch specials.

Two hours later, Lily looked up from the pots of curry boiling on the burners and saw her sister entering the canteen, dressed in a smart black business suit.

Dolly was meeting Charlie at the Science building where he was busy tracking down Pritam Singh's student, Manjunath Reddy. As Charlie was running late, Dolly decided to have lunch with her sister at her stall. She wanted to try out Ashikin's Malay food.

'*What*? Botham asked you about Pritam's retirement plans?' Dolly said, appreciatively eating rice with sayur lodeh and chicken rendang. Lily was updating her on the snippets of conversation she had heard that might be of interest to her sister.

'Yes, such a crude man, not at all like an erudite professor,' Lily sniffed. 'Now if Pritam had been poisoned, Graham Botham would be the chief suspect.' Lily smacked her lips on tasting Ashikin's Malay vegetables.

Dolly tucked into her food and sighed with pleasure. 'Ashikin's Malay vegetables are delicious. She adds just the right amount of coconut milk. I am going to come and eat at your stall as often as possible. We just lost our chief suspect in DW's murder. His sister-in-law, Eun-jin Choi was not in Singapore on the day of the poisoning.' While eating, she proceeded to tell her sister about Eun-jin Choi's bad history with DW.

Lily said, playing with the chicken on her plate, 'DW's life had a lot of drama in recent years. Being jailed and all. Such a pity the sister-in-law wasn't in Singapore at the time of the poisoning. Though there may be another suspect as well. Have you looked at my texts?'

When Dolly shook her head, Lily went on to tell her sister about one of Graham's students dying by suicide in Australia because of unrequited love. DW had told Bill that Graham was the lover of the Korean girl.

Dolly chewed her food, swallowed, and then said, 'I will ask Charlie to look this suicide up on the internet.' The sisters ate their meal in silence for some time, appreciating the Malay cuisine.

'Dolly, something is bothering me,' Lily said, finishing the last of her rice and chicken. 'You don't have the coffee cup and so don't know if the coffee was poisoned. I am just wondering whether DW was poisoned in a different way. Not through the coffee.'

Dolly finished her food and wiped her mouth with a napkin. She sat back in her chair, satisfied after finishing a delicious lunch. 'Well, that's the problem with poisoning cases. We have few clues as to how the poison was ingested since we only find out about the poisoning days later. We must go with what we've got. Look at the evidence of symptoms, though. Two students in the span of half an hour saw the cup of coffee Abdul delivered on DW's table and Salma saw DW behaving drunkenly. I am 80 per cent certain that it was the cup of coffee that had the poison. DW was showing symptoms just after finishing the beverage.' Her mind went back to a past case where she had followed a colleague's dangerous tendency of fixing on one suspect as the killer and closing her mind to other pieces of evidence that could point in a different direction. Dolly decided to keep an open mind and mentally added Graham Botham as a suspect, along with Eun-jin Choi for DW's murder.

Lily nodded. 'Fair enough. You are now after an Indian boy, Pritam's student?'

'Well, we suspect his former student, Manjunath Reddy, of threatening Pritam's life. Pritam received a letter stating he would be the next one to die. Quite dramatic. Manjunath failed his Oral Prelim with Pritam and when told to leave the university, he created a ruckus. Now Pritam thinks he may be enrolled again at Temasek.'

Lily asked, 'Have you heard from Pritam? How is he today?'

Dolly sighed. 'I just received a text from Cheryl. Apparently, Pritam is showing early signs of Parkinson's Disease. The doctors did many tests and came to that conclusion. Not what Preet was wanting to hear but at least he knows he is not going mad.'

The two sisters ate dessert companionably, talking of their families, before Dolly glanced at her watch. 'Well, Lil, I am off now to meet Charlie. That was a nice meal. My compliments to your friend, Ashikin. See you at home tonight.'

Charlie was leaning against a balustrade in the common corridor, sunlight illuminating the strands of grey in his hair. He looked excited as he glanced through his phone text messages.

At Dolly's approach, Charlie looked up and said, 'There is an Indian student called Manjunath Reddy enrolled in the physics department, Madam. I had Student Admissions check his place of birth, home address and all, and they match with the Manjunath Reddy enrolled in the chemistry department two years ago. The boy boards in the same dorm as Cheng Yong. Shall we go and see him, Madam?'

Dolly glanced at her watch. 'We'll go around 8 p.m. today. He is probably in class now. This is a good break, Charlie! We cannot have students going around threatening professors; they need to be stopped. The note for Pritam said he would be murdered next, so we must take this seriously. It may have a connection to DW's death.'

Charlie followed Dolly along the corridors to the lifts. Soon, he was driving the squad car away from Temasek University and on to a busy expressway with the sun warming the city in its golden glow.

18

After the rain in the late afternoon, the setting sun now blazed over Singapore, drying the sheen of moisture off the roads. Having had dinner at a coffee shop in Dover Crescent, Dolly and Charlie drove to the university, passed the Science and Arts buildings, took a left and drove a mile before the student dormitories loomed in front with the staff quarters on the left. Charlie parked the car in an open-air carpark and held the car door open for Dolly to emerge. It was 7 p.m., and the officers figured that Manjunath Reddy was back in his dorm after classes.

Getting out of the car, Dolly peered at her mobile phone and said, 'It seems the students stay in residence halls; there are four of them, and Manjunath Reddy lives on the fourth floor of Raffles Hall.'

'That is Raffles Hall, Madam.' Charlie pointed to a five-storey red brick building in front of them with open corridors winding around it.

There was a security guard at the gate. Charlie showed his warrant card and the police officers were ushered into the housemaster's office. Ronald Freeman, housemaster of Raffles Hall, was seated on a swivel chair in a small office on the ground floor. There was a half-open door on one side, through which could be seen a spartanly furnished living hall. The wail of a child came from within.

Ronald Freeman coughed, rose from his chair, bade the police officers sit in the guest chairs and closed the door leading to his own quarters, where he lived with his family.

'Good evening, officers, I'm Ronald Freeman, the housemaster here. What can I do for you?'

Dolly understood from his drawl that he hailed from the United States of America. She introduced herself and Charlie and added briskly, 'We need to interview one of your students, Manjunath Reddy. I believe he shares a room on the fourth floor with another student. This is in connection with a threatening letter sent to a professor he worked for in the chemistry department two years ago.'

Ronald's blue eyes sharpened. 'Manjunath is a physics student, Ma'am. May I know more about the incident?'

After Charlie narrated the story of the letter and the tale of Manjunath's grudge against Professor Pritam Singh, Ronald Freeman nodded. He ran a hand through his sandy hair and straightened his wire-rimmed spectacles. 'I see. Yes, he had been enrolled in Temasek before. I saw that from the form he filled up when he applied to board here. He has only been here a month; this is his first semester in the physics department. I tell you what, let me vacate my office and send for Manjunath. You can interview him here rather than go upstairs to talk to him in his room where his room-mate would be disturbed.'

'How have you found him?' Dolly asked.

'H'm.' Freeman pressed a buzzer on his desk. 'The guy has a hot temper. He had a run-in with his room-mate, another Indian guy called Chandrasekhar, who is fond of music and likes to play his violin. Manjunath apparently asked him to practise his violin only when he was not in the room, but the lad did not comply. There was a big shouting match and the other students called me.' He glanced up as the security guard came into the office and stood to attention. 'Yeah, Hari, please go upstairs and get Manjunath Reddy from 04-18 and bring him here. Just tell him I want to see him, yeah?' Freeman turned back to Dolly as Hari left the room with a nod. 'Yes, as I was saying, I had to break up the fight and establish some ground rules for music playing. Chandrasekhar is a very sedate boy, immersed in his studies, so I was quite surprised at the venom with which he regarded Manjunath. From what I gathered, Manjunath's parents are very wealthy, they own a factory in Hyderabad, and he is used to getting his own way.' Freeman and Dolly spoke for some more time about the student before Freeman exclaimed, 'Ah, here he is! Come in, Manjunath!'

A medium-height, dark, swarthy youth with black, curly, cropped hair and wire-rimmed spectacles stood by the door, frowning. He was dressed in jeans and a tee shirt with the face of one of India's top cricketers, Sachin Tendulkar, emblazoned on it.

'Manju,' Freeman said with the trace of a smile on his face. 'These are police officers from the Singapore CID, Inspector Das and Sergeant Goh. They wish to talk to you about a threatening letter. Go ahead, Inspector. Have a seat, Manju. I'll be in my apartment if anybody needs me.'

After Freeman had left, shutting the door of his flat firmly, Dolly looked at Manjunath. The youth had begun perspiring and dug out a large white handkerchief from the pocket of his jeans to wipe his brow. He sat down on a chair and glared at the officers.

'But what has this got to do with me?' Manjunath demanded when Charlie had shown him the threatening letter.

Dolly said, 'We understand you had a bad history with Prof. Singh?' Dolly watched the sweat break out on the young man's forehead.

'So, this is what it is about!' Manjunath grew purple in the face. 'You want to finger me as a blackmailer? Wait, wasn't there a murder in that department? Am I a murder suspect as well? Do you know who my father is?'

'No, I don't, young man, and you'd do well not to speak in that tone.' Dolly's voice was like a pistol shot.

'You held a grudge against Professor Singh?' Charlie asked, his voice bland.

Manjunath decided the same laws and rules in his hometown in India did not apply here and said in a more conciliatory tone, 'Yes, Professor Singh failed my oral prelim. We must have an interview with our graduate student committee professors, and they question us on chemistry principles. We must pass this oral exam, or we are out of the PhD programme. Professor Singh asked me a complex question. I ost my nerve and gave a wrong answer. I was upset and I gave wrong answers to all my professors after that and failed.' Manjunath's voice was indignant. 'Professor Singh deliberately asked me a tough question. He was complaining about my research and work ethics before; by failing me in the oral exam, he had the perfect excuse to get rid of me.'

Manjunath had worked himself up and was hyperventilating. Dolly could well believe he had a fierce temper.

'You confronted Professor Singh two years ago?' Charlie queried. His pen was poised over his notebook.

'Yes, I let him have it. We had a nasty showdown in his office, and he told me to pack my bags and leave,' Manjunath said, sullenly. 'I thought of appealing my suspension to the Dean of Science but decided against it. When your supervisor thinks you are not good enough, you'll never get a PhD.' He looked at the police officers, the yellows of his eyes showing. Then, Manjunath glanced disdainfully at the letter. 'This isn't my handwriting. A writing expert can testify to that. Besides, Prof. Singh may have many enemies. He was a wild young man.'

Dolly raised her eyebrows. 'What do you mean? And how would you know?'

Manjunath looked with veiled satisfaction at the police inspector. 'I found out.'

'What did you find out?' Dolly said in a crisp voice.

'When he failed me in my oral prelims, I tried to find out about him, and I got lucky. It's always good to know your enemy, right? Professor Singh's niece was my mathematics classmate and we had interesting conversations about the professor.' Manjunath began picking at a mole on his cheek.

'His niece?'

Manjunath smirked at Dolly's astonishment. 'Devender Kaur is the granddaughter of the uncle and aunt who raised Professor Singh. They were poor relations of Pritam Singh's father and took him in when he was a fourteen-year-old boy, and his father's brother kicked him out of the house. Pritam's uncle threw him out of the house but could not take away the money his parents left him. At the age of fourteen, Pritam was wealthy, which of course may be the reason the distant aunt took him in.' There was a note of envy in Manjunath's voice, and he looked wistfully out of the window, wishing he had the money now that Pritam had in his youth.

Dolly appeared mesmerized by the story of her ex-husband's colourful past. She told Manjunath, 'Go on.'

The boy turned back to the officers. 'Pritam Singh used his father's money for drugs and alcohol. He was very wild. He dropped out of university and spent his time drinking. Then one day he was involved in a car accident, and someone died. His niece said that was the turning point in his life and sobered him up. He went into rehab, sorted himself out, finished his university studies, and went abroad to do his doctorate degree. Then he came back to an assistant professor's position at Temasek.' Manjunath's face was animated. He was enjoying his role of informant and the fact that he knew more about Pritam Singh's life than the police officers. He obviously did not know that Pritam had been married to Dolly. Then his enjoyment would have been even more.

Dolly asked, 'Why was he estranged from the family who raised him?'

Manjunath shrugged. 'Devender did not say much about that. I do have her address if you want to catch up with her.' Manjunath smiled broadly.

Dolly noted down the address on her tablet and said, 'You can go now. We are keeping an eye on you.'

Manjunath rolled his eyes, got up from his seat, and sauntered off.

'I think he is innocent,' Dolly opined as Charlie held the door of the lobby open for her. They had taken their leave of Ronald Freeman.

Charlie nodded. 'I think so, too, Madam.' The officers walked to their squad car.

'If a girl killed herself because of Graham and DW confronted him about that, it's a strong motive for murder. I think it would affect the headship election, and the unfavourable publicity would not be in Graham's favour,' Dolly said, looking around, imbibing the night air tinged with the sweet scent of frangipani.

'It's hard to find out the truth about what happened in an Australian university from here, Madam,' Charlie said, morosely. He was looking at his watch. His toddler daughter had fever and he wanted to get back home.

'Oh, I am sure you will be working on it, though. There are leads. Easy enough to find which Australian university Graham worked in. The news about a Korean girl's suicide would be there on the internet news archives. Besides, since DW knew the girl's family, his daughters may know about this incident. So many leads, Charlie.' Dolly smiled as Charlie looked more enthusiastic.

'I wish Eun-jin Choi were in Singapore when DW was poisoned. She is still the strongest suspect in DW's murder, based on motive,' Dolly said.

'Immigration should call me tomorrow about the dates of Ms Choi's departure and arrival in Seoul, Madam. We are checking everything out, thoroughly.'

The stars were out, and a cool breeze was blowing. Dolly got into the car and realized her stomach was rumbling. She told Charlie to drop her off at Silver Springs and hoped Girlie had prepared a nice dessert. Creamy rice pudding would be nice, Dolly thought.

Tuesday, 6 September 2011

19

Sergeant Charles Goh was in to work bright and early. It was a sunny day with a cloudless sky, and Charlie felt energetic. He swung through the doors of the lobby and walked to the elevator, a spring in his step. His oldest son, James, was studying computer science at Temasek University and Charlie was proud of his boy. After an initial belligerent phase when he had indulged in street gang activities, Jimmy had settled down, much to his mother, Meena's relief, and was concentrating on his studies. He wanted to work as a software engineer in a multinational company—a job that would take him outside Singapore. His craving for adventure sometimes alarmed his father.

In contrast, his younger boys, Jonathan and Govind, were more manageable, their characters styled in a more serious vein. He hoped his toddler daughter, Seema, would follow in their footsteps. He and Meena had not planned the late pregnancy and were apprehensive about caring for a young baby at their age as well as concerned about how her brothers would receive the news of her impending birth. But Seema had proven to be a bundle of joy, lighting up their lives, holding her brothers in the crook of her chubby fingers.

Humming a tune, Charlie entered his cubicle. His phone beeped a message instructing him to call the Immigration and Checkpoint Authorities. Charlie hastily dialled their number. A Tom Ng answered him.

'Ah, yes, Sergeant Goh. Regarding your request to check when Eun-jin Choi had entered and left Singapore the week of 28 August, we have the report. She left Singapore early on the morning of 30 August, which was a Tuesday. She returned to Singapore on Friday, 2 September, in the evening. Anything else we can do for you, let us know.'

After Tom Ng had rung off, Charlie sat in his chair, stunned. Why had Eun-jin Choi lied about the dates she was outside Singapore? Dong-wook Pak was poisoned sometime on Monday afternoon when his sister-in-law was still in town. She could have poisoned him and then left the country. Why had she said she left on Sunday when it was Tuesday? He dialled the number of the firm that employed Eun-jin Choi and asked to speak to the secretary who made travel arrangements. A Belinda Tan came on the line; her voice apprehensive.

'Ms Eun-jin Choi from your company left on a business trip end of August. I need to find out when she left Singapore and when she returned,' Charlie said, his voice officious.

After asking Charlie to hang on the line for a minute, Belinda Tan came back on the phone. 'Yes, I have the details. Ms Choi left Singapore on the early morning flight to Seoul on Tuesday, 30 August and returned on 2 September, Friday, on the evening flight.'

'She told the police she left Singapore on Sunday, 28 August,' Charlie interposed.

Belinda's voice held a timbre of apology. 'I think she mixed up dates, Sergeant. She was scheduled to fly out on Sunday, 28 August but the flight was full, and she was wait-listed. The airlines called and let me know that the flight could not accommodate her and could she take Tuesday's flight. As Ms Choi's meeting with clients was not until Wednesday, I allowed the airlines to change the bookings and let Ms Choi know that her flight schedule had been changed. She left Singapore on 30 August early morning.'

Charlie thanked the secretary and mulled over Eun-jin Choi's assertion that she had left Singapore on 28 August. Had she mixed up dates or was she deliberately lying so as not to become a suspect in her brother-in-law's murder? Charlie called Dolly to tell her the news, and Dolly told Charlie to bring Eun-jin into HQ for questioning. She thought it suspicious

Eun-jin Choi was lying about her whereabouts on the day her brother-in-law was poisoned.

* * *

Eun-jin Choi finished her cup of coffee in her spick and span office cubicle and sighed. She had to attend the first of a day of business meetings, and she was not in the mood for work. The trace of worry in her eyes, ever since the police had informed her of Dong-wook's death, remained. Had the police checked with Immigration the date she left for Seoul? She shook her head. Why had she lied when it was easy for the police to check her embarkation date by talking to Immigration officials? It had been an insane instinct to lie—to remove herself as far as she could from Dong-wook in case she became the prime suspect in his murder. It had been easy to lie since she had been booked on the Sunday evening flight to leave Singapore. It was only later that the flights had been changed.

She had her defence ready and had already briefed the secretary who looked after flight bookings. Sweat sprung up on Eun-jin's forehead. She remembered her conversation with her brother-in-law when she had gone to visit him two weeks ago after learning from Soo-ah where he worked.

Dong-wook had coolly looked at her and said, 'Eun-jin, have a seat. How are you? Soo-ah told me you were working in a multinational here, but I must say I never expected a visit from you. Not after what happened!'

Eun-jin had flushed. 'I did send you a letter of apology and called you after the trial. You had left Korea to work abroad. I am sorry I mistrusted you, Dong-wook.'

Dong-wook had looked at her with icy eyes and said in rapid Korean, 'You thought I could kill Binna with my own hands? No, I believe you knew I would never do that. You wanted to make my relationship with my children tense and full of doubts and suspicions. You were jealous of Binna's closeness to me, and you are jealous of my children's love for me. So, you sent me to jail to become close to your nieces. And you stole your nieces' inheritances from them by influencing your mother to leave you sole owner of her country estate. You are a thorough bad lot!'

Eun-jin cried out, 'My mother left me the country house of her own free will. Binna was too busy with you and taking care of her pretty domestic life to visit our mother when she was ailing. Is it surprising that she left her house to the daughter who took care of her?'

Dong-wook's voice trembled. 'My wife was dying of cancer, Eun-jin. Her mother never knew of her illness because Binna made us promise not to burden her mother with the news. How could she visit her mother when she, herself, was sick?'

'I am talking of the time before she was ill, Dong-wook.' Eun-jin's eyes flashed. 'She visited our mother seldom because you wanted her to be a domestic goddess, keep her in the kitchen cooking and in the nursery taking care of your children. You murdered her career as a scientist, and she was so bright! She could easily have started work when the girls were going to school, but she never did. You were possessive of Binna and kept her chained to you!'

Dong-wook's hands were trembling as he raised his mug of coffee to his lips. He took a sip and said, 'That is not true, and you know it. It was Binna's decision not to work. She was perfectly happy being a housewife. She was not like you, Eun-jin, fixated and ambitious. Yes, maybe she did not visit her mother often enough; we lived far away for one. You went to live with your mother some months before she died, ostensibly to nurse her, but I think it was to make her change her will in your favour. You disinherited my daughters and helped yourself to the house. Get out of my sight!'

Sitting in her office cubicle now, Eun-jin's hands began to tremble, and rage clouded her eyes. She had loved Binna devotedly, only to have Dong-wook take her away. They had been sisters growing up together, two peas in a pod, telling each other their secrets. And then Dong-wook had swept Binna off her feet and she, like their mother, had seen less and less of Binna. How she hated Dong-wook and when the opportunity arose, she had maligned him without counting the cost. Her nieces hated her for putting their father in the dock. So, she had come to Dong-wook to make amends for the sake of a good relationship with her nieces for they were what was left of Binna. And he had spurned her.

There was a knock on the door and the secretary, Belinda Tan, entered. Without preamble, she said, 'The police were on the line asking about your travel itinerary to Seoul the week of 28 August. I told them the truth, Eun-jin, the company should not be embroiled in your personal issues with the police.'

'You told them I requested a change in flight plans?' Eun-jin demanded, her lips trembling.

Belinda sighed. 'No, I did not mention that. I told the police your Sunday flight was wait-listed and then the airlines informed us the flight was full and we requested the Tuesday flight.'

Eun-jin gave a sigh of relief. 'That is all right then. That is what we agreed you should say. Thanks, Belinda. I owe you one!'

When Belinda had left, Eun-jin sat at her desk, her eyes gazing into space. No one must know that she requested the postponement of her flight otherwise she would become a strong suspect in Dong-wook's murder. She mulled over the reason for changing her flight plans and tears pooled in her eyes.

The phone on her desk rang, and Eun-jin Choi knew it was the police on the line. Pursing her lips, she picked up the receiver.

* * *

Bright fluorescent lights beamed down from the ceiling on to the oval desk with five chairs around it. A carafe of water and glasses were placed in the centre of the table. Sergeant Charles Goh looked over his half-moon spectacles at the woman facing him in Interview Room 4. Eun-jin Choi was pale and composed, only the tic near her mouth revealed her nervousness. Charlie wanted to ask preliminary questions and then make her wait until Dolly returned from a welcome meeting for the new head of their division, DAC John Nathan.

'Like I said, I was on the waiting list to fly to Seoul on Sunday, 28 August, but the flight was full. They booked me in on Tuesday morning's flight.' Eun-jin's dark eyes flickered with dislike as she took in the scepticism on the sergeant's face. 'You can check with the company secretary as she notified me of the change in bookings late Saturday evening. I have nothing more to add. I mixed up dates when I first talked to you.' She began fiddling with the leather strap of her handbag.

'You said clearly that you left Singapore on Sunday evening, the day before your brother-in-law was poisoned. It's hard to imagine you couldn't remember the day you left Singapore for Seoul. It was only a week ago!'

Eun-jin continued fidgeting with her handbag without meeting Charlie's eyes. 'I mixed up days, okay? It was fixed in my mind that I was leaving on the Sunday evening flight, and I forgot that it was changed,' she said, her eyes on the table.

Charlie looked unconvinced. 'Were you at Temasek University on Monday, 29 August?' he barked out.

Eun-jin looked up and shook her head. For the first time, fear flickered in her eyes like a hesitant candle. 'No.'

There was silence. The hum of traffic outside on the road faintly reached their ears. Charlie saw Eun-jin lick her bloodless lips. The colour had faded from her face, and she looked like a white ghost. Her black bobbed hair had attractive bronze highlights and her fingernails were manicured, polished and painted a dark red. The space between her pert nose and thin lips was ample, making it appear that she was perpetually pursing her lips.

Charlie said, 'You quarrelled with Dr Pak and so maybe on Monday you went to his office to reconcile with him?'

'That is not true,' she whispered, pleating the belt of her handbag, frenziedly. 'I only visited him once.'

'It would be easier for everyone if you tell the truth before the inspector gets here. The fact that you visited Dr Pak does not necessarily mean you murdered him.'

Eun-jin slowly shook her head. 'Look, I was sorry for my accusations of euthanasia. The nurse was at fault and not Dong-wook. I loved my sister, and my brother-in-law had taken her away from my mother and me. Binna grew distant after her marriage. My mother and I resented Dong-wook's influence over her, making her give up her career to be a housewife. What a waste! My mother had died, and I was working in Seoul at the time. Dong-wook only allowed me to visit my sister twice a month. She was desperately unhappy and extremely sick. I wanted to come to take care of her or take her to our country house. She would have revived in the country air. He forbade all that and restricted my access to my sister. He said she became upset after I visited her. When she died of an overdose, I immediately suspected Pak had something to do with her death.'

Charlie was interested. 'Why?' he asked. 'From all accounts, he was a devoted husband, and his daughters confirm that.'

Eun-jin had tears in her eyes. 'Pak was controlling and dominating, and my sister was timid. Of course, his daughters think the world of their father. Oh, I knew Binna wanted to die. She told me so many times. The pain was intense in her bones and joints. When the doctor said my sister had symptoms of morphine overdose, I thought Dong-wook assisted in her death, that is all. Anyway, all I did was ask the Police Commissioner, who was our father's friend, to start an enquiry into my sister's death. They brought Pak up for trial before properly searching for the nurse and hearing her testimony.' Eun-jin's eyes were wild. 'I was sorry and wrote a letter of apology to Dong-wook after the trial. When I visited him here, I wanted to make amends, but he was still angry. I told you, he was not a forgiving sort. He liked to overwhelm women.'

Charlie drummed his fingers on the table. 'His lady colleagues do not describe Dr Pak as chauvinistic. What did he tell you when you visited him more than two weeks ago?'

'He accused me of manipulating my mother to leave the country house to me on her death instead of to both her daughters. He said I snatched my nieces' inheritances from them.' Eun-jin slowly started weeping. 'I can show you my will, Sergeant. Everything I have, including the country house, I leave divided equally between my two nieces. I loved my sister and I love my nieces, even though they are estranged from me!'

Charlie pushed a box of tissues towards the distraught linguist. 'Can you tell me what you were doing on Monday, 29 August?'

Eun-jin wiped her eyes with a tissue and cleared her throat. She seemed much more composed now and spoke in a stronger voice. 'I came into work in the morning. I left my office around 10 a.m. and went to the malls to do some last-minute shopping for my friends in Seoul. They had asked me to buy certain items for them. I reached home around four in the evening, had some tea, and started packing for my trip. I stayed home the rest of the day.'

'How many times did you visit Dr Pak at Temasek University? Did you ever visit his quarters?'

Eun-jin stared. 'I only visited him once a couple of weeks ago. You think I wanted to visit him again after he shouted at me?'

'You have been working in Singapore for four months and only visited Temasek University's chemistry department one time?' Charlie wanted to know whether Eun-jin was familiar with the department's custom of asking the janitor to deliver beverages to professors.

'Yes, Sergeant, only one time.'

After noting down Eun-jin's home address in Singapore, Charlie got up and checked his phone for text messages. He turned to Eun-jin. 'The inspector is not free to see you yet. We will ask you to come back another day.'

He sighed as he closed the door of the interview room. If they could not change Eun-jin's story of her movements on the day DW was poisoned, and if nobody had seen her in the vicinity of DW's office that day, they had no case against her.

After discussing Eun-jin's interview in her office, Dolly instructed Charlie to show Eun-jin's photo to the students and fellows who worked on DW's floor at the university. Emotion was an unstable entity, Dolly said, and it induced people to do unprecedented deeds such as commit murder. It was obvious Eun-jin was highly strung and deeply resentful of DW's order to his daughters to stay away from their aunt. Did that order ring his death knell?

20

Lily turned away from watching the rain pelting down outside the window of the restaurant and glanced at her husband across the table. Frankie Kennedy looked thin and emaciated, the unhealthy green tinge to his face making Lily feel guilty about abandoning him. His fingers clasped around his wine glass, trembled a little.

She realized with a shock when she met him in front of Saffron Kitchen, a restaurant in Jurong the couple frequented, that he had traded in his spectacles for contact lenses. Without his trademark black-framed glasses, Frankie looked curiously vulnerable. The restaurant was full and the hum of chatter from other diners filled their ears though they sat privately at a corner table. The chandeliers twinkled brightly setting the glasses, hanging at the bar, sparkling. Frankie's brown eyes were lacklustre as they surveyed the menu.

Finally, he set the menu aside and said, 'Why don't you order? I'm not that hungry.'

'We used to love their specials so we will order those. You want the butter chicken set meal or the tandoori chicken set meal?' Lily got busy on the order tablet blinking on the table.

'Butter chicken,' Frankie said, listlessly, 'and no hot beverage for me. I'm okay with the red wine.'

Lily had grown worried when he sat down at the table and ordered wine right away as he had never done that in the past, preferring to drink the teh tarik, one of the restaurant's specials.

Frankie came straight to the point when the waiter removed the order tablet from the table and placed a glass of hot milk tea on Lily's placemat. 'I am seeing a therapist,' he announced morosely, his thick lips pouting, unbecomingly. 'We were scheduled to have a consultation this week, but since two of his appointments were cancelled, he fitted me in last week. We have had two sessions and the consults are helping me. The therapist teaches me relaxing techniques and those are working. I'm not so hyper any more.' The ghost of a smile flitted across Frankie's lips.

Lily studied the tablecloth before glancing up curiously. 'What is the therapy?'

Frankie smiled and for a moment, Lily was reminded of the man she had dated and loved. 'The therapist is doing exposure and response prevention therapy. As you know, I wash my hands repeatedly after touching doorknobs and it drove you nuts. He is teaching me to touch the doorknob at his office every day and refrain from washing my hands. The fear of germs will then be decoupled from doorknobs. Do you get what I mean, Lily?'

Lily, listening intently, nodded. 'Yes, Frankie. So now do you wash your hands less frequently?'

'I have gone from washing my hands fifty times a day to thirty times a day,' Frankie said, triumphantly. Noting Lily's crestfallen look, he said sullenly, 'All this takes time, Lily. You can't expect an overnight miracle. I'm trying my best.'

The waiter appearing at their table with their specials caused a welcome interruption. They ate their meal making small talk about their work lives. When Lily was polishing off the last of her naan with the fish masala, Frankie coughed.

'My therapist said for the exposure and response prevention therapy to be truly effective, it is important to cohabitate with your spouse while the therapy is ongoing. I must become habituated not to fear certain issues with the spouse on hand. If my spouse joins me at the house only after the therapies have concluded, my therapist fears that I will have a relapse. It would be too much of a shock to adjust to the spouse's presence and at the same time maintain therapy goals. He says the spouse being at home and forming a part of the therapy are essential items.' He looked hopefully at his wife.

Lily finished chewing the last of her naan before saying, 'I am sorry, Frankie. My stall at the canteen just opened and my business needs to pick up there, which means I am busy at work. I have also got a partner at work, Ashikin, my friend. She is cooking Malay dishes. So it's all new. I must come home to a relaxing environment, or the stress will be too much for me. Now is not the right time for me to move back home.' Seeing her husband's white and strained face, she hastened to add, 'In another month or so, Frankie?'

Without a word, Frankie threw down two fifty-dollar bills on the table, got up and stalked out of the restaurant without finishing his meal. When the waiter came to clear Frankie's plate, he retreated hastily for Lily was softly weeping into her handkerchief, and the restaurant staff hastened to give Lily privacy.

Lily's face was set and sad as she drove back to Silver Springs.

* * *

Dolly looked with interest at fried pieces of okra burnt at the edges, a dish of which sat within her reach. She was having a solitary dinner at Silver Springs Condo, with Joey away on a business trip in Malaysia and Lily having a meal with Frankie. Dolly raised her eyebrows, and immediately, Girlie snatched the plate away from the table.

'So sorry, I was going to eat that, Ma'am Inspector.' The Filipina domestic helper looked flustered.

Dolly frowned. 'It's not like you to burn okra, Girlie. What is wrong?'

Girlie's large soulful eyes clouded over. 'My Nelson say he love someone else.'

Dolly's brows creased as she tried to recollect Girlie's complicated marital history. 'Last we heard, your husband had lost money gambling, mortgaged your house and that is why you are here working with us, leaving your little girl with your mother. You are Catholic, Girlie, no divorce for him, you go tell him that.'

Girlie placed the okra bowl back on the table, sat down on a low stool by the dining room window and started to weep. 'He lives with her, Ma'am Inspector. My heart is broken!'

There was the sound of a key in the lock of the main door. Soon, Lily appeared at the dining room doorway. Dolly could see at once Lily had been crying.

'What is it, Lily?' Dolly asked, her voice full of concern, setting aside her plate of roti and chicken curry.

Lily sat down on a chair and said in a small voice, 'Frankie is in therapy and the therapist suggested that he does the therapy with me living in the house with him. Otherwise, if he is in remission and then I move in, he is more likely to have a relapse.'

'The therapist has a point,' Dolly said.

'I am not ready,' Lily said, defensively.

Girlie said in a strong voice, 'Ma'am, you should go back to Mr Frankie, or he go love another lady like my Nelson.' Girlie burst into tears and wailed loudly.

'Stop crying, Girlie!' Dolly said, sternly. 'Mummy will wake up. Hush now.'

After Girlie sat sniffling and hiccupping quietly in the corner, Dolly turned to Lily. 'You are not the one in therapy and you need to cut Frankie some slack,' Dolly said. Her mobile beeped two times. Dolly read the messages and smiled. 'Ash is arriving Friday for a two-week holiday from NS camp. I can sleep with you, Lily, and Ash can have the guest bedroom. Ash will have his mother and aunt, not to mention Girlie cooking him wonderful dishes. Yes, Girlie,' Dolly said as Girlie blushed and smiled through her tears, 'my son is a fan of your cooking.'

Lily cheered up. 'Oh, it will be good to see Ash and hear about camp. I'll think about what you said regarding Frankie.' She glanced at her sister. 'What was the other message?'

Dolly said, 'Pritam will be released from hospital tomorrow. He must take a lot of medications. Ashok messaged and is worried about his dad. He says Pritam sometimes sends him weird messages.'

'And the doctor found Parkinson's Disease, nothing more?' Lily probed. Then she added in a low voice, 'It almost seems he suffers from depression. I wonder if there was any mental illness in the family.'

'Pritam never mentioned his family in all the years we were married,' Dolly said.

Lily looked surprised. 'You never visited the aunt who brought him up?'

Dolly reflected, thoughtfully, 'No. Whenever I mentioned his family, he told me they were the source of bad memories and not to mention them again. After a while, I gave up. So, no, I don't know about the mental health of any of his family members, not having met them. But I met one of Pritam's former students who knows the granddaughter of the aunt who raised Pritam, and I have her address. I will make enquiries.'

Girlie had recovered and enthusiastically brought out a dish of bread-and-butter pudding from the fridge and placed it on the sideboard. 'I made this for Auntie. A lot is left.' She turned to the Das sisters. 'I serve you, Ma'am Inspector?' She smiled as Dolly gave a vehement nod.

Lily said, 'I'll have some, too, Girlie. You make good puddings. Mummy goes to sleep so early nowadays. Old age, I think. I miss chatting with her in the evenings. What about the university case, Doll? Are you anywhere near nabbing DW's killer?'

'No!' Dolly looked frustrated. She tasted the pudding and licked her lips. 'The preliminary forensics investigation has yielded next to nothing. The ethylene glycol bottle has many fingerprints, mainly of the undergraduate, Terry Tan, because he uses the reagent for his experiments. And my team has talked to people. No one noticed anyone with a Styrofoam coffee cup near Abdul's office on that Monday. This is the problem with poisoning cases. It's discovered later when the crime scene has been compromised and a forensics investigation can't help. But DW's sister-in-law was in Singapore on the day of the poisoning; she was lying to us before. I have told Charlie to show her photo around to the students and maybe we will get lucky, if someone saw her there the day DW was poisoned.'

She looked at her sister relishing the pudding and said, softly, 'Joey talks to Frankie and told me Frankie is at the losing end of a case involving an abused woman. You know how Frankie takes up abuse causes on account of his mother being abused by his stepfather. It seems he is losing his client's divorce petition in court. And,' her voice dropped to a whisper, 'Joey thinks Frankie is developing feelings for his client. She is a Eurasian married to an Indian. Her name is Nancy.'

Girlie looked knowingly at Lily and said, 'I told you so, Ma'am. All men same.' She suddenly felt better knowing she was not alone in her anguish.

Dolly looked at Lily's white face and said, 'Sorry, Lil, I thought I should tell you. I am sure it's nothing serious, but good if you know.' She gave a yawn. 'I am going to sleep. Lily. Are you coming?'

Lily nodded but could not trust herself to speak. After Dolly had retired to the guest room, Lily rose from her chair and with dragging steps, entered her bedroom and shut the door. Then she lay down on the bed and cried herself to sleep.

Wednesday, 7 September 2011

21

Professor Ursula Botham burped delicately after finishing her morning porridge in her small dining room in the university quarters she shared with her husband, Graham, and son, Tom. Her hands went to her stomach, and she clutched it in sudden pain.

'What's wrong, Mum?' Tom, a ten-year-old with his mother's hair and colouring looked up from his cereal. The sun shone gently through the lace curtains of the window, and sunlight fell on the oval dining table.

Ursula's heart flipped over in love; she would do anything for her son; he was her pride and joy. 'Not to worry, Tommy. Mumsie's ulcers are acting up. The school bus should be here soon. Have you finished your breakfast, darling?'

Tom drank up his orange juice and smiled, his uneven teeth hidden behind braces. 'All done, Mum. Where is Dad?'

Ursula pursed her lips. 'He must have gone to work early,' she lied, not telling her son his father had spent the night elsewhere.

Tom nodded and got up from the chair. 'You're sure you are okay, Mum?'

Ursula opened her arms, and Tom shyly embraced her. 'Mumsie will be all right once she takes her Pepto Bismol. Good luck for the Maths exam, Thomas!'

The door slammed after a string of goodbyes, and Ursula gratefully sank back into her chair. The gentle sun reminded her of her home in Oxford, Banbury Hall. If her father were alive, she would have put a stop to her living Hell here and returned to Oxford. Maybe take up a research fellowship at the university while Tom went to one of the local schools. But her father was gone. Her childhood Colossus had succumbed to a massive cardiac arrest. Without Michael Asquith, what was the point in returning home? He would not be there to comfort her as she licked her wounds, counsel her on the best way to be rid of Graham. Her mother, Bianca, lived in her own world; they had never been close. No, she had to gain strength from her father's wise words that played constantly in her mind and try to live a fruitful life in Singapore. She earned a good income and Tom went to one of the best international schools. With Graham gone, she and Tom would settle down into a peaceful rhythm.

Her stomach hurt but her heart hurt more. Graham's behaviour throughout their marriage had been despicable, but having an affair with her cousin was the limit. She smiled, thinly. She had changed the locks on the front door, locking him out. At least she felt good about that. He would get the message and behave, at least until the Head of Chemistry had been elected. A divorce right now would spell an end to his headship hopes.

Ursula frowned. When she had first met Graham, he had attracted her with his rough charm, sharp intelligence and the absent-mindedness that sparked a maternal instinct in her. With Tom's birth, the maternal instinct transferred to her boy, and Graham's charm evaporated into irritability whenever he was around Tom. The sharp intelligence remained, but you cannot stay in love with a clever boor forever, Ursula mused.

She thought he admired her beauty and intelligence until she saw the look on his face when he visited Banbury Hall. He had married her for her fortune. According to her father's will, the house, estate, and his money were hers and her father had been wealthy in his own right, a self-made building contractor who had amassed millions. The money and the house kept Graham tied to her. Ursula gave a sharp sigh. But Lorna?

Bianca had asked her daughter to keep an eye on her second cousin, Lorna, when she got a job as a lecturer at Temasek University, invite her for a few dinner parties and cocktails. Vivacious Lorna, with her red hair, green eyes and an infectious laugh, had got along all too well with Graham.

Ursula sighed. There was nothing else for it but to divorce Graham after the Head of Chemistry elections were over. For Tom's sake, she would ignore Graham's philandering till the election and not hinder his academic career. Ursula's brows creased. Bill knew about the suicide of the Korean girl in Australia and Dong-wook had known about it. Did anyone else in the department know? The girl had not mentioned Graham in her suicide note though Graham had privately admitted to her that he had gone out with her a couple of times. It was fortuitous the girl was also seeing a Korean boy, and the Australian police naturally assumed he was responsible for her suicide. They had been deaf to the boy's pleas that she was seeing someone else and that was why he had broken up with her.

Ursula gave a heavy sigh. No one must know Graham had caused a student to kill herself: he would lose not only the headship but also his job and disgrace would be heaped on him. She wondered what made Graham chase women in between doing brilliant scientific research. What a fool she had been to have succumbed to his charms all those years ago. Ursula shook her head.

'You sick, Ma'am?' Kamini asked. She was Ursula's part-time maid and had been busy cooking breakfast in the kitchen. She had worked for Ursula from the time she arrived in Singapore, and a warm rapport had developed between them. Kamini was the mother of a boy, too, and the women enthusiastically shared their experiences. Kamini, privy to the Botham shouting matches, was a silent and staunch support to Ursula.

'My peptic ulcers are acting up.' Ursula smiled warmly at Kamini. 'I have my bottle of Pepto Bismol on my office desk, and I will take a spoonful when I am at work. How is Krishnan?'

The women chatted companionably about their sons before Ursula looked at the clock, gave an exclamation and hurried to get her bag from the den. Soon she was on the campus bus heading to the science building.

* * *

Sunlight was streaming into the Singh common room on a bright morning. Latha's father had finally agreed to allow her to finish her degree and return to the laboratories after she had seriously threatened suicide. Krishnaswamy had been mortally afraid Latha would take her own life and allowed Cheng Yong to visit her at their home and counsel her.

She now sat at the long table, telling an interested Salma in a low voice how she had combated her parents. Salma, on the verge of breaking up with her jobless boyfriend, listened intently. Though in Salma's case, if she did cut off connections with Junaid, her parents would heave a sigh of relief.

Kiong Tan looked up from his desk as Cheng Yong rushed in. His face was flushed, his hair tousled.

'What's wrong, CY?'

Kiong's calm voice was like a soothing balm to CY. 'My father is in ICU. In Beijing hospitals, ICU charges are high. I need to send money home. But I have no savings. Do you think Prof. Singh will advance me my next month's salary?'

'Prof. is back in his office. He might advance you the money; it is worth a try. Good luck, CY.'

Filled with his own distress, Cheng Yong did not see the concern on the faces of the other students. He immediately strode off and was soon knocking on the door of Pritam Singh's office. He entered when he heard Professor Singh's booming, 'Come in!'

Pritam Singh looked thin after his stay at the hospital. He waved away CY's solicitous enquiries on his health and said, 'I am fine, CY, and you are just the person I wanted to see. How far have you got in writing the paper for JACS?'

'I am halfway through, Prof.,' CY said. 'I have a favour to ask. My father is hospitalized and is in ICU. I need to send some money to China. If I could have an advance of my next month's salary … are you all right, Professor Singh?'

Pritam Singh was sitting at his desk and clutching his head. He looked up blearily to say, 'A terrible headache. What is it you are asking?' When CY repeated his request, Pritam's eyes flashed with anger. 'We are not running a charity here, and we don't want to set a precedent. You will get your salary when it is due.'

CY recoiled in shock. He had not expected to meet with such a lack of compassion and understanding. Tears threatened to spill over his eyes, and he turned and ran off from the room. He sat on one of the benches in the open corridors of the university and wept. Then he returned to the common room. He limped in, his shoulders sagging and his face haggard.

'These professors are heartless,' he said, slipping into his chair. 'Prof. Singh refused to advance me my next month's salary and my father is going to die without treatment. He had a heart attack, and he can expire any moment.'

The students gathered around CY, offering sympathy and commiseration. Latha's voice rang out, 'CY, I am going to my father. I will make sure he advances you the money you need. Stop snivelling and come with me.'

When the door had closed behind the duo, Salma turned to the other students and said, 'Did you see? Latha taking charge like that.' She giggled. 'Those two are definitely in love.'

Terry nodded, smiling. 'I think so, too.'

The door opened and Bill Eddington entered. He looked at the avid faces of his research group and asked, 'What did I miss? Do tell.'

As the sun slid up the sky, two Korean girls tearfully looked around their father's rented quarters, searching for memories.

* * *

Latha was in a good mood. Her father had been sympathetic and accommodating when approached for a loan to save CY's father's life and had advanced the money. CY was busy sending the money to China and talking to his father's doctor long distance. Humming a tune, Latha jauntily entered the science faculty building and took the lift to the floor where the chemistry professors had their offices.

Latha knocked on Ursula Botham's office door and entered when the professor asked her to come in. Ursula sat behind her desk, rifling through some papers. She glanced at the clock on the wall. It was 2.30 p.m. Her lips lifted in a smile as she asked Latha to be seated. The student noted the professor looking pale and sweaty.

'Are you all right, Professor Botham?' Latha asked solicitously. She liked Ursula and had taken her natural products class for her minor subject.

'Yes, yes,' Ursula smiled tightly. 'It is my peptic ulcers. They give me trouble from time to time.' She pointed to the bottle of pink liquid near her. 'Pepto Bismol saves the day.' She unscrewed the bottle and took a sip of the antacid. After wiping her mouth with a tissue and throwing it into the waste-paper basket, Ursula said, 'Latha, I need to take the photoelectron spectra of some of my organic compounds to determine their electronic structure and bonding. If the spectra are interesting, we shall have a paper and of course, your name will be included. I have talked to Professor Singh, and he has agreed to me paying your salary as a research assistant for this project. I hope you are not too busy with your other projects and can participate in this one.'

Latha nodded. 'Yes, Professor Botham, I can do this project.'

'Good,' Ursula said, enthusiastically. 'Let me give you the details of the project.'

The professor animatedly described the organic compounds and what information was needed from their photoelectron spectra. Latha listened intently. It had grown cloudy outside and rain lashed against the window. Latha got up to close it at a nod from Ursula. When she returned to her seat and looked at the professor, she let out a small cry. Ursula was not seated in her chair. Latha rushed around the desk and saw her sprawled on the floor. She had fainted.

Latha shook the professor's shoulder and cried, 'Prof.! What is the matter?'

Ursula opened her eyes. 'What happened?' She asked in a low voice.

'Prof., you fainted.' Latha helped Ursula up from the ground and sat her back on her chair. 'Shall I take you to A&E?'

'Oh, no!' Ursula said. 'I do faint when the pain from the ulcers is intense. I will be all right soon. But I will take the day off and go home and rest. We will talk about the project tomorrow, Latha. 3 p.m., maybe?'

'Are you sure you will be all right?' Latha was reluctant to leave Ursula alone. 'Shall I call Professor Graham? His office is across the corridor.'

Ursula gave a small smile. 'Whatever you do, do not call him,' she said. 'I will take half a day's medical leave and rest at home. Thanks, Latha. See you, tomorrow.'

Latha nodded and slowly left the room. As she was closing the door, she looked back and saw Ursula Botham raise the Pepto Bismol bottle to her lips.

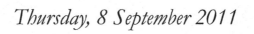

Thursday, 8 September 2011

22

Superintendent Siti Abdullah felt the beginnings of a headache coming on. She sat facing her new superior, the assistant director of the Major Crime Division, DAC John Nathan, in his office. Nathan sat behind his big mahogany desk littered with reports. His jolly face failed to hide eyes snapping with intelligence and the steely resolve to the set of his mouth. He was short and bald with a fierce moustache that he was fond of twirling now and then. The assistant director's suite was spacious with an adjoining room that served as a conference room. The air-con hummed efficiently and on a high floor of CID HQ, the windows afforded a beautiful view of the Singapore skyline, including the distant silhouette of the Marina Bay Sands Hotel. Nathan eyed Siti appraisingly, the smile not leaving his lips.

'Superintendent Abdullah, I called you here to congratulate you on your team solving murder cases with record speed and apprehending murderers quickly. I also called you to ask why your team is lagging behind in the promotions department?' He glanced at some papers on his desk before looking up. 'I see you gave good performance reviews to Inspector Dolly Das and Senior Staff Sergeant Charles Goh last year. I read with great interest how they caught a wily killer in the Silver Springs murder case. Inspector Das has held her current senior position for more than five years, so I am wondering why she has not been recommended for promotion to assistant superintendent?'

Siti's worry manifested itself in the quick tremble of her lips. Her eyes shifty, she said, 'Yes, Inspector Das excelled in the Silver Springs case, and it was during that case I took over this department, Sir. However, my predecessor, Superintendent Royston Chua's notes on Inspector Das were far from complimentary. I took that into account in delaying promotion.'

She avoided his eyes and glanced at the corner of the room where a cosy sofa set was placed with carafes of hot coffee and tea on a low, glass-topped table. Would she ever attain this high pedestal in her career? All her dreams from the time she entered the Police Academy had been to achieve a high position at CID. When Jennifer Tan Ai Li had been appointed deputy commissioner, the first woman in the Singapore CID to hold that post, Siti's dreams blossomed. The days in a poky flat taking care of seven siblings and wondering if there would be some meat with their evening meal belonged to the forgotten past.

DAC Nathan placed his hands in a steeple on his desk and narrowed his eyes. 'I noted Inspector Das and her team solving the Silver Springs triple murder case in two weeks. That, surely, is an exemplary record.' He frowned. 'Whatever Supt Chua had noted, it has come to my attention that Inspector Das builds psychological profiles of suspects and uses that to catch the murderer, and we are recommending this technique as a subject in our on-the-job training courses. I want Inspector Das to teach this subject in a workshop we are going to conduct soon, using her own cases as examples. But before that, I strongly suggest you write her a recommendation for promotion. It is time. After all, we don't want to see you dawdling in your duties, Supt Abdullah, right? What about Charles Goh? It's time he became an inspector. Long years of service and good performance at his job.'

Siti Abdullah swallowed the lump in her throat. She had recruited her niece, Fauzia Khan, to spy on Dolly with the aim of retrenching her when the exercise was executed in a few months, but here was Nathan wanting to promote Dolly instead. She cleared her throat and said, 'Yes, yes, I was going to recommend Charles Goh for a promotion. He has excellent policing skills and solves cases by the book.'

John Nathan's astute eyes bored into her. 'And Inspector Das uses newer methods in her detection, eh? So, they make a good team.' His tone was mild as he said, 'I want to see the promotion forms for both filled up and on my desk by this evening, Superintendent. You are dismissed.'

Siti sat fuming in her office. The room looked puny compared to the DAC's suite. She looked at her computer screen, tapped some keys and retrieved Charlie's notes on the university murder case. Her eyes focused on a name, and she snatched up the phone receiver and dialled a number. 'Fauzia, come to my office at once,' she said.

When Fauzia laconically entered her office and looked at her through her false eyelashes, Siti barked out, 'Professor Pritam Singh's name rings a bell. Something to do with Dolly Das. Do you know, Fauzia?'

Fauzia's eyes gleamed. 'Pritam Singh is Inspector Das's ex-husband and the father of her son. They were married for twenty-five years.'

Siti's eyes were shining, and she exhaled a deep breath. 'Ah, I knew I had heard the name somewhere.' She looked at her niece with gimlet eyes. 'Inspector Das has not declared a conflict of interest in the case she is investigating at the university.'

Fauzia rolled her eyes. 'Auntie, they are divorced, and Inspector Das is married to another man. Her ex is also married to another woman. Water under the bridge.'

'But Pritam Singh is Dolly Das's son's father?'

'Yes.'

'Well, that's a conflict of interest if ever there was one. She cannot investigate this case. You can go now, Fauzia.'

When Fauzia had left, Superintendent Siti Abdullah buzzed for Dolly to meet her at her office. 'Promotion! I will see about that,' Siti muttered to herself, her dislike of Dolly rising like bile in her throat.

'Pritam Singh is my ex-husband!' Dolly protested when Siti confronted her about her potential conflict of interest in investigating the university murder case. 'And he is not a suspect in the homicide. How is my judgement in this case affected?'

Siti's eyes snapped with displeasure. 'I was wondering why you were using unethical methods in this case, like asking Dr Gan to do unauthorized tests. It was because your ex asked you to, is it? Dr Pak was in your ex's employ. Or is it because you wanted to clear your sister, Lily Das's name? There are too many people involved in this case who are your relatives, Inspector. Of course, your objectivity in solving this case will be affected. Professor Pritam Singh is your son's father, and you were married to him for twenty-five years. And right now, we do not have a list of suspects for the murder; everyone who worked with Pak is a suspect, including your ex.'

Dolly's eyes flashed and she shot back, 'With due respect, Ma'am, your close relative, Fauzia Khan, reports to you. Isn't that a conflict of interest and unethical?'

Siti Abdullah's face went purple. 'Fauzia reports to you, not me, Inspector. Do not make allegations you will later regret. As of now, I am taking you off the university murder case.'

Dolly stood up. 'I wish for the DAC to give this order, Ma'am. Please consult with DAC Nathan before you take me off this case. The reputation of a university is at stake, and my years of experience makes me the best officer here to solve this murder. If DAC Nathan asks me to step down from this case, I will, Ma'am.' Dolly gave a nod and left her superior's office.

It was not long before Dolly and Charlie were asked into DAC John Nathan's office. Superintendent Siti Abdullah sat in one of the chairs facing the DAC, her face etched with tension and unhappiness. Nathan looked up as the two officers entered.

His voice boomed across. 'Sit down, Inspector Das and Sergeant Goh. Congratulations are in order. Given your long years of service and outstanding records, Supt Abdullah has recommended Inspector Das be promoted to assistant superintendent and Sergeant Goh be promoted to the rank of inspector. I strongly concur with her recommendation. Long time coming, eh? The promotion forms have been signed, and while paperwork may take some more time, your new designations are effective immediately. Your salaries will be adjusted when the entire paperwork passes through all the channels.' He beamed genially at the astounded police officers. Dolly's eyes were wide with shock, while Charlie could not stop grinning. Siti Abdullah looked furious.

Nathan cleared his throat. 'Ahem, regarding the conflict of interest in the university murder case that Supt Abdullah has brought to my attention. Inspector Das, please declare on one of our forms that Professor Singh is your ex-husband and the father of your son. I note that he is not a suspect in the case, so no further action needs to be taken except for the declaration. Inspector Charles Goh will naturally oversee the case and report his findings to ASP Das, who will in turn discuss all the salient points of the case in detailed emails with Supt Abdullah. ASP Das, please copy me on those emails. With so many senior eyes on the case, objectivity will be maintained. But you are right, ASP Das, the university is our premier one, and I need my best officer working on that murder case.'

He looked at Siti and nodded. 'I have taken your declaration of Corporal Fauzia Khan being your niece in the informative spirit it was intended. However, this is a real conflict of interest, and at no time can Corporal Khan report to you, Supt Abdullah. I will be transferring her to the Serious Sexual Crime Branch; we need good police officers there. Till then, she can oversee the burglary case at Joo Chiat with Inspector Goh, who will report on her activities directly to me until the transfer comes through.' He glanced around at everyone. 'Come officers, let us solve the murder of Dr Dong-wook Pak.'

In her office, Dolly looked at Charlie and heaved a sigh. 'I think we had a close shave. We are lucky DAC Nathan is heading this department. With only the Supt in charge, I would be off this case and soon retired. Congratulations, Inspector Goh!' She beamed at Charlie.

'I can't wait to tell Meena,' Charlie gushed. 'I was thinking I would be pushing sixty when I am finally promoted; so this is a good break. Warm congratulations, Assistant Superintendent Das, and I am sure in two years, you will be Supt Das.'

The two officers shook hands and decided to celebrate soon with a meal at Lily's.

23

After taking her lunch and indulging in half an hour's conversation on the phone with her mother and sister about her promotion to ASP, Dolly stood at the window of her office overlooking New Bridge Road. The sun shone brightly, and she could see the silhouettes of the buildings on the opposite side of the road belonging to Singapore General Hospital. She felt light headed. She had worked hard throughout her career but had resigned herself to the fact that she would retire as a police inspector and not someone of higher rank. Her smile lit up her face, and she could not wait to tell her husband, Joey, the good news in the evening when he was back at his hotel in Melaka after work.

There was a knock on the door and Charlie entered. He looked excited. 'Madam, Mok was showing the photo of DW's sister-in-law, Eun-jin Choi, around to the students in case she was seen at the university the day Pak was poisoned. The postdoc Kiong Tan says he saw her in the corridor near DW's office on the Monday DW was poisoned.'

'What time?'

'Around the time Pak was discovered by Eddington to have fainted in his office. Around 4 p.m. The students and fellows were in DW's office or outside and that was when Kiong saw Eun-jin.'

'Bring her in for questioning, Charlie, and this time I want to speak with her.'

In an hour, Dolly entered Interview Room 4. Charlie was already seated at the table with his tablet. The blinds at the window were drawn and fluorescent lights blazed down. Eun-jin looked fearfully at Dolly as she entered the room.

Dolly seated herself opposite Eun-jin. 'Tell us about your movements on the day your brother-in-law was poisoned. Monday, 29 August. The truth, please, Ms Choi. Please do not waste our time.'

Eun-jin fidgeted with the strap of the handbag on her lap. 'I went to work as usual at eight and left my workplace at ten. If you check the automated entry/exit log at the door of our office, you can confirm my statement. I left work early to go home and pack for my flight the next day.'

'You only came in to work for two hours?' Charlie raised his brows.

Eun-jin nodded. 'I needed to attend an 8.30 a.m. business meeting and it finished at 10 a.m.'

'You did not go to see Dr Pak that Monday?' Dolly persisted.

'No!' Two red spots appeared on Eun-jin's cheeks. 'He told me he never wanted to see me again,' Eun-jin said.

Charlie's mobile rang, and he excused himself and left the interview room.

Dolly said, 'If you didn't go to Temasek University on 29 August, why were you seen near your brother-in-law's office in the late afternoon?'

As naked fear flashed through Eun-jin's eyes, Charlie stormed into the room, his eyes, sharp and accusing.

'That was the travel agent who booked your tickets to Seoul returning my call,' Charlie said, fixing gimlet eyes on Eun-jin. 'You were not wait-listed on any flight. You, yourself, through your receptionist, requested your embarkation flight be changed from Sunday to Tuesday.'

'I am tired of your lies,' Dolly agreed. 'We will detain you here for the rest of the day until you tell us the truth. Why did you postpone your flight from Sunday to Tuesday? It is highly suspicious given the fact your brother-in-law was poisoned on Monday. You were seen in the vicinity of his office as well. Speak the truth, Ms Choi!'

Eun-jin sat pale and stiff in her chair. After a while, she whispered, 'I did not wish to say I had postponed my flight because you would think what you are thinking now. That I postponed the flight to murder Dong-wook on Monday.'

'You have been lying about your movements. We will think the worst of you until you tell the truth.' Dolly glared. Like Charlie, she began to strongly suspect Eun-jin of having poisoned her brother-in-law.

Eun-jin pondered for a while and then said decisively, 'My sister died of cancer. I was afraid I also had the cancer gene, the BRCA1. I had felt a lump on my left breast for quite a while and I gathered up my courage and went for a mammogram on the Thursday before I was scheduled to fly. On Friday, 26 August, the doctor called me to his office with bad news. From the mammogram, he suspected breast cancer and wanted to talk to me on the Monday and do further tests. That is the reason I postponed my flight. You can talk to my doctor. His name is Ronald Tan, and he practises at Raffles Hospital.'

There was silence in the room. Dolly looked at the white-faced woman and said softly, 'Why didn't you tell us this in the first place instead of making us go around in circles? I am sorry you have breast cancer, Ms Choi. Hopefully, you are in the early stages and will be fully cured. Stay strong.'

Dolly's kind voice made Eun-jin Choi's lips tremble. 'I went into the hospital on 29 August, Monday, to do tests that would determine the cancer stage. In the late afternoon, I visited Temasek University. I wanted to talk to Dong-wook. If you check with the hospital and the nurses, they will tell you I was at the hospital from late morning to early afternoon that day.'

Charlie narrowed his eyes. 'So, you were at the university the day DW was poisoned? When and why did you go to see Dr Pak?'

Eun-jin gave a sharp sigh. 'He was family, after all. I was shocked at being diagnosed with the same cancer as my sister. Dong-wook had been her caregiver. I wanted to tell him about my diagnosis.' She began to weep. 'I thought at least then he would forgive me.'

'And did he?' Dolly asked with interest.

'I never got the chance to speak to him. When I arrived, I saw people inside his office. There was a lot of commotion going on. I left.' Eun-jin looked at the table, not meeting the eyes of the police officers. Tears trickled out of her eyes and streamed down her cheeks. Dolly quietly passed the box of tissues to her.

'What time was this?' Charlie asked, making notes on his tablet.

'Sometime after four in the afternoon.' Eun-jin was wiping her eyes with a handkerchief she had retrieved from her handbag. 'I did not wait to find out what was the problem. I did not want to be involved. I had no inkling Dong-wook had taken ill. Even while walking to his office, I had been having second thoughts about confiding my worries to Dong-wook. He and I were not friendly. If I talked to him, he would start remembering Binna and how she had died of the same cancer. Sad memories. When I saw people in his office, it was like a sign telling me I was right not to inform him of my diagnosis. I left.'

'That is all for now,' Dolly said, hurriedly, seeing Eun-jin on the verge of more tears. 'If we want to clarify your testimony, we will ask you back. You are free to go now. Wishing you good health, Ms Choi, and a speedy recovery.'

When Charlie had returned after seeing Eun-jin into a cab, Dolly said, 'Charlie, talk to Ronald Tan, Ms Choi's doctor and double check her story. Talk to the hospital personnel and check whether Choi was at the hospital from 12–1 p.m. on the Monday DW was poisoned. That was when the poisoned coffee was placed on Abdul's table. If she was at the hospital at that time, Choi has an alibi for DW's murder. While I feel sorry for Eun-jin, she had motive and opportunity to murder DW. We only have her word that she came after four. What if she had come around noon and left the poisoned coffee on Abdul's desk? Maybe she was bitter about her cancer diagnosis and DW's attitude towards her still rankled. When they are traumatized, people go over the edge. No one can say what they might do. That's why we need to know where Choi was in the early afternoon. Look at CCTV footage at the hospital as well. If she wasn't at the hospital early afternoon, she becomes our chief suspect again. We have no evidence she poisoned the coffee DW drank. No one saw her in the corridor around noon. All we can do is grill her again and again until she breaks down.'

Charlie nodded and whipped out his tablet. 'The reports on DW's mobile phone and computer are in, Madam. Mok has written out the reports. I've not had time to look through them, yet. Give me five minutes.' When Charlie looked up from his tablet, his eyes were shining. 'DW made no calls from his mobile on Tuesday; he last took a call on Monday night at 8 p.m. The callers were his daughters. There were many missed calls on

Tuesday, all from his daughters. They were calling Tuesday afternoon, but the poor gentleman was in no state to answer.'

'What about his computer? Why are you looking excited?'

'An email from Eun-jin Choi was posted on 29 August, Monday evening. In the mail, she tells him about her cancer diagnosis and asks his forgiveness. He obviously never checked his emails after he was taken sick as there is no reply. This email was posted from a Singapore IP address proving Ms Choi was in Singapore Monday evening. She might have been telling the truth, after all. If she saw so many people in DW's office, she would go away and then she emailed him her news.'

Dolly nodded. 'Anything else?'

Charlie's eyes gleamed. 'Yes, Madam. There was an email DW sent to a Korean email address the Saturday before he died, 27 August. In the email, he asks for details of Ji-woo Kim's suicide in Australia. This mail was to Kim's father, DW's friend. Mok confirmed that, Madam. But here's the thing. In the email, DW vows to his friend to question Graham Botham about Kim's death. Madam, DW was going to make that scandal public!'

Dolly's eyes were shining. 'Now, that *is* a good breakthrough! The question is, did DW have time to talk to Graham Botham before he was poisoned? Monday morning, perhaps? We need to have a chat with Professor Graham. Good work, Charlie!'

Dolly looked at her watch. It was time to go home. She rose from her chair and walked along the corridor with Charlie to the lift lobby.

'I have researched Kim's suicide and talked to the Australian police. The report will be on your desk tomorrow morning, Madam.'

'Anything interesting there?' Dolly and Charlie entered the lift together, and Charlie pressed the button for their office floor.

'The suicide note the girl left behind mentioned no names. She had broken up with her Korean boyfriend a week before her death, so the police assumed he was the cause of her suicide. I did talk to Sergeant Alison Howard on the phone as she worked on this case for the Australian police.' Charlie and Dolly exited the lift and began walking to Dolly's office. 'She said the boyfriend testified he broke up with Kim because she was seeing someone else. He said it was a professor at the university. Ji-woo's dorm room-mate further verified she was seeing a chemistry professor, but nobody claims to have seen her with Graham Botham. Since it was a clear case of suicide, the police closed the case.'

Dolly arrived at her door. Turning to Charlie, she said, 'We need to speak with Graham Botham. I think it is true he was involved with Kim, and she may have killed herself because he refused to marry her. DW was going to question Botham. When we question him, Graham will obviously deny DW ever talked to him on the subject, so we will be back to square one. If only we had proof DW and Graham had an altercation about this girl, Kim. If DW threatened to spill the news about the girl's suicide to the head, Graham may have had reason to silence DW. For the sake of the headship elections.'

Dolly opened her office door as Charlie said, 'Yes, Madam, I think so, too. Have a nice evening, Madam, and congratulations again!'

Dolly smiled and entered her office. She sat at her desk and dialled her husband's hotel number in Melaka to tell him about her promotion. Outside, the shadows grew long, and a long line of cars snaked along New Bridge Road as people drove home from work.

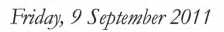

Friday, 9 September 2011

24

Sunlight streamed in through the open windows of the dining hall of the Silver Springs Condominium unit Uma Das owned. Her two daughters and grandson sat at the table, eating an excellent breakfast cooked by Girlie. Ash had booked out from camp on a fortnight's leave. He was a handsome young man, tall, with his father's build and his mother's features. Uma, who had finished her cereal breakfast, sat on a low divan nestling against the dining room wall, peering at the table, and giving a beaming smile whenever her grandson came into her line of vision.

Ash enthusiastically cut up the pork sausages on his plate and sniffed appreciatively the aroma of the back bacon Girlie had fried. 'The breakfast is delicious.' His face grew cloudy, and he looked at his mother. 'Dad is ill. We talk on Skype in the evenings, and I also text him on WhatsApp. Sometimes he doesn't reply and once he did not know who I was and told me he would report me to the police for harassment. Sometimes his words don't make sense. He keeps talking of an accident and how his feet are numb. Is it because of Parkinson's Disease, Mama?'

Dolly shrugged as she bit into a piece of toast. After eating it, she said, 'I don't know, Ash. Cheryl says he sometimes does not recognize her and in the middle of the night calls out for me.'

Lily giggled and Ash gave a lopsided grin.

'It's not funny,' Dolly said with dignity. 'Cheryl was upset over this, as I would be if I were still married to Pritam. Calling out for an ex-spouse is like waving a red flag in front of the present spouse.' She cleared her throat. 'About the accident, I spoke to one of your father's former students and it seems your father was involved in a car crash in his youth. He was also into drinks and drugs but sobered up after the accident.'

Ash's mouth had fallen open, and he brushed away Girlie's offer of more scrambled eggs. 'He never told us! Why? Was anyone injured in the accident?' Ash laid down his knife and fork. 'Does Dad have any relatives? We never visited any when I was growing up.'

Dolly finished her toast and looked disapprovingly at the soggy scrambled eggs on her plate. 'Your grandparents died when Pritam was fourteen years old, and his paternal uncle threw him out into the street because he wanted to inherit the house; it had been your great-grandfather's house. A distant aunt on his paternal side took Pritam in and he lived with the aunt and her family until he left for Oxford to do his doctorate degree. His paternal uncle could not touch Pritam's father's life insurance policy claim and Pritam used this money to fund his education here and in England. And he also used the money on drinks and drugs. After receiving his doctorate degree, he returned here with a position at Temasek University. He did talk to me about being on drugs and an alcoholic a couple of times. Obviously, he wanted to forget that part of his past, so he never spoke at great length about it. I did not know he had been involved in a car accident, for instance. It seems someone died in that car crash and that sobered Pritam up.'

Ash had lost his appetite. 'The distant aunt. Why didn't we visit her?'

Dolly shrugged and looked at her watch. She frowned at Girlie looking guiltily at the eggs untouched on her plate. 'Your father didn't want us to meet his aunt and her family. His former student knows Pritam's niece, her name is Devender Kaur; this is the granddaughter of the aunt who raised Pritam. I have her address.' She dug out her tablet from the handbag on the floor and switched it on. She showed the address to Ash, who quickly took a photo of it with his mobile phone.

Dolly said, 'You can meet her if you want, Ash.' She flicked a glance at Girlie. 'Even Ash can cook good eggs,' she said scathingly and was gratified to see Girlie cringe and sidle back into the kitchen.

Ash was looking at the address. He glanced up and said, 'I want to meet Devender, but will Dad mind us burrowing into his past?'

'No need to tell him,' Dolly advised. 'At least we may have some answers as to whether your father is at risk of inherited mental illness if we know more of his family history. Cheryl is certain your father is mentally ill. Well, I must go off to work. Do finish your breakfast, Ash.'

Dolly scraped back her chair, rose, slung her bag over her shoulder, grabbed her briefcase, kissed the top of Ash's head and was gone out of the door.

Girlie, clearing away plates, said, 'Ma'am Ursula Botham is divorcing her husband soon. I did not want to say this in front of Ma'am Inspector, she is so fierce. She will scold me for gossiping.'

Lily pounced on Girlie. 'How do you have this information? And Girlie, Dolly is now an ASP, not inspector any more.'

Girlie said, 'Ma'am Botham have a part-time maid, Kamini Baskaran. Kamini is my friend, Ma'am. We attend same church. I meet her every Sunday. She cares for Ma'am and the child, Tom, but not like the Sir.' Girlie lowered her voice. 'Once Sir was going to beat Ma'am Ursula, but Tom came in from his bedroom, so Sir ran away. They are fighting all the time, and Ma'am Ursula told Kamini she want to divorce.' Sudden tears flooded her eyes. 'We are Catholic, never think of divorce whatever happens. Look at my Nelson, says he loves someone else.' Girlie burst into tears.

After sending Girlie to her room to recover, Lily returned to the dining room to find Ash dressed and ready to go out.

'I am going to see Devender Kaur, Dad's niece.' Ash waved his mobile phone where he had noted her address.

'Wait for ten minutes. I will drop you in the car. I am ready to go to work, Ash.'

Uma said from the divan. 'Dolly could not eat a good breakfast, Lil. Do teach Girlie how to make eggs.'

'She cooks so many complex dishes. I don't know why she can't cook eggs well.' Lily went to her room to get dressed.

Ash regaled Lily with NS camp tales while they drove along the expressway. Lily took the turning to Toa Payoh and soon they were on a narrow road not far from the Singapore Press Holdings buildings. Ash peered at the block numbers and pointed to a block on its own at the back.

Lily stopped the car and Ash got out. He waved to his aunt and started walking towards the block.

Lily looked at Ash with misgiving. It was not prudent to rake up the past, but sometimes there was no choice. She started her car, reversed, and took the road to the expressway. Angie had become quite adept at frying pratas for the breakfast crowd at the canteen, and Lily could afford to come in late for work.

* * *

Lily was enjoying a quiet meal at the canteen after the lunch crowd had dispersed when she saw Latha enter and look around. Spying her, Latha waved and after ordering from Vernon at the counter, came over and asked if she could join Lily for lunch.

'Of course, dear,' Lily said, smiling. 'A late lunch today? I saw CY and the others have their lunch awhile back.'

Latha settled herself into a chair and smiled. 'Yes, Auntie Lily. I have an experiment going on in the fume cupboard. Right now, the solution must be under UV light for an hour, so I told Salma to keep an eye on it and took my lunch break.'

Vernon appeared, looking disgruntled. He wanted Angie to see a gynaecologist and Angie refused to do so because of the added expense. Lily thought Vernon and Angie were having far too many tiffs for a happily married couple, but not wishing to interfere in their marital lives, she kept her peace. He banged down a vegetarian thali in front of Latha and left.

'What's got into him?' Latha, who liked Vernon, looked worried.

'Tiff with wife,' Lily said, shortly. 'Vegetarian today?'

'Yes, Amma told me to fast, but I compromised by going vegetarian, some inauspicious day today in the almanac,' Latha said, vaguely. She continued, 'Did you see Professor Ursula Botham at your stall today?' When Lily shook her head, Latha looked worried. 'I was with her in her office on Wednesday and she fainted. She may be on sick leave and staying home. She has peptic ulcers.'

'Um. Painful,' Lily agreed. Smiling amiably, she asked, 'And how is your friendship with CY?' She winked. Lily now supported Latha in her decision not to marry her fiancé after Latha told her he was a gambler, spending his father's money thoughtlessly. Lily liked CY and her romantic nature yearned for an interracial marriage.

Latha blushed. Lowering her voice, she said, 'Oh, Auntie, I think I'm falling in love with him. When his father took ill and Prof. Singh was mean to him and would not advance him any money to send home for his Pa's treatment, my heart melted. It was then I realized that I am in love with him.' She enthusiastically mixed her rice with the palak paneer and ate a spoonful. She licked her lips appreciatively.

'Pritam has always been a miser,' Lily said, an edge to her voice, the memory of her ex-brother-in-law not loaning a penny for her husband's cancer treatment still rankling.

'I asked Appa to loan CY some money, and surprisingly, he agreed.' Latha frowned. 'Why did Appa agree so readily?'

'So you don't threaten suicide again?' Lily gave a full-throated laugh and signalled to Vernon to bring over some coffee for them. 'Ah, here is Dr Eddington!'

Bill came to their table and after being invited, sat down. 'I need a coffee and still no coffee dispensers in the common room,' he said. He picked up his mobile phone from the table and dialled a number. After a while, he switched it off and said, 'I keep calling Ursula and she never answers. She has not come in to work today. I must attend a dinner party hosted by one of the physics professors tonight, but if I can't get in touch with Ursula by phone tomorrow, I'll pop over and see what's wrong.'

He sighed and looked penetratingly at Lily. 'Does your sister have any idea who could have murdered poor DW? He was a nice guy, and he did not know many people here. Why would someone want to murder him?' He added, 'Kiong said DW's sister-in-law was here the day of his poisoning. The one he hated so much. Does your sister think she is his killer? Kiong recognized her photo when the constables were showing it around.'

'There has been no arrest yet.' Lily adroitly evaded the question, and they began to talk of the debate on whether CCTV cameras should be installed in the university common rooms and offices.

Latha swallowed a mouthful of rice and said, 'It's privacy issues. I would hate for a camera to be installed in the common room. We would feel someone is always watching us.'

Lily pointed to a camera near her stall. 'Well, we do have cameras in the canteen and, of course, also in the carparks and elevators. Look at it this way. If there had been a camera in Uncle Abdul's room, my sister would have known who placed that cup of coffee on his table for DW and the murder would be solved.'

Bill sipped his coffee and nodded. 'I think soon we will have to forgo our desire for privacy and agree to the installation of cameras everywhere. In the light of DW's poisoning. It was all right when the university was deemed a safe place. One could argue against installing cameras in offices and the inner corridors. But not now.'

They talked about the headship election until Latha finished her meal. Bill and Latha then bid goodbye to Lily and left to go back to work. Lily went into her stall and, to her dismay, found Angie weeping bitterly.

'Oh, Angie, what is wrong?'

Angie sniffed and wiped away her tears with the back of her hand. 'Vernon and I fight all the time. Baby place so much stress and not born yet. Imagine what will happen later. It is money worries, Mrs D. We have too little of it. We are still saving to pay a deposit for a government flat and move out of V's Pa's condo. I want to see a gynae only later, but V is fighting with me over it. He wants me to see one now.'

'No financial help from V's father?' Lily enquired.

Angie shook her head. 'Pa gambles, Mrs D. And he is thinking of selling condo. Downgrade. Take Granny with him. No room for Baby in new flat. What for they open casinos in Singapore. It is so easy to gamble and lose money. Look at Pa! And you don't pay us much,' Angie added, accusingly.

'Well, my stall is not exactly the Ritz,' Lily said. 'It's hard enough for me to make any profit. With Ashikin chipping in, the business is doing better now. It's true she does not work on Fridays because she visits the mosque for prayers, but on all the other days, her dishes are sold out.'

'What for you worry, Mrs D? You have rich husband waiting for you,' Angie shot back, getting up and going to wash the dishes in the sink. 'I would go back to him. No money, no honey, Mrs D.'

Lily sat down on one of the chairs outside her stall. Her thoughts dwelled on Frankie. She felt guilty for abandoning him. Her phone beeped and she glanced at the text message from her brother-in-law, Joey, who was on a business trip to Melaka.

'*Have been talking to Frankie. How do you feel about adopting a baby? He is all for it. I think having a baby on his hands will make Frankie forget his OCD for good.*'

Lily stared at the message and later Angie found her employer gazing into space, a silly smile on her lips.

'You don't regret being pregnant, Angie?' Lily said, snapping out of her reverie.

Angie's face lit up. 'No, Mrs D. Baby's father is the one I don't like,' she said, waspishly.

Lily giggled. 'Oh, Angie, the future will right itself for all of us, don't worry!'

Angie saw her employer smiling as she furiously typed a message on her phone. Angie shrugged and hurried back to hose down the stall.

25

Ash climbed the stairs of a walk-up apartment in Toa Payoh, to the fourth floor, and knocked on one of the two doors. It was an old housing complex with paint peeling off the walls and dust floating around the landing, sparkling like tiny fireflies in the sunlight streaming in through a window with bars. When there was no response, Ash knocked louder. He waited after hearing a faint female voice crying, 'Coming!'

The door opened a crack and Ash found himself looking at a young girl in a dressing gown, her hair in a towelled turban. She had clearly run from the shower to open the door. She looked enquiringly at Ash.

'I am looking for Devender Kaur,' Ash said, his face apologetic.

The door opened further, and the girl said with a faint smile, 'That is me. Who are you?'

'My name is Ashok Singh. I am Pritam Singh's son. I understand your grandparents took care of my father when he was young.'

Devender's eyes were wide as she opened the door fully and waved Ash in. 'Pritam Singh's family finally visiting us, wait till I tell Mummy! Here, come into the living room; sorry, it's in a bit of a mess. I will clear the sofa for you.'

Devender yanked a snarling cat off the double sofa and slid some books to the floor. 'There you go, have a seat. Don't mind Gurmit if he crawls up on the sofa again. He seems to think he is its owner. Tea or Pepsi?'

Devender was tall, plump with broad shoulders, and big eyes fringed by curly lashes. Her nose was long and undulating, ending in a small rosebud mouth. She appeared older than him, Ash thought. 'Pepsi is fine, thanks,' he said.

Devender returned from the inner sanctums with two cans of Pepsi. She swept newspapers off the untidy low table and placed the cans there. She yanked Gurmit off the single sofa and sat in its place. Gurmit glowered from the worn, tattered carpet, showing his claws.

Devender ignored the cat and took a sip of Pepsi. 'What brings you here?'

Ash had rehearsed what he wanted to say. 'I wanted to get to know Dad's family. We know his paternal uncle threw him out of the ancestral home when his father died, but we also learnt a kind paternal aunt gave him shelter at a vulnerable age. I was wondering why, when I was growing up, we never saw any of Dad's family.'

Devender laughed. 'You are looking for family gossip, Ashok, is it? My grandmother was a distant cousin of Pritam's father but had been close to him. When she heard Pritam did not have a roof over his head, she convinced her husband to allow Pritam to make his home with them. My mother was older than Pritam and an only child. My grandfather was quite a character, and I don't think he treated Pritam well. Anyway, that is what Mummy says. My grandmother was the one who took care of Pritam, and he was fond of her, according to Mummy.'

'Your mother was not close to my father?' Ash was curious. 'Call me Ash,' he added.

Devender pondered. 'And I am Devi. No, I don't think Mummy and Uncle Preet were close. She was older than him. Mummy was pampered by her father and since Pritam was wild in his youth, my grandfather asked Mummy not to have much to do with him. Pritam had his own money, his father's life insurance, which was substantial. He paid for his own education. He was into drugs and alcohol when young.' Devi looked at Ash through her lashes.

'Yes, I know.'

Devi nodded. 'There was an accident. In those days, my grandfather was wealthy, and the family lived in a big apartment on Dempsey Road.

We had a car, and Nana employed a driver. Pritam was maybe seventeen years old at the time and he was an alcoholic. Without permission, he used to take the car out on joy rides. And one night, he was in a hit-and-run. The other car driver's wife died. Nani cried a lot as she had been fond of Pritam's father and did not want to see Pritam in jail. The police were closing in on our car. Nana paid our driver a large sum of money to confess to the police that he had been behind the wheel. The other car had been at fault in a big way, so our driver got only a few years in jail. The other car driver and his little son were injured. Anyway, the incident sobered your father up, and he never touched drugs and alcohol again while he lived with us.'

'Yes, that's what Mama says.'

Devi nodded, soberly. 'He soon went off to England for his doctorate degree and Mummy says they never saw him again. When Nani died, Mummy called the university and got in touch with Uncle Preet. He said he would attend the funeral, but never came. Mummy gave up on him after that. She said if he did not feel any gratitude towards someone who had been like a mother to him, she did not want to know him any more. Mummy was five years older than Pritam and already married when the car accident occurred. Nana died a year after Uncle Preet went abroad for studies, and Mummy brought Nani over to live with us. Nana left behind debts, his business was floundering, there was not much money, so they sold off the Dempsey Road apartment. I was born when Mummy was forty, a late bloom.' Devi gave a tinkling laugh. 'But I remember Nani. She died when I was ten years old. She was a gentle person.' Devi looked at Ash and asked, 'How many siblings do you have? I don't have any.'

'Oh, I am the only one, at least for now.' Seeing Devi's raised brows, he said sheepishly, 'Dad's second wife is expecting a child in two months.' He assimilated Devender's baffled look and continued, 'Dad married Mama in his thirties. Mama is a police superintendent,' he added, proudly. 'I came along eight years after their marriage. Two years ago, my parents divorced and both remarried. Dad is married to a Chinese girl, Cheryl, who is expecting a baby. Mama is married to Joey, a nice easy-going Eurasian. I have finished JC and am doing my National Service.'

Devi nodded and asked, 'Why did you really come here?' She smiled to take the edge off her words.

Ash's hair fell engagingly over his forehead, and he looked apologetic. 'Dad has Parkinson's Disease, and he is also behaving strangely. He hallucinates about the accident in his youth and is driving poor Cheryl nuts. I wanted to learn about his young days, about the accident and wanted to know if there is any mental illness in his family. Dad, sometimes, becomes clinically depressed.'

Devi frowned. 'Mental illness? No, I don't think so, but I will ask Mummy. She still teaches at a school part-time though she should be retired. My dad died young, and Mummy single-handedly raised me. I need to get a job, but it is tough to do so these days. Leave your address and phone number with me. I will talk to Mummy and get back to you.' She continued, 'Mummy did sometimes chat with Pritam after he returned from England and took up the teaching post at Temasek.She told me Pritam had visited the hit-and-run victim, Johnny Tan, and paid him a large sum of money. Compensation for his guilty conscience, I guess.'

'I wonder where Johnny Tan lives,' Ash mused.

'Not far from here, in a two-room rental. Johnny works as a cleaner in our estate. Small world, eh?'

'Thanks for filling me up on Dad's youth.' On a whim Ash added, 'Are you free for dinner this evening? You could meet Mama. She has recently been promoted to assistant superintendent, and we are celebrating since Papa Joey just got back to Singapore as well. His work takes him abroad. Join us for dinner, it will be fun.'

Devi thought it over, then nodded shyly. 'Mummy is on librarian duty tonight at the nearby library so yeah, why not? Thanks, Bro.'

Armed with Johnny's address, Ash walked out into the sunshine.

* * *

Girlie, laden with dishes of Indian food, tottered into the dining room from the kitchen. The family was celebrating Dolly's promotion to assistant superintendent. Snatches of laughter and talk came from the living hall as Girlie carefully laid the table. She glanced out of the window and saw darkness had fallen.

The dinner crowd consisted of Dolly's husband, Joey, Lily's husband, Frankie, Lily, Dolly, Ash, Uma, and Devender Kaur. Lily looked curiously at Pritam's niece as she laughed at a remark Ash made and took her seat at the dining table. She was good-looking, with the Pathan features common among Punjabis, stocky and well-built. Her smile was her best asset; she had a small mouth and uneven white teeth.

Lily smiled at Girlie and turned her attention to the dishes her helper was laying out on the table. She frowned. The okra looked burnt, and she wondered why Girlie bothered to cook it when there were so many other vegetables she could make. The biryani smelt good, although Girlie had been liberal in her use of saffron, the rice looked bright yellow. She peered at the chicken drumsticks floating in a green gravy and rolled her eyes. *Girlie's version of 'Spinach Chicken'.* The yellow lentils looked appetizing as did the mutton kebabs. She directed a look of approval at Girlie, who blushed happily. Lily smiled at Frankie as he pulled out a chair for her and took her seat. Frankie sat between his wife and his mother-in-law.

Joey, his eyes happy behind wire spectacles, and sitting on Uma's other side, said, 'Before we start on the feast, I would like to congratulate my wife on her promotion at work. Everyone, here's to Assistant Superintendent Dolly Das.' He grinned and raised his glass of orange juice; the others following suit.

Uma wiped her eyes with a small handkerchief. 'I am happy to see this day,' she quavered. 'A superintendent! Dolly's papa would have been so proud!'

Dolly, sitting between her husband and son, laughed in her pleasant baritone. 'Thanks, everyone.' She started on her spinach chicken. Soon, she was licking her lips. 'Girlie, whatever this *looks* like, it tastes good.'

Uma leant forward from her chair and peered inquisitively at Devi, seated on Ash's other side. 'So, Devi, you have never met Pritam?' She bit into a chilli with her dentures thinking it was okra and quickly gulped down lemonade.

Devi looked at Uma and smiled. 'No. My mother married young and left home and by the time I came along, Uncle Pritam no longer lived with my grandparents. Mummy really expected Uncle Pritam to come to Nani's funeral as they had been fond of each other, but he never came. Uncle Pritam put his past firmly behind him. I am glad, though, that Ash looked us up. It is nice to have a cousin, even a distant one.'

Joey, enthusiastically doling biryani rice on to his plate, said, 'And the accident Ash was telling me about? The victim is known to you?'

'Johnny Tan? Yes, he is our estate cleaner. Small world.' Devender attacked her mutton kebab with gusto.

'I am going down to meet him next week,' Ash said, tentatively. 'Papa Joey, can you come with me?'

Dolly who had been enjoying the spinach chicken with rice, stopped eating. She intervened. 'Ash, do you think that's a good idea? It was all right to get in touch with Pritam's family, we needed to know of mental illness in the family, but talking to the crash victim? If your dad finds out you've been speaking to the other car driver without first talking it out with him, he may be upset. Why do you want to meet Johnny Tan? After all, Pritam did give money to the family.'

Devi nodded. 'Yes, Uncle Pritam gave a lot of money from his inheritance to Johnny Tan when he found out Johnny had become an invalid after the accident. Fifty thousand dollars, I think.'

Frankie served mutton kebabs to his wife and turned to Devi. 'What was Johnny Tan's profession before the accident?'

Devi frowned before smiling at Ash serving her spinach chicken. 'Mummy said Johnny was an engineer and worked at a reputable firm before the accident. There was brain damage, and he was in hospital for many months. The doctors performed surgery, but Johnny was never the same again. He could not think right.'

'What about the other crash victims?' Frankie asked. 'I take it Pritam escaped unscathed?'

'Yes, Uncle Pritam only had a few bruises. Johnny Tan's wife died instantaneously, and his little son was injured, too, but not seriously. I do not know what happened to the son. I've never seen Johnny with a young man.'

Uma looked angrily at the chicken stew Girlie had served her. Eating bland food with the aroma of mutton kebabs floating around the room, was hard on her. Leaving the stew and rice untouched on her plate, she turned to Dolly. 'Pritam *killed* somebody! Daddy was right all along, did not want you to marry him.' She looked at Ash's stricken face and cackled. 'Don't mind your dida, Ashok. We, old people, are full of prejudices. I will say this for Pritam, though. Whatever he was in the past, he is the best dad to Ash. Loves him so much. Who was at fault for the accident?' she demanded in a shrill voice that arrested Girlie on her way to the kitchen with the dirty dishes. Girlie looked at the untouched chicken stew on Uma's plate and frowned. *After she had taken such pains over it!*

Devi helped herself to more mutton kebabs. 'Johnny Tan was at fault, but if Uncle Pritam was not intoxicated, he could have swerved away from the other car. Uncle Pritam sped away from the accident site, not bothering to stop to see who was hurt.'

Uma nodded, her white stringy hair standing out on her head in spikes. 'He was always a coward. Never occurred to Pritam to give himself up.'

Ash's handsome face was distraught. He laid his spoon and fork down on his half-eaten food and said, 'Dad hallucinates about this accident, Dida. It's not as if he isn't punished for it every day of his life. I want to learn about the Tan family to assure Dad the crash survivors are all right. It seems he cannot forgive himself.'

'I will go with you to meet Johnny Tan,' Joey decided, ignoring Dolly's frown.

The conversation lightened, turning to the subjects Ash was thinking of studying at university when his NS stint finished. There was good-natured bantering and laughter when Lily teased Ash about his new girlfriend, Amita. In half an hour, all the dishes on the table were empty, the faces of the diners contented. Girlie heaved a sigh of relief at the success of the meal.

After the two youngsters had gone to Ash's room to listen to music and the others had settled themselves in the living hall with cups of coffee, Joey took out an envelope and several photos of babies fell out.

'This is the photo of the baby my agent in India has chosen for you to adopt.' Joey grinned from ear to ear, passing the photo to Lily. 'She was born a month ago, and if all goes well with permission from the Ministry of Community Development, she can arrive in Singapore in two months.'

'Look, Frankie, she is smiling!' Lily exclaimed, making cooing noises.

Frankie, sitting on a chair by himself, looked stern and Lily raised her eyebrows. Frankie stated, 'We have no hope of getting approval from the ministry if we continue to live apart and be estranged. The first thing they look at is whether we are a happy couple able to provide a good home for the baby. They will find out we live apart and then that's it.'

Joey nodded vigorously at Lily. 'I'm afraid that's true. You need to repair your marriage before you adopt a baby. You should at least start living together again.'

Lily's face fell. 'So soon?' Seeing Frankie's thunderous face, she said, 'Okay, okay, I do understand. I will return home, Frankie.'

Frankie's shoulders relaxed, and he gave Lily a dazzling smile. Curbing the unease in her mind and her fear that she would still be unable to cope with Frankie's OCD, Lily smiled back uncertainly.

Saturday, 10 September 2011

26

It was 7.45 a.m. Jauntily humming a Tagalog tune, Girlie walked briskly between the kitchen and the dining hall of Uma Das's unit in Silver Springs Condominium, laden with dishes from which steam was rising. She placed the dishes on the long buffet table at one end of the hall. Girlie was in an ebullient mood after receiving a text from her philandering husband asking for forgiveness and another chance with her. As she sizzled sausages in the kitchen, Girlie felt that this was a good start to the day.

The bell outside the main door pealed and Girlie frowned. She could hear Ash singing in the bathroom and sounds from Lily's bedroom indicated she had woken up. Uma slept late nowadays and was unlikely to wake up until nine in the morning. Dolly had returned home with her husband, Joey. Who could be at the front door at eight in the morning? Expertly ladling the fried sausages on to a plate, Girlie sauntered to the main door as the bell pealed urgently again.

'Coming!' Girlie shouted as she unlocked the door and peered out. 'Kamini!' She cried in alarm. 'What are you doing here?'

In the well-lit corridor outside, a plump Indian woman in a Punjabi suit blinked, clutching the hand of a young boy with blonde hair.

Kamini, Ursula Botham's home help, found her voice. 'Girlie, help me, please. When I come to work at 7 a.m., Tom open the door. Ma'am Ursula's bedroom door was closed and locked. No sound from inside. And Sir not home. Tommy call his mobile but voice message only. Your employer police inspector, she can tell me what to do. Go to police post, is it? I don't know.'

Girlie stammered, 'My employer is a police inspector's sister. Not the same thing, Kamini.'

'What is going on here?' Lily was tying the tassel of her dressing gown flung over her nightclothes. 'Girlie?'

Girlie moved aside and said, 'Ma'am, this is Kamini, my friend who works for Ma'am Ursula Botham. Ma'am lock herself in bedroom and won't open the door. They don't know what to do.'

Lily peered at Tom and said, 'You'd better come in. Did you call university security, Kamini? They are the ones to call. They will come and open the door, and if Prof. Botham is sick, they will call for an ambulance.' She looked at Tom and smiled. 'Hi, I'm Lily. Have you had breakfast?'

Tom mutely shook his head, tears pooling in his blue eyes.

'Here, why don't you sit at the table and let Girlie get you some breakfast? My nephew will join you. You will like talking to him.'

Tom nodded, and after a few words with Ash and a hurried phone call to Dolly, Lily got dressed. She left Ash and Tom breakfasting together companionably and told Girlie to keep Tom in the flat while she and Kamini went to the university campus.

* * *

Lily drove Kamini to the staff quarters where a heavily built Indian man was waiting at the gate.

'ASP Das called me,' he said, looking reproachfully at Kamini while talking to Lily. 'I am from university security. Shall we go upstairs?' He jingled a set of keys in his hand.

The lift took them to the fourth floor and Kamini led the way to a corner unit with flowerpots lining the path to the door. She fished a key out of her handbag and opened the main door. They entered the hall that led to a bright dining room with all the windows open. There was a kitchen at one end and three doors opening out of a narrow, carpeted corridor leading away from the dining hall.

'This one is living hall and study room,' Kamini babbled as they passed a dark room with bookcases and sofas. She pointed to an open door through which could be seen posters of British rock stars. 'That is Tom's room.' She moved hesitantly towards a closed door at the end of the corridor as though afraid of what she might find when the security guard opened it. 'This is Ma'am and Sir's bedroom. The door locked from inside.' She turned the handle and the door remained locked.

The security guard looked at the keyhole and then rummaged among the many keys on his chain. After some minutes, he picked out a key and nodded. 'Yes, this should open the door. Stand back, please.'

Kamini edged away, her dark face shining with fright. Lily held her place behind the guard, trying to peer over his shoulder, her short height hindering her. The key fitted into the lock, the guard turned the handle and the door opened into a dark room.

'The light switch is beside the door,' Kamini whispered with dread.

The guard flicked the switch on, and the room flooded with light from a small chandelier hanging from the ceiling. Lily, peering from around the guard, could make out the end of a bed and a pair of feet. The guard uttered a startled exclamation.

'Please stay back,' the guard warned in a guttural voice. Kamini shrank into the shadows of the corridor, but Lily entered the room, undeterred, her eyes swivelling curiously to the bed.

Ursula was lying on the bed in her nightgown, her arms stretched out wide, her blue eyes gazing lifelessly at the ceiling. Her blonde hair framed her face in a serene halo.

'Check for life,' Lily ordered the guard, shortly.

The guard went to the bed and felt for Ursula's pulse, pushed his hand underneath her nose and silently shook his head. Lily crowded in behind and gazed at the body.

'Why, she is yellow all over,' Lily exclaimed. Ursula, indeed, did look like an overripe banana. There were no signs of trauma on her except for her lips twisted bitterly as though she had been recollecting a nasty incident before death claimed her.

The guard got busy on his mobile phone, calling the ambulance. There was a wail from behind them. Kamini stared at Ursula's still form, lamenting her death.

'I will call my sister, she is a police superintendent investigating the murder of Dr Pak from the same department Professor Botham worked in,' Lily said, shepherding Kamini out of the room.

'Ma'am is *dead*?' Kamini whimpered, bewilderment etching her face.

'I think so. The guard has called for an ambulance and doctor. Do you want me to make you a cup of tea? I need to call my sister.' Lily whipped out her handphone from the bag slung over her shoulder.

'No, Ma'am, I make tea for you.' Kamini dried her tears, gaining some comfort from making herself useful.

On the phone, Dolly instructed Lily to remain where she was; Charlie and she were on their way. She also told Lily to tell the security guard who had found the body to wait inside the flat for the police to come.

Lily conveyed Dolly's instructions to the guard, who nodded and went into the small balcony off the dining room to wait for the police. Lily sat on one of the chairs in the dining room to wait for her sister. She looked around the stark room typical of university temporary accommodation. A table for six, wooden chairs, a sideboard and a landscape print on the wall. Lily rose from her chair and made her way to the living room. She switched on the light and noted a more personal touch here.

The sofas were covered with flowery prints reminiscent of English homes and the walls were decorated with not only British landscapes but also family photos. Bookcases stacked with books covered three sides of the room. Lily began examining the family photos on the wall. In one photo, a smiling Ursula was hanging on to the arm of a stocky man in overalls while a woman with a pinched expression on her face looked on. Lily took them to be Ursula's parents. In another family photo, Ursula was a bride, in what was obviously a registrar's office, a sprig of white flowers in her hands, and a hat with a veil covering her face, her baby bump clearly showing. Beside her stood a young Graham, smiling into the camera. There were landscape paintings on the wall, not quite with the professional touch, and Lily deduced that either Ursula or Graham painted as a hobby.

She moved on to the bookcases. The one nearest to the window was crammed with chemistry books, manuals and journals. The bookcase opposite the window and next to the door was filled with fiction novels, the readers in the family obviously favouring crime thrillers. Some books by South-east Asian authors were there and several classics by Dickens and Austen. The small bookcase on the farther side was stacked with travelogues and some non-fiction self-help books.

The wail of the ambulance siren sounded outside and soon there was the noise of footsteps. Lily came to the door of the living room and was relieved to see a police sergeant from the nearby post asking the ambulance personnel to take care as the bedroom could be a crime scene. Lily knew Dolly had sent the policeman ahead before she and Charlie got to the apartment.

Kamini hovered with a tray on which there was a plate of heavily buttered toast and a cup of tea. Lily came inside the living room and sat on a chair. The maid's eyes were red from weeping, and she mumbled, 'I disturb you before breakfast, Ma'am. You must be hungry. Have some toast, Ma'am Lily.'

Lily thanked Kamini and waved her to a chair. 'What time did you leave Ursula yesterday? Did she go to work?' Lily bit into the toast and began to chew. Her heart was beating fast. Had Ursula Botham been poisoned like DW?

'No, Ma'am stay home. She was sick. It was her stomach ulcers,' Kamini said. 'She phone university for sick leave. I come in the morning. I give Tom his breakfast and send him to school. I take dry toast to Ma'am in the bedroom. She look very sick, Ma'am Lily. But she still working, reading papers, and resting. She eat dry toast only. I tell her to visit doctor, but she shake her head. I spend morning cleaning house. I take in soup and sandwiches for Ma'am's lunch. Ma'am was sleeping but wake up to take soup. Yes, Ma'am Lily, come to think of it, she look yellow yesterday already. I leave house at noon after I make sure Ma'am know there is frozen pizza in the fridge for dinner. She tell me she cannot take sandwiches. I throw them away. I wash the dishes and leave.' Tears had pooled again in Kamini's eyes. 'I should have called doctor yesterday already,' she wailed.

'No need to blame yourself, Kamini,' Lily said, kindly. 'Anything strange happened yesterday?' Lily probed, finishing her toast.

Kamini reflected, her dark face gleaming in the light of the chandelier. Her large kohl-lined eyes widened before her mouth shaped into a moue of indecision. 'When I put lunch tray on bedside table, Ma'am was sleeping. I smell garlic on her. I think Ma'am take her garlic pills again. She used to before but stopped because she said it was not helping her get better. She used it to make the fat in her body go away, she said. I think her doctor give allopathic pills, later.'

There was a sound in the hall, and Lily spied Charles Goh directing policemen to the bedroom and soon enough, she observed her sister and the forensic pathologist, Benny Ong, making their way there, too.

Lily quickly gulped down her tea. Fifteen minutes later, Dolly arrived in the living hall.

Lily wanted her sister alone and, standing up, tentatively suggested, 'Maybe some tea for the police officers, Kamini?'

Kamini nodded and walked away to the kitchen. Dolly looked spry in a navy-blue pantsuit. Her eyes still held a degree of wonderment at being promoted to Assistant Superintendent.

Dolly said, 'That was the maid? Girlie's friend?'

Lily nodded and then burst out, 'Was Ursula Botham murdered?'

Dolly frowned. 'The pathologist found no visible injuries on the body. He is still examining her. From a preliminary examination, Benny Ong, the doctor, thinks Ursula suffered a cardiac arrest. Her heart stopped beating. She is also yellow, suggesting jaundice.' She seated herself on a sofa and waved Lily to the seat next to her.

'DW's heart stopped beating, and *he* was poisoned. You need to do a PM, Dolly. Ursula Botham is from the same department as DW,' Lily said while sitting down.

Dolly nodded. 'Yes, I know, Lily. I have brought the forensics team with me. DW was poisoned and maybe Ursula as well. It is hard to imagine Ursula dying naturally, being so young. Do you know if she suffered from any disease? Did the maid say?' She looked at the closed windows and got up to switch on the ceiling fan. It was hot in the room.

Lily's brows were creased. 'She suffered from peptic ulcers, the maid said. But one does not die from peptic ulcers. Ursula was young and there is a poisoner about, Dolly, I think the doctor should look for poison. It is logical. Besides, Kamini said she noticed a garlic odour from Ursula's breath yesterday, and I seem to remember from the crime thrillers I've read that garlic breath is a symptom of a poison. I don't remember which poison.'

'You and your crime thrillers!' Dolly rolled her eyes. 'But I will talk to Benny about it. Ursula's death is suspicious.'

Lily looked keenly at Dolly. 'I thought this was Charlie's case. The inspector in charge comes to the crime scene, right. You are now Assistant Superintendent, Dolly. Old habits die hard?'

Dolly looked defensive. 'You could say that. Some ASPs are more hands-on than others. I guess I'm one of them.'

There was an excited shout and Charlie appeared in the doorway. 'Madam, there is vomit in the master bathroom, and it is glowing. Professor Ursula Botham could have been poisoned by phosphorus.'

Dolly rose from the sofa while Lily stared. 'Secure this apartment as a crime scene, Charlie, and I will ask Graham Botham to give immediate permission for an autopsy.' She glanced out of the door and saw a Caucasian man in the dining room, looking scared. 'I think I see him outside. Mok went to get him from his girlfriend's residence; he was not answering his phone. Really!'

Lily cried, 'I remember! Garlic breath is a symptom of phosphorus poisoning! I read it in one of the crime novels.' Seeing Dolly paying scant attention to her, Lily sighed and looked at her watch. 'I must return home and rescue Ash from entertaining Tom. Now his father is here, Kamini can come with me and bring the little boy home.'

* * *

Lily found Ash and Tom playing video games on Ash's laptop in his bedroom. Seeing Lily at the door of the room, Tom immediately jumped up from his chair and came forward.

'Mummy is sick?' he asked.

Lily had told Kamini that Graham should break the news of his mother's death to Tom, and both women mutely nodded in answer.

'Was she sick yesterday?' Lily asked gently.

Tom nodded. 'I had enrichment class yesterday and came home after six in the evening. Mummy was sleeping and I had to wake her up. She had forgotten about dinner. She dragged herself up and sat at the dining table telling me how to defrost and warm the pizza. She only had one slice and later, I heard her retching in her bathroom. She told me to do my homework and said she would go to sleep early as her ulcers were still acting up. Before I went to sleep, I wanted to say goodnight, but her door was locked from inside. I knocked but there was no answer. She must have fallen asleep. There was no line of light underneath her door.'

Kamini blinked back tears, clutched Tom's hand, and took her leave of Lily after profusely thanking her for taking charge. Lily remained standing at the door of her condo unit even when the lift door had closed and Kamini and Tom were out of sight.

27

The university had made available a conference room on the ground floor of the staff quarters where the CID officers could question Graham Botham and his lover, Lorna Asquith, since the forensics team had yet to finish their work at Ursula's home and it was out of bounds to the bereaved husband.

There was a desk with four chairs in the white-washed room and no other furniture. Sunlight streamed in through a wide window. Dolly and Charlie sat next to each other, facing Graham and Lorna across the expanse of the desk.

Dolly thought Graham looked tired and tense, his long, unruly brown hair falling all over his rugged face, his eyes unfocused and afraid. In contrast, Lorna Asquith, a tall, willowy redhead, was calm, her green eyes coolly clocking Dolly. It was Lorna who broke the uncomfortable silence stretching on as both sides appraised the other. She looked at Charlie.

'In case you want to know about Graham's whereabouts this week, he was living with me in my staff quarters. I am a visiting lecturer at the geography department and the U kindly leases me accommodation. He came to stay with me on Tuesday after work. He left Ursula.' She raised a shapely eyebrow on hearing Graham cough.

Graham cleared his throat. 'I would not say I left Ursula. The truth is that Ursula kicked me out of the house. She changed the locks. It was a spousal tiff. It would have been resolved if Ursula were alive. She objected to me spending time with Lorna. We would have made up.' His voice shook with traces of the emotion he still felt for his dead wife.

Lorna's green eyes flashed, and she turned to Graham. 'You're just saying that because you want to maintain a good image of the devoted husband on account of the Head of Chemistry election.' She narrowed her eyes and looked at Charlie. 'Graham is pitted against Pritam Singh for the headship, Inspector.'

Charlie found it interesting that Lorna was providing alibis for Graham. Or was it a streak of possessiveness that made her broadcast to the officers that *she* was the woman in Graham's life? 'But this is not the first time you have cheated on your wife, right?' Charlie asked pleasantly. 'In Australia, you had to leave your job because of an affair with a student?'

Lorna bristled and turned an outraged face to Graham. 'Really? I did not know that. Who was she?'

The colour returned to Graham's pale face. 'Her name was Sheila Wright, if you must know,' he said, waspishly. 'She was an heiress to a shoe empire.'

'Then why didn't you marry her?' Lorna's voice was like a pistol shot.

'There was Tom,' Graham said, his voice soft. He looked down at the table.

'Prof. Ursula did not think of Tom when she broached the matter of divorce?' Charlie asked, noting with interest that Lorna had stiffened, turning her face away from Graham. It was obvious she had been unaware of Graham's past infidelities.

'We never talked of divorce! Who has been spreading rumours?' Graham shouted. 'We would have reconciled, we always did. Husbands and wives fight, right. That was all it was.'

Charlie shrugged. 'Mrs Botham told one of her friends that after the headship elections were over, she would divorce you. She was waiting so as not to harm your career prospects.'

Dolly looked appreciatively at Charlie. He was asking the right questions and truly deserved his promotion.

Graham sneered, an ugly look on his face. 'Inspector, I would not listen to gossip and rumours, especially if Bill Eddington is your source. He never had the courage to propose marriage to Ursula and resented our marriage. Ursula and I used to laugh about him. Ursula thought he was a wimp.'

Dolly intervened. What she had to say was of a sensitive nature, and it was better if these questions came from her. 'You had more than one affair in Australia, right. What about the Korean girl, Ji-woo Kim? Didn't she kill herself because you refused to divorce Ursula and marry her?'

There was pin-drop silence in the room. Graham took a sharp breath, the colour leaving his face. 'I had nothing to do with Kim's suicide,' he finally whispered. In a stronger voice, he added, 'Kim broke up with her boyfriend just before the suicide. Why would you think I was involved?' He tried to look outraged, felt Lorna's incredulous eyes on him and looked down at the table.

'Dong-wook Pak, your research fellow, knew Kim's family. It seems Kim told her family that she was in love with you, and you were spurning her. After the suicide, her boyfriend told the police that he had broken up with Kim because she had fallen in love with a professor of chemistry.' Dolly held Graham in a steely glare.

Graham looked up at Dolly with angry eyes. 'But she never said it was me! There were so many chemistry professors there. The police closed the case, and the coroner ruled the death a suicide. You have nothing on me. I would appreciate it if you did not accuse me of wrongdoings before checking facts. I could complain to your big boss, eh? For defamation of character. Don't think I won't.'

Dolly was unfazed. 'Dr Pak recently wrote to Kim's father that he would question you about Kim's death. Did he, Dr Botham?'

Graham's face was white. He mutely shook his head. His hands on the table, began trembling. He finally found his voice. 'Absolutely not! DW said nothing to me.'

Dolly signalled to Charlie to continue the interrogation, and Charlie's rough voice bit into the sudden silence. 'We understand Prof. Ursula was wealthy in her own right. She owned a manor in England and had inherited money from her father. Who is the legal heir to her fortune?'

'Tom and me,' Graham said readily, though his eyes would not meet those of the police officers. 'She left everything to us.'

Dolly, noting Lorna sitting back with the hint of a smile on her face, said, 'She left a last will and testament?'

'No, I do not think so.' Graham scratched his head distractedly. 'That is why I said that our son and I are her heirs. That is the intestate law, right?'

Charlie nodded. 'Yes, if she did not leave a will.'

Lorna's voice was sharp as she held Graham in a sharp stare. 'Are you sure there is no will? You could ask Aunt Bee; she would know if Ursula made a will.'

'I don't want to talk to Bianca. You know I don't get along with her, Lorna. To the best of my knowledge, Ursula left no will.' Graham looked around. His eyes grew worried. 'Where is Tom?'

'He will be here in a minute. Your maid, Kamini, brought him over to my sister's house when she could not open Prof. Ursula's bedroom door.' Dolly looked straight at Graham, who immediately looked away. 'Were you aware your wife was sick?' When Graham slowly shook his head, she barked out, 'You were not aware that she had peptic ulcers and pain from that?'

'Oh, *that*,' Graham said, dismissively. 'Yes, she did suffer from ulcers, a good dose of Pepto-Bismol usually set her right again. It was nothing serious. She never had heart problems. The staff at Temasek are checked every six months by the hospital, and a heart problem would have been picked up. To the best of my knowledge, she did not have liver problems, either. Maybe she ate something in the hawker stalls and contracted jaundice. I only saw her for a moment before your men pushed me out of the room, Inspector, but her skin looked yellow.'

'We would like an account of your movements yesterday,' Charles Goh said, whipping out his tablet.

Graham frowned. 'I never went near my quarters or my wife, if that's what you're asking. My wife died of natural causes, right? I am being questioned as though she was murdered.'

'We would like your permission to conduct a post-mortem on your wife,' Dolly stated formally. 'There were some indications she may have been poisoned. Given that a postdoctoral research fellow was poisoned only a few days ago at the chemistry department as well, we would like to ensure the cause of death was natural and that there was no foul play involved.' She did not mention the glowing vomit in the bathroom; the less a suspect knew of investigations, the better.

Lorna gave a gasp and the colour drained from Graham's face. 'I guess I have no choice but to agree. Go ahead, ASP Das, you have my permission.'

There was a knock on the door. It opened and Tom stood there, Kamini protectively holding on to his shoulder. On seeing his father, Tom ran to him and asked, 'Dad, where is Mummy? We could not open her door this morning.'

Dolly nodded to Charlie and said to Graham, 'We will leave you now. It would be good if you stayed somewhere else till the evening. Gives our forensics team time to do a thorough job in your flat.'

'We will go to my apartment, of course,' Lorna said. She gave Tom a tentative smile. 'I have some video games. Want to play?'

Charlie saw the couple and Tom out of the door. The police officers got into the squad car, thoughtfully. If Ursula Botham had been murdered, they had to nab the killer roaming Temasek University before any more murders took place. It wasn't looking good for Graham Botham: he seemed to have motives for both murders.

28

At HQ, Dolly followed Charlie into his new office. It had a small window overlooking greenery and was on the same floor as her previous office. Charlie had arranged the office neatly, and Dolly looked over the room approvingly. She sat in the guest chair and motioned Charlie to sit in his swivel chair.

Dolly smiled. 'So, I am now going to let you take over the case as an inspector, Charlie, which means you do all the legwork. I am always here to give advice. As ASP, I have extensive administrative duties. Supt Dragon Lady has piled a lot of work on me. I do miss field work, though. Admin is boring.'

Charlie looked confident. 'Yes, Madam. We have secured the crime scene and we wait for the forensics team to update us and for Benny to confirm Ursula Botham was poisoned.'

Dolly drummed her hands on the table. 'You think the crime scene is Ursula's apartment?'

Charlie shook his head. 'Not necessarily, Madam. We have sealed her office and our team is searching for phosphorus in the staff offices and laboratories.'

'Good,' Dolly said. 'What did Benny say? How was the phosphorus administered to Ursula? We will assume for now that Ursula was poisoned by phosphorus.'

Charlie stared at Dolly. 'Benny never said anything, Madam.'

'Here's the first rule as an inspector, Charlie. You ask questions of the forensic pathologist when he is examining the corpse at the crime scene as well as when he has done a preliminary examination of the corpse at the morgue before autopsy. And you need to be present at the morgue during autopsy. You've seen me questioning Benny a few times, right?'

'I asked for the time of death,' Charlie said, readily. 'Benny said sometime late last night. That figures, Madam, since the lights were switched off in the bedroom, and the lights would have been on when the door was opened if she had died earlier in the night, say before Tom went to bed.'

'We already know Ursula's room was dark when Tom went to bed. He knocked on her door, received no answer, and told us there was no line of light underneath Ursula's bedroom door. The time of actual death does not help us much in poisoning cases since it does not tell us *when* the victim ingested poison. Poisons take a bit long to act on the human body,' Dolly said. 'The victim could have been taking the poison for two or three days. We need to find out how Ursula Botham was poisoned. What you needed to ask Benny was whether the victim had inhaled the poison, ingested it, or absorbed it through skin.'

'How do you know all this, Madam?' Charlie was incredulous.

'I looked up phosphorus poisoning on the internet as soon as our team discovered the glowing vomit in the bathroom. According to the articles I read, if the poison entered through skin, there should be burn marks. I already called Benny. There were no burn marks, and he thinks the victim ingested the poison. If the victim were exposed to poisonous vapour and inhaled it, death would have been fast. Ursula was ill for several days. So, now, we must think about how Ursula Botham could have ingested phosphorus. In her coffee, tea, or something else? This is mirroring DW's murder. We think his poison was in the cup of coffee left anonymously on Abdul's table.'

Charlie looked crestfallen. 'I should not have been promoted, Madam. I still have so much to learn.'

'Rubbish, Charlie! You will do great. Was there anything found on her bedside table?'

'A bottle of Pepto-Bismol.' He looked at a text on his phone. 'Mok just texted that there is also a bottle of Pepto-Bismol on Ursula Botham's table at her office. She was taking medicine from both bottles.'

'Tell him to send both bottles to the forensics lab for testing.' Dolly's eyes were shining. 'It was common knowledge Ursula suffered from peptic ulcers and had Pepto-Bismol at her office. The offices are not locked. So, the killer could have slipped some phosphorus into Ursula's Pepto-Bismol. Pepto-Bismol is an emulsion and when Ursula took sips of it, if there was phosphorus inside, she could have been ingesting it along with the medicine. As far as I know, phosphorus is not soluble in water. An emulsion medicine would well mask the white phosphorus particles.'

Dolly looked at Charlie's respectful face and laughed. 'Always do your research, Inspector. Benny told me they do not have specific tests to detect phosphorus poisoning. If there is such a poisoning, it results in high phosphate levels in the blood, liver failure, heart failure, but as you know, they can be from natural causes as well though not all at once, of course. It is important to know how she took the poison. If we find poison, say in Ursula's Pepto-Bismol bottles, we can classify Ursula's death as murder. Keep talking to Benny as he proceeds with the autopsy. Doctors may be able to determine when exactly the victim ingested the poison. Two days or more like three days? I think they can roughly determine the time of ingestion from the deterioration of the organs and the levels of phosphate in the blood. Charlie, have lunch and then go and supervise the two crime scenes. Both the apartment and Ursula's office. And then go to the morgue and have a chat with Benny.'

'Madam, thank you so much for the pointers. I will have a quick lunch and leave for the university. I want to personally get that bottle of Pepto-Bismol from Ursula's office to the forensics lab for testing.'

Dolly left Charlie's office and took the lift to her floor and office. She found her boss, Superintendent Abdullah, seated in her office chair, her face unhappy.

'Ma'am.' Dolly stood stiffly to attention.

'I had the home minister and the foreign affairs minister on the phone, together in a conference call. We are in the spotlight, ASP Das, with the spate of poisonings at our premier university. The murdered victims were foreigners working at the university. I will have the prime minister on the line next. Have you sealed the dead professor's office?' When Dolly nodded, she asked, 'What about the PM?'

'We did get permission from the husband for a PM and the pathologist is expediting it as we speak.'

Siti said, 'Good. I do not want these ministers breathing down my neck. And clues are not going to go on waiting for you, ASP Das. Ask Benny Ong to do over-time, we will pay for it. PM results Tuesday morning latest.' Siti looked probingly at Dolly. 'Allow Inspector Goh to do the interviewing, ASP Das. I heard you were there during Graham Botham's interview, and you were at their house as well. Adjust to your new role, Assistant Superintendent, and in that way, you will also retain your objectivity given your ex works in the chemistry department. We agreed to all of this with DAC Nathan, but I don't see you following orders. Remedy that.' The superintendent gave a curt nod, rose from the chair, and left Dolly's office.

Dolly immediately buzzed for Charlie, who had grabbed a quick bite to eat and was getting ready to go to the university.

Dolly motioned Charlie to a chair and said, 'Expedite Corporal Fauzia Khan's transfer to the Serious Sexual Crime Branch, Charlie. She is spying on my activities and feeding information to her aunt. Otherwise, how did Boss know that I was at Ursula's house!' Dolly sat on her chair, turned on her computer, and looked at some papers on her desk. Her face was grim when she looked up at Charlie. 'We need to know if Ursula left behind a will. Her husband seems to think not, but he may not know; they were not on good terms. How do we go about finding out if she left a will? She is a British citizen.'

Charlie was scanning his tablet. 'Although it is early hours in the morning at Oxford, I have booked a call to Ursula's mother, Bianca. She may be able to help and give us information on Ursula's lawyer. I have told her to call your number. You may get a call anytime now.'

'Great work, Inspector Goh.' Dolly's smile hid the fact that she felt pressured and flustered.

Dolly's phone rang, and the operator told her that a Bianca Asquith was on the line from the UK. Dolly cleared her throat and spoke. 'Mrs Asquith, I am Assistant Superintendent Dolly Das from the Singapore CID. Please accept my condolences on the death of your daughter, Professor Ursula Botham.' Dolly switched to speakerphone so that Charlie could hear the conversation. Charlie listened intently.

Bianca Asquith's voice quavered over the line. 'Thank you. I will be arriving in Singapore next week to take my grandson, Thomas, back to England. When Graham gave me the news of Ursula's death, he was vague as to the cause. Is it foul play? She was so young.'

Dolly replied, 'I will meet you, Ma'am, and update you on that. Meanwhile, if you can assist us in a small matter?'

'What is it?' This time Bianca Asquith's voice was sharp.

'Did your daughter leave behind a will? Her husband, Professor Graham Botham seemed to think not.'

There was a hollow laugh over the phone line. 'What does he know? My daughter was an extremely wealthy woman, Superintendent. She did make her will last time she was here in Oxford for a holiday. Her lawyers are from our family firm, Galbraith & Sons, they have an office in Oxford. I can give you Andrew Galbraith's number, will that help? Please hang on to the line while I hunt for the number.'

After five minutes, she was back on the line and Charlie diligently noted down the phone number of Ursula's lawyers. Bianca's voice crackled over the phone and Dolly could have sworn there was mirth in her voice. 'I can tell you its contents as my daughter did discuss her will with me. She leaves the manor house to her son, Tom, and Galbraith and I are her trustees. The bulk of her monetary assets, which are ample, is left to her son. She left me 500,000 sterling pounds and permission to make Banbury Hall my home until my death.'

Dolly's voice was excited. 'Do you have any idea as to the value of the monetary assets, Ma'am?'

'Several million sterling, I imagine. My husband was a wealthy man and Ursula was his heir.'

Dolly's voice was sharp. 'Prof. Ursula did not leave any money to her husband, Graham?'

Bianca snorted. 'Only a paltry sum, the value of which you would have to ascertain from Andrew Galbraith, the lawyer. If there isn't anything more, I need to get back to sleep otherwise I will wake up with a sore head. I will see you next week, Superintendent. Give Andrew Galbraith my regards when you speak to him.'

Dolly slowly replaced the phone receiver. She looked at Charlie, speculatively, 'I wonder how many millions exactly were at stake? You go ahead to the university, Charlie. See that the antacid bottles are sent safely to the forensics lab. Galbraith will take a while to call.'

Dolly remained deep in thought after Charlie had left the office. The murderer was a wily one, poisonings were the hardest crimes to solve. If Ursula's death turned out to be a poisoning, Dolly could not help wondering about a serial killer being at large in the chemistry department with two back-to-back murders. She had recently been teaching a suspect psychological profiling workshop to new police recruits, and the topic was serial killers. She had read Ann Rule's book on the serial killer Ted Bundy, and described to her class some traits of a serial killer and how they operated, before setting them the task of applying these traits to other known serial killers as a homework assignment. When multiple murders occurred, Dolly was trained to keep in mind the existence of a serial killer.

29

Dolly was doing further research on phosphorus poisoning on the internet when Charlie knocked on the door and entered. He looked damp as he sat in the guest chair.

'It's pouring outside,' he said, 'and the university really should have more covered walkways, especially to the carpark. I got drenched in the rain, Madam.' He smiled. 'It's good I have a change of clothing in my office.'

Dolly glanced outside her window at a grey world and nodded. She had been so engrossed in re-reading Pak's autopsy report and researching poisons that the change in the weather outside had gone unnoticed. The phone rang, blinking lights indicating a long-distance call.

'That will be the British lawyer,' Charlie said, settling into the visitor's chair.

Dolly picked up the receiver, switching to speakerphone once she had verified that Ursula's lawyer was on the line. After exchanging pleasantries with Andrew Galbraith, Dolly asked, 'How much was Ursula Botham worth?'

'Five million sterling pounds,' was the lawyer's cryptic answer.

'How much was left to Professor Graham Botham?' Dolly asked.

Andrew Galbraith's voice was precise with a sad undertone. 'Ursula stipulated in her will that he would receive 50,000 sterling pounds for every year they stayed married. They were married for a little more than ten years, so he is entitled to about half a million sterling pounds. I was extremely sorry to hear of Ursula's death. I knew her since she was a little girl, and I handled all her father's affairs. I will see to it Tom is taken care of as Ursula wanted. Her little son meant the world to her. Bianca is going to Singapore to bring him back, I presume.' A hard note crept into his voice. 'If Graham Botham creates a problem regarding Tom returning to England, Bianca will let me know and I will travel to Singapore to sort out matters. I am the second trustee of Ursula's fortune and one of the executors of her last will and testament.'

'Still, half a million pounds is a lot of money,' Charlie mused after Dolly had finished the call.

Dolly leant back in her chair, thinking hard. 'Graham told us there was no will and therefore he thinks he will receive millions of sterling pounds. He thinks he will receive half of Ursula's fortune so two and a half million pounds. Ursula was going to divorce him, so Graham murdered her to hang on to her fortune. There's a big difference between half a million pounds and two and a half million pounds. Yes, Graham had a motive to murder his wife, but first we must determine whether there was a crime in the first place.'

Charlie rose from his chair. 'Yes, Madam, and Lorna Asquith is also a suspect. She is the poor relation and hankers after Ursula's fortune, so she courts the husband thinking he will get her the fortune if Ursula is killed. Lorna was looking smug when Graham said he and Tom would share Ursula's fortune. Lorna could have poisoned Ursula, but, yeah, she had no motive to poison DW. Okay, Madam, I will go now and expedite Fauzia's transfer. What a pest!'

Dolly nodded, and Charlie went back to his office.

It was still raining outside, the raindrops rattling the glass of the window. Dolly worked quietly inside.

* * *

Dolly met her husband, Joey, at Silver Springs for dinner. Frankie arrived, too, and the meal was filled with talk and laughter. Ash had gone out to have dinner with his girlfriend. For a change, Girlie cooked Filipino food, and the family enjoyed her delicious paella. Uma was nursing a cold and had taken to her bed, electing to have soup and toast on a tray in her room while avidly watching Hindi serials on Zee TV. But feeling better and being naturally garrulous, she came into the living hall and settled herself on her usual divan after she had finished her meal. Girlie hurried over with a mug of Milo for her.

Joey and Frankie retired to the small den off the hall with two whiskys, and Lily and Dolly trooped into the living room, each pecking their mother on her cheek before taking their seats on sofas. Girlie served them steaming mugs of coffee. Sipping her Milo, Uma beamed at her daughters.

'So, was it phosphorus poisoning?' Lily could not contain her excitement as she turned to Dolly.

'Another person has been poisoned?' Uma stared. 'Who? A fellow again?'

'No, a British professor,' Lily said.

Uma nodded sagely at Dolly. 'Pritam is next on the list.' She gave a vicious cackle.

Lily laughed. 'Mummy, if you were mobile and Pritam was murdered, you would be the chief suspect. You sound like the person who wrote the threatening letter to Pritam saying he would be the next to be murdered.'

Dolly said, soberly, 'Ursula Botham was a young mother.' She looked at Lily. 'It seems there is no definitive test for phosphorus poisoning, and one must go by the deterioration of organs and whether the victim had exposure to phosphorus. The forensics team is busy testing Ursula's bottles of Pepto-Bismol in case the poison was in there.' Dolly frowned. 'The chemicals cupboard is locked now, and the students and fellows have to check out the chemicals. We will look at Bill's log. See if anyone signed out phosphorus.'

Lily said, while sipping her coffee, 'I thought it was the solvent cupboard that was locked, and a log made for that. White phosphorus is a solid substance, right. Maybe it is kept separately with other solids.'

Dolly nodded. 'You are right, Lily.' She got busy on her phone while saying, 'I am telling Charlie to make sure all cupboards with chemicals are locked.'

After Dolly had finished texting and was sipping coffee, Lily said, 'There is a similarity between the two poisonings. The poisons are both industrial poisons, and while you would think you could access them in a chemistry laboratory, you can buy antifreeze, which is ethylene glycol, in car shops. And isn't phosphorus the main ingredient in rat poison?'

Dolly jumped up from the sofa in so much excitement that Uma, who was beginning to doze off, sat up, straight. 'Rat poison is kept in the janitor's office. He said so.'

Uma said sleepily, 'Eh, I don't think they use phosphorus in rat poison any more. I forget where I read that. They use something else. But yes, in my time, rat poison was phosphorus. One had to be careful handling it.'

'You could always test the rat poison in Uncle Abdul's office for phosphorus,' Lily suggested, helpfully. She frowned. 'Dolly, how are these two poisonings connected? The chief suspect in DW's murder is Eun-jin Choi, but why would she kill Ursula unless Ursula saw her hanging around Abdul's office with the cup of coffee. And the prime suspect for Ursula's murder is Graham, but why would Graham kill DW?'

Dolly settled back on the sofa. 'Well, there was the case of the Korean girl's suicide in Australia.' Dolly proceeded to tell her mother and sister about DW's email to Kim's father saying that he would confront Graham about the affair. 'DW had started digging into Graham's past. We don't know if DW had an altercation with Graham about Kim's suicide before he was killed. It's possible. We can't rule it out and that makes Graham the chief suspect and connects both murders.'

'It could also be a serial killer, murdering for fun since he has free access to so many poisons,' Uma supplied, before giving a big yawn. 'Girlie, I am sleepy. Make my bed,' she shouted so that Girlie, who was cleaning the kitchen, could hear her.

'Goodnight, Mummy,' Dolly said as Uma went towards her bedroom leaning on Girlie.

The den door opened, and Frankie and Joey appeared. Joey looked at his wife and pointed at his watch. 'Time to go?'

'I have a client visiting early tomorrow morning, so I need to get a move on,' Frankie said. He glanced at Joey. 'It's Nancy. Her case is coming up for a hearing next week, and we need to prepare her testimony.'

Lily pricked up her ears. Nancy must be the physically abused client Frankie was defending and for whom Joey thought he was developing tender feelings. 'Nancy injured her husband?' she asked innocently.

'In self-defence,' Frankie said, hotly. 'He was coming at her with a golf club. She grabbed a kitchen knife and stabbed him. You should see the marks on her body. He abused her for many years. That guy is better dead. But he recovered from his wounds and refuses to divorce Nancy. So he can beat her some more.'

Seeing Frankie make a move towards the front door, Dolly raised her brows at Lily. 'I thought you had moved back to your condo so you can adopt the child from India?'

'I am moving back tomorrow,' Lily smiled at Frankie. 'We both agreed on that.'

When Lily lay down on the bed in her bedroom, she found it difficult to fall asleep. Frankie could be in love with Nancy. How passionately he had defended her! It was all her fault, she thought. She just could not live with Frankie's OCD. She heard the main door opening and heard Ash talking to Girlie. Soon there was silence, but Lily lay awake.

Sunday, 11 September 2011

30

It was a cloudy and windy day when Joey drove Ash to Toa Payoh in the hope of having a chat with the car crash victim and estate cleaner, Johnny Tan. Ash and Joey found Johnny sitting in a small room beneath Devender's apartment complex carpark. They had asked around before being directed by one of the other estate cleaners to this small, dingy room reeking of petrol fumes. Johnny Tan was a slightly built individual with a disproportionately large head covered by wispy hair through which could be seen dark scar marks. He wore black-framed spectacles that slid down his bulbous nose and when shadows darkened his doorway, he peered, myopically, out. He sat on a stool by a desk on which there was the photo of a young man.

'Uncle, can we buy you a cup of tea?' Joey asked, pleasantly, taking in the shoddy bearing of the man and the room.

Johnny pondered. 'I had kopi five minutes ago.' He suddenly smiled showing even white teeth.

'Then a curry puff, maybe?' Joey persisted. 'We go over to the coffee shop?'

'Okie,' Johnny said, obligingly and then added, childishly, 'I like chicken curry puff, not the veggie one.'

Ash had been looking curiously at the photo of a young man on Johnny's desk and now looked up. He noted Johnny had difficulty speaking and seemed to deliberate before articulating words aloud. As they walked to the coffee shop, Ash watched Johnny shuffle along, looking at the ground.

Johnny looked dazedly around him when Joey led him to a chair in the coffee shop, asked him to sit down and went to the stalls in search of chicken curry puffs.

'Uncle, I am sorry about the accident forty years ago,' Ash said, his voice soft.

'Eh?' Johnny asked, looking blankly at Ash when he repeated his statement in a louder voice.

A man from the next table laughed. He was thin and wiry with a foxy look. He said some words in Mandarin to Johnny, who looked frightened and half-rose from his seat in alarm. The man came over and sat down on a chair at the table.

'I am Shiny Lee,' he said, 'air-con repairman. Johnny does not remember. You mean car accident?' he asked of Ash and smiled at Joey, who had joined them. 'I was going to tell your son the car accident took away Johnny's brain.' He became garrulous. 'I lived next door to Johnny in a three-room housing board flat at the time of the accident. My wife was friends with his wife, Mabel.' He looked momentarily sad before continuing, 'Mabel died in the crash.'

Ash frowned and looked at Johnny wolfing down his curry puff. 'Did Johnny own a car? I thought there were three people in the car, Johnny, his wife and their little son.' Ash cast his mind back to the news article about the crash he had read at the National Library.

Shiny nodded. 'Johnny was smart. An engineer. Buy the car on loan. Good thing it was insured. He had many plans, of upgrading to a larger flat, switching his boy's school to a posher one. They remained dreams. He was taking his family out to dinner when the accident happened. We all think Johnny die, too. He hit his head on the steering wheel. His brain was mush. So many operations! No money left. Johnny never got back his brain, eh, Johnny?' Shiny slapped his friend's back, affectionately.

'And the little boy?' Joey asked, surreptitiously slipping a second curry puff on to Johnny's plate. Johnny's eyes gleamed.

'The boy hurt his leg. One operation. Walked with a limp. Nothing more. He was sitting in back with seat belt on. Mabel had no belt on, and what's more, sitting in front seat. She was thrown right out of the car and

another car run her over. Dead on the spot. It was horrible.' Shiny's eyes
flickered with the terror of yesteryear.

'What a tragedy!' Joey said, looking at Johnny, who was paying no
attention to them and eating his second curry puff with gusto.

'Worse. It was a hit and run. The driver of the other car never stop.
But the police track car down. It was a young Indian boy driving that
night, but his family pay their regular driver to take the blame. Rich family.
There was a court case and all. In those days, no car cameras, but the
drivers of the other cars on the road say Johnny make illegal right turn.
He was in the wrong, sure, but Indian boy drunk, too. Never see car
coming or stop. When you belong to rich family, you are never punished.'

'You are punished in a different way,' Ash said softly. He looked
around at the busy coffee shop, his eyes glittering with unshed tears. The
hum of conversation rose and fell around him.

'Mind you, the Indian boy come to see Johnny, later. He had good
job. He give Johnny lots of money. Blood money. Cannot bring Mabel
back.' Shiny patted Johnny on the shoulder.

'What happened to Johnny's son?' Joey sipped his cup of tea,
ruminatively.

Shiny sighed. 'Children, eh? You never know with them. My boy,
now, he is filial, raised a Taoist by my dear wife. When he get married, he
leave our house, but every Sunday, he and his family eat with us. We get to
play with our grandson.' Shiny's smile lit his face.

'And Johnny's son?' Ash prompted.

A shadow fell over Shiny's face. 'The boy was not right in the head
after Mabel die. He loved his Ma. He would not eat and sleep for months.
We did not know what to do. My wife tried to get the little boy to eat. He
cry and cry for his Ma. The boy was sensitive. He was ten years old, but
still wet his bed. Then one day, his Ma's sister come to take him away.
Johnny was in rehab by then. I never see the boy again. Johnny say his
son visits him. He say his son pay Johnny one thousand dollars pocket
money every month. We don't know true or not. Johnny lives alone in
a two-room rental, and we moved to another block. My wife wanted to
meet Johnny's boy, but the boy does not come here. He meet Johnny in
the city, take him out to a posh restaurant for lunch and to kiddie movies
in the theatres. Johnny can take care of his basic needs at home, but that is
it. His brain is gone. Johnny say his son ask him to stop work as soon as he

have steady job and can buy a flat for them. Who knows what to believe? It can be Johnny wishfully thinking. When he lived with his aunt, the boy never come to see his father. So, who knows, eh.'

Johnny had finished his curry puffs and was now looking at the group, contentedly. 'That was good curry puff. I had only one.'

'You had three, actually,' Joey smiled.

Shiny shook his head as he got up. 'The town council give Johnny cleaner job here long ago. He clean well. Mechanical tasks, he can do. Poor Johnny has forgotten to think and him with an engineering degree. All gone to waste in ten seconds. That's life.'

'What a sad story,' Joey observed as he walked with Ash to the carpark. 'Your Dad did give Johnny money, though, and I think Pritam is tormented by the accident.'

'I can well understand that. Poor Uncle Johnny and his son. I hope the son does take Johnny to live with him. Johnny deserves a good break in life.' Ash walked slowly, his mind on his father's past. Ash felt some comfort knowing Johnny had contributed to the accident by making an illegal turn. It had not been all his father's fault.

The sky was darkening, and a sharp wind whipped up. As Joey and Ash got into Joey's car, they saw Johnny shuffling slowly from the coffee shop back to his dingy petrol-fumed room, his eyes peering at the road, a dazed look on his face. Joey revved up his car and it sped away from the brain-damaged lonely man looking forward to his son taking care of him in his old age.

Monday, 12 September 2011

31

The grey morning reflected the sombre mood prevalent in the Singh common room. The students had liked Professor Ursula Botham, and she had been their lecturer in some courses. Latha could not hold back her tears. As rain poured outside, so did a rivulet of tears from her eyes.

'I was about to start a project with her, and she had asked me last week to her office to discuss the project. She had these organic compounds, and I would take their photoelectron spectra. She wanted to discover details of their bonding properties.' Latha gave a big hiccup, and Salma, sitting next to her, patted her shoulder.

CY entered the room with a plastic bag of beverages. He took in Latha's distress and asked softly, 'Tea, Latha?' He gave her a cup as she nodded.

'No, thank you,' Terry, the undergraduate student said, as CY offered him a cup. He shrank away from the proffered beverage, looking frightened.

CY stepped back. 'What's got into you, Terry? I was being friendly. No one told me to buy beverages for everyone when I bought my own.'

Kiong Tan looked up from the journal he had been reading at the desk in the corner and gave a small smile. 'Terry probably thinks there is poison in the coffee.'

CY's face lost colour before he turned beet-root red. 'You think I put poison in your coffee?' he demanded taking a step towards Terry, who hastily pushed his chair back.

Salma said, 'Don't be silly. Terry just doesn't want coffee, right?' She turned angrily to Kiong. 'Stop teasing, Kiong. We are all sad and worried. We have lost two people we know in two weeks. We are all on edge, don't make it worse.'

'Don't bring beverages for others from now on, CY,' Latha advised. 'It's not appreciated, and you'll get hurt.'

Bill Eddington entered the room and the tense atmosphere defused. He looked haggard. He had loved Ursula and could not help reflecting on their friendship in Oxford. How carefree those days had been! 'I knew Ursula well,' he said, sitting on a chair and accepting without hesitation a cup of tea from CY. 'We were at Oxford together, and I was invited quite often to her manor house on the outskirts. I knew her parents well. Then we lost touch after we left Oxford. We reconnected here and I went often for dinner parties at their apartment in the staff quarters. This is a terrible shock. She was a young mother! Poor little Tommy!'

'Was she poisoned, Dr Eddington? Do you know?' Latha asked in a small voice.

Bill's spectacles flashed in the overhead fluorescent lights. His blue eyes were ruminative. 'I went up to their apartment last Saturday, and police officers had cordoned off the flat. So, it was a crime scene. Ursula was too young to die from natural causes. She must have been poisoned like DW. Graham is holed up with his girlfriend, Lorna, in her quarters and Tom is with them.' He looked around, his face anxious. 'We seem to have a serial killer in this department, and the police are clueless as to his identity.'

Kiong looked uncomfortable under CY's accusing gaze. 'Look, CY, I am sorry I said the coffees were poisoned. It was my attempt at a joke. We have all been so sad.'

CY nodded coldly. He turned to Bill. 'I talked to some members of Prof. Ursula's research group. They said she died in her bed of a heart attack. Like DW. Poisoning is hard to detect. I wonder what poison was used this time.' He turned back to Kiong. 'You saw DW's sister-in-law here on the day of his poisoning? Mrs D from the canteen said you set the police on to her.'

Kiong adjusted his spectacles, which were slipping down his nose. He said defensively, 'The constable was showing her photo around and yes, I had seen her outside DW's office right after Bill found him slumped over his desk and gave the alarm. There was a crowd in there and she was loitering outside. She went away, though.'

Salma's eyes were wide. 'But DW must have been poisoned earlier, right? He was slurring his speech when I went in at 1.45 p.m. Did you see this woman then?'

When Kiong shook his head, Latha said, 'The sister-in-law would not know that students put coffee and teacups on Uncle Abdul's desk for teachers. I don't think the sister-in-law murdered DW. It must be a serial killer because who else had a motive to kill both Ursula and DW?'

'A serial killer also has to have some motive. Maybe a grudge against this department?' Salma looked thoughtful.

'Graham Botham had motives for both murders,' Bill whispered and narrated the story of the Korean girl's suicide in Australia and of Ursula's plan to divorce her husband.

Terry said excitedly, 'Have you told the police all this, Bill? I think Professor Graham is the killer. I never liked him, snooty and all.'

Salma interrupted. 'But DW hadn't confronted Prof. Graham about the Korean girl, right. Prof. Graham did not know DW knew about the girl in Australia. So why would he kill DW?'

Bill nodded. 'Maybe, Salma. DW told me about the Korean girl before lunch and then he was poisoned right after lunch. Unless, of course, DW had already spoken about it to Graham and never told me.'

'The police need evidence,' Kiong said, 'before they arrest anyone. It's a pity no one saw anyone with a coffee cup near Abdul's office from from 12 to 1 p.m. the Monday DW was poisoned.'

'We were all having lunch,' Latha said.

There was a whisper. 'I wasn't.' Salma's eyes were wide and scared. 'I was working in the laboratory down the corridor from Uncle Abdul's office.'

'Did you notice anyone in the corridor?' Terry asked, sharply.

Salma looked around at everyone and quickly lowered her eyes. 'Not really. I did go from the lab to the common room to look up something at around 12.45 p.m. When I was returning to the lab, I thought I saw someone near Uncle's office.' Salma's voice trailed off.

'Who?' CY asked in a loud voice.

'He was too far away. I could not make him out; he kept to the shadows.'

Latha sighed. 'At least, it's a man and not a woman. Gosh, Salma, you saw DW's killer!'

'This is where it would have been useful to have a CCTV camera in the corridor,' Bill said and sighed. 'The department will definitely pass the proposal now to have cameras in corridors, common rooms, and offices and to hell with privacy.'

Salma said in a soft voice, 'Yes. I, for one, will feel safer working here with cameras everywhere. It's sure to deter the madman who is wreaking havoc in our department.'

The rain had stopped, but the day continued dark and gloomy.

* * *

Inspector Charles Goh looked appreciatively around his office. His cubicle days were over and now he had an office all to himself as befitting an inspector of police. He also liked the rise in his monthly salary, and he and his wife, Meena, were already planning on taking a holiday in Bali during the December school holidays. The phone on his desk rang. It was Benny Ong.

The pathologist's voice crackled from the other end. 'Inspector, Ursula Botham had liver and kidney necrosis, a failed heart and the phosphate in the blood was elevated. I was liaising with the forensics testing team, and there was a small amount of phosphorus powder in the Pepto-Bismol bottle. Taken together, Inspector, my preliminary findings point to Ursula Botham being poisoned with phosphorus. It's a murder.'

'Which Pepto-Bismol bottle?' Charlie squeaked.

'The one from her office. It is possible she took the poison over several days. I will tell you more after full PM. Bye, Inspector.'

A voice came from the open doorway. 'Anything interesting?' It was Corporal Fauzia Khan, standing there in a smart business suit. Her eyes were shining.

Charlie's face became wooden. 'Your transfer has come through, Fauzia. You can go and join the Serious Sexual Crime Branch today. No need to update me on the Joo Chiat case. There are other officers working on it.'

Fauzia's face became stiff. 'Okay.' She shrugged. Her eyes flashed. 'When Auntie becomes fixated about something, she usually gets her way,' she said, ominously. She added, 'The journos are waiting downstairs to be updated. They hang around the university, too, and they have found out someone else has died.'

'No need for you to say anything,' Charlie said hastily. 'Our department will deal with the journalists. Good luck, Fauzia.'

Charlie gathered up his briefcase, walked to the lobby and waited for the lift to take him to Dolly's office.

* * *

Lily looked glum as she surveyed the contents of the pot boiling on the stove in front of her in the canteen. She had moved to her husband's home in the early hours of Sunday morning. It was hell living with Frankie, she thought, and tears clouded her eyes. As far as she could see, there were no great changes in her husband's habits, and she thought he was wasting money on the counsellor. She now had second thoughts about adopting a baby as she did not think Frankie would change his habits even with its presence.

Her phone beeped, and she glanced at her sister's terse text. Lily's eyes gleamed. Dolly had just informed her of the pathologist's findings. Lily sniffed. Not a word of thanks from her sister, just the message. After all, she had provided pointers to the phosphorus poisoning like garlic odour on the breath.

Ashikin was glancing into the pots on the stove and gave a sigh. She looked at Lily and smiled. 'My food is all gone, Lily. We are making good money?'

Lily nodded and smiled. 'Thanks to you, Ashikin. We have so many more customers now because of your Malay food. Where are you going?'

Ashikin looked shifty. She cleared her throat and said, 'Having my lunch with Naheed, Lily. I buy lunch from her stall.' She giggled, nervously. 'Keeps her happy, I think. We share distant relatives, so, yeah, we have become friends.'

'Good for you,' Lily said, smiling insincerely. She had been looking forward to having lunch with Ashikin.

Vernon sauntered into the stall, his bad eye rolling madly. 'The police are back in the science department searching the laboratories and staff offices. Poor British lady did not die natural, Mrs D. The Singh gang are frightened. Latha has decided to stay home until your sister solves the murders, Mrs D!'

Lily nodded. 'Yes, Dolly texted me that Ursula Botham was poisoned by phosphorus. The poison was in the Pepto-Bismol bottle in her office.'

Angie, who had been cleaning the counters at the back, gave a small scream. 'Oh, the poor lady! Taking sips of poison and thinking it was helping her ulcers get better. Mrs D, this murderer is very scary!'

Lily nodded. 'The phosphorus must have been taken from one of the chemical cupboard shelves. It is easy to commit a murder in a chemistry laboratory, so many industrial poisons at one's disposal. Note that two different poisons were used for the two victims. The chemistry lab is a murderer's treasure trove.'

Angie shivered. 'I would not like to work there.' She jerked her head at the lunchtime crowd. 'The husband is back at work, not look sad. There he is with Dr Eddington having lunch. He is having our butter chicken special.'

Lily glanced at Graham. Other than appearing untidier than ever, he did not look different. Bill looked sadder than Graham, Lily thought. They were deep in conversation with Graham gesticulating with his hands.

'How is it living with Mr Frankie?' Angie whispered, conspiratorially. Vernon was busy washing dishes in the sink at the back.

'Terrible.' Lily did not bother to whisper. 'He is still the same and it was a bad idea about the adoption. Nothing is going to change.'

'Aw, don't break Mr Frankie's heart again, Mrs D! I was having a beer with him last night. He is so excited about Baby Kennedy. We are going to be Daddies together.' Vernon had come over, anxiously.

'Look, V, you don't have to live with him. You don't know what it's like,' Lily said, frowning at her assistant with annoyance.

'Considering our baby keeps Angie and me together, I say a baby is a blessing.' Vernon frowned darkly at his wife who glared back.

'Wait, what happened to all the love?' Lily demanded. 'You two are still not getting along?'

Angie showed her back to Vernon and resumed cleaning the counters. 'Yeah, Vernon drinks a lot. Money wasted. Why you think he go over to Mr Kennedy's all the time? To drink beer together.'

Before Lily could speak, Vernon strode out of the stall, his shoulders stiff. Lily watched him saunter over to the drinks stall.

'Oh, I didn't know he has a drinking problem,' Lily said. 'Frankie, though, was always a hard drinker from even before marriage. Never listens to me to limit his alcohol intake, and I am sure he will die from liver cirrhosis. Come, Angie, let's have lunch, the crowd has thinned out. Tell me everything.'

The two women helped themselves liberally to butter chicken and biryani, and set the trays on a table right in front of their stall so that they could serve any customers wanting a late Indian lunch.

When Lily had finished her lunch and had started sipping her sweet lassi drink, her mobile rang. It was Dolly and her voice was frantic.

'Ash is at Silver Springs. Go there and bring him to Temasek Hospital. Pritam lost consciousness in his office and was found by one of his students. I have just been informed that he is now in ICU and in a coma. I am going there. Please bring Ash!' The line was cut off.

Lily gave the news to Angie and rushed to the carpark. She got into her car and sped towards Silver Springs condo. Her heart wept for Ash. He loved his father, and this time Lily was sure, something was terribly wrong with Pritam.

32

The harsh fluorescent lights of the hospital waiting room beamed down on the Das family and Cheryl. The ICU doctor did not have a prognosis since the medical staff could not find out what was wrong with Professor Pritam Singh. The doctor agreed with Lily that Pritam's stage of Parkinson's Disease would not induce a coma. Lily looked at Dolly who was comforting a visibly shaken Ash. Beside him, Cheryl sat weeping, her stomach bulging in front of her. Lily hastened to comfort Pritam's wife.

'I don't know what is wrong with Preet,' Cheryl sobbed, her make-up smudged and her face looking old and worn. 'He is forgetful, has strange pains and numbness all over his body. I almost thought he was in the early stages of dementia when the doctor diagnosed Parkinson's Disease. But why did he slide into a coma? He is so ill and it's frustrating when the doctors don't have a diagnosis. I don't know how much of this I can take.'

Lily agreed. Ever the practical one, she said, 'Are you staying on your own, Cheryl? Is there someone you can go to? Your mother, perhaps?'

The tears continued to flow. 'My parents are dead, and I am an only child.'

Lily thought fast. 'You can stay with my mother at Silver Springs, Cheryl, given your condition. You can move into my room. It is empty as I have moved back with Frankie. Cheryl, you should not be alone.

We all want the baby safely delivered. Ash will keep updating you on Pritam. Sounds like something you may want to consider?'

Looking at Lily gratefully, Cheryl nodded. Dolly, who had overheard the conversation, glared at her sister, but Lily pretended not to see the fire shooting from Dolly's eyes. Suddenly, an idea struck Lily. She quickly got up and went over to her sister.

'What with the murders at the university, do you think Pritam was poisoned as well?' Lily's mind was whirring like a busy machine. 'Ursula did not expire from the poisoning immediately; she took time to die from the effects of the poison. Could it be possible there is poison in Pritam's body?'

Dolly gave Lily an odd look. 'I am a bit suspicious,' she admitted, her hand still on Ash's shoulder as he sat on the next chair with his head buried in his hands. 'But not all poisons show up in the blood. We would have to know the type of poison that was used. I can ask the doctors to check for phosphorus and ethylene glycol, the poisons used so far, but if it is attempted murder, this killer is one smart person, Lil. He uses different poisons every time, almost as though he were experimenting with human life.'

'A psychopath!' Lily was nodding her head. 'When you question Graham, bring Pritam into the conversation. After all, they were competing for the headship, right? Graham kills Ursula for her money and Pritam for a headship. And poisons DW to stop him from spreading the scandal that would affect his headship candidature. Graham's your man.'

'Killing for money is a sound motive but to kill for a headship?' Dolly looked dubious. 'Anyway, I will grill Graham thoroughly, and I will also have a chat with the present HOD.' She looked shrewdly at Lily. 'You have invited Cheryl to stay at Mummy's house. I think you should ask Mummy first whether Cheryl can stay there. It's *her* house.'

Lily bit her lip. 'Yes, I think I should have done that. But I already invited Cheryl to stay. I was only trying to help.'

Dolly shrugged. 'Mummy would probably say yes though I would not bet on it given her equation with Pritam. With Cheryl at Silver Springs, someone has to supervise Girlie and the running of the house.'

'I was thinking of moving back for a while,' Lily said innocently. 'I can sleep with Mummy in her room on a sofa bed.'

Dolly laughed. 'Oh, now I know why you invited Cheryl. Frankie is getting too hard to handle. Lily, you just moved back with him! Don't escape from your marriage issues by moving back and forth between homes. Stay put at your husband's house or you will be facing a divorce soon.' Dolly looked seriously at her sister, who avoided her eyes.

Lily tossed her head and went to a corner to call her mother. Soon she came back, smiling.

'Mummy was shocked about Pritam being in ICU. She is worried for Cheryl's baby and said Cheryl can stay with us at Silver Springs. I will take Cheryl to her home, let her pack some clothes, and go home, myself, and pack my own suitcase.'

Lily began walking towards a tearful Cheryl, pretending not to hear Dolly's warning, 'Don't forget to call Frankie and update him.'

Rain clouds had gathered in the sky and the first drops fell as Lily shepherded Cheryl into her car. Soon the landscape was a hazy blur as the rain lashed down in torrents.

* * *

Abdul was locking his cupboards up for the night in his small office. Glancing at the door, his eyes widened in fright. Inspector Charles Goh stood in the doorway.

His eyes narrowed, Charlie said in Malay, 'You mentioned you keep rat poison here. Where is it?'

The whites of Abdul's eyes showed. 'We hear rumours. The British professor was poisoned. And the janitor is the killer. He poisoned her with rat poison, is it?'

'We don't know who killed Professor Botham,' Charlie said unhelpfully. 'We did identify the poison used to kill her. And we need to test the rat poison you keep here to see if this poison is the same. Come on, man, where is the rat poison?'

Abdul jingled a bunch of keys in Charlie's face. 'I lock up the rat poison in the cupboard. The keys are always with me, even at home. There is no way to get to the poison other than to force the lock.' He ambled over to a small cupboard, selected a key, fit it into the lock and opened the cupboard. He took out a small tin with a skull and crossbones sign. He looked at the cupboard lock and shook his head.

'The lock is not broken,' the janitor said, his eyes triumphant.

Charlie took the tin from Abdul and said, 'I will take this for testing. Thank you. Here is the receipt saying the tin is with the police.'

Charlie took a piece of paper out of his pocket and passed it to Abdul.

'I didn't kill anyone!' Abdul cried in a shrill voice.

But Charlie was already on his way to the lifts and paid no attention.

* * *

Ash was trying to be helpful to Cheryl as she sat on the lounger in the living hall of his grandmother's unit at Silver Springs Condo, sipping green tea. To obtain Cheryl's preferred green tea, Ash had to go to the supermarket and pay for the atrociously priced High Mountain brand of Chinese green tea. All the way back home, he worried whether he should ask Cheryl for the money for the tea, and after intense procrastination, decided he would pay for it out of his pocket money, hoping fervently she would not send him to buy more items.

Girlie was painting Cheryl's toenails as she sprawled on the lounger while Lily sweated over the kitchen stove. Ash decided Cheryl was vain and spoilt. After settling herself in Lily's room and plonking herself down on the lounger, she had not once mentioned her ailing husband. Her tears had miraculously dried up from the moment Lily had invited her to stay in Uma's flat.

Ash could not help asking, 'Do you have a domestic helper at home to help you with chores?' He could not imagine Cheryl doing housework.

Cheryl pouted. 'Preet said we could hire a full-time helper in my ninth month of pregnancy. You know your father is a miser, Ash. But of course, I do have home help. I have a part-time maid who cleans the house. We eat from outside.' She leant forward conspiratorially. 'I heard you have talked to Preet's niece, Devender. So, your father killed someone in a hit-and-run, is it? It was so long ago. Why does he keep having nightmares about it now? It's almost as though someone or something has triggered those memories.'

There was the sound of a key in the lock and Dolly arrived, perspiring furiously and looking tired. Ash jumped up to go to the door and give his mother a hug. Dolly looked at her son, who was not demonstrative by nature, in surprise.

Cheryl's voice piped up. 'Hi, Dolly! Do you have any news on whether Preet was poisoned?'

Dolly shook her head and sat down on the sofa. She frowned at Girlie painting Cheryl's toenails. Girlie caught her look.

'Oh, Ma'am, I will be done in five minutes and then I will get a cup of tea for you,' Girlie fawned.

Dolly asked sharply, 'Are you paying Girlie for the pedicure, Cheryl?' She noted the bowl of water and pedicure tools on a cloth near Girlie.

Cheryl smiled. 'Yes, the going rate, forty dollars for a full pedi.'

Dolly's voice was cold. 'If you pay Girlie any money, I will report her to the Ministry of Manpower for working and earning money in jobs outside her scope of work in this house. You will receive no money for this, Girlie, understand?'

Cheryl sat up on the lounger looking frightened. 'Oh, but she has been working so hard on my toes and feet, see how clean they are. It would be a pity not to pay her for her hard work. She will do a manicure for me tonight as well.'

'Girlie can do your nails, Cheryl, no problem with that. She is a helpful person,' Dolly said, sweetly, her eyes fiery. 'She cannot receive any remuneration, that is all.'

Girlie hurriedly finished her task, her face red. 'It's done, Ma'am,' she said in a faint voice. 'No money needed, Ma'am. I go clean the kitchen and the common toilet tonight, Ma'am Cheryl. I have no time to do your manicure, so sorry.'

Dolly smiled thinly at Cheryl's dismay and said, 'Girlie, fetch me a cup of tea and help Lily in the kitchen. Why aren't you doing that?'

'Vernon have fight with Angie and come here, Ma'am. He will sleep on the sofa bed in the living room tonight. He is helping Ma'am cook dinner.'

Dolly raised her eyebrows. 'More than one couple fighting with their spouse and bedding down here then.' She grinned at Lily as she came into the living hall. Her grin turned to a frown when she saw Lily dressed in a green silk saree with a gold border. 'Why aren't you changed into your housecoat, Lily? I feel hot just looking at you.'

'I will be going out soon. I am meeting Frankie later for a snack.'

Dolly nodded and turned to Cheryl. 'Pritam was having neurological symptoms for how long?'

Cheryl frowned. 'Two months? Yes, it would be around that. It started as short-term memory loss. He would forget to take his hypertension medicine and keep repeating sentences. He was foggy-brained, too. I thought it was stress. He is working hard to publish articles in prestigious journals as he is under heavy scrutiny. You know, for the headship.' Cheryl looked proud.

Dolly grunted. 'Let us hope he comes out of the coma.'

'About a month ago, the nightmares started and for about two weeks, he had severe depression. He even talked about taking an overdose to end it all.' Cheryl's voice trembled and Ash looked distressed. 'The funny thing was that when he was at the hospital undergoing tests for Parkinson's Disease, he was alert, jolly, his old self. After he returned to work, all his neurological symptoms returned.'

'Strange,' Lily observed. 'Intermittent symptoms.'

Cheryl looked askance at Ash. 'Did you ask Devender about mental problems in Pritam's family?'

Ash said shortly, 'She has not heard of any.'

Lily interrupted, 'Okay, dinner is ready. Girlie has laid the table. It's simple Indian fare today. Fried rice, lentils, spiced cauliflower and a simple chicken curry.'

'Your simple chicken curry is full of cream,' Dolly grumbled good-naturedly, as her stomach rumbled in anticipation.

They trooped into the dining room and sat down. Vernon appeared from the kitchen with dishes in his hands.

'V, Girlie will serve us dinner. You come on and sit down. Have a good meal. It will clear your brain and make you realize that running away from a marriage is not a good thing,' Lily scolded. 'Especially when your wife is pregnant.'

Dolly laughed. 'Look who's talking!'

A breeze blew into the room billowing out the curtains. It was a sombre meal for everyone. Their thoughts were on Pritam hovering on the threshold of death.

At Temasek Hospital, a nurse quietly changed Pritam's intravenous drip and checked the heart monitor. She went to the nurse's station and wrote 'no change' beside Pritam's name on the patient log.

33

It had been more than ten years since he had last met Bianca Asquith, Bill Eddington thought, as he sat at a corner table in Orchard Road's Marriott Café with the tired, jet-lagged Englishwoman and her wayward niece, Lorna Asquith. The clock's hand was moving to eight and Lorna was on her third helping from the restaurant's buffet station. Bianca, despite her haggard appearance, still managed to convey her anger and displeasure at Lorna. Bianca ate sporadically from a breadbasket and a bowl of soup, while Bill fiddled with the chicken rice on his plate. The restaurant was moderately crowded and snatches of laughter and conversation from other diners interrupted Bill's thoughts. The air between the two women tingled with such tension that Bill felt he was a spectator in a silent duel of wills. Bianca broke the silence.

'Do you intend to marry Graham, Lorna?' Her voice was raspy and hoarse, like a forgotten, disused harpsichord. 'Ursula told me you made a beeline for him as soon as you landed in Singapore. It is one thing to be cuckolded with a stranger and another with one's own cousin. Don't tell me you are in love with him, Lorna.'

Lorna greedily finished the shrimp scampi on her plate and glanced at her aunt out of cool green eyes tinged with a shadow of doubt. Her long auburn hair fell over her shoulders in waves and in a plain black frock, she looked a thinner version of the screen legend Greer Garson.

'Would it be so unthinkable for me to be in love with Graham, Aunt Bee?' She raised a pencilled eyebrow, her eyes wide.

'For one, he was the husband of your cousin, a married man with a child. You seem to have given no thought to your nephew, Tom? You were doing your best to break up his parents' marriage!'

Lorna laughed, and it was a hollow sound. 'Come on, Aunt Bee! You know as well as I do, love had died between those two if it ever existed in the first place. In Australia, he was deeply in love with a shoe heiress, and it was the thought of Tom having to go through a break-up that stopped Graham from filing for divorce. He told me he vowed to himself that if he ever fell in love again, he would leave his marriage and co-parent Tom, not waste his life tied to Ursula. Well, I came along and yes, Aunt Bee, I think I will marry him now. He is a widower and free to marry whoever he pleases.'

'Did you kill Ursula?' The sentence sprung out like a slingshot. Bianca Asquith now leant back, her soup and bread finished. The shot struck home. Lorna dropped her fork to the floor with a clatter. A waiter quickly picked it up and rushed to the kitchen to get a clean set of cutleries.

Her face pale, Lorna squeaked, 'How can you say such a thing, Aunt Bee? Who told you Ursula was murdered?'

Bianca seemed to have regained her energy, the jet lag was passing. Her voice gaining strength, she said, 'Ursula was too young to die a natural death. You are the focal point of a love triangle. Yes, I am sure the police officers consider you a suspect, Lorna.'

Lorna's mouth twitched, and she asked shrilly, 'Bill, is this true?'

Bill's appetite was gone; the chicken rice remained untouched on his plate. When Bianca requested they have dinner at Marriott Café, he had agreed as he had known Bianca from his Oxford days with Ursula. He hardly imagined Lorna would be at the dinner table, his role that of a mediator. He said in a tired tone, 'I don't know about Ursula. But a Korean scientist in our department, DW, was murdered. Poisoned.'

Bianca sat up, straight, her eyes flashing. 'My daughter is dead at forty. It is tragic. She was brilliant and had so much to live for. She was a loving mother, and my grandson has been left motherless.' A tear trickled down Bianca's withered powdered cheek. 'Granted you and Ursula had a bad childhood history, Lorna, it's still not an excuse to have an affair with your own nephew's father. Although five years younger than Ursula, you were always after her boyfriends, even Bill.' Her face lightened as Bill shifted uncomfortably in his chair. 'Lorna, you were jealous of Ursula's wealth and brains. Your bad upbringing is due to your mother, of course. Polly Asquith was a barmaid and God knows why your father ever married her.'

Lorna stood up, sparks flying from her eyes. Her thin lips trembled. 'How dare you belittle my mother? Money is not everything. My parents loved each other and still do. Don't bring my mother into this.'

'Then why were you always coveting what Ursula had?' Bianca demanded. 'You should have been happy and satisfied with the love your parents gave you. You were after money, weren't you? And so was your mother, forever sending you to stay with us during your school holidays. To see if you could get a slice of the pie. Let me tell you one thing, young woman. You can marry Graham, but he is not inheriting Ursula's fortune. My daughter made a will leaving her wealth to Tom. You can kiss goodbye to all the fortune you were dreaming of grasping by murdering my daughter!'

Lorna gave a stifled scream and rushed out of the restaurant. She tripped over the carpet and would have fallen if not for the steadying hands of one of the waiters.

Bill looked after Lorna's retreating form and sighed. 'Bianca, we don't know yet that Ursula was murdered.'-

'Then how did she die?' Bianca said, her eyes shards of blue ice. 'Lorna hated Ursula though my daughter tried to be nice to her when they were children. If I were the police, I would look at Lorna's movements and search her home and office for poison. You, yourself, said someone else in the department was poisoned. So was my daughter, I'm sure. Lorna has the cold heart of a killer, Bill.'

'If Ursula was murdered, Graham and Lorna both had motives,' Bill agreed. 'Yes, Bianca, the police are aware of Graham's attachment to Lorna. In fact, when Ursula was ill and dying, Graham was staying at Lorna's quarters. The Korean scientist who was killed was my office mate, a postdoctoral fellow like myself. He was killed with a chemical poison.'

'You mean a serial killer could be on the loose at the university? Whom did the Korean gentleman work for?' Bianca's eyes were round.

'Graham.'

Bianca smiled thinly. 'Then Graham is the murderer. If you dig deep enough, you will find Graham had quarrelled with his postdoc or had a grudge against him.'

'Or DW knew something that had the potential to damage Graham's reputation,' Bill agreed. 'Graham thought he would inherit Ursula's wealth, half at least. He thought Ursula had left no will. He told me this when I had lunch with him.'

Bianca's eyes sparkled. 'He is wrong. My daughter was not so foolish. She did make a will and it will be probated. Graham only gets some money. Tom gets the bulk of Ursula's fortune. You are not going to leave, are you, Bill? I am feeling ravenous. I want to sample the buffet. You will have to see me home. I am staying at Ursula's quarters, and you stay nearby, don't you?'

Bill sat back and sighed. He looked at Bianca peering into the dishes at the buffet station and felt tears prick his eyes. Her family was not mourning Ursula, but he was. His thoughts roamed into the comforting realm of the past when he and Ursula had gone for walks and laughed together at Port Meadow, a beautiful park in Oxford.

Tuesday, 13 September 2011

34

The day was gloomy and overcast outside, but the chandelier in the dining room of the Silver Springs unit shone brightly on the family gathered there for breakfast. Lily looked askance at Cheryl wolfing down eggs, bacon and sausages, her face fresh and shining. Girlie, bringing in more fried sausages, wiped the grin off her face on seeing Lily's stern glance. Girlie tossed her head in defiance. A pregnant woman needed to eat for two, she thought, as she offered a second helping of sausages to Cheryl. Ash seemed preoccupied, deep in his thoughts.

'When do you go back to camp, Ash?' Lily asked. She worried for Ash. He was close to his father and was taking his illness badly. The same could not be said of Cheryl after settling in at Silver Springs.

Ash snapped out of his reverie. 'Next week, Mashi. I am so worried for Dad.' His voice trembled.

'We must hope for the best,' Lily soothed, swatting away Girlie's offer of more scrambled eggs.

Uma, sitting hunched over her cereal, looked up. She cleared her throat. 'Cheryl!'

Cheryl nearly jumped out of her chair. It was obvious she had been concentrating on her food, her mind elsewhere. 'Yes, Auntie?'

'Do you have relatives or friends you could stay with next week? Joey will be abroad, and Dolly is coming to stay here.'

Cheryl opened her eyes wide, a piece of sausage speared on her fork. 'Ash will be leaving for camp next week, right. I can move into the guest bedroom and Dolly can bed down with Lily. Who knows how long they are going to keep Pritam at the hospital?' She popped the sausage into her mouth and chewed enthusiastically.

Ash laid down his knife and fork. He had lost his appetite. 'If Dad makes it out of the hospital, that is. He is in critical condition.'

Lily's eyes shone with fleeting dislike as she glanced at Cheryl, and her mother coughed. 'Ash doesn't go back to camp till the end of next week, and Dolly is arriving this weekend. Dolly is stressed over the university murder case, and she is worried about Pritam, too. After all, he is her ex. I would really like to have her stay with us.' Cheryl had got on Uma's nerves in the short time she had been staying at her house.

Cheryl's face puckered. She laid down her cutlery and said apologetically, 'I really don't have any friends or family I could stay with. I am so worried about Pritam. What if he dies?' she wailed.

Uma sighed and clamped her mouth shut giving Lily a glare, annoyed that her daughter's good nature had landed them with an annoying guest at a worrying time.

Ash was speaking on the phone to his mother. After he had switched off his mobile, he turned to Lily. 'Dad has some physics journals in his office at the university he said I could borrow. I am thinking of applying for the physics honours programme at Temasek after my NS is done. I was asking Mama if it was all right to visit his office this morning? I was wondering whether it was locked. Mama said the staff are keeping their offices locked because of the murders. She said to get the keys from a janitor called Abdul.'

'Abdul is a nice guy,' Lily smiled. 'His office is at the end of the second floor of the science building.'

Ash nodded and rose. 'Right. I will go to the university after, ahem, I run an errand.'

Uma cackled loudly and observed, 'Ash, you can tell us you are going to see this girl. There's no need to be shy. Now, whatshername? Girlie?'

Girlie, who was solicitously serving fruits to Cheryl, looked up and sniggered. 'Amita Singh, Auntie.'

Lily smiled at her nephew. 'Is it serious between you two?'

Ash went red and muttered, 'No, of course not. We are friends, that's all.'

Cheryl looked up from her fruits and smiled conspiratorially. 'We will speak later, Ashok. I'll give you some pointers on dating.'

Ash did not meet her eyes and muttered, 'Bye.' He went over to his grandmother and pecked her cheek, bringing a beaming smile to her old face.

After Ash left, Lily rose and went to her mother's room to get dressed. She wished she was back in her old room and Cheryl was not occupying it. She hoped Cheryl would take the hint that she was unwelcome and go home, then she would have her sister with her in her old room and look forward to long gossiping sessions.

Angie had become so good at frying pratas, she nowadays single-handedly saw to the Indian breakfast at the stall and Lily could afford to come in to work only to cook her lunch specials. Lily went to her mother's bathroom to take a long hot shower.

* * *

Lily was surprised, on entering the canteen later, to see her sister eating nasi lemak at a table with Ashikin in attendance.

Dolly smiled at Lily, the tinge of worry never leaving her eyes. 'I need to do some interviews early, Lily, so I decided to breakfast here. I was telling Ashikin how much I love her coconut rice.'

Ashikin smiled and said, 'Thank you, Dolly. Taken your breakfast?' She turned to Lily.

'Yes, but I will have a cup of coffee. What about you, Ashikin?' Lily asked.

'Oh, I will take breakfast with Naheed, she comes early to work just for my nasi lemak, she says.' Ashikin gave a tinkling laugh and turned to leave.

Lily's face was dark as she sat down at Dolly's table with kopi she had bought at Uncle Wang's stall. 'I'm afraid Naheed will poach Ashikin from my stall. They are so buddy-buddy.' She shrugged and looked at her sister. 'How is the case going? I cannot get rid of the feeling Pritam may have been poisoned. Look at the department's history. A postdoctoral scientist and a professor were murdered, Pritam was next.'

Dolly said, 'We are not close to solving those two murders. Do you think there are two murderers? And after the second murder, I can't help wondering if there is a serial killer in the department.'

'You mean Eun-jin killed her brother-in-law and Graham Botham murdered his wife?' Lily asked. She took a long sip of her kopi. 'Maybe. But Eun-jin may have an alibi for the time DW was poisoned. If Pritam was poisoned as well, I think Graham Botham is fitting the murderer's profile. He is the only one with motives for all the poisonings. Serial killer? Hmm. What makes you think so, Doll?'

Dolly immediately said, 'One of the traits of a serial killer is that he seeks thrills and so murders people without remorse. I've always thought the university killer is brazen, going about his business in broad daylight, showing how clever he is not to be caught.'

Lily looked doubtful. 'Usually, killers have concrete motives or kill for revenge, greed or love. Graham Botham does have motive. He is greedy for Ursula's money, and he is ambitious and wants the post of Head of Department. And may have poisoned Pritam.'

Dolly said, 'DW emailed Kim's father saying he would talk to Graham about Kim's suicide. From that email, Charlie tracked the father down and gave him a call in Seoul. Kim's father said he had not received any mail from DW. He checked his computer again and found DW's mail in his spam filter. Kim's father told Charlie Kim had told him via a phone call that she was in love with a chemistry professor called Graham Botham. The father had cautioned his daughter not to go through with this alliance, that it would be a recipe for disaster to date a married man with a son. Kim apparently agreed on the phone to stick to her boyfriend. But, without her father's knowledge, she broke up with her Korean boyfriend. When Kim killed herself, the father spoke to the boyfriend and to Kim's dorm-mate and both confirmed Kim had been pursuing a married professor. Her suicide letter said she was dying for love and by her own hand. She did not name anyone, so the Australian police closed the case.'

Lily was shaking her head. 'You have a serial cheater and a serial murderer, and they may be one and the same!'

Dolly giggled. 'Evidence! We need it.' She looked at her watch. 'I think we can rule Eun-jin Choi out as the murderer; she really did not have any motive to kill Ursula. The murderer is either Graham or a serial killer. It's important to build the murderer's psychological profile.' Dolly finished her rice and chicken and began eating the *ikan bilis* with pickle. 'A serial killer targets certain types of victims. While Ursula and Pritam are professors, DW was a fellow, no commonality.' She took a sip of her hot milk tea.

Lily nodded and her eyes shone with excitement. 'In a university, many people can have grudges. There are disgruntled students who may have been rusticated, like Manjunath Reddy. There are fellows who lost their fellowships because their professors wanted someone else. And there are professors who were denied tenure.'

'But not getting tenure and early curtailment of fellowships are part and parcel of academic life, Lil,' Dolly objected. 'It's hard to imagine someone roaming around poisoning people for that. To give the department a bad name? Stop student enrolments, maybe?' Dolly pondered. She had finished her meal and was drinking her tea.

Lily said, 'If I were you, I would ask the chemistry HOD if he can think of anyone having a bad grudge against the department in general.'

Dolly sighed. 'Poisoning cases are hard to solve. Supt Dragon Lady has been a bit quiet and that is suspicious. It was not easy for her when the DAC forced her to promote me. Her spy niece is gone from our department, but I am uneasy. Supt wants me out, Lily. And I need to solve this high-profile case to be in the DAC's good books.' Her tea had cooled, and she began gulping it down.

'Don't worry about your job, Dolly. The Singapore Police Force is known to look after its officers; retrenchment is rare. I wish Cheryl had somewhere else to stay,' Lily sighed. 'I know you'll stop coming to see Mummy because of Cheryl. We used to chat together about your last case and that's how we solved it.' She gave her sister a smile. 'At least, you will be at Silver Springs next week while Joey is away.' She finished the last of her kopi.

Dolly rose from her seat. 'Well, I'm off to speak to the chemistry HOD, Lil. See you later!'

Lily looked at her sister making her way to the building where the faculty had their offices. She frowned at Ashikin and Naheed giggling together over their long breakfast, before entering her stall to prepare the lunch specials with Angie and Vernon.

35

Dr Michael Wong, Head of the Department of Chemistry, was a man with a head of silver hair, a pleasant smile and bright eyes behind gold-rimmed granny glasses. His face was sombre as he seated Dolly in the visitor's chair. She glimpsed the sea through the windows of his twentieth-floor office.

'Dolly, good to see you again, though under such sad circumstances,' Mike said. While married to Pritam Singh, Dolly often accompanied her husband to parties at Michael Wong's spacious bungalow. 'Ursula was one of our brightest stars. Her research skills were excellent and such a well-liked teacher, too. She was doing ground-breaking research in natural products.' His eyes sharpened. 'Are you sure she was poisoned?'

Dolly nodded. 'Yes, with white phosphorus. The pathologist confirmed it. We tested the janitor's rat poison tin, and the rat poison did not contain phosphorus. It contained another chemical. So, the white phosphorus probably came from the inorganic chemistry laboratory shelf. Professor Singh's lab, for example. Professor Ursula suffered from peptic ulcers and there was always a bottle of Pepto-Bismol on her office desk. The poison was in there. She had been ingesting it over several days.'

Professor Wong looked shocked. 'The solvent cupboard was kept locked after Pak's poisoning. I wish similar precautions had been taken then for the cupboard containing solids and powders.' He seated himself in his swivel chair. 'Some tea or coffee for you, Dolly?'

Dolly said, 'Thanks, no, I just had breakfast. Can you shed any light on professional rivalries? Did Ursula Botham have enemies?'

Mike frowned. 'This is an academic institution and a research facility. We do chemical research, and each professor has their own area of expertise. We apply for funding for our research proposals so there is, in general, healthy competition for these funds. A professor who has published more research work will have a better chance of securing funds. Ursula was among the top five in our department with extensive research papers. She had recently secured funding for research work that would have entailed a collaboration with Dr Pritam Singh. Ursula's new research funding involved half a million dollars from Galaxy Pharmaceuticals, a big haul for the department. She would have been studying compounds that occur naturally but have potential as drugs and for that, she needed to study their electronic structural properties, hence the collaboration with Pritam who runs the photoelectron spectral analysis laboratory. As far as I know, no other professor was in contention for that funding.'

Smoothing his hair, Mike continued, 'Ursula was well-liked in the department. She was friendly with both staff and students. Look for a personal angle, Superintendent, for I do not think it was a work-related murder.'

'Which brings me to Dr Graham Botham,' Dolly said, promptly. 'I understand that he is in contention for the headship.'

Professor Mike Wong smiled, thinly. 'The headship is a rotating position, and yes, my time is up next year. The staff all have a vote, including me. There are two candidates in the running, Professor Graham Botham and Professor Pritam Singh. I don't see, though, what that has to do with Ursula's death.'

'Probably nothing. We are covering all angles. Are you aware of any tensions in their marriage, Professor Wong? Or was Ursula a hindrance to Graham securing the headship?'

'Graham is never going to get the headship,' Mike said, hotly, his eyes glowing behind the granny glasses. 'See, we look for stability, too. Pritam has been working here for years and we all know him. The older professors understand what tenure under his headship will entail. Graham is new.

He is full of ideas but lacks longevity in the department and a certain calmness, which in my opinion, is the department head's main asset.'

'If Pritam was out of the way, then Graham would secure the headship?' Dolly raised her eyebrows.

Professor Mike Wong's face saddened. 'If Pritam was no longer working here, then yes, Graham would secure the headship. Graham heads the Surface Science section, which is our pride and joy. He brings in more than a million dollars in funding every year and the electronics industries use his laboratory to do testing for large fees. His research is lucrative for the department. More than Pritam's, but overall, Pritam is the best candidate in my opinion for the headship. It will go to the vote. We will see whom the staff want.'

Dolly swallowed a lump in her throat. On the fabric of her mind was the fear of her ex-husband dying. 'Mike, a fellow and a professor from this department have been murdered. We can't connect the two murders in the sense we can't find a suspect who had a solid motive to commit both murders from a personal angle. We must look into the idea of a serial killer with a grudge against this department.'

Mike Wong's voice was sharp. 'What kind of grudge?'

Dolly looked candidly into the his eyes. 'Loss of tenure, loss of a fellowship, rusticated students, you get the picture, Mike. If you can think of any such person or a list of people, we can further our enquiries into the murders.'

Mike's face was white. 'Academic life, like others, has its ups and downs, but surely murder is a drastic step. Loss of tenure is part and parcel of academic life. Surely it's not cause to go around killing people in the department and give it a bad name?' His voice trembled. 'If you can't catch the murderer, Dolly, our student enrolment will suffer.'

'Mike, think about what I said. If anyone comes to mind with a big grudge against the department, let me know. Better still, give us a list of professors who lost tenure in the last five years, fellows whose fellowships were terminated early, and students who were expelled. You are right, a normal person would not be a serial killer. Serial killers are all mentally impaired, Mike, you know that.'

Mike looked blankly at the table, nodding. At least three professors were refused tenure recently, he thought. The ghost of a smile flitted across his face, and he looked up at Dolly. 'Now if you asked me if Graham wished Pritam dead, I would have to think about it. Pritam has not been poisoned, has he?' His voice shook. 'He is on medical leave and in the hospital. I thought it was something to do with Parkinson's Disease?'

'We don't know if Pritam was poisoned, Professor Wong, we hope not. He is in ICU as you know. He collapsed in his office.'

Mike Wong nodded and looked at Dolly shrewdly. Fond memories of dinner parties at the Singh condo apartment came to him and he said, 'Dolly, this must be a difficult time for you. Alison and I extend our sympathies to you. How is Ashok holding up?'

Dolly blinked back tears and said, 'Ashok is doing his NS and is home on leave. He is worried for his dad, of course. Thank you for your concern, Mike. Please give my regards to Alison. You are aware Graham Botham was disgraced at his last university? He was told to leave the university in Australia. I am surprised you hired him given the fact he was let go because of having an affair with a student.'

There was pin-drop silence in the room. The way Mike stared at her left Dolly in little doubt he had been unaware of Graham's bad reputation at his last place of work.

'I do not know what you mean,' stuttered Mike Wong. 'He had impeccable references from the head of department and other professors at the Australian university. There was no reason for me to doubt their word. Are you sure of your facts, Dolly?'

Dolly nodded. 'Dr Pak's poisoning, now. Someone left a cup of poisoned coffee on the janitor Abdul's desk to be delivered to Pak. A CCTV camera in Abdul's office would have nailed the culprit. Same with Ursula's poisoning. Someone entered her office and put phosphorus in her Pepto-Bismol bottle. Again, a camera in her office would have been of great help. Mike?'

Dr Wong was nodding vigorously. 'This debate about privacy of staff and students versus safety in installing cameras in offices has gone on long enough. Obviously, our department is not safe from this madman. We have unanimously voted for cameras to be installed in individual offices, common rooms, and corridors. Currently, we are vetting vendors for this job, Dolly. Rest assured in some months, there will be more cameras everywhere.'

Dolly nodded. 'I'm glad to hear that, Mike.'

There was a loud knock on the door, and it opened to reveal Ash's frightened face along with the scared faces of Kiong Tan and Cheng Yong Lee.

Ash entered and came straight to his mother. 'Mama, Dad's office was locked, and I went in search of the key since Uncle Abdul was not in his cubby hole to give the keys to me. Kiong, Terry and CY helped me locate the key in a key cupboard in the lab. They came with me to Dad's office. This time the door was ajar, and someone was screaming inside. We rushed in and found Uncle Abdul screaming in pain. There were burn marks on his hands and CY immediately took him to the washbasin in Dad's office and asked him to wash his hands with soap and water. Abdul said his hands started burning when dusting the lamp on Dad's desk. We called the ambulance and Terry is with Uncle Abdul. He needs to go to hospital, Mama, and you need to find out what chemical is lying around in Dad's office. Maybe Dad was poisoned, too, Mama?'

'Wait! Are you talking about our janitor, Abdul Latif?' Mike Wong screeched.

Dolly rushed to the door, closely followed by Professor Wong, who was asking Ash, 'Who is your dad, boy?'

Dolly turned around and said, 'Mike, you don't recognize him? This is Ashok. My son went to Pritam's office to collect some journals.'

The group half walked, half ran to the lifts, Dolly on her mobile calling Charlie to come immediately to Pritam's office with the forensics team and NEA officers who supervised the removal of hazardous waste. She was sure a chemical poison was on the lamp Abdul was dusting and the forensics team needed to identify the chemical in case it had been poisoning Pritam.

'Oh, I hope Abdul is not seriously injured by the chemical.' Professor Wong's voice shook. 'He has been working here for thirty years and was going to retire next year. What is happening in this department? Wait, Pritam was *poisoned*?'

As they waited for the lift, they glanced outside. The sky was darkening, and a storm was about to break.

36

Lily had placed a pot of chicken do piyaza to boil on the stove in time for the lunchtime crowd when Vernon, who had been running an errand, rushed in, his hair wild and his eye rolling randomly. Angie, washing dishes at the back of the stall, stole a glance at him before continuing with her work.

'Mrs D!' Vernon cried, 'Uncle Abdul was dusting the table lamp in Prof. Singh's office. He has burn marks on his hands. Touched a chemical when dusting filament of table lamp. White chemical, they are saying. He scream so loud. Ash and the Singh group found him. Everyone is talking about this! I hear from the Singh research group, Mrs D. The ambulance took Abdul away. Mrs D, this means Prof. Singh being poisoned by this chemical, isn't it? In his office and all? But on a lamp, Mrs D?'

Lily's eyes were as round as saucers. 'Ash?' she stuttered.

Vernon nodded. 'He came to take books from his Pa's office. Madam Dolly has sealed off the office and policemen are all over the place. The forensics team is on the way, Inspector Goh told me. They are going to wear masks and protective gear to remove poison from office. NEA is involved, too, Mrs D. They oversee hazardous material removal, right.' He stuttered gamely over the word 'hazardous', unsure of its use and pronunciation. He continued, 'The head, Professor Wong, give go-ahead for poison removal. The whole floor sealed up already. Can't go to look-see.' Vernon looked crestfallen.

Lily was staring and Angie came over, her eyes wide.

Angie spoke, not looking at her husband. 'What kind of poison is it?'

Vernon tried to gauge his wife's mood. He felt sorry for himself and knew he had to curb his alcoholism for the sake of his family. He had spent a restless night on Lily's sofa bed and yearned to return to his own home. He said ingratiatingly, 'They will test the one that burnt Abdul. They need to know what poison, then can reverse its effect. I did not catch what that's called. Same as reversing snake venom.'

Lily turned off the flame underneath the pot of chicken do piyaza. 'Antidote. Yes, this may mean Pritam was poisoned by the chemical that burnt Abdul's hand. But how? I don't understand. I called the hospital and there has been no change in his condition. He has not worsened, which is a good thing. Who could be poisoning everyone?'

'I don't think the killer meant to poison Abdul,' Vernon said, thoughtfully, one eye on his wife, who was deigning to look at him again after showing her back to him for the past two days. 'Charlie said the ASP believes her ex was poisoned in his office and he was the target. The poison was left over, and Abdul accidentally touched it.'

Lily's eyes were shining. 'I think Dolly is right. If it is a slow-acting poison placed somewhere in the office, Pritam would have intermittent exposures and that explains why he showed neurological symptoms only when working from the office.' She frowned. 'But the chemical was on the lamp filament? Pritam would hardly touch the filament. Abdul touched it to dust it. So, *how* was Pritam poisoned?'

'What a scary killer!' Angie exclaimed. 'And so near us as well.' She moved a step in Vernon's direction, which Vernon accepted as a positive sign towards the mending of his marital relationship.

'I hope they identify the poison,' Lily said grimly. 'Until then, the doctors won't know what antidote to use for Pritam and let's hope the poison has an antidote. I looked up phosphorus. No real antidote. If Pritam dies, Cheryl will surely miscarry their baby. I was trying to get her to leave my house, but not now, after hearing this. Her husband may really have been poisoned; it's not Parkinson's Disease that has landed him in hospital.' Her eyes misted over. 'Poor Pritam. I hope he gets better. He is family.'

The dark clouds parted, and the rain came pelting down.

* * *

In the late afternoon, Girlie pressed the bell on the front door of Ursula Botham's quarters. After some minutes, Kamini opened the door and ushered her in. She took her friend to the kitchen and waved her to a seat on the two-seater table there.

'I got your text. What is it, Kamini?' Girlie's eyes were apprehensive. 'Tom is in school?'

Kamini busied herself making tea for Girlie. The kitchen was small but pleasant with modern appliances, a linoleum floor, laminated cupboards, a steel sink, and granite countertops. Yellow downlights beamed down from the ceiling.

With a worried face, Kamini told Girlie that Tom was crying in his bedroom because his father was preventing him from leaving with his grandmother for England. Graham was fighting with Bianca, Kamini said, from the time he returned from police interviews, and ranting about the police impounding his passport. With tears in her eyes, Kamini said that Graham had demanded to be shown Ursula's will that left her fortune to Tom, and Ursula's lawyer had arrived from England. A tear trickled down Kamini's cheek as she told Girlie that Graham had threatened to set the police on Bianca for attempting to take Tom away and that had made Tom cry even more. Kamini said, 'I am worried about Tom. Should I tell ASP Das about him? This is so bad for him.'

Girlie sighed. 'What can the police do? This is a family problem.'

'There's more,' Kamini said while pouring hot water from a kettle into two mugs. She dipped two tea bags in and sat opposite Girlie, allowing the tea to brew. 'The day before his Mum die, Tom tell me he come home from school at 6 p.m. And Lorna Ma'am was in the house. She was in Sir's study and looking inside table drawers. She see Tom and leave. Is it important?' She went to the kitchen counter, threw the teabags into the dustbin, gave the tea a stir with a spoon and brought the mugs of tea to the table. 'Have tea, Girlie.'

Girlie's eyes were gleaming. 'Thanks. Yes, it's important about Lorna Ma'am. I give you Inspector Goh's phone number. Call him and he will know what to do. Oh Kamini, you think Ma'am Lorna killed Ma'am Ursula?'

Kamini's face lost colour. 'Possible. They not like each other. One day, Ma'am Lorna come to the house, oh, about two weeks ago, and Ma'am shout at her. Told her she was breaking up a home and to go back to England. Ma'am Lorna say Ma'am lose Sir long ago. Ma'am order Ma'am Lorna to leave house. Yesterday, I hear Ma'am Bianca talk on the phone with her lawyer in England. Tom get all his mother's money and house, not Sir. I am worried for the little boy, Girlie. What if Ma'am Lorna kills Tom, too? I cannot watch him night and day. Have to go home to my family. Tom is rich now, so in danger.'

'Where is Ma'am Bianca?' Girlie asked, sipping her tea. She pointed to Kamini's cup. 'Your tea will get cold, Kamini. Drink up.'

'Ma'am Bianca go shopping. She say she return to England soon with Ma'am's body.' Her voice trembled and she took a sip of the tea. 'She bury Ma'am with her father in England grave. I miss Ma'am, Girlie, she so nice to me, like friend, not employer.' Kamini burst into tears. 'If Sir not allow Tom to go to England, the she-devil Lorna will kill him. I love Tom like my own Krishnan, Girlie. What to do?' Kamini sobbed brokenly, her mug of tea forgotten.

'I will talk to Ma'am Lily and you speak with Inspector Goh. Stop crying, Kamini, it won't do any good.' Girlie pushed the mug of tea towards Kamini, and for some time, the two maids sipped their tea in silence.

There was the sound of a key in the lock and voices and laughter came from the hall.

'Sir and Ma'am Lorna,' Kamini whispered. 'Use the back door to leave, Girlie.'

But Girlie was too late. Graham had come into the kitchen to get a drink of water and spied Girlie trying to ease out of the back door.

'Hey! Stop! Who are you?' he shouted, his spectacles askew. His hair was untidy, and a lock fell over his broad forehead. His eyes were sharp and accusing.

Girlie stopped in her tracks and slowly turned around.

Kamini stood her ground. 'She is my friend. Come for a chat. She is leaving now.'

'You were supposed to prepare lunch and here you are gossiping with your friend. You do not have permission to have your friends over. In fact, you are fired, Kamini!' Graham's face was red, his eyes glowing with displeasure. 'You can leave with your friend and not return. I paid you your salary yesterday, and I no longer need you.'

The colour had fled from Kamini's face. Standing by the kitchen table, she said stoutly, 'I wait for Ma'am Bianca to come home. Then I leave.'

'There is no need for that,' Graham said. 'Lorna is here with me. We can take care of Tom.'

Kamini went over to the counter and set about cutting vegetables. 'No,' she said. 'I prepare lunch now.'

Graham began to splutter in anger, and Lorna appeared in the doorway. She looked beautiful in a green suit and pants that matched the colour of her eyes. She had overheard the heated argument.

'We can call the police and remove you from the premises,' Lorna told Kamini in a cold voice.

Kamini turned. 'Please do,' she invited. 'My friend go call the police, anyway. Girlie, go. Now.'

When Girlie had disappeared out of the door, Lorna asked, 'What do you mean by saying your friend will call the police?'

Kamini remained quiet, and Lorna began to look uneasy. 'Come on, Graham. Let's go through those papers Bianca wanted signed. In the den.'

In an hour, there was a knock on the front door and Graham opened it to find Inspector Goh standing outside, looking solemn. 'Is Ms Lorna Asquith here?'

Lorna came out of the den and raised an eyebrow. 'Yes. Why?'

Charlie flashed his warrant card and said, 'Your nephew, Tom, says you were here in this house the day before Professor Ursula was found dead. We want to question you. Please accompany me to HQ. Corporal Sim?'

A petite policewoman came forward and said to Graham, 'We wish to question your son, Tom, Professor Botham. I understand he is in the house. Ah, there he is.'

Kamini brought a frightened Tom to the hall.

Charlie said formally, 'We will question your son, Professor Botham, and then arrange for his accommodation at a hotel with his grandmother until he is ready to fly to the United Kingdom. Your mother-in-law, Bianca Asquith, has lodged a police complaint with us stating you are restraining your son here against his wishes. She feels that after his mother's death, the best place for him is his country of residence and citizenship. He is traumatized by his mother's passing and needs care. Since your passport is impounded and you are a suspect in your wife's murder, you are not the best person in the circumstances to take care of your son. When we question Tom, it will be in his grandmother's presence.'

Graham lost his temper. 'I had nothing to do with my wife's death! You have also not charged me. And I am Tom's father and have rights. He is staying with me. I will get a lawyer to stop Tom leaving.'

Tom burst into tears and cried, 'I want to be with Grandmama! Mum always said to go to Grandmama if something happened to her. I want Grandmama!'

Graham looked at his son weeping into Kamini's shirt and glanced away.

'Tom, please accompany Corporal Sim. Kamini, you can come as well. You can go home when Tom is safe with his grandmother.' Charlie watched as Kamini led Tom to Corporal Sim. At a nod from Charlie, the trio went to the lift lobby.

When they were gone, Charlie looked at Lorna Asquith, whose nostrils were flared with anger. 'Ms Lorna Asquith, please accompany me to Headquarters, where Assistant Superintendent Dolly Das will question you on your whereabouts the day before Madam Ursula's death. Come with me, please.'

Lorna glanced wildly at Graham. 'Do something! They are going to pin Ursula's murder on me, Graham! The newspapers reported Ursula was poisoned!' Her eyes widened when Graham turned his back and returned to his den.

'Coward!' Lorna hissed at his back and then turned to Charlie. 'Do your worst, Inspector. I will answer your questions, but I will complain to your superiors if I am hassled or bullied in any way. I am not afraid.'

When there was silence and the door had closed, Graham sat in the den, his head buried in his hands, weeping bitterly. After the bout of tears, he looked up, saw Ursula smiling serenely from a photo, and viciously took the photo frame from the table and smashed it on the ground, his face a mask of hate.

37

Dolly sat in her well-furnished office on a high floor of CID HQ and looked at the phone, eagerly waiting for the forensics team to identify the chemical in Pritam's office. Only then could Pritam's doctors treat him with an antidote and there would be a chance of recovery. Superintendent Abdullah, when updated, had told her in no uncertain terms that finding a poison and how it was administered meant nothing if it could not pinpoint the killer. Siti said with flashing eyes that if Dolly did not have the Temasek University poisoner under lock and key in a week's time, she would pass the case to a more experienced and astute officer. And one knows who that will be, Dolly thought viciously, her old foe, ASP Brendan Gan. He was breathing down her neck again. Promoted to Assistant Superintendent a year ago, Brendan was a rising star and one of the primary candidates to head the Major Crime Division in a few years' time.

Dolly was in a bad mood when she entered Interview Room 2 to talk with Lorna Asquith. Lorna's taciturn and belligerent attitude did nothing to lighten her frame of mind. She was going to be an uncooperative suspect as she sat in her chair, glowering at the officers. Charlie sat next to Dolly, his fingers on his tablet, ready to note down salient points from the interview, his eyes worried. It was really Charlie's interview to do, but given the gravity of the case, Dolly had offered to be Lorna's interviewer.

'What were you doing in Professor Ursula Botham's apartment on the day before her death?' Dolly barked out.

'She was my cousin. I heard she was ill and went to visit her.'

'How was she?' Charlie intervened. 'What time did you visit her?'

'Around 5 p.m.,' Lorna said, shortly. 'No one answered the door. There is a key that Graham keeps on a ledge near the front door, and I tried that. To my surprise, I found the key did not work. Later, Graham told me Ursula had changed locks so he could not get in.'

Charlie looked puzzled. 'Then how did you enter?'

A thin smile flitted across Lorna's lips. 'The flat has a back door connecting the kitchen to the corridor. The maids use this door to come and go. You must skirt the apartment to reach it. I went around and tried that door. It was unlocked. Obviously, Graham had not figured out that he could have entered through the back door.' Lorna smiled more broadly. Then she sniffed. 'The back door should have been locked. The maid forgot to lock it. Careless! Ursula was fast asleep in her bedroom. I did not disturb her. There was a bottle of Pepto-Bismol on her bedside table, and I thought her ulcers were giving her trouble.'

'So, what did you do?' Charlie asked.

Lorna looked sullen. 'I went to the den and browsed through some books, waiting for Ursula to wake up.'

'The little boy, Tom, came home from school at 6 p.m. and found you rummaging through drawers in the den,' Dolly accused in a sharp voice.

Lorna shrugged. 'Tom is known to lie,' she said, dismissively.

'Were you looking for your cousin's will?' Dolly raised an eyebrow, watching with interest perspiration springing up on Lorna's forehead.

'I did not know she had a will. Graham said she didn't.'

'Andrew Galbraith, Professor Botham's lawyer, has arrived in Singapore, and I talked to him briefly on the phone before coming here. He said you called him ten days ago at his office to ask if your cousin had made a will.'

Lorna's green eyes flashed. 'You do your homework, Assistant Superintendent. So what if I was looking for Ursula's will? I did not believe Graham when he said there was no will. I knew my cousin. She would plan for Tom's future, and her relationship with Graham was fractured. It was probable she had made a will. There was no point in asking Aunt Bee. She can't stand me. I thought there might be a copy of the will in the desk

Ursula used in the den. I started my search, but Tom came home from school. I left and that is all there was to my visit to Ursula on the day before her death.'

'You did not wake your cousin?' Charlie persisted. 'To ask her if she needed anything?'

'No.' Lorna ran a hand through her red hair falling over her shoulders. 'It was obvious that she was not well. I did not want to wake her.' Her green eyes rested speculatively on Dolly. 'I heard the Pepto-Bismol bottle in her office at the university contained the poison. She had ingested poison at her place of work.'

'Which also happens to be your place of work,' Dolly said, her eyes cool.

'Yes, but the Science and Arts faculty buildings are a mile apart. I do not visit the Science buildings.' Lorna's lips lifted in a smile. 'Is that all you have on me?' She looked at her watch. 'I need to get back to work.'

'What were you planning to do if you found the will?' Charlie asked.

'Read it, of course, see who Ursula's beneficiaries were.' Lorna looked at the window and the sunlight outside. 'I was interested to know what would happen to Graham if Ursula divorced him as she was threatening to do. Did he get any money for the years he had remained married to her? Galbraith wouldn't tell me anything. He said whether Ursula made a will or not was confidential information. I had to find out.'

Dolly's eyes bored into Lorna like a laser beam. 'A will is only interesting to someone if they know that the person who made the will would die soon.' Her voice was sharp. 'Why were you so interested in Ursula's will while she was living?'

The colour fled from Lorna's face. She looked frightened. 'Look,' she said in a shaking voice, 'I did not poison my cousin. Graham did not want the divorce. He did not want to lose Ursula's wealth. He went on telling me Ursula still trusted him and that is why she had not made a will. Finding the will and reading its contents would give me ammunition to show Graham that Ursula mistrusted him. If the will benefited Tom and left Graham little of her wealth, then there was no point in him hanging on to her. He was not going to get her money anyway. Then he would be free to be with me.'

'On the other hand,' Dolly said, 'according to her will, the money Ursula Botham left for her husband was directly proportional to the years he stayed married to her. Hanging on to her would have helped him financially.'

Lorna shrugged. 'I did not know that. I wanted to get married to Graham, and if I could show him Tom was Ursula's sole beneficiary to the bulk of her fortune, he would have agreed to the divorce Ursula suggested. That is all I have to say.' She nodded and rose from her chair.

When Lorna had left, Dolly looked at Charlie. 'I find her suspicious.'

Charlie nodded. 'We will keep an eye on her, Madam. She obviously suspected Ursula Botham had made a will that did not benefit Graham financially.'

Dolly frowned. 'First, I thought Lorna was after the money Graham would inherit from Ursula. If Lorna suspected Ursula did not leave Graham that much money and she was still interested in him, then she may really love him. And if she already suspected Graham would not benefit financially from Ursula's death, why would she kill Ursula?'

Charlie said, 'Well, she said Graham was refusing to divorce Ursula and maybe Lorna killed Ursula to get Graham to marry her. Money, as you say, Madam, may not have mattered as much to Lorna Asquith. Graham remains the chief suspect in Ursula's murder. He thought he would get a lot of money if his wife died, and he wanted to marry Lorna, so he kills Ursula. His office, Madam, is right across from his wife's office in the Science Faculty building. Easy enough for him to slip poison into her Pepto-Bismol bottle.' He said in a worried voice, 'Right now, though, we need to find out if Professor Singh was poisoned. If he was, then Graham Botham had motives for murdering his wife and his rival at work, and he had opportunity. He will be our man. And maybe he wanted to stop DW from affecting his career prospects and killed him so he would not expose his affair with a student who later killed herself.'

Dolly asked, 'No phosphorus was found in the Pepto-Bismol bottle on the bedside?'

Charlie shook his head. 'Only in the one in her office, Madam. And do remember, Graham Botham had no access to his home that whole week. Ursula locked him out.'

Dolly nodded. 'But the kitchen door was unlocked and provided access to the flat. I talked to the hospital doctors about phosphorus poisoning. There are three stages of symptoms. First, vomiting and diarrhoea, then cardiopulmonary effects and, finally, organs like the liver are affected. Ursula was yellow; she was in the last stage and died.'

Charlie was looking at his notes. 'Ursula Botham was last at her place of work on a Wednesday, and she died sometime Friday night. During this time, she took Pepto-Bismol from the bottle by her bedside so was not exposed to poison. Does that mean whatever she ingested up to Wednesday at her office killed her?'

Dolly nodded. 'Yes, because she was untreated for the poisoning. The doctors told me only a little phosphorus can do the damage. The Pepto-Bismol emulsion at her office masked the presence of poison. I wish a forensics officer would call with the name of the poison in Pritam's office. It's urgent! Pritam may die otherwise. No change in Pritam's condition?'

Her eyes teared up as Charlie silently shook his head.

The phone rang sharply, and Charlie picked up the receiver. Dolly looked up, tense.

After listening for a few seconds, Charlie, his eyes round with wonder, passed the phone receiver to Dolly. It was Jason Teo, the forensics head, who was on the line.

'Mercuric chloride? But how did that act as a poison for Pritam, Jason? He would not touch the lamp filament.' Dolly listened intently and the colour faded from her face. 'My God! This poisoner is diabolical! So, the mercuric chloride was laced over the filament cover? It would decompose from the heat of the lamp when it was lighted and release mercury vapour. And that would be poisonous?' She listened for some time and said, 'Chronic mercury poisoning over time? What would be the symptoms?' She listened and nodded, vigorously. 'Yes, yes, Jason, Pritam had all the neurological symptoms you describe. Depression, memory loss, trembling, and hallucinations. Good work, Jason, thank you!'

Dolly replaced the receiver, lifted it up again and dialled a number. In a minute, the forensic pathologist Benny Ong was on the line. Dolly told him the news and urged, 'Benny, you need to go to the Temasek Teaching Hospital. You need to talk to Pritam's doctors. How long will it take to detect the mercury in his body? Any antidote that can help him recover from mercury poisoning?' Dolly listened for some time and then bid goodbye to the doctor.

She turned to Charlie and said, 'There is no real cure for mercury poisoning except to remove the victim from the poisonous environment and that has been done. The forensics team will contact the industrial waste group from NEA who will remove the poison and clear Pritam's office. My God, I wonder if the poisoner has laced other lamps in the department with mercuric chloride? We are dealing with someone familiar with chemistry, Charlie, to know that mercuric chloride, when heated, gives off poisonous mercury vapours. I think we can rule out Eun-jin Choi and Lorna Asquith as suspects. No, it's a chemist who is killing people! Charlie, send Mok to the hospital to find out how the janitor is doing. I think he touched the chemical, but the students made him wash his hands. So, hopefully, no poison is in his system via the skin? Tell Mok to talk to Abdul's doctor and find out.'

Charlie nodded. 'Is there an antidote for Prof. Singh?'

'Benny talked about chelating agents. Ingesting those may remove the poison from Pritam. Charlie, take Corporal Sim with you and supervise the removal of the poison from Pritam's office and see to the disinfecting. I am going over to the hospital to see Pritam.'

'Until we find the poisoner, there will be no stopping this madness.' Shaking his head sadly, Charlie went in search of Corporal Mok and Corporal Sim.

Dolly slung her bag over her shoulder and raced for the elevator.

Wednesday, 14 September 2011

38

When the bell rang in DW's apartment, Seo-yeon rose from the dining table, where the sisters were having lunch, to open the door. Seeing her sister about to close the door on their visitor, Soo-ah quickly went to her aid. Through the crack between the door and the frame, she saw the apprehensive face of their aunt, Eun-jin.

'You are not welcome.' With her sister by her side, Seo-yeon found her voice. 'Please go away.'

'Do not send me away, girls, please take pity on your poor aunt. I was wrong to go after your father when Binna died. I was devastated to lose my sister without being on good terms with her. I was wrong to accuse Dong-wook of performing euthanasia. I come for forgiveness. You are my only family, girls.' The spate of sentences was fired off in rapid Korean. In a trembling voice, Eun-jin added, 'Take pity on me, for I now suffer from the same illness that took your Ma.'

Soo-ah whispered to her sister, 'Let her in. We need to find out who murdered Papa, Sister. Bill told us Aunt visited Papa in the U.'

Seo-yeon reluctantly nodded and opened the door. The sisters stepped back when their aunt opened her arms to embrace them.

'We were having lunch. You are welcome to sit at the dining table,' Soo-ah said, curtly.

Eun-jin bent her head and nodded. At the table, while her nieces finished their bowls of noodles, she said, 'Please accept my condolences, girls. You have lost your parents, but rest assured I will be there for you. Do not turn me away like Binna did.'

'We have to question why our mother turned away her own sister,' Seo-yeon said.

Eun-jin nodded and said, 'Yes, I want to explain that. Do you remember our country house, a big mansion bordering a forest? You spent your holidays there when you were young. My mother owned the mansion and lived there. She lived on her own with servants as I was working in Seoul, and Binna was married and busy taking care of you. Well, your mother stopped visiting your grandmother after some time. Our mother was angry. She forbade me to have anything to do with Binna. I visited Binna in Seoul and quarrelled with her. She told me your father did not like her visiting the mansion.'

'Why?' Soo-ah asked, her eyes unfriendly. 'Yes, I do remember we went to the country when very young, but then stopped our visits.'

'Do you want some tea?' Seo-yeon asked reluctantly, and pushed a cup and the teapot towards her aunt when she nodded.

Eun-jin poured tea into the cup, took a sip, and said, 'Your parents never told you how they met? Our country estate was huge with some tenant farmers tilling the land. Dong-wook's father, your paternal grandfather, was a tenant farmer on our estate. He tilled a few hectares of land and lived in a cottage on the estate. When young, we played with the farm children, and Binna became close to Dong-wook. We all went to the nearby school and Dong-wook excelled in his studies as did we. We all won places at the university in Seoul. When Binna married Dong-wook, his father expected my mother to sell him the land he tilled for a nominal sum so he could own his land. Our father had died so it was in our mother's hands. At first, our mother was agreeable, but later she changed her mind and your paternal grandfather had to leave our land and relocate to another part of the country. Dong-wook never forgave our mother for what she did. He discouraged Binna from visiting our mother. When our mother was on her deathbed, I visited Binna and pleaded with her to see our mother one last time, but she declined. Dong-wook did not like me because I supported our mother.'

Her two nieces were listening with wide eyes, and Eun-jin's tea was getting cold. Gulping down her tea, Eun-jin said, 'I take it your mama never told you all the family history.'

Seo-yeon shook her head. 'No. Soo-ah and I were always wondering why none of our grandparents ever visited us. But you did visit, Aunt.'

Eun-jin nodded. 'Yes, Binna and I were close when young. Even though Dong-wook did not approve of my visits, Binna and I continued keeping in touch and having meals in the city whenever we could, to catch up. When she was diagnosed with cancer, I was devastated.'

'We lived without much contact with relatives,' Soo-ah mused. 'The four of us would go on holiday and our world revolved around our little family. But we did have contact with you.'

Eun-jin's voice was warm. 'Yes, Binna allowed that, and I am happy about it. I love both of you, dearly. Please do forgive me for accusing your father of performing euthanasia on my sister. I have suffered dearly for it.'

'What happened to our paternal grandparents?' Seo-yeon asked. 'I do not remember visiting them.'

'We heard your grandparents died in poverty. Dong-wook did not earn much money as an academician and could not take care of them well. They died very soon after they relocated to the distant district after your parents married.'

Soo-ah cleared her throat. 'We heard you visited Pa at his workplace a month ago. Why?'

Eun-jin said, 'I was sorry for putting him through the trial and wanted to mend our relationship. Seo-yeon had stopped talking to me, and I thought she would talk to me again if Dong-wook forgave me.'

'You were heard quarrelling.' Seo-yeon's voice was matter of fact.

Eun-jin sighed. 'Yes, Dong-wook was not welcoming. He accused me of using my influence on my mother to leave the estate to me. He felt it should have been divided between Binna and me. I reminded him that he did not allow Binna to visit our mother on her deathbed. Yes, we quarrelled bitterly and now I cannot repair my relationship with him. He is gone. Although our mother left the estate to me, both of you are my heirs, named in my will. I tried explaining that to Dong-wook, but he was just so angry.'

Soo-ah said, 'Pa never mentioned your visit, Aunt.' She looked speculatively at Eun-jin and said, 'Did you visit him on the day he was poisoned, Aunt?'

Eun-jin's face paled, and she whispered, 'You suspect me of murdering your father. Yes, I did visit the university on the day the police said he was poisoned, around 4 p.m. I wanted to tell him about my cancer diagnosis. He would take pity on me and give me pointers on how to beat the cancer. He was a devoted caregiver to Binna, after all. But I saw people in his office and there was a commotion going on. I left. I did not kill your father, girls.'

'But you were there!' Seo-yeon cried. 'And you could have visited earlier and left that poisoned cup of coffee with the janitor.'

Eun-jin rose abruptly from her chair and said, politely, her face composed into a white mask, 'I was wrong to come and disturb your lunch. I will leave now.'

'Wait,' Soo-ah said. 'You mentioned you are ill.'

Eun-jin nodded, her eyes dark. 'My diagnosis of Stage 2 breast cancer was confirmed on the day Dong-wook was poisoned. I should be cured with a mastectomy and chemotherapy. Your mother was diagnosed in Stage 4 when there was little one could do. We have the same breast cancer gene. Girls, you should check if you have the same gene and take precautions.'

Soo-ah stretched out her hand and Eun-jin grasped it. 'We are sorry you have cancer, Aunt.'

Eun-jin nodded, turned on her heel and left.

When she had gone, Seo-yeon looked at her sister. 'Do you think she killed Pa?'

Soo-ah sighed. 'It is hard to view one's own aunt as a killer. But she had motive. She hated Pa. She is our aunt, but she is a cold person inside out. I can imagine her putting ethylene glycol in his coffee.'

'Aunt is a linguist; would she know about poisons?' Seo-yeon's voice was doubtful.

'Anyone can read about it from the net,' Soo-ah scoffed. 'But then, when Bill visited us last night, he said a professor died of poisoning and a second one is in the ICU fighting for his life. So, maybe there is a serial killer in the department. Pa was unlucky.'

Seo-yeon said, 'Aunt is cold and calculating. What will she want in return for the country house?'

'For us to take care of her when she undergoes chemotherapy?' Soo-ah said.

Seo-yeon sighed. 'We will, though, won't we? First Ma and then Aunt.'

'Oh, look at the rain, how it comes shimmering down. I am homesick, Sister.' Soo-ah rose from the dinner table, walked to the window, closed it, and stood looking at the rain.

'We cannot leave until we see Pa's murderer hanged,' Seo-yeon said in a cold voice, and for a moment Soo-ah was reminded of the steeliness of their aunt.

'It is good the Dean has allowed us another month's rent-free accommodation in Pa's quarters,' she said, easily.

The two girls sat, companionably, while the photo of their parents smiled benignly on them from the wall.

39

Ash rose from one of the benches in the open corridor of the university, closed the physics journal he was reading, and packed it away in his backpack. He slung the pack over his shoulder and took the lift to the ground floor. With a worried face, he entered the science canteen, making a beeline for his aunt's food stall.

Lily sat on a high stool taking a breather, while Angie and Vernon served customers. Hearing her nephew's voice, she looked up in surprise.

'Ash, you haven't gone home for lunch?' she asked, her voice anxious. 'Are you all right? You look worried, Ash.'

'Mashi, I'm hungry. Can we talk over lunch?'

Lily nodded and told Vernon to serve them fish masala and palak paneer with steamed rice. She grabbed hold of her nephew's arm and shepherded him to a corner table right beside a crop of banana plants. The mild breeze gently blew over them as they seated themselves. After Vernon had served them with a smile, and Ash had eaten half his meal, Lily spoke.

'What's wrong, Ash?'

In a soft voice and after looking around furtively, Ash told Lily what he had discovered.

Lily laid down her cutlery and looked at her nephew, breathing hard. Her eyes were round with wonder. 'Are you sure, Ash? We have to be certain before telling your mother.'

Ash nodded. 'Yes, I am sure. Mashi, we can verify by you coming along with me and looking at the photo. Two pairs of eyes are better than one.'

Lily nodded and the two finished their lunches, excitement making their eyes sparkle. Vernon sauntered over, his bad eye rolling in happiness. He and Angie had made up and Vernon was coming home, with the terse command from his wife that he had to wean off alcohol or else, ringing in his ears. Angie, in return, had agreed to consult a gynaecologist through her pregnancy term.

'What's up, Mrs D?' Vernon asked, noting the excited sparkle in Lily's eyes.

Lily glanced at her assistant and turned to her nephew. 'Ash, V can come as well. Three pairs of eyes will be best.'

'What?' Vernon looked surprised.

'I will tell you in the car. Come along, Vernon. The lunch crowd has thinned out and Angie can manage on her own. I will tell Ashikin to supervise the stall while I am away, she is a partner after all.' Lily bustled towards her stall to instruct Angie to lock up at 2.30 p.m. She dragged Ashikin away from her gossiping session with Naheed, with strict instructions to look after her *own* stall.

* * *

Lily drove her car through lunch-time traffic towards Toa Payoh. Vernon sat in the front passenger seat, his eyes sparkling with excitement. Once he had been informed of their mission, he could not wait to be a part of the sleuthing team as of old.

It was nearly three by the time Lily turned into a road that led to the walk-up complex where Pritam's cousin and niece lived. She parked adroitly in the carpark in front of the complex while Vernon looked with interest at an old man wheeling a barrow of rubbish from the bins to the incinerator. Ash, his nose buried in a book, looked up, closed the book, and kept it away in his backpack.

Ash had brought with him a bar of chocolate and some cigarette packets, and when they were out of the car, he walked over to Johnny Tan, who was rummaging in the recycle bins.

'Uncle, do you remember me? I came the other day to chat.' Ash opened his palms so Johnny Tan could see his offerings.

Johnny peered at Ash through his thick spectacles, spied the gifts and gave a smile. Showing no recognition at all on his face, he said, 'Yes, yes.'

'Why don't we go over to your office, Uncle? I am doing a college project on estate cleanliness, and I want to ask you some questions,' Ash lied, glibly. He nodded at Lily and Vernon. 'These are my friends.'

Johnny did not move his eyes from the chocolate bar and cigarettes and nodded, absently, not bothering to look at Lily or Vernon. 'Okay,' he said trustingly, and led his visitors to a small room under the sheltered carpark. He put his hands in his trouser pocket, took out keys and fumbled with the lock of the door. Finally, he had it open, and everyone crowded into the office. Ash gave the chocolate and cigarettes to Johnny, who turned the gifts over in his hand in wonder.

Lily and Vernon looked around the dark office, their eyes alighting on a photo prominently displayed on a table.

'Is there a light switch?' Vernon asked, tired of myopically peering at the photo.

Ash looked around, spied the switch by the door, and pressed it. The room flooded with light, and Johnny blinked.

Lily and Vernon were by the table and both uttered exclamations as they recognized the boy in the photo. Johnny, however, had recovered from his fogginess.

He said to Ash, 'I do not really remember you, but I thank you for the gifts. It is a long time since I had chocolates.' He spoke slowly and laboriously.

Vernon asked in his most officious voice, pointing to the photo on the table, 'Is that your son?'

Johnny followed Vernon's pointing finger to the photo and nodded. Sadness filled his face. He said slowly, 'My boy, Terry. He does not come to visit me any more. Busy with his studies.' Pride touched his face. 'He is a scientist. Like I was.' Tears clouded his eyes.

Lily said in a kind voice, 'I am sure you are proud of him. You are Christian, Uncle?'

Johnny peered in Lily's direction and nodded. 'My wife, Mabel, insisted on going to church every Sunday. Mabel is no more.'

'We have recognized him,' Lily whispered to Ash. 'You were right. Let us leave Johnny in peace.'

Ash dug out a bag of peanuts from his pockets and offered it to Johnny. 'Bye, Uncle. Be well.'

Johnny grabbed the bag with childlike gratitude. 'You live here on the estate?' he asked, looking up at the door. But there was no one there and Johnny sighed. His eyes lighted up when he spied the chocolate bar, and eagerly, he began to tear at the wrapper. After he bit into the bar, a happy smile filled his face. His barrow lay unattended outside as Johnny Tan did full justice to his surprise snack.

* * *

It was 4.30 p.m, and Dolly and Charlie were sitting in a booth in the police canteen, eating curry puffs and drinking tea. Dolly's face was tense. She had visited the hospital and learnt from Benny that Pritam had been treated with chelating agents to reverse the effect of mercury poisoning but there was only a 50 per cent chance of the treatment working. She had also visited Abdul, whose burns had been treated and who seemed none the worse for wear other than being very frightened. The doctors were keeping him in the hospital for two days and monitoring his vitals just to be safe.

If Pritam died, there would be three murders and the killer was still at large. Dolly felt a tension headache coming on. Charlie looked worried, too; this was his first case as an inspector, and he knew how important it was to solve the case. While they understood how the victims were being poisoned, they still did not know who the killer was. Even if Graham Botham had motives for all the murders, where was the evidence that Graham was the murderer? As they discussed the case, Corporal Fauzia Khan stopped by their table.

Dolly had been brainstorming the case with Charlie and stopped talking on seeing Fauzia. 'How are you doing at the Serious Sexual Crime Branch, Fauzia?' Dolly asked pleasantly.

Fauzia smiled, tentatively. 'I want to return to you, ASP Das. Please! I want to help solve murders, not work to defend abused women. I can come back now. Auntie is leaving Major Crime.'

Charlie perked up and shifted towards the wall, making room for Fauzia on the booth seat. 'Sit, corporal.'

Fauzia sank gratefully into the space made for her and deposited her cup of tea on the table. Her undulating nose quivered with emotion as she looked at Dolly sitting opposite her, looking stunned. Without preamble, she said, 'Auntie is being transferred to head the Liaison and Training Branch. The deputy commissioner feels she is a great teacher and would be ideal to train new recruits. Please, Ma'am, let me return to your team. No ethics laws will be broken now that Auntie won't be here. It is true I really admire you and your police work, Ma'am. I know I was not open with you before, please let me make it up to you. It is not as though I agree with Auntie on everything. It's just that my dad gambles, and I am a single mother staying with my parents. We need occasional monetary handouts from Auntie, and she got me this job at CID. We owe her, Ma'am.'

Dolly, who strongly suspected Siti Abdullah used her niece to spy on her, wondered whether the aunt would still be pulling the strings from the training department to oust Dolly and reinstate herself. She found it hard to believe Fauzia though she conceded to herself that Fauzia could be speaking the truth.

Dolly said, coolly, 'Why don't you work at Sexual Crimes for at least six months before we have this conversation again? It's not fair to your supervisor if you change jobs so fast. How does Supt Abdullah feel about her transfer?'

Fauzia rolled her eyes. 'How do you think? She is furious!' She flicked Dolly a glance. 'She feels DAC Nathan is setting the stage for you to become superintendent and that is the reason for her transfer.'

'Well, I can't be a full superintendent for at least two years, so I don't think I am the reason for your auntie's transfer.' Dolly's eyes were amused.

'Maybe they do need a good trainer for the recruits,' Charlie said with a bland face and Fauzia sniggered. It was apparent Fauzia was trying her best to show that she was not loyal to her aunt and was looking to her career prospects. But like Dolly, Charlie mistrusted Fauzia.

Corporal Mok appeared at their table. He looked with surprise at Fauzia before his face darkened. Then he said, 'ASP Das and Inspector Goh, you are both wanted at DAC Nathan's office at five.'

Dolly glanced at her watch. 'Let's go, Charlie!'

40

DAC Nathan's office was on the top floor of the CID building with bay windows and a wonderful view of the Singapore skyline. Dolly and Charlie stood to attention near the door, while Siti Abdullah glared at them from a chair pulled near to Nathan's big desk.

DAC John Nathan sat in his swivel chair, peering at reports on his desk. He glanced up and motioned Charlie and Dolly to two chairs opposite him. Supt Abdullah looked like a glowering bystander to the action.

John Nathan flicked a glance at Siti before looking at Dolly and Charlie. 'Supt Abdullah is needed in our Operations, Investigation Policy Division, so she is transferring there from Major Crime. The Liaison and Training Branch there needs an overhaul, and the DCP feels Supt Abdullah is the best person to give birth to a brand-new department the CID can be proud of. ASP Das, you will report directly to me for the time being and this meeting is a transitionary one for me to become more familiar with the university poisoning case.'

Nathan spent two minutes looking through reports and then barked out, 'Let me get this straight. Three victims were poisoned by different industrial poisons. Is the murderer playing a game with us? Or is there more than one murderer? And what about this university? They do not keep their industrial poisons under lock and key?'

Dolly said, 'These are chemicals used in experiments and research. Some are kept under lock and key, but the staff and students have keys and can access the chemicals.'

Nathan shook his head. 'What you are then saying, ASP Das, is that staff or students are murdering each other.'

Dolly said, 'The first murder, that of Dong-wook Pak, could have been done by an outsider. The poison, ethylene glycol, is readily available in car shops and other places. You would not need to break into a chemistry laboratory to get hold of the poison. A cup of coffee was poisoned with ethylene glycol and kept in the open office of the janitor with instructions to deliver it to Dr Pak.'

'How much ethylene glycol would be needed for it to be fatal?' Nathan mused.

'Enough to fill a large Styrofoam coffee cup. And it would be sweet to the taste. The postdoc would think the coffee had extra sugar in it,' Dolly said.

Nathan shuddered. 'You say the sister-in-law had motive?'

'The victim and his sister-in-law had bad blood between them, and she had previously visited him at the office, and he had asked her to leave.' Dolly said. 'They had a big quarrel. Relatives often dislike each other, but Eun-jin Choi went the extra step and tried to get her brother-in-law convicted in Seoul of performing euthanasia on his cancer-stricken wife, Eun-jin's sister. That shows a deep degree of animosity. But she could have been hasty or may have tried to get Dr Pak jailed because she sincerely believed he helped his wife to die, and she may have loved her sister very much. But why would she want to murder him now?'

'Especially when diagnosed with cancer the day Dr Pak was poisoned. One would think she had other things on her mind than killing Pak,' Charlie said. 'I have talked to Dr Ronald Tan, Eun-jin's doctor and Ms Choi spent the late morning and early afternoon of the day Pak was poisoned at Raffles Hospital, undergoing tests to determine her cancer stage. We have CCTV footage from the hospital showing that she was in one of their clinics from 11 a.m. to 2 p.m.'

Dolly sighed and said, 'The poisoned coffee was placed in Abdul's office sometime between 12 p.m. and 1 p.m., so that lets Eun-jin Choi out of having poisoned her brother-in-law. We have proof she was at the hospital.'

Superintendent Siti Abdullah, her eyes flashing at Dolly, acidly said, 'There have been two murders and one attempted murder. Obviously, you need to look for connections between the murders to catch the killer.'

'Wait a minute, Supt. Let us be thorough. Now the second victim was Professor Ursula Botham.' Nathan peered at a report on the desk. 'She was poisoned by phosphorus. It was in her bottle of Pepto-Bismol in her office. I take it this poison has no taste.'

'That's correct, Sir,' Dolly said. 'And you would need very little for a fatal dose. Pepto-Bismol is an emulsion; the phosphorus was well-masked there. We are after a very clever killer, Sir.'

Nathan looked up with wide eyes. 'Are the offices locked? Who had access to Professor Botham's office?'

'The offices were seldom locked during the day, Sir,' Charlie said, apologetically. 'My men have asked the professors with offices on Ursula Botham's floor if they saw anything suspicious. They all said it was business as usual. They said students and professors come out of each other's offices all the time. They discuss projects in the offices. No help there.'

Nathan sighed. 'So, a wide net of suspects, eh? Who benefits from Ursula's death?'

'The husband was having an affair with her cousin, and he thought Ursula did not leave a will. She was a wealthy woman and if what he thought was true, he would have inherited several million pounds after her death. She was talking of divorcing him because of his philandering and then he would not get the money. So, he kills her and thinks he will inherit millions and can marry his lover. But, according to the mother of the victim, Dr Ursula Botham made a will leaving nearly all her money and assets to her son.' Dolly stemmed her speech to catch her breath.

Nathan nodded. 'The husband had a good motive then. Why would Graham Botham want to kill Pak? Wait, did Pak work for him?'

Charlie nodded. 'Yes,' he said, reluctantly. He proceeded to tell Nathan of Ji-woo Kim, the student in Australia who died by suicide after Graham broke off his affair with her.

Dolly said, 'Dr Pak emailed Kim's father saying he would confront Graham about Kim's suicide. This mail was sent a day before the poisoning. We don't know if Dr Pak confronted Graham before he was poisoned. Graham denies it, of course.'

Nathan's eyes shone. 'Maybe Pak did talk to Graham! And Graham murdered Pak to stop him from spreading a scandal that would spoil his chances of becoming HOD. And Graham tried to murder Pritam Singh because he was afraid the staff would elect Pritam, and not him. Graham Botham has motives for murdering all three victims. Do you think Botham will confess if grilled?'

'No,' Dolly said. 'We don't have evidence to initiate a successful grilling. Look at Pritam's poisoning, Sir. A small amount of a mercuric salt was placed on his table lamp filament cover. The heat and light from the lamp decomposed the salt into poisonous mercury vapour, inhaling which Pritam was going slowly crazy. So, I agree with you, Sir. The killer knows about chemical reactions. The killer is not, say, Choi or Lorna Asquith.'

Nathan looked at his watch. 'Yes, I said so. I need to go to a meeting. I agree Professor Graham Botham is our chief suspect since he benefited both from his wife's death and that of his colleague. And maybe Pak, as well. Botham is a chemistry professor so knows about chemical reactions. Professor Singh is still hanging on, I hear.' He shot a quick look at Dolly. 'We are hopeful Dr Singh will recover with the antidotes to mercury administered at the hospital. Mercury, eh? What a ruthless murderer! Three poisons. ASP Das, you need a breakthrough in this case. Hope to hear you have nailed the murderer sooner rather than later.'

After Nathan had left, Dolly and Charlie stood up. Dolly looked at Superintendent Siti Abdullah and said, 'Congratulations on the transfer, Ma'am. I hope you will be happy at the Training Department. Thank you for guiding us, Ma'am.'

Charlie nodded. 'Ma'am.'

Siti Abdullah sat in her chair, her eyes pinpoints of animosity. 'Thank you,' she said, stiffly and then added spitefully, 'Don't think DAC Nathan is not watching you like a hawk, ASP Das. I have already fielded the name of ASP Brendan Gan to take over the university poisoning case if you are unable to solve it in two weeks. ASP Gan is much better than you at grilling a suspect and extracting a confession. Don't expect favouritism, ASP Das.'

'Of course not, Ma'am, why should I?' Dolly said and went out of the office, Charlie following hard on her heels.

'Supt Dragon Lady has not finished with us, Madam,' Charlie said in a low voice while waiting for the lift in the lobby.

'Yes, and that is why we should never take Corporal Fauzia Khan back into our team.' Dolly's voice was decisive. 'Supt Dragon Lady has a hold over Fauzia's family and Fauzia will change sides quickly. We don't need the hassle of second-guessing her motivations all the time if she is back with us. I do not think Graham Botham will break under our grilling but bring him in for questioning tomorrow. I am off to Lily's. See you tomorrow, Charlie!'

The lift door opened, the two officers entered and stepped out at their respective floors. Dolly entered her office, collected her handbag and briefcase, and was soon driving her car to Silver Springs Condominium.

41

Lights twinkled in the apartments of the Silver Springs Condominium as Dolly walked along the covered walkway to the lift lobby of Block D. Getting off the lift on the fifteenth floor, Dolly walked the few yards to her mother's unit and rang the bell. Her stomach rumbled gently with hunger.

Girlie opened the door and smiled, ingratiatingly. Dolly immediately asked, 'What have you been up to, Girlie? Doing something illegal?'

Girlie rolled her eyes. 'Oh no, Ma'am. I am happy! The police take Tom to stay at hotel with grandmother. They fly home, soon, Ma'am. If not, Kamini worry about Tom's safety with killer father on the loose.'

'There is no proof, yet, the father is a murderer,' Dolly said, waspishly. 'Really, Girlie! If we knew for certain he is the killer, we would lock him up. But yes, he is the chief suspect.' She entered the living hall and stopped short on seeing the entire household assembled there.

Lily's eyes were shining. She rose from the love couch where she had been sitting with her nephew and approached her sister. 'Dolly, we have some important information, but have a cuppa first. Girlie, get my sister tea.'

Vernon and Angie were sitting on the large sofa, and Uma was looking alert on the divan. Uma smiled toothlessly at her older daughter, glad to see her. Cheryl was nowhere in sight.

'Where's Cheryl?' Dolly demanded, seating herself on the roomy single sofa after dutifully pecking her mother on the cheek.

'Pritam is coming around and the hospital called. Frankie has taken her there. It's good news, Doll,' said her sister, beaming at her from the love couch.

Dolly went to Ash and hugged him. 'The chelating agents must be reversing the poisoning. Daddy will be all right, Ash. Don't worry.' She wiped tears from her eyes with a tissue she grabbed from the box on the table. She returned to her seat and smiled her thanks at Girlie, who was placing a cup of tea on the table next to her sofa.

Ash, though, was looking concerned. 'Mama, please listen .to what Mashi has to say. We made an important discovery.'

Uma cackled. 'Lily has solved the case yet again before you could, Doll.' She shook with merriment.

Dolly's eyes widened. 'What's going on?' she demanded. 'We know the identity of the murderer. We need to get evidence and a good link to the first murder. Then the case is sewn up.' She raised the teacup to her lips and took a sip.

'Whom do you suspect, Madam Supt?' Vernon asked, his good eye fixed on Dolly.

'Professor Graham Botham. He is the only one with motives for the two murders and one attempted murder.' Dolly took another sip of tea.

Lily said, 'You must look at human emotions.'

'We *are* looking at human emotions, in this case greed and jealousy on Graham's part,' Dolly replied. 'Greed for Ursula's fortune and jealousy of Pritam over the headship. What are you on about?'

'There are deeper human emotions, Mama,' Ash said, his eyes pensive.

'Come on, talk,' Dolly urged. 'It's obvious you all have someone other than Graham in mind.'

Girlie came and sat at Lily's feet, her eyes round with curiosity.

'Maybe there was one intended victim, and the other victims were red herrings to deflect attention from the murderer?' Lily asked. 'And Graham is the scapegoat.' Lily's eyes were luminous.

'And who was the intended victim?' Dolly asked.

'What if it was Pritam?' Lily said, readily.

Dolly frowned. 'Other than Graham, who would want to murder Pritam?'

Lily nodded. 'There *is* someone. The way the other victims were killed is different from how Pritam was poisoned. He was being slowly poisoned over a month and suffered greatly. To think you are losing your mind must be one of the worst fears one can feel. Think back, Dolly. Pritam began hallucinating about the accident in his youth. His legs went numb, one of the neurological symptoms of mercury poisoning. When driving, he lost his bearings. He was terribly frightened. He thought he was going crazy. Then came the depressive episodes. I read up on mercury poisoning, Dolly. One victim was depressed enough to kill himself. The murderer was driving Pritam to the point where he would have no choice but to take his own life. Of all the victims, Pritam was the one who suffered the most with the slow poisoning. Dong-wook died one day after he was poisoned, and Ursula was ill for two days before she died. Not so, Pritam. The murderer wanted Pritam Singh to suffer horrendously and that shows the killer was after Pritam; the other murders were committed to throw us off the scent.'

'I want to know something,' Uma said from the divan. 'Lily explained to me how Pritam was being poisoned by mercury vapour and that it was intermittent poisoning. Why would it be intermittent, though? Didn't Pritam have his lamp on all the time?'

Dolly shook her head. 'Pritam's office is well-lighted by overhead fluorescent lights like other offices. Pritam is long-sighted, he has glasses to help him read fine print. When he was working at the computer, which would be most of the time, writing papers and proposals, he would not need the table lamp to be on. He probably only used the table lamp when he was reading journals. This is a reasonable explanation of intermittent mercury vapour inhalation.'

Lily nodded. 'So, the murderer is someone who knew Pritam used the table lamp only sometimes. A student? They go in and out of the offices, and they see what the professors are doing.'

'Or a member of staff,' Dolly said sharply. 'Graham Botham. Let's get back to your theory, Lily. Who had such a grudge against Pritam that he would want him to suffer like this? Not Manjunath Reddy, surely?'

Ash spoke. His voice was low and trembling. 'The little boy whose mother was killed in the car crash Dad was involved in years ago. Johnny Tan's son. The boy was about ten years old when the accident took place.

He was attached to his mother who died in the crash. Not just that, his father became incapacitated. The brain injury Johnny Tan suffered maimed him for life. His neighbour told me Johnny was an engineer working in a multinational firm. He was made redundant after the accident and the only job he could keep was that of a garbage collector in a housing estate. The boy's mother died, and his father became an idiot. It is possible the boy was simmering with resentment inside, and the grudge blossomed into a hot emotion that made him decide on revenge. Make my dad suffer like his did.'

Dolly's eyes were shining. 'But where is this boy? We heard he was raised by relatives and secretly meets his father. Anyone know his whereabouts?'

Lily's voice was excited. 'What if we told you this same boy works in the chemistry department at Temasek University?'

Dolly sat up and Girlie uttered a terrified scream.

'What? Johnny Tan's son is a student there? Who is he and how do you know?' The police superintendent demanded.

'Mama,' Ash said, his voice soft and sad. 'I visited Johnny Tan with Papa Joe, remember? I saw Johnny Tan's son's photo on the table in his office. Then when I went to the Singh common room to ask for the keys to Dad's office, the boys there helped me find the key. Johnny Tan's son was among them. I recognized him from the photo. I was shocked and told Mashi. Also, I was not sure if I was right, and since Mashi and Vernon know the boys well because they frequent the canteen, they came with me to Johnny's to verify this was the same boy.'

Vernon chimed in. 'One and the same. No question about it.'

'But who *is* he?' Dolly demanded.

Lily said a name softly and Dolly's eyes rounded. Her face grew excited before it fell. 'Even if this is the same boy, there is no way to prove he harmed Pritam. And murdered the others. There is no proof, Lily! No evidence!' Dolly wailed in anguish.

Vernon's eyes were shining. 'I watch criminal cases on TV, Madam Supt. How about trapping the boy? CCTV?'

Girlie squealed. 'Yes, Ma'am Dolly. Like in the movies.'

Dolly frowned. 'He has already harmed Pritam, so why would he kill again?'

Lily looked sad. 'If Pritam recovers and it seems he will, I don't think Johnny Tan's son will let Pritam live. He will come after him again. Then you can catch him. Have a CCTV in Pritam's office?'

Uma said in a sharp tone, 'Don't do this, girls! Pritam's life will be in danger. What if this boy throws acid on his face or something dangerous like that?'

Dolly was thinking hard. 'The boy is a poisoner, so he may approach Pritam with a poisoned beverage. CCTV will capture him giving Pritam the beverage and then we will test the beverage for poison. Then we have the evidence to nail the boy.'

Lily nodded. 'I don't think the boy will smear poison anywhere in the office. He will bring a poisoned beverage to his professor. You're right, Doll. What?' she asked seeing Dolly shaking her head.

'This boy had a grudge against Pritam, granted,' Dolly said. 'But why kill the others? What did he have against DW and Ursula? Especially, Ursula. He wasn't even in her research group. Just to make Graham the scapegoat. In case we find out the identity of this boy and that he is Johnny Tan's son? And suspect him of poisoning Pritam? Looking ahead, then? Remember DW and Ursula died before Pritam was hospitalized. So, you're saying this boy was planning ahead to the time we find out he is Johnny Tan's son?'

Lily was thinking hard and said, 'Or he has some of the traits of the serial killer you were talking about. I now believe you were right about the murderer being a serial killer. Look at the murders. Committed in broad daylight when anyone could have seen the killer. Isn't this something a thrill-seeker would do? Someone who has fun evading the police and someone without any iota of remorse. Just because he has a grudge against Pritam does not mean he doesn't have the traits of a serial killer.'

Dolly's eyes were shining. 'Yes, and serial killers are drunk with power. They think they have someone's life in their hands. Yes, this boy could have the traits of a serial killer, Lil.'

Uma was still shaking her head. 'Don't use Pritam as bait. It's too dangerous, Doll. This boy is the devil himself.'

Ash said, 'Mama, can't you have plainclothes police nearby? If Dad is attacked, someone can quickly come in and arrest the boy. And Dad must agree to being the bait. And take care.'

A smile flitted through Dolly's face. 'Your father is quite brave. I think he will agree to being the bait. When he realizes he was the intended victim of the poisoner.'

Uma said hotly, 'It's all conjecture. For all you know, Graham Botham is the murderer. And this boy is just working at the department, minding his own business. After all, Pritam did pay a large sum of money as compensation to Johnny Tan.'

'The only way to trap the murderer is to have Pritam back at work and see what happens,' Dolly decided. 'If Graham wants to remove Pritam and be the head, we will know and if this boy wants to take revenge for what happened to his family, we will know. I will discuss all this with Charlie, but I think trapping the murderer is the only way to get evidence.'

Uma asked in a trembling voice, 'If this boy is the killer, what was he doing murdering innocent victims like the Korean gentleman and the British lady? Just for fun?'

Lily shivered. 'Mummy, we explained, didn't you hear? He placed the poison on Pritam's lamp a month ago and watched Pritam suffer. That made him feel powerful, and he developed a taste for murder. And killed the others.' Lily continued, 'He is a psychopath. Only this sort of person would kill for fun. They feel no remorse.'

Girlie's eyes were wide with terror. 'And he has a taste for poisons.'

'If he isn't a psychopath, we are back to Graham Botham.' Dolly said, gulping down her cold tea. 'Motives matter and Graham had motives for all three murders and this boy has motive for only one murder.'

Angie spoke up. 'Sometimes a strong motive makes one kill,' she said, wisely. 'Dr Singh spoil this boy's life forty years ago. His mother die and his father become estate cleaner from engineer. The boy angry inside, Madam. I tell you all a story. In my village in Malaysia, two fishermen catch fish together and sell fish in market. They become partners. Their business do well and one day, one come home in boat alone in the morning. Say partner fell from boat and drown in the night. How to know, huh? This man never give money to partner's family, take all for himself and grow rich. Twenty years later, he go on a cruise with his family. He disappear from ship and people think he drown. The family call the police and who was on the ship as crew but son of killed partner. My granny tell us this story when we were young. I never forget. Like elephant, man never forget.'

There was silence as all digested Angie's story.

Lily's words cut through the sudden silence. 'Admit it, Doll, you do not have any evidence against Graham or this boy. Do you think either will confess if grilled? You need to trap the murderer.'

Dolly sighed, nodded, and dialled Charlie's number on her mobile. When he was on the line, she asked him to join them at Silver Springs Condominium.

After switching off her mobile, Dolly said to Lily, 'Charlie says he has not had dinner, so I invited him over for a meal.' Her eyes swivelled to Girlie, who was loitering by the door, her eyes still wide with terror. 'Anything good you cooked today, Girlie?'

'Oh yes, Ma'am.' Girlie focused on the present. 'Mutton do piyaza, spiced potatoes, buttered lentils and pulao rice. The inspector likes all those.'

'Good.' Dolly glanced around at everyone. 'Look, I want to thank all of you. You used your deductive powers well with Lily leading you. We will see what Charlie has to say. Of course, if this university had CCTV cameras in the rooms, these poisonings would not have happened. You all realize that, right?'

Ash shook his head. 'The killer would have found other means to kill. He just may not have had it so easy.'

Dolly rose. 'I'm going for a shower before dinner.'

When Dolly had left, Vernon said glumly, 'I don't think Madam Supt likes the trapping idea. Professor Singh's life in danger and all.'

Uma rose to Dolly's defence. 'And can you wonder? Dolly is a police officer, her job is to protect people, not place them at risk. But even though she is not happy about it, Dolly may have little choice in the matter. Now that I have thought about it, what else can Dolly do? She can't tell the university to ask this boy to leave so that Pritam is safe. No evidence the boy is the killer.' Then she added in a theatrical whisper, 'The trapping will be just like a movie, eh? I wish I could see.' She launched into the details of a Bengali detective movie she had watched on TV as Girlie went to the kitchen to warm up dishes. Charlie did not live far from them and would soon be here.

After Uma finished her story, Lily said, 'Dolly is conservative, and she also needs time to think. Let Charlie come. He will be game for the trapping idea and provide Dolly with the push she needs to set the scene to trap a killer. I will say this, though. Poisoning DW with ethylene glycol, killing Ursula with phosphorus and attempting to murder Pritam with mercury makes this boy one messed-up guy.'

Suddenly a cool breeze blew into the room, and Ash hurried to shut the window. It was pitch dark outside.

Monday, 3 October 2011

42

The sun was shining brightly, its rays filtering through the blinds of the Singh common room creating patterns on the floor. It was ten o'clock and the entire group was present, avidly discussing Professor Pritam Singh's health status and return to work. They were sitting around the long table in the middle of the room, sipping beverages. A brand-new coffee dispenser, bought by Professor Graham Botham, stood in the corner of the room.

'Oh, I am so glad he is back.' Latha's eyes were shining with joyful tears. 'I was panicking. I only need six more months of research data and I will be ready to write my doctoral thesis. But Prof.'s death would have meant an end to my dreams.' She sipped her tea.

Cheng Yong glanced around. 'Prof. was poisoned with mercury and the doctors at the hospital had to inject an antidote of chelating agents to cure him. He was poisoned like Dr Pak and Prof. Ursula.'

Terry, the undergraduate, leant forward, his metal spectacles glinting. 'Who told you that, CY?' he asked sharply. 'The newspapers said nothing about mercury poisoning. What was the chemical that burnt Abdul's hands?'

'A mercuric salt. I was talking to Vernon and Inspector Goh told him Prof. had mercury poisoning. That means a murderer is still roaming around here.' Cheng Yong's face was flushed, and his eyes flashed.

'The police better catch the murderer or there will be an attempt on Prof.'s life again.'

A sudden silence descended on the group until there was a sob from Latha.

'I thought all this was over,' she cried.

Kiong drank his tea and demanded, 'How can it be over? The murderer didn't get to kill Prof. Singh, right? Anyone know how Prof. came to ingest mercury? Did he ingest mercury or the mercuric salt?'

Salma frowned. 'Ingesting liquid mercury is not that dangerous, is it? Not in small amounts. It's mercury vapour that's highly poisonous.'

Cheng Yong looked soberly at his colleagues. 'Prof. did not ingest mercury. The police discovered a coating of the mercuric salt on the outside of the filament cover of the table lamp on his office desk. When the light was on, the heat decomposed the salt into elemental mercury vapour. Prof. inhaled the poisonous mercury vapour slowly over time and that's why he was experiencing neurological symptoms like loss of memory, numbness, and depression. Slow poisoning! We've seen Prof. put on that lamp when he is reading a journal. He didn't light the lamp all the time. So, he only inhaled the mercury vapour when he switched on the lamp and not otherwise.'

Salma uttered an exclamation. 'What a diabolical murderer! He was driving Prof. slowly mad.'

'Exactly,' CY said, shaking his head in horror.

Bill Eddington asked, 'What about Uncle Abdul? How is he?'

CY said, 'Uncle Abdul has recovered and gone home. He has taken early retirement. It was fortunate he only had chemical burns. The mercuric salt did not enter his bloodstream much.'

'Oh, Allah be praised,' Salma said. She had been particularly fond of the janitor and treated him as a family friend. 'I am glad he can take rest at home with Auntie. What an experience for poor Uncle Abdul. But because he had those burns, everyone knew there was poison in Prof.'s office, and they could identify the poison and save Prof.'s life.'

Cheng Yong said, 'The department has assigned Prof. Singh a new office. Same floor but the end room. A smaller room with just a desk, chair and cupboard. I visited him early this morning to discuss my project. He was his usual jovial self, and it was good to see that. Well, I am off to the laboratory, I have some experiments running.'

CY and Bill went out of the room and the others bent to their work, reading journals and books.

* * *

Professor Pritam Singh sat in his swivel chair staring at the computer screen. He felt uncomfortable in the small office assigned to him, but Dolly said it was necessary since the room next door was large and a few police officers were stationed there, manning the CCTV. Pritam glanced up. On the ceiling, partially hidden behind a cornice, a small red light from a CCTV camera blinked, gently.

Pritam felt uneasy. Dolly had explained Lily's theory of Johnny Tan's son being the murderer and the need to catch him in action. He was diabolical and did not leave any trail behind, so this was the only way to put him behind bars. Sweat sprung up on Pritam's forehead. The judgement he had evaded in his youth when he sped away from the accident was now being meted out. He was sitting in his office, a lamb to the slaughter, waiting for Johnny Tan's son to poison him.

He thought about Cheryl and the baby. He had cheated on Dolly with Cheryl, made her and Ash unhappy; judgement on those actions were being passed, too. If anything happened to him, Cheryl would miscarry the baby. Tears clouded his eyes. He had sinned in life, but he loved Ash, his son, with all his heart. And he was looking forward to being a father again. He wanted another chance, dear God, just another chance. He did not want to die. Pritam buried his head in his hands.

He remembered his aunt's gentle voice telling him the family driver would take the blame for the accident. He was horrified to learn a woman had died. But he was afraid of jail and of taking responsibility. His aunt had smoothed the hair on his head and told him not to worry. Why had he not gone to her funeral? She had been like a mother to him.

And then his guilty conscience guided his steps to that poky room underneath the carpark and the broken man who sat there, looking blearily at him. An engineer became an idiot because of him. He had recoiled from Johnny with a smothered cry, but then slowly moved forward to talk to the man whose life he had destroyed. He knew no amount of money could compensate for anything he had done to this man, but he had paid him handsomely.

There was a sound near the door, and Pritam's heart thudded with fear. Dolly had not told him the identity of the killer and with wide eyes he watched the door open.

Kiong Tan stood there, a small smile on his face and a cup of beverage in his hand. He came into the room and closed the door, but not before Pritam had glimpsed a janitor with his mop and pail in the corridor outside. Pritam faced the man who had come to kill him.

'Prof., I brought you some iced coffee,' Kiong said, his voice pleasant, but his eyes boring into Pritam. 'I thought we would discuss our project over the coffee. I have got some good results.'

Pritam watched Kiong deposit the Styrofoam coffee cup on the table. Without being asked, Kiong sat down in the visitor's chair.

Pritam cleared his throat. 'Thanks, Kiong. I'm a bit busy now. How about an appointment at 3 p.m.?'

Kiong pushed the coffee towards his mentor. 'Why not now? Drink your coffee, Prof.' His voice had become menacing.

Pritam looked at the cup of coffee in dread.

There was a clatter outside and the door opened to reveal the janitor, the peak of his cap pulled low over his forehead. He had his pail and mop on the floor next to him.

'Can I mop your office now, Sir?' the young man asked in a gruff voice.

Kiong looked at the janitor in annoyance. 'No, can't you see we are busy?'

Pritam cleared his throat. 'Yes, please clean the office now. Kiong,' he said in a loud voice, 'I will see you at three, okay?'

Kiong looked at the cup of coffee, shrugged his shoulders and left the room. When the door had closed, Corporal Mok pushed back his cap and took a thermally insulated evidence bag out of the roomy pocket of his janitor's uniform. He swept the coffee cup into the bag and zipped it up.

'Please go and drink a cup of coffee at the canteen, Sir. Take your time,' Mok said, apologetically. 'We need to dust for fingerprints and send the coffee for analysis. Your room will be ready in an hour, Sir.'

Pritam mopped his brow with a large white handkerchief. He looked at Mok and said, 'You mean Kiong is Johnny Tan's son?'

'He is Johnny Tan's son, but unless we find poison in this coffee, we don't know if he is our murderer.'

Pritam left his office, his head in a whirl. He took the lift down and made his way to the canteen. He needed to talk to his sister-in-law, Lily.

In the room next to Pritam's office, two constables manned the video output of the CCTV camera on a computer. The officers wore headphones, and the conversations were being taped on a device. Corporal Mok entered the room just as the phone rang.

'Madam,' Mok said respectfully into the receiver.

Dolly's voice came over the line. 'Any luck, Adrian?'

'Yes, Madam. Kiong Tan came with coffee for Professor Singh. My men are sending the cup for forensics testing. Fingerprint officers will soon be here, Madam. Everything is under control. The images from the CCTV are clear, and the conversations audible.'

'Good.' Dolly rang off. She rose from the chair in her office and got ready to go to the forensics laboratories to expedite the testing of the coffee Kiong had offered Professor Pritam Singh. She hoped the results were positive for poison, and they could nail a murderer.

Friday, 7 October 2011

43

The morning sun slanted in through the serrated blinds of Interview Room 1 in CID HQ, the flickering light playing over the prisoner's face. The tests on the coffee had come in and last night, Charlie and Mok had driven to Kiong's rented apartment in Novena and arrested him for murder.

Charlie closed the blinds and switched on the overhead light. Kiong Tan sat straight, his face imperturbable, his blank eyes looking at the wall opposite, bypassing the eyes of Dolly and Charlie, who were facing him across the desk. Two constables stood at the door while Corporal Mok stood behind the prisoner, leaning against the wall.

Charlie switched on the tape recorder and said: 'Terence Kiong Tan is in the room with ASP Dolly Das, Inspector Charles Goh, and Corporal Adrian Mok. The interview starts now at 10 a.m.'

Dolly drummed her fingers on the desk before looking into the prisoner's eyes. 'Kiong Tan, we are formally charging you with the murders of Dr Dong-wook Pak and Professor Ursula Botham. We are also charging you with the attempted murder of Professor Pritam Singh. Do you confess to the murders?'

'No. I have no idea what you are talking about.' The voice was emotionless, remote.

Charlie flushed with annoyance at Kiong's wooden face. He would be hard to crack. 'You gave Professor Pritam Singh a cup of coffee last Monday. We tested the coffee and found the industrial poison carbon tetrachloride in the coffee. You were going to kill Professor Pritam Singh.'

'I never visited Prof. Singh with a cup of coffee.' Kiong's voice was a monotone.

Dolly shifted in her chair. 'Prof. Singh's office was equipped with a CCTV camera. It has captured you entering the office and offering Prof. Singh a cup of coffee.' Dolly was buoyed up by seeing a flicker of emotion cross Kiong's face. She rammed home the advantage. 'Are you Johnny Tan's son? Your mother was Mabel Tan?'

To her surprise, Kiong did not deny his roots. His face became warm and alive. His eyes gleamed. 'Yes, I am Johnny Tan's son, and Pritam Singh killed my mother and disabled my father. He maimed me, too.' He pointed at his leg. His voice rose. 'I had to have a major operation to fix my leg. And I still limp. I do not deny Pritam Singh destroyed my family. That does not mean I attempted to kill him. You need concrete proof of my involvement, Superintendent, not some flimsy video footage. That is not solid proof and will not stand up in a court of law. You know that as well as I do. Okay, I did go to Prof. Singh's room, but a janitor came in while I was there. He gave Prof. the cup of coffee.'

Corporal Mok said from the back, 'That was me. I was the janitor.'

Kiong was looking at the table and Dolly felt frustrated at being unable to read his face. 'I am afraid that cup of poisoned coffee nails you as a killer, Kiong. You wished to drive Pritam mad for the injuries he inflicted on your family. That is why you did not use a lethal poison that would have killed him instantly. You used a small amount of mercuric chloride smeared on the filament covering of his office table lamp so that the salt vaporized into poisonous mercury fumes, inhaling which, Pritam Singh would slowly die. And in the time, it took to kill him, he would think he was going crazy. He would become more and more depressed through the chronic poisoning to the point he would think of taking his own life. Then you would have your revenge.'

Charlie said, 'If you are innocent of wrongdoing as you claim, why did you put carbon tetrachloride in the coffee?'

Seeing Kiong's head still bent, Dolly said sharply, 'Your plan backfired, though, didn't it, Kiong? Pritam Singh recovered from the mercury poisoning, and he is still hale and hearty while you are behind bars. All that effort wasted, Kiong.' Dolly clicked her tongue, her voice oozing sympathy.

Colour rushed into the boy's face and his lips trembled ominously. He looked up, his eyes flashing.

Charlie chimed in, bent on breaking Kiong's resolve. 'Professor Singh has gone back to his life. These few months will fade from his memory and very quickly, too, when his baby is born. His wife is pregnant. You could do nothing to Professor Singh, Kiong!'

Kiong's face was as white as that of a ghost, and he spoke in a cracked whisper. 'Pritam Singh suffered! I could see it. At first, he would forget small things and then one day I saw him at the carpark, weeping behind the wheel of his car. He had forgotten how to get home from the university. I saw him using the car's GPS after that. I often visited him at his office,' Kiong said, conversationally. The colour had returned to his face, and his eyes gleamed with malice as he recalled how he drove Pritam mad. 'I would make up lies about my research and tell him. He would look surprised, but he could not contradict me.' Kiong laughed. 'He thought he had forgotten what work he had given me to do. I gave him a research proposal of a completely different line of work to what I am doing now, and I copied his signature at the bottom. You should have seen his face when he read the proposal. He looked like an idiot before he started crying.' Kiong began shaking with silent laughter.

Dolly's eyes widened with horror. Charlie remained unfazed.

He said reasonably, 'I am sorry about the trauma and death in your family. You are a filial son, and it is right you should be angry. But why kill Prof. Botham and Dr Pak? They had not harmed you.'

Uplifted by Charlie's kind voice, Kiong shrugged. 'It was fun to do it,' he said simply. He added, 'I am a scientist. I like to experiment. I wanted to find out how easy is it to kill a person with poison. They were experiments. Prof. Singh was already suffering, and nobody understood I was behind it. I wanted to see how far I could go.' His matter-of-fact voice chilled his listeners.

Charlie continued, his tone admiring, 'Dr Pak now. That was quite clever, really, leaving his poisoned coffee with Abdul. The janitor would take it to Pak, it was part of his job. You knew Pak liked sweet coffee.'

'It was a cinch,' Kiong agreed. 'Though there was a chance DW would question Abdul as to why he was being served the coffee. He probably assumed Bill had sent it along. DW could not resist sweets and sweetened coffee. He could drink more than two cups at one go. I took care not to be seen when I took the cup of coffee to Abdul's office. Later, Salma said she saw a man's figure near Abdul's office. I was relieved she had not recognized me. I did keep to the shadows and wore black clothes that day. It gave me great satisfaction that I got away with killing Pak.' He added, seriously, 'Poisons are the best lethal weapons as they are hard to trace and their effects mimic health disorders. They are also readily available in a chemistry laboratory. I saw Terry working with ethylene glycol for some experiments, and I decided to use it.' He laughed silently. When he had curbed his mirth, he said, 'I went to visit Pak the next day, on the Tuesday, at his apartment. I wanted to know how he was doing. I saw him dying. He asked me to call for an ambulance. Those were the last words he ever said.' Kiong wiped the sweat off his face with the back of his hand.

Charlie looked puzzled. 'What was the selection process in choosing your guinea pigs? You had no issues with Dr Pak, right? No quarrel?'

Kiong's face became sullen. 'I did resent him if that's what you're asking. When I applied to Professor Graham Botham, it was for a senior research fellow position and I wanted university accommodation as well since I did not live with my father. Prof. Botham told me his funding was used up in paying DW's salary and the slot he had for postdoc accommodation was also being utilized by DW. He promised me when DW left, he would offer me the senior research fellow position, but for now, he could only give me a junior research fellow position. I was offered half the salary I should be getting. I was educated at Harvard!' Kiong's eyes were pinpricks of indignation.

'Oh, so DW's death benefited you?' Charlie was more admiring than ever.

Kiong's face went white with rage. 'You'd think, right? But Botham went back on his word. When I asked to apply for DW's fellowship after his death, he fobbed me off. He said he had someone else in mind from Australia. And that person would be allotted the quarters as well.'

'What a cad,' Charlie agreed. 'So, you killed his wife.'

Kiong's face had become bland. When he spoke, his voice was composed and matter of fact. 'I was angry with Graham. I felt my experience at Harvard was not being appreciated. But I chose Ursula because it was easy to poison her. I happened to visit Ursula to discuss a chemistry problem. I saw her drinking out of her Pepto-Bismol bottle in front of me and thought it was an easy place to put poison in. The staff offices remain open, and it is easy to go in and out. Many of us had heard the quarrels between Ursula and Graham, and I knew he would be the chief suspect for his wife's murder.' Kiong was out of control again and ground his teeth in anger. 'But the police never arrested him.'

Dolly did not know how much more of this she could take, but Charlie continued speaking, intent on extracting a full confession from Kiong Tan. 'When did you put the mercury salt on the lamp filament cover on Prof. Singh's desk?'

'Oh, about a month before school opened for classes. Abdul is lazy, he seldom dusts the lamps and furniture. But I came into Prof. Singh's office at least two more times to replenish the poison as it was being vaporized over time when he switched on the table lamp. He used the lamp when he read journals. We all had seen that when we visited his office. I was careful to place only a small amount of salt each time, otherwise Singh would die fast without suffering.' Kiong was distracted now, for the first time taking in the tape recorder whirring on the table.

Charlie said, 'Did you write a threatening letter to Prof. Singh saying he would be the next one to be killed?'

Kiong giggled. 'Yeah, I know that was childish, but the state he was in, I wanted to see his reaction to a letter of that sort. I went into his office after he had picked up the letter and he was sitting at his desk, trembling. He could not recognize me and told me to leave. He was flustered and on the verge of tears. It was fun!'

Dolly shuddered. 'Your name is Terence. Your father called you Terry. You do not use your Christian name?'

Kiong's eyes sharpened, and he gave a dismissive shake of his head. 'No, I had it removed from my certificates and IC. I lost my faith when my mother died.' Suddenly, a tear formed and hung like a dewdrop at the corner of his left eye.

Without warning, Kiong went berserk. His hand began to shake, and he cried, 'You have no idea what it was like to lose my parents and live with people as a poor relation. Sure, my aunt took me in when Pa was incapacitated, but my uncle hated me. He was a sadist. He used to cane me for the slightest offence. I suffered emotional and physical abuse at his hands. What could I do, huh? I depended on them for a roof over my head. I took in all the barbs directed my way and decided to get out of the house as soon as I was able. I concentrated on my studies; they were my gateway to independence.'

'What happened to your uncle?' Dolly asked, a trace of fear in her voice.

A smile lifted Kiong's lips. 'He died of liver cirrhosis. I used to slip him bottles of whisky on the sly when his doctor forbade him to drink alcohol.' He smiled at the look of disgust on Dolly's face.

Charlie was curious to know how premeditated Pritam's murder had been and asked, 'Did you study chemistry so that one day you would work closely with Pritam Singh and kill him?'

Kiong laughed. 'No, it was pure coincidence. I liked chemistry. After doing my postdoc at Harvard, I wanted to return to Singapore with a job to take care of Pa. I applied for a fellowship to Graham Botham and when I joined the department, I was told to work on some projects with Dr Pritam Singh. The past came rushing back then and I could not stop hating the man who had destroyed my family.'

Charlie said, 'You blame Pritam Singh for the accident. Isn't it true that your father made an illegal turn on the road?'

Colour rushed into Kiong's face. 'So? Pritam Singh could have avoided our car if he had been sober. And he had the audacity to offer my father a large amount of money later. You think money can buy back my mother's life?' His voice cracked on the last words, and he buried his face in his hands, weeping bitterly. 'I loved my mother!'

Dolly nodded at Charlie, who went through the motions of a formal arrest. They now had a full confession on tape from Kiong Tan for the murders at Temasek University.

After officers had taken Kiong away to be remanded in custody, Dolly strode to the window and pulled the blinds up, allowing the sun into the room, dispelling the darkness there. 'Vengeance is mine,' she muttered, on the tail of a sad sigh.

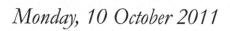

Monday, 10 October 2011

44

Corporal Fauzia Khan entered the Police Canteen and made a beeline for the booth where Constable Janine Chu was sitting having her lunch. The crowded canteen resounded with the clatter of cutlery and the hum of conversation. Constable Chu was the recruit who had taken Fauzia's place in Dolly Das's team.

'Hi, Janine!' Fauzia stood at the table and smiled. 'Do you remember me? We went to the Academy together.'

Janine looked up and smiled, warmly. 'Sure, Fauzia. You aced all your exams. How is life at Serious Sexual Crime? Take a seat.'

Fauzia sat opposite Janine and smiled. 'Thanks. The newspapers reported the university killer has been apprehended. I heard rumours there was a daring stakeout at the university by your team to find evidence to nail the killer. It sounded exciting. Were you a part of the stakeout?'

Janine Chu nodded. 'Yes, I was there, and I can tell you, Fauzia, it was exciting and chilling at the same time.' She explained to Fauzia how she and other police officers had hidden in the room next to Professor Singh's office as he offered himself as bait to the killer. A cup of poisoned coffee had clinched the case.

After congratulating Janine warmly on catching a wily killer, Fauzia rushed to her aunt's office. Barely knocking on the door, she pushed it open, saying, 'Auntie, you don't know what I just heard!'

* * *

The afternoon sun cast a warm glow over DAC John Nathan's room contrasting with the frosty silence with which the Assistant Director of Major Crime was regarding his two subordinates, ASP Dolly Das and Inspector Charles Goh, seated opposite him.

'I have it on good authority that you placed Professor Singh's life in danger to catch his killer.' Nathan's eyes were angry and his face worried. 'Why was I not updated and informed of what you were planning to do, ASP Das?'

Dolly said, 'Sir, I did send you email updates, but you were out of town.'

Nathan said, 'Yes, I was attending the Criminal Justice conference in America. The DCP wanted some of us to attend so that next year, we can present our own cases there to the CID worldwide community. It was an important conference. And I had limited email access. I only arrived back last night. Why didn't you wait for me to return to Singapore before setting the trap for the murderer?'

Dolly said, 'We had no choice, Sir, but to act when we did. Pritam had to return to work; he had run out of medical leave. His life was in danger at the university. Kiong Tan had failed in his attempt to take Pritam's life, he would try again and eventually he would succeed. We had to apprehend Kiong Tan. We could not ask the university authorities to tell Kiong to leave the university. On what grounds? And if he remained there, Pritam's life would always be in danger. Currently, there are no CCTV cameras in the offices and common rooms to catch the killer on videotape. So, we did the next best thing. Put Pritam in an office with a camera, next to which was an empty room where my team could hide and man the CCTV camera and audio conversations. With permission from Professor Wong, the Head of Chemistry, of course.'

Nathan bristled. 'You could have brought Tan in for questioning and grilled him until he confessed. Why act out this dangerous drama to nail him? You could have used the STAR team. We need them to apprehend dangerous criminals as you well know, ASP Das.'

Charlie said, 'Sir, with due respect, Kiong Tan is highly intelligent. He would not have confessed when grilled. In the stakeout, we were confident he would bring along a poison with him to use on Professor Singh and that evidence could be presented in court to convict Kiong Tan. Sure enough, Kiong presented a cup of poisoned coffee to Professor Singh. He is a poisoner and not someone who uses weapons to kill. We felt we could manage without the Special Tactics and Rescue unit.'

Nathan was looking calmer and asked, 'What poison did he use?'

'Carbon tetrachloride,' Dolly said. 'It is a colourless liquid and he had put it in the cold coffee. It has a distinctive odour, but the coffee smell masked it. We can use this evidence to help the prosecutor win a conviction, Sir. Although he will spend the rest of his life in a mental institution. Kiong is mentally unhinged. I have sent the audio transcript of his interview to your email, Sir. He was laughing about the murders.'

Nathan turned to his computer and opened his emails. There was silence in the room as he keenly read the transcript of Kiong's police interview. He gave a heavy sigh after he had finished and turned to Dolly with bleak eyes. 'What a sad story, eh? Such a bright young man with a great brain and good prospects in life. To be consumed by the desire to take revenge. What a waste! It's as well his poor father cannot understand what his son has done!'

Nathan continued, 'Yes, yes, I see why you had to trap the boy. No choice, eh? And Professor Singh and Professor Wong agreed to this mode of nailing the killer. Yes, yes, otherwise, who knows how many more that deranged young man would have killed.'

Dolly nodded. 'The criminal is insane, and he had many traits of a serial killer, Sir. What's more, his traumatic childhood followed the typical blueprint experienced by serial killers—bed wetting into adolescence, watching his mother killed in the car crash, and suffering emotional and physical abuse from the uncle who took him in after the crash. By catching him, we saved lives and brought justice to the families of the deceased. Dr Pak's daughters are flying home to Seoul with his body tomorrow, and they are grateful the killer has been caught. Professor Graham Botham is not a suspect any more and he has conveyed his thanks to the police force.' Dolly's eyes were teary.

DAC Nathan nodded and said softly, 'I can see you took great precautions not to endanger Professor Singh's life and yes, you did catch the murderer. Is Kiong Tan under psychiatric evaluation?' When Dolly nodded, he looked at his computer and went through her email again. His eyes shone with amusement. 'Mok a janitor, eh?' He recovered from his mirth and said, 'I wish to congratulate you on nabbing a dangerous killer and solving the university murder case. Superintendent Siti Abdullah reported to me you were using unethical methods to nab the killer. I hope she pays more attention to training the cadets and does not meddle any more in my department.'

Nathan coughed, took a sip of water, and cleared his throat. 'We have a replacement for Supt Abdullah. Superintendent Geraldine Ang is transferring from the Bomb and Explosive Devices Branch to replace Supt Abdullah. This is taking place with immediate effect, which is good as now you will have someone to supervise you when I am out of town on police business. No more stakeouts without our permission, eh? And more senior eyes on murder cases. All to the good. Okay, officers, you are dismissed.' Nathan smiled at his subordinates and nodded.

Dolly faced Charlie in her office. 'Only our team knew of the stakeout. Someone from our team talked to either Fauzia Khan or Siti Abdullah. Find out who it was and give strict instructions to our team not to gossip about the methods we use to nab killers to anyone else in the police force.' Dolly's face was set in anger as Charlie left the office.

After lunch, there was a tap on Dolly's office door. Fauzia opened the door and slouched in. 'You wanted to see me, ASP Das?'

When she was seated, Dolly said pleasantly, 'I heard you talked to Janine Chu from my team and asked her details of how we nabbed the killer in one of our cases. Why is this so, Corporal? Not enough to do in Serious Sexual Crime?'

Fauzia smiled. 'I was interested, that is all. I'm always interested in how you solve cases, ASP Das. I am a fan of yours.'

Dolly's eyes were cool. 'And you told Supt Abdullah about what you heard, and she told my boss, DAC Nathan. Look at yourself! Spreading tales right up to the top instead of doing your work?'

Fauzia looked puzzled. 'But you, yourself, must have informed DAC Nathan about all the details of the case.'

Dolly pursed her lips. 'Of course, but he was out of town with limited access to his email.' In a cold voice, she continued, 'I have lodged a complaint with HR that you are meddling in a department you don't belong in, and harassing Charlie Goh and myself by spreading tales and rumours. They will be having a chat with you, soon. And keep out of my way, Corporal. I don't want to see you anywhere near my officers again. You are dismissed.'

Fauzia got up from the chair, glared at Dolly and rushed out of the office. Dolly sat back, brows drawn together, knowing Fauzia Khan and her aunt were not done with her and her team yet. She gathered her handbag and rose from her chair. Her face showed stout resolve. She would not let Fauzia or Siti lessen the happiness and relief she felt after solving a difficult murder case.

45

Girlie was happy. She peered into the butter chicken bubbling on the stove. A snatch of an English song came on the air through the open kitchen window, and Girlie began to hum the tune. The family were gathered in the house for a dinner celebrating the end of a particularly gruelling case. She felt relieved that her friend, Kamini, though out of a job at the Botham household, was happy little Tom had left for England with his grandmother.

According to Kamini, Graham Botham was in a foul mood after learning from Ursula's lawyer that she had made a will leaving the bulk of her fortune to her son to be held in trust for him until he was twenty-one years old. Lorna Asquith had broken off with Graham and had resigned from the Geography Department, intending to leave for home soon. Girlie wondered if Graham would go back to England too. As a slight burning smell attacked her nostrils, Girlie hurried to the gas burner on which okra was cooking. She frowned. She had to get the okra right this time or she would not hear the end of it from Lily.

In the drawing-room, brightly lit by the chandelier and lamps, Dolly was telling everyone assembled how Charlie had extracted a confession from Kiong. Charlie sat on the love couch with his wife, Meena, a grin on his face. Ash sat with his mother on the sofa with Joey on her other side. Frankie and Vernon sat on chairs, and Lily sat on the long ottoman with

Angie. Uma gazed at everyone avidly from her divan. Cheryl lay on the chaise lounge, her eyes wide. Girlie had served everyone with appetizers and the group ate with gusto.

Cheryl squeaked, 'That killer drove Preet crazy and would have finished him off if he were not caught. He is young and so cruel.'

'He is not right in the head, Cheryl,' Dolly said, sadly.

Charlie speared a chicken tikka with a fork and said, 'If Madam Lily had not put us on the scent of poisons, we would have thought all the murders were natural deaths. There was no evidence of murder. We owe a debt of gratitude to Mrs D.' He popped the tikka into his mouth and began chewing enthusiastically.

Lily finished eating the onion pakora from her plate before saying, 'Well, if Ash had not recognized Kiong from the photo on Johnny Tan's desk, Dolly would have arrested Graham Botham.'

'It would have served Botham right. He is such a rude person and so competitive with Preet,' Cheryl opined. She smiled, gleefully. 'The head, Professor Wong, removed Graham's name as a candidate for the new headship elections. Now that everyone knows his true colours. Pritam will be elected head, uncontested.' She tentatively popped a vegetable tikka into her mouth and winced when she bit on a green chilli embedded in the appetizer.

Girlie entered with a fresh plate of potato tikki, which she placed on the side-table next to where Meena Goh was sitting and nodded encouragingly.

Uma said, 'That young boy, Kiong, must have nursed the grudge against Pritam for so many years.' She shook her head. Her eyes avoided the appetizers; her daughters' eyes never missed the moment when their mother was about to steal one of the 'forbidden foods'.

Cheryl said, 'It's good Preet is back at home, and I am not alone. I keep thinking of the murders and how Preet was nearly killed. And I keep imagining mercury vapour curling out of his desk lamp every time Preet lighted it. And he would come home confused and bewildered. At one point, I thought he was close to suicide.'

Vernon said darkly, 'All along, I feel something not right with Kiong. His eyes were cold. So different from CY, who is jolly.' He dipped the chicken tikka on his plate into a bowl of mint sauce before popping it into his mouth. Angie was so busy finishing the potato tikkis on her plate that she barely looked up.

Lily dimpled. 'Cheng Yong will make a good husband for young Latha. They are going steady and are serious about getting married one day. I hope Savithri and Krishna do not oppose the marriage.'

Vernon said, 'I feel sorry for DW's daughters. Such a nice gentleman, and the girls are surely missing him.'

'Well, when they heard who the killer was, they forgave their aunt and reunited with her. They are all flying back tomorrow to Seoul with DW's body. Eun-jin is giving up her job here to be close to her nieces. Her nieces will take care of Eun-jin while she undergoes treatment for breast cancer,' Dolly confided.

'It was Bill Eddington who put me on the scent of poison,' Lily mused. 'He pointed out that DW did not reek of alcohol even though he appeared drunk. I was curious to know DW's alcohol levels and when Dolly started making enquiries, they found the ethylene glycol.'

'Poor Dr Eddington,' Girlie sighed, her eyes looking far away. 'No happy ending with Ma'am Ursula. He came to the Botham home for dinners. Sometimes, Kamini served the food. She told me he would look at Ma'am Ursula with gooey eyes.'

Dolly said, 'Ursula was murdered because Kiong was angry Graham went back on his word to give him DW's fellowship and university accommodation. I think Kiong was devolving into a maniac by then. Remember, he had already put the mercury salt on the lamp one month ago. He had seen Pritam suffering and had got away with it. He has many traits of a serial killer. So, just a little anger against Graham was enough for him to kill Ursula. He probably liked the idea that Graham would go to prison for the murder. So, yes, Kiong wanted revenge against Pritam, but normal people do not act in this way, especially killing the first two victims. Maybe, the traits of a serial killer lay latent in Kiong and once he began poisoning Pritam, his urge for thrill, evading capture, all surfaced. And he felt no remorse at all for killing DW and Ursula. It's ironic that the one whom he really wanted to kill is now alive—Pritam.'

'I feel sorry for Kiong, though,' Ash, who had been silent, spoke now. He had barely touched the appetizers on his plate. 'Imagine how traumatic it was for him as a ten-year-old to be in a car crash, look at his mother's dead body and go through the anguish of watching his father, who had been an intelligent engineer, reduced to a mentally deficient cleaner. Dad destroyed Kiong's life in one single moment.'

'Surely, you are not siding with a murderer, Ashok?' Cheryl's voice held layers of indignation.

'No, he became a killer because he had mental issues but there is always a trigger, and this was it.'

Joey had finished his appetizers. After giving a gentle burp, he observed, 'He will not hang. He is too mentally gone to stand trial for murder. He will spend the rest of his days in a mental institution.'

Charlie said, 'Kiong said he killed Ursula and DW for fun. No need to have any pity on him. Ursula was a young mother.'

Cheryl's mobile trilled and she switched it on. Her face was radiant as she sang, 'Hello, Preet!' In a few minutes, her face lost colour and became chalk white. She stuttered into the phone, 'If you think that's best. I'll be home soon, right after I finish dinner.' She switched off her mobile and burst into tears.

Lily hastened to her side and patted her shoulder. 'What's wrong, Cheryl? What did Pritam say? Is he okay?'

Cheryl blubbered. 'He has withdrawn his name as a candidate for the headship election. He spoke to Michael Wong and wrote a formal letter.'

Dolly asked, 'But why?'

Cheryl raised tear-stained eyes. 'Everyone knows he was a hit-and-run driver when he was young and killed Kiong's mother. He says it tarnishes his character, and he is not fit to be Head of Chemistry!'

Uma said in a high-pitched voice, 'He has a point. Even I said, what a cad he was to run away from a crash scene.'

'Maybe this is for the best,' Lily said kindly. 'Preet has gone through a trauma, Cheryl, slowly being poisoned like that. And now the baby will arrive, which is sure to put a lot of pressure on both of you. It's best to be relaxed right now.'

Dolly said brusquely, 'Let's have dinner. Then you can go home and comfort Preet, Cheryl. He is sure to feel down. The headship meant a lot to him. But he has done the right thing. People may have pointed fingers at him. You know how people are.'

When the delicious dinner had been consumed and Charlie and Meena had left with Cheryl, Charlie offering to give Cheryl a lift back to her house, the family gathered in the living hall with Vernon, Angie and Girlie to drink their after-dinner coffees. Uma lay on the divan, her eyes droopy.

Lily glanced at her mother and then looked at her sister. 'I finally got Mummy to agree to cataract surgery. She has an appointment with a doctor at the National Eye Centre.'

Girlie nodded. 'Soon your eyes good as new, Auntie.'

Uma flashed her eyes at her helper. 'Yes, and that's not good for you, Girlie. I will be able to see all the dust on the furniture. Don't think I don't know how you dust the furniture.'

Everyone laughed and Joey looked at his brother-in-law. 'Hey Frankie,' he said. 'You look sad. What's up?' He took a long sip of his coffee, his eyes mischievous.

Frankie stirred and looked at Lily with hurt eyes. 'We will never get to adopt the baby. Every opportunity she gets, my wife is back at her mother's house. We may as well get divorced!'

Lily blushed guiltily and murmured, 'No, no, I will move back, don't worry, Frankie.'

Uma said in a strident voice, 'It's true what he says, though. Why are you always here, Lily? You are married and should now lead your life with your husband. Girlie looks after me well. You use the excuse of my old age and bad health to run away here all the time. Stop it!'

Joey looked kindly at Lily and said, 'Frankie and I had a good discussion about his mental health with his therapist. You will notice, Lily, that Frankie's OCD is limited to his own place of residence, right? For example, he does not fuss around in this apartment, correct?' Joey gestured to Frankie. 'Go on then, Frank, tell them your plan.'

Frankie gazed into Lily's eyes. 'I really love you, Lily, and want to have a family. The only way to do that is for each of us to have our own space and at the same time stay connected. I will be selling our big condo unit. I will buy two studio units next to each other with a connecting door in the Silver Springs complex. You will live in one unit, me in the other. How does this idea grab you, Lily? I will have meals with you and come over for chats, but we will each have our own space. My OCD will be limited to my own studio apartment.'

Lily cried, 'Oh, you don't have to go to such lengths, Frankie! I will return to our apartment, no need to sell it. It's your dream home.'

Dolly said, 'Frankie's idea does have merit, Lil. Think it over. Many people live close to their relatives, even next door to each other. This way, you will be near Frankie and at the same time, Frankie and you will be close enough to Mummy in case she takes ill. You *are* getting on, Mummy!'

'I clean both your units, Ma'am,' Girlie offered, her eyes shining. 'And when the baby come, I become nanny.' She giggled, pleasurably.

Dolly fixed stern eyes on Girlie. 'You know the rules, you can only work for Mummy at her place of residence, Girlie.'

Girlie looked downcast before perking up. Her eyes shining, she said, 'Okay, Ma'am Dolly, but when baby come, Ma'am Lily will be working so she can leave Baby with Auntie and me for the day?' She grinned happily as Dolly nodded and smiled.

Lily looked guilty but smiled when Frankie nodded at her, encouragingly.

Dolly looked at her son glued to his mobile phone reading a text and asked, 'Your girlfriend mad at you, Ash?' Her tone was indulgent. 'When will we meet her?' She gently sipped at her cup of coffee.

Uma immediately said, 'Ashok, I want to meet your girlfriend. Why aren't you bringing her here?'

'Mummy,' Lily intervened, 'Maybe they are not serious yet. They've only been out on a couple of dates.'

'I can't believe it!' Ash cried, looking at a text. 'Amita's parents are arranging her marriage to a Sikh groom.'

There were exclamations from everyone, and Uma bristled. 'You are Sikh, too, Ashok Singh.'

Lily said, 'There's no time to be wasted, Ash. If you are serious about her, bring her here to meet the family. Are you serious about her or not?'

Ash raised his flushed face to his aunt. 'Yes, Mashi, I never told you, but we were dating from JC. We've been dating for two years.'

'Ashok, you're too young to think of marriage,' Dolly said, sharply. 'You have your education to finish.' She knocked her cup on the saucer in agitation and some coffee spilt on to the glass top of the side-table. Girlie, who had been sitting at Uma's feet rushed to the kitchen to get a damp cloth to clean up the spill.

'Amita is too young to marry; she is a year younger than me. She is only eighteen.' Ash looked so upset that Joey who was sitting next to him, patted him on the back.

'I got married at eighteen.' Uma smiled toothlessly at her grandson.

'Mummy, that was ages ago,' Dolly said. 'The kids nowadays don't marry until they are in a stable job at least. And that's years away for Ashok.' She took two sips of her coffee and handed the cup to Girlie who was hovering over the side-table with a cloth.

'I don't want to get married now,' Ash assured his mother. 'Don't be upset, Mama. We should both graduate and secure jobs before thinking of marriage. Singapore has a high cost of living. But that's what I mean. Why are Amita's parents marrying her off now?'

'Old-fashioned like Mummy,' Lily said and finished the last of her coffee.

Dolly smiled at her son. 'Well, Ash, okay, please invite her to a family tea. We will talk with her and formulate a plan to ward off this unwanted marriage.' Dolly laughed and caught Joey's eye.

Joey said, 'We finally get to meet Amita Singh. I am in Singapore next week, so I will be part of the planning party to get Amita out of her arranged marriage. It's great that the Ministry of Defence said your unit does not need to return to camp for another week, Ash.'

Dolly blew a kiss at her husband as Ash exclaimed, 'Thanks, Papa Joe!'

Dolly walked to the window and lifted the curtain. It was dark outside. She turned back in, to light, warmth, and jollity. The case had been difficult and the killer wily, but she and Lily had managed to solve a difficult case, yet again. She was glad she had Ash's girlfriend troubles to think about next week. It would take her mind off Siti Abdullah and her niece, Fauzia.

She glanced up and saw Lily looking at her, puzzled. Dolly gave a slight nod, a signal between the sisters that soon they would meet for lunch to discuss whatever was troubling Dolly. Lily and Dolly smiled conspiratorially at each other, while their mother extracted Amita's family details from Ash.

Outside, residents bustled about or sat on benches around the fountain, talking and laughing. The next morning, they would read from the newspaper how a young boy allowed his anger and resentment to simmer inside until he became a serial killer.